BELLES & MOBSTERS BOOK FOUR

ALEXEI

EVA WINNERS

Visit www.evawinners.com and subscribe to my newsletter.
FB group: https://bit.ly/3gHEe0e
FB page: https://bit.ly/30DzP8Q
Insta: http://Instagram.com/evawinners
BookBub: https://www.bookbub.com/authors/eva-winners
Amazon: http://amazon.com/author/evawinners
Goodreads: http://goodreads.com/evawinners
TikTok: https://vm.tiktok.com/ZMeETK7pq/

ALEXEI PLAYLIST

https://open.spotify.com/playlist/1u5AcXCDNS3Dm5yBpHtscy?si=
0K3mPqiOTJeWRrKU9FRatA&pt=
096ec0420341156bd9362269449424d1

PROLOGUE
AURORA

There has to be another way, I thought for the millionth time.

My heels clicked against the pavement of the dark alley-way. It was creepy, and I'd feel uncomfortable walking down it without my gun or Alexei. Though I'd never admit that to the cold, stoic asshole next to me.

An unassuming location and a plain building. You'd never guess there was a kinky sex club off this quiet, dark street. A large, brick house, two stories tall, dark and quiet. There were no cars around and no traffic. It reminded me of a dead end, the dingy, alley street in horror movies where serial killers took their victims to torture, rape, or kill.

A cold shiver ran down my spine; the eerie silence of the night broken up only by the barely coordinated clacking of my heels. I was still unclear what the expectation would be once we entered through the club door.

"We didn't even practice," I muttered under my breath, my heart thundering nervously. I'd felt better going into combat, not to a fucking sex club. "Are you sure there isn't a better way?" I hissed quietly.

I was losing my shit and freaking out while Alexei Nikolaev acted like we were going for ice cream. *Icicles more like it,* I thought wryly. The man never showed any damn emotions.

"Yes." His answer was short, curt. No surprise there. The man barely spoke and was cold as ice. Stoic as a damn statue.

I didn't feel comfortable with this plan. There was talk of possibly performing to fool them. Performing! I wasn't a performer for fuck's sake. I was an FBI agent. I never dreamt going to a sex club would be part of my job. But here we were, on our way to one.

But I couldn't let the chance at capturing Ivan Petrov slip through my fingers. He was my case. And supposedly, there was a man who ran this joint who would be our ticket to get to him. We had to gain Igor's attention! Some fucker who was in Ivan's favor.

Wrapping my arms around my waist, I gripped at the silky material of my short, red minidress. The top of the dress fit me like a corset and was by far the tightest thing I had ever worn. Each time I took a breath in and released it, I was sure my boobs would burst out of it. The dress was short, too short for my liking, and clung to every curve of my body. Combining the dress with the red pumps, only made me look more like a high-dollar escort.

I didn't pick any of it; it came with the assignment. Courtesy of Alexei bloody Nikolaev. I'd rather take the fucking heels and throw them at his pretty face.

How a man so bleak, so cold, could pick something so bold was beyond me! But then, it wasn't him wearing this shit. It was me.

We walked side by side, his steps slower to allow me to keep tempo in my heels. It was the first time I'd seen him in a suit. Usually, he wore his black cargo pants, plain black shirts, and combat boots. I didn't like the man and his physical appearance wasn't something I'd take notice of... usually. Yet, today, it was harder than normal.

Fuck. This. Shit.

My ankle quivered as I took a wrong step, and I almost lost my balance. But before I could stumble, his inked hand wrapped around my upper arm and caught me. My eyes shot to where his touch seared my skin, sending hot waves through my blood.

Then my eyes snapped to his face. The same stoic, unmoving

expression. Same frigid, pale blue eyes. It was the first time he'd touched me. I focused on his body disturbingly close to mine; so close that I could smell his cologne. An odd mixture of citrus and pine. It actually smelled very nice.

I swallowed hard. "Thanks," I murmured softly, my voice slightly breathless. How was it possible that such a searing, suffocating heat could come off such a frigid person?

No response. Barely a nod.

We continued, our steps slightly slower. *Clack. Clack. Clack.*

It took another ten steps before we stopped in front of the discrete black door. A fleeting glance my way by those pale blue eyes, and I swallowed the lump in my throat. If it didn't bother him, it didn't bother me either.

A jerky nod by me and he knocked on the door. One. Two. Three.

"One more," I rasped. He cocked his eyebrow. "Three is bad luck," I explained.

He knocked one more time and the door swung open the next instance.

In front of us stood a woman dressed in an extravagant, black cocktail gown. Everything on her was exactly right—from her formfitting dress, her jewelry, makeup, down to her shoes. It was all perfect.

Her brown eyes locked on Alexei. Desire flickered in them. And recognition!

I threw a side glance in his direction, wondering how often this man actually came here. Returning my eyes to the woman, I found her eyes on me, assessing me. She nodded and stepped back to let us in.

Alexei's hand came to my lower back, his touch burning through the material of my dress as he nudged me. *I don't like this*, my mind played on repeat, over and over again. My steps were hesitant as I moved forward, but there was no going back now. The door shut behind us with a thud and my heart raced faster.

I scanned the room with each step. The walls were painted black, yet the reception area was marble white, making the contrast stark.

"Welcome to the Eve's Apple," the woman purred, her eyes hungry on Alexei. And her smile! It was so bright, it might power the entire club.

A strangled laugh bubbled in my throat, but I quickly swallowed it. *That fucking name is so goddamn stupid!*

Alexei's big hand on the small of my back nudged me forward. I took a step, heading toward a hallway with burgundy walls and a mirrored ceiling. That, with the dim lights, gave it some serious porn-set vibes.

We kept on walking until we made it to the end of the hallway, which opened up to a large room with a bar to the right. The room was painted black with dark crimson accents, from thick Oriental rugs hanging off the walls, to the red marble floors, to the ruby chandelier hanging from the ceiling.

My eyes traveled over the people in the room. They were mingling, men's eyes hungry on the women, as if they were shopping.

"Drink?" Alexei's frigid voice brought my attention back to him. I nodded, when in fact I just wanted to shout, *"FBI, motherfuckers, where is this goddamn Igor?"*

We walked through the crowds, and it was impossible not to notice the leers from women and men alike. Despite my dislike of Alexei, I found myself stepping closer to him. I didn't want anyone to get the wrong idea, and he better not get a bright idea and leave me alone for one bloody second.

As we sat down on the barstools, he signaled the bartender.

"Vodka spritz for the lady and cognac for me." Alexei's voice was disinterested and cold, with a low timbre. I gave him a fleeting look, that little scar on his lip somehow fascinating. I often wondered how he got it.

The moment the drinks were brought, I reached for mine like a lifeline and took a gulp of it. I'd need it tonight. I glanced around the room and suddenly felt Alexei's lips against my earlobe.

"No eye contact." His breath was hot against my skin. "Otherwise, it's an invitation."

My eyes widened, and I immediately returned my gaze to him. We were here as a supposed couple. That was bad enough; I wasn't interested in inviting any additional attention from other men.

Another drink was placed in front of me.

"Jesus, Mary, and Joseph," I muttered under my breath. I gulped down my second drink. Before I could even open my mouth, a third drink was placed in front of me. I didn't grab it; otherwise, I'd be on my way to getting drunk.

"Alexei Nikolaev." A heavily accented voice came from behind us, a big hand landing on my shoulder. I flinched at the unfamiliar touch.

Alexei uttered something in Russian, his voice unmoving and the cold tenor unmistakable.

A shiver ghosted down my spine. Before I could blink, the man's hand fell from my shoulder.

"Are you enjoying the club?" the man asked us both, but his eyes never wavered from me. He was leering at me and not even trying to hide it.

I cleared my throat. "It's great," I answered, forcing a smile.

Alexei stood unmoving, his eyes locked on the man with professional disinterest.

"Introduce us, Alexei."

"Aurora. Igor." The way my name rolled off Alexei's lips did something to me.

Igor the Peeper was pretty much undressing me with his eyes, giving me the creeps. Alexei must have seen the same because his hand came to rest on my thigh, and his heat had me fighting back a delightful shiver.

Wait. What?

"Would you like a tour, Aurora?" Igor offered, his eyes never leaving me.

My hand covered Alexei's and I patted it awkwardly. "Ah, thank you. Alexei already offered." I smiled sweetly. At least I hoped it was a passable, sweet smile.

Igor smiled, but it didn't reach his eyes. Who was this Igor? Something about him rubbed me the wrong way. I went through Ivan

Petrov's file in my head, but I didn't recall the name Igor nor his face in the records.

According to the Nikolaev men, Igor was our ticket to get to Ivan Petrov. Supposedly he was part of Petrov's inner circle. The part that concerned me was that I didn't know the connection between the Nikolaev men and this guy and Ivan Petrov. The FBI had never even heard of Igor.

Granted, I had only recently received this case. I took it on for personal reasons and I suspected I'd been paired with Alexei Nikolaev because I was the only younger female in our office. My tender age of twenty-five usually worked against me, until they needed someone for a sex club. Fuckers!

I scanned over Igor memorizing his features. I'd go through the FBI database later and see if I could get any kind of match. His hair was dark, cut short, military style. He wasn't bad looking, until you locked eyes with him. His eyes were dark, almost black, and something unnerving in his gaze didn't quite sit well with me.

Then I remembered what Alexei said. Do not make eye contact; otherwise, it was an invitation.

I immediately turned my head and focused on Alexei's hard face. Those cold eyes could freeze back our melting polar ice caps.

"I have a VIP room ready for you," Igor added, breaking a slightly tense, uncomfortable silence. Alexei Nikolaev was more than okay with the silence. Me, not so much. It drove me fucking nuts. Growing up in a big home, with four brothers, it was never quiet. You could hide in the bathroom and you'd still not get privacy.

"Do svidaniya." Alexei dismissed Igor with one word. Or was it two in Russian?

With a final flicker of his eyes my way, Igor scurried along. I watched him disappear among the people through the dance floor in the center. On each corner of the dance floor, there was a small elevated platform with a naked dancer shaking her body like her life depended on it.

Several couples sat in lounges along the edge of the dance floor, watching people dance. I followed their gaze and my eyeballs just about popped out of my head. A woman lifted her dress up to her waist, flashing everyone her bare ass.

I turned to Alexei to see if he'd noticed it too, but there was no reaction on his face. His inked face with that unusual blond hair and those pale blue eyes was an unmoving mask. Just like his brother Vasili Nikolaev, Alexei had this darkness oozing from every pore of his body.

"Is that the guy?" I asked Alexei.

"Da."

I nodded slightly, keeping our talk to a minimum. Awareness trickled down my spine and the atmosphere thickened. A group of men came to the bar, their tones hushed, and their eyes on me. I felt like prey, available for hunting.

"VIP room. Now." Okay, maybe Alexei wouldn't allow an open season on my ass. His voice was cold, dark; a tone that made me wonder what his true story was. All I knew was what his file said, but I knew there was so much more.

Though, it wasn't something I should concern myself with.

He stood up, offering me his hand. I took it, without remark, and we strolled past all the gawking men and women. It didn't escape me that there were also men swooning after my date.

No, not my date, I quickly corrected myself.

Alexei led me down the short hallway and then through a doorway. To our VIP suite. The room had glossy, black marble floors, three red velvet walls, and one entire wall with two-way glass.

There was the St. Andrew's cross mounted to one wall, and I swallowed a breath, my eyes flickering to the stoic man behind me.

"Don't even fucking think about it," I warned, my voice trembling.

"Relax." His one-word answers were driving me fucking nuts. I was falling apart here and this guy… nothing. Nada. Zip.

My gaze shifted to the rest of the room, hoping to settle my nerves. There was one black chair with a golden wooden frame, facing the window that overlooked the stage. I watched him unbutton his jacket, taking it off, tossing it carelessly onto the side table.

He sat down in the chair, looking like a king. Nervously, I shifted from one foot to the other. Where was I supposed to be sitting? The dimmed lights gave this whole situation a bow-chick-a-wow-wow vibe.

"Sit." One-word command, his voice indifferent, and yet, it sent shivers down my spine.

"Where?" I choked out.

No answer. He probably thought me stupid. This was a couple's club, as it was explained to me. Closeness was expected.

I took a step towards him. And another one. I turned around slowly, like in a haze, and sat down on his lap. With my back stiff, my eyes flickered out the window and locked with a dark, piercing gaze. Igor!

"He's watching," I muttered under my breath.

"Da." Fuck, his Russian voice was sexier than his English voice.

Two heartbeats, and his hands came to my waist. He squeezed just tight enough, tempting me to turn around to see his face. Though I knew I wouldn't find anything there. This man was too good at hiding behind his mask.

His hands slid down my waist and my thighs. Goosebumps broke over my skin, and I clamped my teeth to hold in a moan. Alexei was the coldest man I had ever met, a criminal. Then why did my body burn? I felt like I was on fire, the feel of Alexei's hard body behind me made the ache pulse between my thighs.

This is just for show, I reminded myself. We had to give the impression of being a real couple. But his touch was real, too real. I focused my eyes outside the window, where two men and a woman gave us a show.

I watched the two men touch the blonde woman like their lives depended on her, my eyes fixated on the three of them. Her skirt was bunched around her waist, her shoulder strap off, exposing her breast. The men's hands were all over her, hungry and rough. The expression on her face was that of pure bliss. Blood in my veins burned like an inferno; my skin buzzed with an unfamiliar sensation. I couldn't breathe, the air too thick, my lungs too tight.

In one thrust, one of the men entered her and the woman's moan vibrated through the glass. My soft gasp echoed through the dark space. Electricity crackled in the room and my mouth went dry as I watched her.

Her palms flattened against the glass. Jesus, they should get a room, not do it out in the open, I thought to myself. Though the purpose of the sex club was to do it in the open. God help me out of this mess!

Her moans became piercing, I heard them loud and clear from here. One of the men wrapped his hand around her, his fingers pinching her nipple and her breathy whimper traveled through the glass. I felt my own nipples tighten.

I shifted, trying to get comfortable, feeling too hot for my own good. Then I shifted again, my ass grinding slightly against Alexei and I froze.

Alexei was hard.

My head snapped back to his face. Nothing but the same expression met mine. My heart pounded against my rib cage, my breathing labored and this man showed nothing. No emotion. No flicker of desire.

Except he is hard. The thought pierced through my lust-infused brain.

All thoughts evaporated from my brain, leaving me only with this flame of lust that licked at my skin. I shifted on his lap and a flicker of depraved hunger flashed in his eyes. Flames in his pale blue gaze that threatened to swallow me.

Then he snapped. One second I was sitting on his lap, the next my palms were against the window, and I was bent over with my ass in the air.

Alexei

I was so fucking hard, my cock strained against her ass. The moment she ground against it, my control snapped. The blood roared in my brain and rushed straight to my groin. I fucking snapped.

Bending her over, her palms braced against the glass, my hands pushed her red dress up, baring her ass to my view. The woman wore the tiniest string I had ever seen. I pressed my body against hers so she could feel my cock against the soft curve of her ass.

Pressing my lips to her fragile neck, I enjoyed her soft skin, the racing pulse beneath my mouth. Licking the skin over her collarbone, I brought my palms to her round ass.

"Ready?" I asked. A small whimper escaped her mouth, her breathing labored.

She glanced over her shoulder, our eyes connecting. Those deep, warm brown eyes. The color of chocolate. She smelled like chocolate too.

"Ready, kroshka?" It was her last chance to stop me.

"Y-yes." Her voice was breathy, her lips pouty red, and her eyes hazed with lust. Fuck if I knew whether it was for me or what she saw that threesome couple do.

The petite, dark-haired FBI agent was full of surprises. I shouldn't take it too far. Everything that touched me ended up broken. Everything I touched ended up ruined. Filthy.

But unless we played this right, Igor would rat us out and our ticket to Ivan would go to fucking hell. The way he leered at her pissed me off. It sent cold fury down my spine and made me want to murder him.

Aurora was *mine*. Her breasts. Her ass. Her pussy. All fucking mine. Her mouth, though, wouldn't be. I didn't kiss.

I reached around and parted her thighs, pushing the flimsy material aside and sliding my finger past her folds. She was soaked. So fucking wet that my fingers were drenched within seconds.

God help me, but she was intoxicating and maddening at the same fucking time. Unlike anyone I had ever met before.

Even her arousal smelled like chocolate, like a drug you inhaled and it forever remained in your system. I pushed my fingers deeper in and her pussy clenched around my fingers. Her head fell backwards, her eyes watching me over her shoulder, through her heavy eyelids and her cheeks flushed.

With my free hand, I fisted her hair and tugged it backwards, aware others from the club were watching. They could barely see us though.

Only the outline of us would be visible because I dimmed the lights just right to ensure they couldn't see us clearly.

Her pussy kept clenching around my fingers, eager for more as I thrust my fingers in and out. Her moans grew louder, her ass pushing against me. Then without warning, I retreated my fingers and brought them to her mouth. Without my asking, her lips parted and she sucked them clean.

Fucking beautiful!

Still gripping her hair with one hand, I unbuckled my pants, pushed her thong aside, then slid my rock-hard cock along her hot folds, then slammed into her. She was tight, her pussy clenching around my cock like a stronghold. Her moans vibrated straight to my chest as I fucked her hard. For the past two weeks, ever since she opened her sassy, smart mouth, this was all I wanted, and it was better than I envisioned.

She felt like heaven. My own personal heaven that I had no right to, but I stole a taste of it anyhow. All my control disintegrated as I fucked her hard and relentless. She matched each one of my thrusts with a whimper.

I worried I'd break her, forcing myself to ease up when her low warning growl had me spurring on.

"More." I was more than happy to oblige, picking up my pace and pounding into her mercilessly. Her soft moans turned into gasping, urgent cries. She was close. I felt it as if it was my own orgasm. I turned her head, so I could see her face as she shattered with pleasure. For me.

Her dark eyes glazed with desire, her mouth parted, and I fucked her faster and deeper until I felt her fall apart, her pussy milking me for all I had. She was fucking gorgeous.

A shudder rippled down my spine and I blew my load right into her tight, hot pussy, and the most powerful orgasm of my life cut through me.

Fuck. Me.

Her body slumped back into me as if she sought out comfort from me. Little did she know, I only brought havoc. Never comfort.

I used my hand to turn her head towards me, and for the first time in my life, I was tempted to kiss a woman. Not just a woman; this woman.

She must have felt the same urge, because her eyes lingered on my mouth.

I was fucked. So fucked!

ONE
ALEXEI

Two Weeks Ago

Vasili drummed his fingers on the surface of his desk. He liked to keep his hands busy. I preferred when people didn't move and definitely didn't talk. I fucking hated talkers. I leaned against the wall, waiting, my arms folded.

"I have an idea," Vasili finally broke the silence. When I didn't move, he continued, "Do you want to hear it?"

I cocked my eyebrow. It must not be a good idea if he had to voice it. Usually Vasili was about telling, not sharing ideas. And definitely not about asking for input. It was probably why Sasha rebelled all the time. I didn't care either way. If I liked the idea, I'd help him. If I didn't, I wouldn't.

Just as I did with Cassio and his gang, which is the reason I liked working with them.

"No?" Vasili questioned.

"You're going to tell me your idea anyhow," I clipped. "So why ask?"

Tap. Tap. Tap.

Vasili was agitated. It was a rare occurrence these days. Isabella, my half sister from my mother's side, eased him. *She made it all worth it*, Vasili said. Good for them. I was happy both of my half-siblings found each other. And no, Vasili and Isabella had no blood connections. I shared a father with Vasili and mother with Isabella.

Tap. Tap. Tap.

Vasili had a cool head, but he didn't handle threats to his family well. Truthfully, none of us did. Not Cassio or his brother. Not Luciano. Not Nico. Every single one of us went ballistic when our family was threatened.

The Belles and Mobsters agreement was one of those threats, and we all worked hard to eliminate it. It ended with Marco King and things had eased up on women's trafficking. Mainly because the entire coast refused to accommodate anyone smuggling humans. Killing Benito and Marco King served as a good example to any other idiot who thought they'd run an agreement like that. Or any kind of human trafficking.

But there would always be a villain who didn't get the memo and someone for us to fight. Ivan Petrov was our current target. The shadow ghost that the FBI had been chasing for years. The man I personally wanted to see dead. The man who now threatened my family.

"We can't keep letting that fucker take boys," Vasili growled. "And he goes too far by even insinuating he'd take Nikola."

Another boy was kidnapped. In broad daylight, surrounded by people. In the middle of a busy street in New Orleans. Ivan Petrov was behind all the kidnappings. It was his signature. The kidnapped boy was the right age and physique for what that bastard looked for. Besides, the message Ivan left behind was clearly directed at me.

You didn't pay your debt.

Your nephew will.

No signature needed. I knew Ivan would eventually come to collect. He never left a debt unsettled. The only way to avoid paying a debt to that bastard was with death. But then you kind of paid the ultimate debt, didn't you?

Fucking twisted psychopath!

Though to this day, I didn't regret my decision from all those years ago. He wanted the little girl with dark eyes and even darker hair. She was supposed to be a lesson used to teach her father, who happened to be governor then and was a senator today, what happened when you double-crossed Ivan Petrov. But it wasn't the little girl's debt to pay. So I betrayed him. The little girl and I escaped Ivan's clutches.

But the boy didn't. Her brother.

Guilt about it still clawed at me. Knowing that the boy had to go through the same goddamn hell I lived through. Nobody should have to endure that shit. And I was responsible for the kid's hell by leading Ivan to him and his sister.

That knowledge alone had a chokehold on me. A dead weight tied to my legs as I sank to the bottom of the ocean.

To this day, there was no doubt in my mind that Ivan knew exactly what he was doing. Usually, he used me to kill men who had double-crossed him. And those men were just as despicable as he was. It didn't bother me to end them. But that one time, he sent me to stalk the kids of his rival just because he refused to sell him a piece of land.

It fucking burned me that I didn't kill him all those years ago when I had a chance. A fraction of a moment. A missed chance. But he played on one single emotion and manipulated me. He hinted at knowing my family, giving me a lead to follow. And then he fucked me over.

Fucking emotions.

If I could burn those and never feel anything again, I'd jump on that train.

I worked best alone, in the shadows. It was what I'd been trained to do even before I learned to kill. Probably why I was best at killing. And hunting men down.

When I found Cassio and his gang, or they found me, it was a calculated move on my part to work with them. My fucking choice. They let me do my thing, expected nothing in return, and *asked* if they needed my help. There were no demands of blind allegiances. I'd never give those to anyone but my own fucking family. Though I always had the gang's back and they had mine, on more than one occasion.

"The FBI is hot on the case," Vasili explained. No fucking wonder. This time it wasn't a stray boy. This kid was on his way home from school... on his way to his family. It was the only thing that didn't match Ivan's MO. But that was the jab at me. And he had been ramping up kidnappings all over the States. He was desperate for more little boys for his fucked-up games.

"I have a contact in the FBI." No surprise there. Vasili had contacts everywhere. "He owes me one. We could have him give us his team and work with us."

Okay, as far as plans go, it wasn't a bad one. The FBI had vast resources and taking advantage of those would be to our benefit.

"I want you to work with the team," my big brother added. "Find a way to get closer to Ivan. He has to be stopped."

There was *a way*. Except, I had no partner to take there. And I had to ensure I didn't kill anyone when we got there.

"Do you know who the FBI has working on the case?" I asked him, knowing the answer already.

He shrugged his one shoulder. "Does it matter?"

It did. It was who saved me. *A little hand that slipped into mine and gave me light to hold on to.*

Yes, to me it mattered a great deal.

My eyes traveled out the big window of Vasili's office. The view of the city stretched, like a sinful empire. It was quiet here, but I knew the city was noisy. I grew accustomed to the constant buzz of this city. New Orleans was eclectic—a perfect melting pot of the old world, new world, and many in between.

In Washington, D.C., I stood out like a sore thumb among the clean-cut politicians and businessmen. Here, I was part of the city that embraced the dark, the light, and the paranormal through myth and magic, as part of everyday life. My face wasn't any more unusual than that of the next guy.

The tattoos on my face—normal. Scars—normal. Fucked-up past—so goddamn normal, it was sad.

New Orleans became *home*.

It didn't matter that the air reeked of must from the muddy waters of the Mississippi, mixed with the sweet scent of beignets, spicy aroma of crab boil, and a block over on Bourbon, the smell of urine filtering through the streets. I belonged here. I fit in here as just another member of society.

The people I cared about lived here. For the first time in my life, I had a family. *Family!*

It was a reluctant thought. Home and attachments to anything and anyone was long extinguished in me. Courtesy of the old Nikolaev bitch. It was thanks to her, Vasili's mother, that I grew up never knowing my mother and father. Vasili's mother had sold me out to Ivan. Her form of punishment bestowed on her husband, my father, for cheating on her. The woman's jealousy was cruel, tearing my own mother apart and sending her into the clutches of the old Santos, Raphael's father.

He was supposed to help my mother find me, but all he managed was to get her pregnant. At least she was smart enough to get away from him before his own wife hurt Isabella. Lombardo Santos wasn't much better than Vasili's mother. He trafficked women from South America and didn't care about sampling them. In the most brutal ways. A few years back, I put a target on his head, and Sasha, being the good brother that he was, killed him.

One of the better days of my life. Life had been good lately. My siblings were protected and safe. So were my nephew and niece. Yet, over the last several years, that long-forgotten feeling lingered somewhere deep. Fear of losing what I loved.

I fucking hated it. It made me extra paranoid and extra murderous.

I blamed Isabella for it. The anxiety became worse once she had the little ones. Nikola and Marietta, named after Vasili's father and Isabella's mother. I didn't think of either one of them as my own parents.

Thank fuck Tatiana hadn't had babies. There was only so much worrying I could handle. The familiar cold feeling crept up my spine, but I ignored it. In my thirty-eight years of life, I had become accustomed to it.

It seemed the whole gang was popping out babies and getting

married. Cassio was the latest one to fall. And soon, he'd become a father himself. Just several months ago, Luciano's baby girl was christened. Nico and Bianca had their twin boys, along with the little hellion twin girls. The men had settled down and focused on their families. Something we all craved for years. Except, the family wasn't just connected by blood but also tight friendships.

But now we had so much more to lose. It wasn't just about us any longer. It was about the families we'd created.

"What do you think, Alexei?" Vasili asked. "He's got to be stopped."

He was right, we had to stop Ivan. Every single boy in this fucked-up world was in danger from that motherfucker. Áine King, Cassio's wife, saved a group of boys in Russia almost a year ago. It started a chain of events that must have pushed Ivan over the edge because he made his attacks more personal. He targeted the cities of his enemies— New York, New Jersey, Baltimore and the D.C. area, Miami, and most of all New Orleans.

In fact, it seemed the state of Louisiana became Ivan's main playground for kidnapping boys. And he didn't even bother to be subtle about it. He must have grown desperate for more stock, as he called the little boys he used for his fighting rings and other despicable things once old enough. That fucker ensured he made hefty profits, draining us all dry—emotionally, mentally, and physically. Living through that kind of shit left a mark.

It was what drove me. My goals coincided alongside Cassio's and all his gang. Elimination of anyone who dealt in moving flesh. The unfortunate part was that each time we killed one human trafficker, there were two more stepping up.

But right now, I was focused on Ivan Petrov, the evil that still walked this earth. I wanted to gouge out his eyeballs, cut his fingers off, then cut off his balls, toes, ears, and end with his dick. So he could feel all the pain he inflicted over the years on everyone else.

For the past year, Vasili, Sasha, and I had traveled to all known locations trying to get eyes on Ivan and end his life. Cassio, Luca, and Nico helped too. Even Cassio's wife. We all wanted to end Ivan's organization. But he had become very good at hiding. And it would seem he no longer used the shelters I knew about.

Except something kept coming back to the forefront of my mind.

"There might be a way to get to Ivan," I told my brother with finality.

"**M**acchiato and a latte, please."

I stifled another yawn. Goddamn it, I was exhausted. Since my team found ourselves in downtown New Orleans chasing a lead, a fake one, and wasted all night, I decided I'd at least treat myself to coffee before we got back to headquarters.

All night and it led nowhere.

Another boy went missing. Blond hair and blue eyes. It was very specific over the last few months. Then we got an anonymous tip that a boy of similar age and physical attributes was seen on the outskirts of the French Quarter. By the cemetery. It was an odd place any boy would find himself, but we followed up on all the leads at this point. Any one of them could mean the difference between life and death.

"Here you go, officer." I scrunched my eyebrows, my mood prickly from lack of sleep. What the fuck was he talking about? I wasn't a cop.

Then I remembered, I still wore my FBI vest and my sidearm secured in the holster on my hip. It was on the tip of my tongue to correct him and tell him the right term was agent. Special agent if he wanted to be exact. It was a common mistake many made. But then I shrugged. It wasn't worth it, and I was too tired to lecture someone on correct titles.

Grabbing the coffee off the counter, I murmured my thanks and headed back to the car. The second I exited the coffee shop, the hot, humid air hit me. July in New Orleans was no joke. It was humid as fuck and I swore the smell of alcohol, beignets, and some unidentifiable musty scent constantly lingered in the air. No amount of breeze could get rid of that scent.

I only moved to New Orleans about six months ago when the cases of kidnapped boys became more prominent in this area. I couldn't quite decide if I liked it here or not. New Orleans always buzzed with life, but I was lonely here. It was a different kind of loneliness from the political and social life of D.C.

Besides, I always had my brothers and my best friends Willow and Sailor there. It was bearable with them around.

Here, it was too apparent what a loner I'd become. But the thoughts of my brother Kingston kept pushing me forward. I had to atone for my wrongdoings, make things right, find out what happened to him. I wouldn't rest until I found him.

Shoving those dark thoughts aside, I strode to the black Ford Expedition where Jackson sat, waiting for me. He had been my partner for the last month, and before then, only whenever I went into the field. Over the last thirty days, I had been reassigned to work full-time in the field.

My brothers, being who they were, ensured that when I joined the agency, I got the safest possible job. Behind a desk. I worked my butt off over the last several years, and once I transferred over to New Orleans, I finally got my break. I was out in the field. Being a profiler, I was only allowed to gather information from the crime scene. But with this case, I took more of an active role. I was searching for the kidnapper.

It required a lot of convincing, but thankfully McGovan, my boss, was understaffed and I was willing. Yes, he worried about what the powerful Ashfords would do to him if they found out, but they'd never know. Not my father, nor my brothers, who were excessively protective. The former only cared about himself. Selfish bastard. Yes, he was my father, but only in name. He'd sacrificed his children and his morals for his political career.

Putting one coffee-to-go on top of the car, I opened the car door, then grabbed the coffee off the top of the car and slid inside.

"Here you go."

I offered my partner his latte.

"You are a saint," he muttered, stifling a yawn.

Both of us would be exhausted today. And we weren't the best kind of cranky people. Hopefully we survived the day without killing each other. At least it was Friday. The best part was my brother and girlfriends were spending the weekend with me. Byron, my eldest brother, was checking up on me. I guess it was his turn—Royce, Winston, and Byron rotated with big-brother duties. On some occasions, they'd get a bright idea and come together. Talk about overprotective, but they did it with love, so I couldn't complain too much.

I shut the door behind me and brought my macchiato to my lips.

"It's going to be a long day," I muttered.

"You can say that again," Jackson complained. "And if goddamn Milo talks to me today, I might kill him."

My lips curved into a smile. Milo was our tech guy. He could hack into anything, obtain information on everything. Well, except the identity of the man who was kidnapping boys in Louisiana.

I suspected the same man was responsible for kidnapping boys all over the States. I had been after him for as long as I could remember. Almost like an unhealthy obsession, but I needed to solve it.

For Kingston, my fourth brother.

Goosebumps broke out all over my skin, just like they did every time I thought of him. It was guilt that was eating at me, I knew it. He was taken because of me. And my father, but I was there. I didn't listen to him... I didn't listen to my brother.

A lump formed in my throat, the fierceness always the same. My heart squeezed in my chest, and I'd have thought it a heart attack if I hadn't experienced it before. But I had. Guilt was a powerful thing.

Atone for my sins, my soul whispered.

This predator could be connected to the man who took my brother. So there'd be nothing to keep me away. I was doing this for all my brothers. None of us had been the same since Kingston was taken from us.

Usually, it was boys ages ten to twelve that disappeared. Various ethnic backgrounds, usually without a family. Except for rare cases here and there, like Kingston, but my gut feeling told me it was the same guy.

And recently something had changed.

The kidnappings suddenly felt personal. Blond hair and blue eyes. Over and over again. Age no longer seemed to play a part. Though the MO remained. This man was now singling out a specific type of boy. In the U.S. and all over the world. And no longer "strays" but now also boys who had families. Like my brother.

Twenty minutes later, we were back at the FBI headquarters in New Orleans. The three-story, brick building sat tucked away on Leon C, right off the river.

Honestly, I never imagined I'd be working for the government growing up. I thought I'd be an artist or maybe a freelance artist. Yet, here I was. Kingston's kidnapping affected each of us differently, and we all had our own way of dealing.

This was my way.

I swiped my badge and walked through the security check, then waited for Jackson. Once he was done, we strode through the large, marble lobby towards the elevators.

Two men stood there, and I did a double take. They were large. Extremely large. Six foot five-ish if I had to guess. Their backs were to us, so I couldn't see their faces. Just as I was about to nudge Jackson about them, a familiar voice called out behind us.

"Hey, guys."

Both Jackson and I groaned in unison. "I'm taking the stairs," Jackson told me and disappeared before I could even say a word.

"Traitor," I called after him.

The elevator binged and the door opened. The men in front of me strode inside and I followed, pushing the button for the third floor urgently.

"Too slow," I grunted as Milo rushed into the elevator at the last minute, nearly getting jammed by the door. Fucking moron.

"Hey, Aurora. How was your night?" He grinned widely, his eyes sparkling with mischief or something else. I could never quite pinpoint it. Like he knew some secret that the rest of us weren't privy to. Not to mention, the vibes from him always rubbed me the wrong way. It made me want to scream *"peeper the creeper."* Maybe because he was a hacker.

I rolled my shoulders to ease the tension. "Great."

"Did you see anyone?"

Just because I have a firearm, it doesn't give me the right to kill him, I reminded myself silently. We took an oath to serve and protect, not kill annoying little hackers that give you the wrong vibes.

"Yep."

His eyes widened. "Who?"

"People." I cracked my neck. Fuck, this tension was killing me. "You should try getting out sometimes. There are a shit ton of people out there."

Milo actually looked pensive, as if he was debating whether he should do it. Man was smart as a whip, but awkward as fuck. He was about my height, five foot six, brown hair and brown eyes. Wore suits that were a size too big, so it made him look even shorter. I wasn't certain how old he was, maybe just a few years older than me.

His hand reached out and I narrowed my eyes on him. What was he—

I swatted his hand away. "That's my coffee."

"Don't you and your brothers share? You should be used to sharing."

Bum. Bum. Bum. Bum. Bum. Bum. My heart sped up at the painful speed, hammering against my ribs.

"Don't you know sharing is caring," he continued. My spine went rigid. A memory flashed. I blinked my eyes, hazy images in my mind playing.

"Run, Aurora!" My brother's voice shattered the beautiful sunny winter day. "Run and don't look back."

"I don't want to go alone," I whimpered, my fear keeping me glued to my spot.

"Don't worry, little girl." The old man's voice was creepy. His English sounded weird. He smiled, his teeth yellow, and it widened with each step he took toward me. My little heart thundered so fast, I thought it would explode out of my chest. "Sharing is caring."

"Leave her alone!" Kingston's eyes bore into me. "Run, Rora!" he screamed at the top of his lungs; his demand was clear. For the first time that day, I listened. I ran as fast as my legs could carry me.

My lungs burned, my muscles shook, but I kept running.

Ding.

I blinked. The elevator came to a stop. I shook my head, shoving the memories aside. Somewhere dark and deep, where they festered until I could make him pay.

"Fuck sharing and caring," I hissed. I hated those words. "Don't you have someone to stalk?" I snapped at Milo, his eyes widening at my words.

I rushed out of there before he could answer. Lack of sleep made me extra sensitive, and another word out of him, I'd lose my shit.

It would not be smart to get called by HR just as I was placed in the field.

THREE
ALEXEI

S he had grown up.

Of course, I immediately recognized Aurora Ashford, daughter of Senator George Ashford, who had been eyeing the presidency. I'd kept tabs on her, on and off, over the last twenty years. I knew she worked for the FBI. And only recently, I found out she was in New Orleans, my city. All those years and life brought her back to my doorstep.

She was part of the plan. Vasili had the general idea of what we needed, but when it came to my connection to the Ashford family, I kept that to myself. Certain things were hard to forgive.

I watched the petite woman smack the man's hand and my lips twitched. Actually twitched! My sisters, nephew, and niece were the only human beings who ever made me want to smile. The scar on my lip had stopped me from smiling since I was a teenager. It didn't seem worth the physical pain it brought, and there was rarely ever anything to smile about back then.

Actually, scratch that—there was never anything to smile about. Yet now, I felt the urge to smile.

I focused my eyes on the woman in front of me. Her back was to me, the top of her head barely coming to my chest. She was tiny. Too fragile. What was the FBI thinking, sending her into the field? Obviously she worked in the field, she still wore her bulletproof vest. Last time I checked on her, she was in D.C. working for the FBI as a profiler, seated behind a desk.

And now here she was, within my reach. That little girl was gone, in her place was a beautiful, grown woman.

Her blue jeans hugged her hips and her round ass looked tempting in them. She wore a white shirt underneath her FBI body vest and black combat boots. Sidearm too. Her long black mane was pulled up into a silky ponytail and that same olive skin tone as her ancestors from her mother's side. The DiLustros, Italians, and part of the Kingpins of the Syndicate.

When she uttered her next words, I was convinced she inherited her mother's temper. I had been around my fair share of Italian women lately, and their tempers flared faster than bullets. Though the Irish could be just as bad. Bunch of damn hotheads. Though I'd rather see Agent Ashford have the Italian temper than her father's qualities. He was more of a smile-as-he-stabbed-you-in-the-back type of a conniving son-of-a-bitch.

"Fuck sharing and caring. Don't you have someone to stalk," she snapped at the guy who dared to talk to her. The words from twenty years ago rang in my ears. My part in all that clawed at me, the guilt burned right into my heart.

The elevator opened and she disappeared, her scent fading without her in the small space. Much to my disappointment. She smelled like chocolate. My favorite sweet. Unfortunately, my body couldn't process that dessert. It was what happened when chocolate was used as a method of torture.

Chocolate. I must have imagined it. It wasn't a normal scent, definitely not a perfume.

No, it couldn't be. Her coffee had to be some mocha shit or something. As she disappeared from my view, a sense of loss lingered.

Fucking ridiculous.

The girl never even glanced our way. A woman of her status probably had men lined up. Smart. Capable. Beautiful. Rich. The Ashford family held sway over everything. They were the royal elite of the social and political world. Her brothers were referred to as the Billionaire Kings. Except underneath all their shine, they had secrets and skeletons, just like anyone else.

Either way, a woman like Agent Ashford didn't fuck around with men who dealt in shady businesses, had a fucked-up past, and scars marking their body and mind.

Vasili and I strode out of the elevator. He didn't even glance at the woman in front of us. Not that he ever looked at any other woman since Isabella. He had been texting with her since we left the house. My brother left her barely twenty minutes ago. It was a mystery what they could possibly be saying to each other.

Scratch that. I really didn't want to know.

Just as we got to the office door, he shoved his phone into his pocket.

George McGovan.

The name neatly printed on the office name plate outside the door. It opened on cue and a man in his forties came face-to-face with us. His eyes lit up in recognition. Vasili and McGovan first crossed paths over a decade ago when Vasili saved his ass in some Russian prison. Ever since then, Vasili had been using him for information. He even managed to have McGovan wipe out some of my activities flagged by the FBI. Of course, McGovan didn't rank high enough to be able to wipe out all my shit.

"Mr. Nikolaev," he greeted us, extending his hand. "Two Nikolaevs."

He grinned like it was the best joke ever.

"Special Agent McGovan," Vasili greeted him, accepting his handshake.

I never moved. I fucking hated touching people. I'd much rather break his hand than shake it. It had nothing to do with being a germaphobe and everything to do with what that fuck Ivan had done to me.

The special agent readied to extend his handshake my way, but Vasili interrupted him.

"Can we get right to business?" Vasili demanded more than asked.

"Of course, of course." The special agent glanced around, his eyebrows scrunching. "I see my secretary has disappeared again."

Both Vasili and I kept our gaze on the man. We wanted to get this done and get the fuck out of here. We weren't on the wanted list, but it wasn't as if we were strictly legal either. God knew I wasn't. The FBI had been sniffing around me since the moment I stepped foot on U.S. soil. Ivan Petrov was known for his criminal activities; although nothing had ever been pinned on him. He had enough scapegoats to pin crimes on.

And unfortunately, my name had been part of his crimes. After all, I was the executioner. His personal killer.

McGovan stepped out of the way as we strode into his office. Vasili sat down opposite the FBI director, while I remained standing, leaning against a cheap gray stand-up file cabinet that protested at my weight. It was hard to get rid of some habits, one of them being the need to be close to the exit. When you grew up surrounded by enemies, it was ingrained into you. If not, you were dead.

The moment we were all situated, Vasili didn't waste any time.

"Like I mentioned on the phone," Vasili started. "We have some valuable information that will help with solving the kidnappings of young boys in New Orleans and throughout Louisiana."

What the FBI didn't know was that these kidnappings were happening all over the United States. In fact, all over the world. Most of the boys who were taken were never found again.

"I see." McGovan rubbed his hands, like he was already mentally counting what solving this case might do for his career. "Can you send over what you have?"

"No." It was the first time I spoke. The special agent's head snapped my way.

"The only way this will work is for you to assign your team to work with us," Vasili explained, ignoring his question. "Once the culprit is captured, he is all yours."

This wasn't a capture mission.

This was a kill-the-fucking-bastard-and-the-FBI-could-have-his-dead-body type of mission. The FBI had no idea who was responsible, but they had a team and resources. I knew exactly who was responsible but needed access to their resources. One resource in particular.

"And you will remove Alexei out of your database completely," Vasili added. "I don't care how. I just want it done."

I didn't move to look at him. I told him I didn't give a shit if I was on the FBI radar or not. They'd never catch me or find anything that could be upheld in court. But my brother was stubborn and adamant about fixing his mother's sins. They weren't his to fix. If that bitch was still breathing, I'd skin her alive.

"That's not exactly how it works," McGovan explained, pulling my thoughts back.

Vasili stood up, fixing his impeccable suit, pretending to wipe off nonexistent specs of dust. He was giving the idiot time to realize this would go only one way.

"Hold on. Are you leaving?" McGovan asked with a slight panic in his voice.

"Yes." Vasili pinned him with a stare. "There is only one way this is going to go. We have information that will help end these kidnappings. You have the resources. Assign the core team to us. We'll take care of the rest. The only thing you need to take care of is wiping Alexei out of your system."

His beady eyes widened. "I'd lose my job if the higher-ups get wind of it. And I don't have the proper authority."

"Only if they find out," Vasili agreed. "And they won't."

Vasili turned to leave when McGovan frantically stopped him.

"Wait, wait." He shoved his hands into his hair, making it a disheveled mess. We had barely been here two minutes and he was already a mess. How in the hell did he ever succeed in this career? "Let me introduce you to Agent Ashford, who has been tracking this case for a while."

Vasili's eyes flickered my way. A shared nod and he sat back down. She was who we needed.

McGovan picked up his handset and pushed a single button.

"Ashford. My office."

He hung up and his eyes came back to Vasili, then darted to me. "I need to know my agent will be safe."

"We'll keep him safe." Vasili didn't know one thing about Agent Ashford. He had his secrets; I had my own. *She* was my secret.

"He's actually a *she*," McGovan replied. "Agent Ashford has been chasing leads for the past six months in New Orleans. She can give you a quick rundown. But I need reassurance she won't be put in harm's way. Her father is..."

Knock. Knock. Knock. Knock. McGovan trailed off and his eyes darted to the door.

"Come in," he called out.

I knew who it was before the door cracked. The smell of chocolate. The door opened and Agent Ashford walked in. She no longer wore her FBI vest but still kept her sidearm.

She strode in, softly shutting the door behind her. She stood straight and firm, but something, everything about her was soft. She wasn't that short, except that compared to Vasili's and my frames, she seemed petite and fragile. Her lips were full, rosebud-like, and dominated her delicate face right along with those big dark eyes. Those same dark eyes as her brother Kingston.

Her gaze traveled over her boss, then Vasili, and ended on me.

Our eyes connected and she stole my breath. Literally. For a fraction of a second, I forgot to breathe and the only thing I felt was my heartbeat and the darkest, softest chocolate eyes on me.

This woman had no business being in the field. The thought was loud and clear in my brain.

Her expression was too soft, too innocent. It burned right through my skin and straight to my dick. And for the first time in my life, I actually *wanted* to touch. For the entirety of my adult life, sex was just another exercise. A necessity to relieve the steam.

Nothing more; nothing less.

But I hated any form of touching. Yeah, I was all kinds of fucked up. Courtesy of our parents' triangle, revenge, and jealousy. Yet as I watched Agent Ashford, it all faded away.

Past. Present. Future.

It was dangerous. Repercussions would be deadly. And her family was powerful. Her brothers protected her at all costs, and had torn into quite a few families to keep her out of harm's reach over her lifespan.

Especially since they lost their one sibling.

I watched her tilt her head sideways, studying me, and to my dismay, I wondered what she saw.

Riffraff. A thug. A killer.

She'd be right on all accounts. I was all that and worse. If she'd remember, she'd know I was worth less than a speck of dirt on her boots. Though she still offered comfort twenty years ago. To a mere stranger; a killer.

"Ah, Agent Ashford," her boss called out, but her eyes never strayed away from me, watching me warily. "Meet Vasili and Alexei Nikolaev." The moron chuckled, and I kind of wished I could just shoot him so he'd stop talking. "They are brothers."

Another idiotic chuckle.

Her lips tugged up and I'd bet all my money she almost rolled her eyes and then stopped herself.

She glanced at Vasili, then back to me, then back to Vasili. I didn't fucking like it.

"Hello." Then as if she couldn't stop herself, her eyes came back to me.

That's right, little girl. Keep your eyes on me.

FOUR
AURORA

Holy smokes.

    It was the only thought I could conjure. What an amazing gene pool! My eyes traveled over the man who sat in the chair. Even sitting down, he looked like a damn giant. He wore an expensive suit; Armani if I had to guess. Custom made. Though it didn't take away from his aura of danger. The man was a fucking beast.

My eyes darted back to his brother. He wore black cargo pants, military grade… an expensive military grade. Black combat boots. A black, button-down shirt with the sleeves rolled up that exposed his muscles. And those damn tattoos.

What the fuck was up with those?

He had them on every visible inch of his skin. Even on his face, under both his eyes. I shifted forward, as if pulled by an invisible force, or curiosity, to examine those tattoos. Personally, I hated tattoos, but there was something intriguing about his. They didn't seem random either. The profiler within me wanted to dissect them and understand the meaning behind each one of them.

"Ah, Agent Ashford. Meet Vasili and Alexei Nikolaev. They are brothers."

I had to fight the urge to roll my eyes at my boss. *No shit, Sherlock.*

Anyone with one eye, never mind two, could see these two were related. Even if their coloring wasn't the same, and it was, all you had to do was look at their eyes. I had never seen such pale blue eyes in my lifetime.

A distant, foggy memory flashed in my mind but dissipated before it could clear.

"Nice to meet you," I greeted them both.

Though the way my boss uttered their last name, it sounded important. The last name didn't ring a bell, but then, I wasn't exactly from this area. Though I'd be sure to look them up.

"You too, Agent Ashford," the guy sitting down replied, his voice deep and accented. The one standing remained silent.

"You and Jackson will be working with the Nikolaev men." I cocked my eyebrow. These two were clearly not agents. My eyes roamed over the two brothers. Their expensive clothes didn't conceal the predators underneath, nor ruthless intelligence hiding behind those pale glaciers. These men were dangerous. "I want you to share all the information you have with them. And this is to remain confidential." My head snapped to the Nikolaev brothers and then to my boss. Okay, something was definitely up. "Can you do that?"

Again, the urge to roll my eyes was strong. My boss was the classic example of the man who thought women couldn't do a job as well as a man in this organization. I could show him women did it even better, but why waste my energy on it.

"Which part?" My voice dipped with sarcasm. I couldn't resist. Sometimes McGovan talked to me like I was a moron. "It kind of seems overwhelming."

Both Nikolaev men's lips twitched. Though I wasn't sure whether it was in distaste for my sarcasm or insubordination. My eyes darted to the brother who was sitting down. I noted tattoos on his fingers.

A cross, queen of hearts, and pointed star.

Kind of hot, though tattoos were not my thing. Mentally, I made a note to look up what those symbols meant. There was no mistaking the Nikolaev origin. That last name screamed Russian.

"Don't worry, Ashford. These men will help you, so you don't get overwhelmed." Okay, this time I just couldn't stop myself. I rolled my eyes.

"Wonderful, then we're all set," I sneered.

Usually, information wasn't shared with outsiders. I glanced back at my boss and noted him pushing the button on the device, which jammed any electronic device, making eavesdropping by anyone outside this room impossible.

Yeah, something was up with all this shit.

"Though considering these two are not cops nor agents, it's illegal to share information about an active, ongoing case," I continued icily.

McGovan's bushy eyebrows jumped up to his receding hairline. "Excuse me?"

God, did he want me to spell it out?

"I said—"

"I heard you, Ashford," McGovan bit out. I should have known he'd turn on his asshole mode. He was good at that and fucking hated that I could make one phone call to my brothers, or God forbid to my father, and he'd be on a fucking bench. Not that I ever would, especially not my father. "This is a highly visible case and these two offered help that we clearly need since you still haven't identified the predator."

I narrowed my eyes on my boss. "Considering this predator has been around for the past four or five decades, I wonder what kept you or all your elderly associates from identifying him," I snapped.

Maybe I sounded like a spoiled-ass brat, but he couldn't pin this predator on me. I had been busting my ass and chasing all the leads. Yes, I did it for personal reasons, but also because I didn't want another boy taken. To disappear without a trace, leaving his loved ones wondering whether he was alive or dead. Praying that he was alive and yet scared to wish that on him.

"Ashford, we're on the same side here." McGovan must have sensed my mood. This predator and these kidnappings were my sore spot. "I got the authorization from up above that we can work with these two men."

He was lying; I knew it without a doubt. The way his left eye twitched, the way he tapped his pen against the table.

"They have the identity of the predator," he added and I returned my attention to the two Nikolaev men, eyeing them suspiciously. They just happened to have the identity of the predator that lurked in the shadows for the past five decades? But unlike other men, it wasn't as easy to read the Nikolaev men. Their faces were unmoving, identical masks.

There was no question about them being dangerous. They projected the same kind of energy as my brothers, though my brothers concealed it a bit better under their polished manners and seductive smiles. Or maybe these two just didn't give a crap to hide their nature.

"Fine," I acknowledged my boss. Though he was crazy if he thought I'd blindly trust them. I trusted my partner to have my back, not these two whose appearances screamed that their ways were unscrupulous.

More than following the rulebook, I wanted the predator captured. Something about this specific case told me it would answer questions that lingered for the past twenty years.

"Good, good, good," McGovan gleamed. I could practically see him mentally rubbing his hands together. "I want you to start with them this weekend. This case is high visibility and—"

"I have plans this weekend." I let out a heavy sigh. "I've been following this case nonstop for six months and haven't come any closer to figuring out who's taking these boys. I need some time off. To reset, to clear my mind, or I'm not going to be any good to anyone. And I have family coming in. I'm going to spend time with them. Come Tuesday morning, I'm here with bells on, ready to do what needs to be done to find this asshole in charge, but until then... I'm off the clock."

"You can cancel them," he barked out. My best friends Willow and Sailor were coming and so was my oldest brother, Byron. There was nothing on this planet that would make me cancel those plans.

I narrowed my eyes on my boss.

"No," I told him firmly, and held eye contact with his beady eyes.

"So if you need someone this weekend, find someone else." Then to ensure he understood me, I added, "It. is. Nonnegotiable."

Okay, so insubordination might get me fired one of these days. Except, not seeing my eldest brother wasn't an option. This was the first weekend he'd had off in months, and I refused to miss the chance to spend time with him. And my best friends.

Besides, McGovan was too scared to fire me, considering he was an ass-kisser and scared of my father's influence. The great Senator Grayson Ashford, the future of our country.

Thinking about Dad always left a bitter taste in my mouth. I owned up to my mistakes and my sins. My brothers did the same, but not our father. He used and abused, regardless of the cost to others. Even as a kid, I sensed it. I saw it in the way he treated my brothers. Like they were disposable.

I hadn't learned until much later just how true that was. We were all disposable to him, including his illegitimate son and daughter, and my mother who had ties to the infamous Kingpins of the Syndicate. I learned about his illegitimate children while in high school. The rest I learned after.

My brothers kept me in the dark about it all, but eventually the little girl grew up. I learned my father's sins, how much he cost our mother, and all my siblings. Especially the little sister who didn't even know I existed.

Bottom line was that the Ashford family was just as ruthless and filthy as the criminals of the underworld.

"Okay," he caved, just as I thought he would. "Can you give these men a summarized rundown of the kidnapping cases and your thoughts? You can send them details via email."

I must have hesitated a heartbeat too long because McGovan started talking again, agitation clear in his tone.

"Keep in mind, Agent Ashford, they have knowledge of the poten-tial individual behind this. Their information will help us capture him," McGovan added, thinking he was explaining everything when in fact he only triggered more questions.

These men were outsiders and shouldn't be getting information from the FBI. McGovan wanted me to share confidential information with visitors so this case could be solved as soon as possible and he could look like a hero.

God, I fucking hated politics. I knew he wanted to move up to D.C., and if this case came to a close under his supervision, he'd probably get that promotion. The entire country was watching him because the volume of kidnappings no longer skated under the radar and McGovan's office was the one actively working the case.

I strode to the opposite side of the room and leaned against the wall, keeping myself close to the exit and my eyes on both men. I didn't trust them.

My eyes connected with their gazes. Frigid. Pale glaciers. Their eye color was kind of freaky. They were so pale, there was something unnerving about them.

I shook my thoughts of their physical appearance. If they could help point us to the right culprit behind the kidnappings, I'd take it. It was the least I could do to make up for my wrongdoings.

"In Louisiana, the boys have been disappearing for about two years," I started. "Random and far apart, geographically and time-wise, so it was never picked up by the FBI. Until recently. But there are similar cases all over the country. Actually, I'm pretty sure even outside the U.S." A short nod from the one in the suit, and suddenly, I had to agree with McGovan. These men knew something. "Specifically in New Orleans, the cases started, or maybe picked up, about seven months ago. First month, five boys went missing while roaming the streets, pickpocketing. They were mostly boys from disadvantaged families. Whoever is doing this specifically targeted those boys so it could be chalked up to the boys being runaways. Unfortunately, they are the type of troubled boys last to be noticed when they've gone missing. So it remained under the radar. Then the escalations started—boys pulled out of school by supposed friends, never to be seen again. Or drawn off the playground. Like this predator suddenly wanted his actions noticed. But only his actions, because nobody ever remembers a single thing about any of these men I believe are working for him. Either they are excellent at blending in with the shadows or the predator's features are not memorable."

Another nod. I felt my heart rate pick up at the possibility of bringing the man guilty for so many tragedies to justice.

Sharing is caring, the creepy voice whispered in my brain, the reminder unwelcome.

Yet, a shudder ran down my spine as a revelation slammed into me. The man who took Kingston had an accent. A Russian accent! Much heavier than the man in the suit before me, but I was certain it was a Russian accent. Until today, I hadn't spoken to anyone with such an accent.

"I believe the cases here and throughout the U.S. are connected." My voice had a barely noticeable tremble to it. "I have absolutely no evidence to support it, but the MO is exactly the same. Every single time. Whoever is doing this targets boys who are lost, for lack of a better term. Nobody will notice if they are gone, at least for a few days." I swallowed hard. "They are taken from public places, but no one ever notices a damn thing." I've seen it firsthand. Our own nanny stood nearby. And Kingston and I were not strays, we came from the Ashfords. Crème de la crème of elite society, as the papers wrote. "Until these recent cases."

And at least one other, I added silently.

"What makes you think these last cases are special?" the Nikolaev man sitting down asked, though I had a suspicion he knew the answer. His voice was deep, the accent clearly there.

Just like the one I remembered in my nightmares as I screamed for my brother.

"The last boy's disappearance was alerted to authorities within an hour. He didn't get home from school. Same with several prior cases. He or she wants to be noticed. If you look through the last five to ten kidnappings, you'll see certain things have shifted. The kidnapped boys have exclusively light blond hair and light blue eyes."

A thought pierced through my brain. These two men had light blond hair and blue eyes. Maybe they had sons and were concerned for them?

"In all other cases, coloring wasn't a factor. It feels like a message," I continued. "A very specific message. Though the question is to whom—the general public or someone specific? Or maybe he is preparing something big and wants everyone to spin their wheels in the wrong direction."

Though I didn't think so. And my gut feeling warned me that the specific targeting of blond-haired, blue-eyed boys was somehow connected to the two Nikolaev men in front of me.

"Preparing for what?" It was the first time I heard the Nikolaev man with tattoos on his face speak. His voice was guttural, like he had been choked too many times and his vocal cords damaged. He barely had a hint of an accent though.

"Trafficking," I told him. "And maybe adding a bit of flavor for personal revenge." Okay, saying it like that, it seemed far-fetched, but deep down, I knew I was right. Just like the moment my eyes landed on the man who took my brother, I knew he'd tear our family apart. "I know trafficking women and young girls is more common, but it happens to young boys too. I think whoever is taking these boys has a standard trafficking business going. If you look through the past three, four decades, you can see a similar MO pop across the U.S. Never as big as this, but it has been going on right under our noses."

McGovan chuckled and resentment slithered through my veins. I hated that this was just a case for him. For me, it was a matter of life and death. For any one of the boys who went missing.

"Okay, as you can see, Agent Ashford gets excited and has some theories. But we are just focusing on the kids in New Orleans. There is no merit to her theory."

My eyes shot to my boss, glaring at him. "Yes, there is," I snapped back, my voice hoarse with emotions. "The connections are plain as day. Every single kidnapping has similarities. Did you even read my file?" I narrowed my eyes on McGovan, trying to get the point across.

I studied each missing boy's case, from their circumstance of birth until the day they disappeared. I lost count of the people I interviewed in order to gather bits and pieces of information, because it seemed every single time whoever was orchestrating the kidnappings was invisible to the people around.

"This predator is a master manipulator and has vast resources. Not only in the States but also in the world. Where in the fuck do you think he puts all those boys? In his four-bedroom, single-family home in the suburbs?"

God, McGovan was such a jackass. All he had to do was read my files and he'd see the connections. Except he didn't want to go save the world. Just his own damn career. In my eyes, McGovan was no better than Senator Ashford. Both just looked out for themselves and no one else.

I had to take a calming breath or risk losing my cool. If I went off on my boss, no matter what my connections might be, it wouldn't look good for my record. There was only so much my brothers could wipe out, and I hated asking them for special favors. Not that they'd ever hesitated to help me.

Vasili Nikolaev stood up and my eyes snapped his way, watching him warily.

He extended his hand with an unreadable expression on his face. My eyes lingered on his hand for a heartbeat too long. Jesus, his hands were huge. He'd crush me with just a small squeeze.

Reluctantly, I put my hand into his and his inked fingers wrapped around my hand, then squeezed firmly.

I wished he'd give me some clues on who he really was. Yes, he reeked of ruthlessness, danger, and money, but underneath it all there was more. So much more. The same was true with his brother, except there was an unnatural coldness in him.

"I'm happy we'll have you on our team." Okay, he sounded sincere. Maybe these guys would be the answer to stopping this crap. And then finally, I'd find answers and avenge Kingston. "I'm Vasili."

Nobody had to tell me this man was a force to be reckoned with. It was in his every move, every look, every word.

"Aurora," I murmured, not quite sure why I gave him my first name. Usually, I only offered my last name. Even Jackson called me Ashford, never by my first name.

My eyes darted to his brother but he said nothing. His face was an unmoving mask, marked by tattoos. His eyes were frigid on me. Unlike his brother, he didn't attempt to shake my hand.

"Okay, then," I muttered sarcastically. "Nice to meet you too."

He remained staring, the icy silence creepy. Yet, it didn't make me uncomfortable. It did, however, pique my curiosity. As well as something else, a memory or a feeling I couldn't quite latch on to.

For a fraction of a second, I drowned myself in the pale glaciers, voluntarily submerging into the icy waters.

Then he looked away and left without another word, moving like a panther. Vasili was right behind him.

Both silent and deadly.

FIVE
AURORA

S o sue me.

After the Nikolaev men left and McGovan gave me an earful, I came back to my own desk. Then got straight to work.

I typed in Nikolaev's name into the database and information started streaming in.

Nikola Nikolaev.

Father to Vasili, Sasha, Alexei, and Tatiana Nikolaev. Alexei Nikolaev was their half brother. Mother Marietta Taylor.

Not surprising. Men often had women on the side. Just look at my father.

My eyes roamed the screen, consuming the information.

Nikola and his wife moved to the States along with their children— Vasili and Sasha. Tatiana and Alexei were born in the States.

"Jesus Christ," I muttered. The old man had ties to the Russian mafia, suspected of possibly leading it. Though it was never confirmed and no proof was ever found.

What is McGovan thinking? Having any kind of deal with these men could tarnish the credibility of the case once solved.

I swallowed hard. The idea of dealing with any member of a criminal organization sent dread through my veins. It was normal considering what I'd witnessed happen to Anya, Sailor's sister, by a member of the cartel. Or knowing how my mother was murdered.

I forced myself to continue reading.

Vasili Nikolaev took the reins of the business fairly young and set up what appeared to be legitimate businesses, at least on the surface. Or maybe they were fronts, it was hard to tell without digging into each business and their financial records. The Nikolaev men were so successful, they had become some of the top real estate tycoons in the world.

"Impressive," I murmured, slightly awed.

The Nikolaevs ambition and success rivaled my brothers. In fact, in the business real estate market, they were often competing against each other. It was odd that I never heard my brothers mention the Nikolaev name before.

Not that I ever asked about any of their business dealings. My brothers were intent on building an empire so we could be untouchable. I was intent on capturing my brother's kidnapper.

I clicked the arrow, flipping to the next screen of information.

Sasha Nikolaev. Forty-two years old.

My eyes narrowed.

"That can't be right," I rasped. "U.S. Navy SEAL... sniper."

What. The. Fuck?

His father already had a reputation by the time Sasha Nikolaev joined the Navy SEALs and trained as a sniper. Lunacy. It was almost as if the government personally trained a member of an organized crime family.

Then there was Alexei Nikolaev.

The most intriguing Nikolaev who only joined the family six or so years back.

He was born in Louisiana, in a private hospital. For about two years, his mother lived in the New Orleans area until she started moving around a lot. She finally settled in Florida where she had a baby girl.

But there were no more mentions or traces of Alexei. It was as if he'd disappeared. Yet, there were no mentions of foul play.

It wasn't until about twenty years ago when he popped up again; this time on the FBI's radar due to his connections to Ivan Petrov, the suspected and reclusive Russian human trafficker.

Except, nobody had ever seen the man. Ivan Petrov was basically a criminal ghost.

Alexei Nikolaev apparently had a highly sought skillset. By the Bratva, Cosa Nostra, Irish mafia, Greek mafia… Fuck, he worked with all criminal organizations.

My heart thundered as I read Alexei's dealings with other questionable members of the society—Nico Morrelli, Cassio King, Luciano Vitale, Raphael—

And the screen went blank.

My head snapped around, eyeing the lights. The electricity was still on. No flickering. Everyone else seemed to be deep into their work.

I returned my attention back to the screen and pressed the refresh button. When nothing happened, I clicked the enter button.

Still nothing.

So I restarted the search, typing in the name. *Nothing.*

"That can't be," I hissed. "I was just reading the damn thing. I know there is shit in here."

I tried again. Still nothing.

I reached for my desk phone and dialed up Milo.

"What's up?" His standard answer.

"Hello, Milo," I started, trying to keep my voice even. "I was in the midst of reading a file on Alexei Nikolaev, a person of interest, and then it just disappeared. Just fucking disappeared."

He chuckled and my teeth clenched. I knew my lack of sleep usually made me more irritable. It wasn't fair to take it out of him, though at this moment, his chuckle irritated me unlike anything else.

"That's because I wiped it clean," he deadpanned.

My blood pressure spiked up. "Why in the fuck would you do that?" I snapped.

He chuckled again, and I gritted my teeth or risked saying something very inappropriate.

"McGovan ordered it and had authorization by the higher-ups in Washington," he explained.

It made no fucking sense. What fucking horseshit!

"Well, get it back," I hissed. "I wasn't done and I need the information." When he didn't answer, I lost my shit. "Fucking now, Milo!"

"The wipeout is permanent."

Then he hung up. He fucking hung up on me.

I took a deep breath in and exhaled, then repeated it again. Calmness slowly crept through me.

So I inhaled and exhaled one more time before I resorted to looking through the damn internet. Though the Nikolaev men seemed to be idolized by the media, almost as much as my brothers, for their looks, wealth, and intriguing rumors of their connections to organized crime, it didn't provide me with any substantive information.

I'd never understand the appeal. It was suicide to get involved with one of those men. I've witnessed firsthand how destructive and disgusting men in organized crime were.

It destroyed Anya.

My cell phone alarm went off, halting a trip down memory lane. Glancing at the clock, I noted the time. It was almost three—time to pick up big brother from the private airport.

I promised him I wouldn't be late.

"How is my baby sister?" Amusement glowed in my brother's eyes. It was half past three and I probably looked as tired as I felt. My brother, on the other hand, looked like a million bucks. "Who do I need to kill?"

Byron's greeting to me was always the same. He was the most predictable unpredictable person on this planet as strange as that sounded. From the moment I was born, I could always count on my brothers. To them, I was the baby to protect and cherish. To me, they were gods.

Though in a slightly different way than the rest of the female population. To the whole world, the Ashford brothers were the most eligible bachelors to walk this earth. All of them shared certain physical qualities. Thick, wavy hair. Cheekbones that could chisel ice. Height and broad shoulders that spoke of grace as well as lethal strength.

And the women's favorite was my eldest brother with his wealth, power, and sex appeal. Not my words. *People* and *Forbes* magazine printed those exact words, immortalizing them for the world to read. They were often in the spotlight, political and social. I was never part of that world, and it was thanks to my brothers. They sheltered me from that shallow, glittering world.

"No need to kill anyone," I scoffed, rolling my eyes with a soft smile. "I'm quite capable of killing the bad guys myself."

I winked playfully as he bent his head to press a kiss on my cheek.

At thirty-eight, Byron was my oldest brother. Four brothers could be overwhelming. There was also another half brother roaming this earth. As horrible as it sounded, I had plenty of brothers and that piece of information didn't shatter me as badly as learning I had a half sister. Snooping through my brother's desk while in high school gave me a preview to our family. Specifically to my father. And not a good one.

"Nice to see you again, Agent Ashford." My brother's arms wrapped me into a bear hug. "My favorite sibling, though don't tell that to the other ones. They might get jealous."

I chuckled and returned his hug.

Women passing by eyed me enviously, not realizing I was hugging my brother. Byron looked good in his jeans, a black, button-down shirt with the sleeves rolled up, and aviator shades. It was his dress-down style, but he still attracted women's eyes like bees to honey.

To the world, Byron was a cold, ruthless businessman with cutthroat tactics. Years ago, a reporter jokingly called my brothers the Billionaire Kings who ran their empires with cold heads and even colder hearts. The name stuck, but what the world didn't know was that when it came to the family, no amount of money or power mattered to my brothers.

Unfortunately, the same couldn't be said for our father.

I bet it burned Senator Ashford to know his sons surpassed him a million times over. The accumulated wealth of my brothers rivaled Jeff Bezos. My brothers weren't politicians or aiming for the presidency, but the fact of the matter was that if they wanted it, they'd get it. They were charismatic and successful in everything.

They were often compared to the Kennedys. At least the papers stated it, and we all knew the papers never printed anything wrong.

Either way, to me these men were my brothers. My family I'd give anything to protect. Just as they'd protected me their entire lives.

"And you, Mr. Ashford. An infamous Billionaire King," I teased. "Ready to have some of your standards lowered?"

He chuckled, showing me a perfect set of white teeth.

"My sister has the highest standards when it comes to taste," he retorted. Then as if he remembered something, he continued, "Except when it comes to food. I am starving, but if you take me to one of your suspicious food trucks, I'm afraid I'll demand my pilot come back and pick me up."

I shoved my shoulder into him, but he barely budged. "How was I to know you'd order seafood?"

Six months ago, I dragged my dear brothers to a food truck on L'Enfant Plaza in D.C., right before I moved to New Orleans. I ordered a veggie sandwich; they ordered crab cake sandwiches. I mean, everybody knows not to order seafood from food trucks. Right?

Well, apparently my brothers didn't. And as I talked to a friend I ran into, my brilliantly smart brothers ordered exactly that. All three of them ended up with food poisoning. And let me tell you, my brothers were the biggest babies when they were sick.

They swore up and down they'd never eat crab again. It was a running joke that I tried to poison them. So they'd assured me as they rolled on my bathroom floor, clutching their stomachs that I was no longer in any of their wills, and there was no need to take them to food trucks... ever again.

Like I cared about their damn money. I'd threatened to record them if they brought up a will one more time. Just the thought of losing them sent cold fear right to the marrow of my bones.

"Don't tell me I have to take you out to a fancy restaurant for dinner with my measly government salary?" I complained, though I couldn't stop smiling.

Byron's smile broadened. "Don't worry, Rora. I'll get the check." My smile faltered for a mere second, but Byron caught it. Only Byron and Kingston ever called me Rora.

His arm came around my shoulder in understanding, and we walked to my car in silence, both of us probably lost in our own memories.

Kingston would forever be a shadow we missed.

We had dinner at Emeril's, much to Byron's satisfaction.

The place buzzed with life, and thanks to the Ashford name that Byron gave, they seated us immediately. My brothers were always recognized, I wasn't. And it was by design.

For a moment, I worried that being seen here with Byron would attract unwanted attention, but as always, Byron took care of that too. He ensured the hostess gave us the most private table, and he spoke to the owner asking that no pictures be taken. Of course, he was more than happy to oblige once Byron offered to have his PR provide an acceptable photo and written article he could use for advertisement, free of charge.

"How are Winston and Royce?" I asked him as I sipped my glass of wine. Thank God Byron would pay for it because he ordered a five-thousand-dollar bottle. "I haven't talked to them yet this week. It's been busy."

"They wanted to come." Byron smirked. "But I sent them off on an assignment, so I could have you all to myself."

"So sneaky." I chuckled, shaking my head. "Though it does make me wonder how you found time out of your busy schedule."

The food came at that moment. I had ordered Emeril's "Who Dat" burger while Byron got the chargrilled petite filet. It was only for his benefit that I didn't get the fish of the day. He still couldn't stomach the smell of any seafood.

"You talk to them all the time," he complained, feigning distress. He didn't fool me or make me feel guilty, so I just bit into the burger. "You haven't seen me in over six months and have been sending me short, cryptic messages." I rolled my eyes. There was nothing cryptic about them. "You keep giving me one excuse after another why you can't call me. Therefore, baby sister, I decided to pay you a visit to ensure you're okay and to take care of some business while here."

Being the youngest of the siblings had its perks but also its disadvantages. My brothers could be so damn overbearing. Winston and Royce hid it better than Byron. My oldest brother wanted to make everything better for me, even before I realized I needed something. He demanded my happiness, the same way he conquered the world. By making everyone bow to his demands.

Though, I wasn't surprised to hear Byron had business to attend to. He had business everywhere.

Swallowing my food, I took another gulp of my drink, then lowered my glass.

"They weren't excuses," I told him. "I've been busy with this case at work. So what kind of business do you have here? Taking over New Orleans?" I joked.

He waved his hand, discounting the notion. I wouldn't put it past him though.

"Is McGovan giving you a hard time?" he asked instead, the question seemingly casual but, underneath it, there was a hint of his ruthless, protective streak. He'd make my boss's life hell if I so much as uttered a single complaint. So, of course, I wouldn't. I was an adult and could deal with my own problems.

"Of course not," I noted. "He's too scared of my brothers and our father."

"If he's smart, he'd be more scared of your brothers than the old man," he sneered. He was right, my brothers were a lot more lethal. He continued eating his entrée.

An awareness slid down my spine and the back of my neck prickled with something cold. I glanced over my shoulder, my eyes skimming the room, but I didn't see anyone. The restaurant was crowded but guests paid us no attention.

I turned around and met Byron's gaze. He sipped on his glass of scotch. "You feel it too?"

Byron had a way of making you feel at ease, but he saw everything and had a sharp sixth sense. It must have been ingrained into him as a SEAL. All three of my brothers served in the military for two tours. They ensured they didn't serve at the same time so one of them could take care of me.

"Yeah," I muttered. "Probably paranoia." He placed his glass down and pulled out his phone. "Please tell me you're not alarming Winston and Royce."

"Of course I'm not alarming them." He didn't even glance my way. "And I'm not asking them to put some eyes on you."

"Byron," I protested, my voice rising a notch. "Don't you dare."

I heard the swish from his cell, signaling the sent message, as he placed it on the table.

"Now tell me about this case you are profiling," he said, ignoring my other comment.

"Well, you're a civilian, so I cannot discuss it with you." It was funny that I had to say it twice now on the same day. "You know the rules."

He tilted his head, observing me and probably seeing way too much. Luckily his phone beeped and he turned his attention to it.

"Can we box this up?" I asked him when he raised his eyes to me. "I chased a lead all night. I'm tired, and as exciting as your company is, brother, my face might end up planted on this table."

He must have expected it.

"Anything my sister needs."

SIX

AURORA

L oud squeals traveled through the airport and every single pair of eyes turned our way.

I couldn't stop the smile that spread across my face even if I wanted to. And I didn't want to. Yesterday, I picked up my brother. Of course, he didn't squeal like a little girl when he greeted me. He strode over to me with sure steps, importance oozing with his every movement.

With him in town, Sailor along with little Gabriel, who wasn't so little, and Willow, it almost felt like my entire family was with me. If my other brothers were with us, it would feel complete. Like old times. Especially during college. Sailor, Willow, and I struggled figuring out having a baby in the home. My brothers were there to help us through.

As the three of them ran to me, I opened my arms, hugging them all at the same time. Our words stumbled over each other's, our high-pitched voices mixing together, reflecting the excitement we all felt. Poor little Gabriel was smothered in between our three bodies, giggling.

"Oh my gosh, I am so happy you're here," I exclaimed, showering all three of them with kisses. "I was so worried something would come up and none of you would be able to come."

"Mom said the same thing," Gabriel blurted out, grinning. "She said she needs this to keep her sanity."

I chuckled, ruffling his dark curls. "We all need this to keep our sanity, my little man."

Gabriel just turned seven and was my godson. I had never been more proud than the moment Sailor asked me to be his godmother. And I took that responsibility seriously. Just as Sailor took her responsibility seriously. When Anya passed away, right after giving birth, Sailor adopted Gabriel. Being she was only nineteen at the time, I begged my brothers to use their connections and make it happen. And they came through, like always.

They even funded her tuition and all financial needs to ensure she finished college since her family cut her off completely. The world didn't know my brothers for the wonderful men they were.

Of course, Sailor couldn't live on campus anymore, but she refused to accept more help than was needed from my family. She insisted her job could pay for her living expenses. So my wonder-fully sneaky brothers got me a beautiful five-bedroom apartment, more like a penthouse, in the heart of downtown Washington. The three of us left the Georgetown University dorms and lived off campus for the last three years of college while caring for little Gabriel.

Now, for all intents and purposes, Sailor was Gabriel's mother, and we were his aunts.

"You three are crazy?" Gabriel asked seriously, prompting us all to chuckle. I guessed it all depended on the definition of crazy.

"Shush, little man," Sailor scolded him softly. "We need our little getaways to keep going in life. And we never went so long without seeing each other. Besides, didn't you just tell me last week how you missed Aunt Aurora?"

Unlike Gabriel who had dark brown curls and the darkest blue eyes that always shone with mischief, Sailor had a golden mane full of soft curls and ocean eyes. I always thought she looked like the best version of any princess I had ever seen. Even more importantly, she was the most beautiful person I had ever met, inside and outside.

"What?" Willow pretended to be heartbroken. "You didn't miss me, little guy?"

Gabriel's grin widened, ear to ear, and his dark blue eyes sparkled. "I did, but we live together. I saw you last week before your business trip."

"Oh, that's right," she agreed. "It just seems too long to go without seeing you all." I agreed. It was hard, after years of seeing each other every single day, going to not seeing each other for weeks and months. "I really need this," Willow sighed, hugging us all. "Looking forward to this weekend has been the highlight of my life."

"We will make it the best weekend of our lives," I announced, grinning. Then immediately winced. Sailor's and Willow's eyes snapped to me, and I knew exactly what they were thinking. The last time we made that announcement was during our spring break the last year of high school. "And Gabriel will keep us in check," I added assuringly. "Besides, Byron is here for the weekend, so no wild things will be happening," I assured us all.

Willow, Sailor, and I giggled like high school girls as we armed ourselves for a night out. Byron was staying behind with Gabriel, and I caught them both rolling their eyes several times.

Typical boys.

"Woman, you gotta put some pictures on the walls," Willow complained. "It is freaking me out how impersonal this place is. It's not you."

I shrugged my one shoulder. It was a place to lay my head, that was it. But she was right. My apartment in D.C. had paintings from our travels on the wall, pictures of my brothers and best friends, along with Gabriel. It was the same apartment the three of us lived in during college years, so it was probably the reason it felt like home.

Since I arrived in New Orleans, this case had kept me busy, consuming all my thoughts and time. I spent more time at work than at home, hence the minimal décor. Besides, the condo was too quiet and my thoughts too loud. So sitting home alone was a major pain in my ass.

Though now that my girlfriends, my brother, and Gabriel were here, the three-bedroom condo brimmed with life. Just like my apartment back home.

My plan wasn't to stay in New Orleans permanently. It wasn't home. Both Sailor and Willow stayed in D.C., so I planned to go back. My brothers had penthouses there too, though they were rarely there anymore. But when they were, they'd come and visit, so it was home.

"Uncle Byron, I don't want to watch *Star Wars* again," Gabriel complained, and I had to bite the inside of my cheek. I guess the little guy didn't realize there were six of those movies when he picked out the movie. Or was it seven? "It's boring."

A loud gasp traveled through the flat, while Willow, Sailor, and I shared amusing glances. Byron was a *Star Wars* fanatic. Imagine if the reporters got ahold of that little piece of information.

From a Billionaire King to a Star Wars fanatic, I mused silently.

"Gabriel," I heard my brother's tone take on a serious note, "*Star Wars* is a classic. A form of art." I snorted and Byron's head snapped in my direction, narrowing his eyes into glaring slits. I'd bet my little salary he'd make it a life mission to convert the little guy into a fan. "It is an American classic. You have to give it a chance and learn to love it."

I scoffed at that lame explanation. That was not the way to attract children to like something.

"You either love a movie or you don't," I objected, ignoring my brother's scowl, as I applied makeup. "Not everyone loves it. I mean, do you like *Lord of the Rings*?"

It was my brother's turn to snort. "That is a New Zealand movie."

"Umm, just because it was filmed in New Zealand doesn't make it a New Zealand movie." For all his genius IQ, he wasn't that bright.

"New Line Cinema is an American film production studio," Willow chimed in. "They produced *Lord of the Rings*." She would know. She worked for the entertainment industry. Willow went the entertainment route, while Sailor and I opted for the careers that'd probably give us a shorter lifespan. I wasn't sure who was crazier here. Though neither one of us would give up. Both Sailor and Willow were great at their jobs.

Sailor was passionate about reporting on the underdogs.

Disadvantaged victims of the corporate world.

The invisible women who experienced the brutality of human trafficking.

She never hesitated to write a story about sensitive topics that should be known. Unfortunately, some people in D.C. minded that. Though it'd never stop her. And it helped that the Ashford brothers had her back.

Just as Sailor reported on sensitive topics, Willow wanted to produce movies about them, bringing their stories to a larger platform. We were certainly a trio.

"No matter," Byron protested. "They filmed it in New Zealand; it's not an American movie in my book, and that's all that counts."

The three of us rolled our eyes in unison, then dismissed him. They knew Byron well enough by now to realize it wouldn't make any difference to convince him otherwise. He'd let us believe we almost succeeded and then he'd tell us how idiotic we were.

An hour later, Willow, Sailor, and I ended up in the quietest restaurant we could find in the French Quarter. It would seem our party days were behind us because none of us could stomach crowded bars or streets. And the French Quarter was nothing if not crowded.

So we sat in Tableau, a classic French-Creole restaurant in an elegant three-story historic building with balcony seating. It was situated on St. Peter Street, between Jackson Square and Preservation Hall. We were right in the midst of all the entertainment in the heart of New Orleans but away from the noise, mayhem, and drunks on Bourbon Street.

"Well, your brother is getting hotter with age," Willow broke the silence as the three of us stared at the wild parties passing us by.

We used to be wild. For one week straight. An unforgettable spring break, in the worst way possible. We were know-it-alls. Spring break in Miami was a party playground with access to everything and anything.

We snuck into the hottest nightclubs, got drunk as fuck, and Anya, Sailor's older sister, who watched over us, joined in. Some nights I had no idea how we got back to the hotel.

Until that last night when we didn't. Instead, we broke into the house of the supposed cartel we heard about. On Anya's suggestion. She was a drunk with the worst ideas.

That backfired, and ever since, we'd paid the consequences for it. We lost Anya, though we had Gabriel, and he was worth the heartache. We'd never tell him how he came about. That he was a product of some fucked-up day.

Willow took a sip of her cocktail, then casually added, "I'd bang him."

"Shut up," I choked out, cringing at the image. It killed me to admit it, but all my brothers were good looking. They always had women swooning after them—for their looks, money, power, and charisma. All my brothers inherited their height from our father. I wondered if Kingston was somewhere on this earth, tall like him too. Both Byron and Winston had Father's eyes, while Royce, Kingston, and I had dark eyes like our mother. Apparently, I was the spitting image of her.

Not that I knew her. She died before I turned three. The official story was a robbery gone wrong, a case of "wrong place, wrong time." The unofficial story was that a rival gang of her brothers, the infamous members of the Kingpins of the Syndicate, killed her.

All I had were her pictures and my brothers' memories. Maybe it was good that she died before everything turned into a nightmare. She didn't have to live through all the fucking crap that happened. Sometimes I wished I didn't remember.

"I don't want to have that picture in my mind," I added. "Yuck. Makes me wanna barf."

Sailor grinned and leaned forward with wide eyes. "Would you fuck him this weekend?" I kicked Sailor under the desk and a yelp escaped her. "Hey!" she complained as I glared at her.

"Don't give her ideas," I warned her with a frown. I'd heard Willow having sex once. You couldn't unhear that shit. My eyes narrowed on my best friend, and I pointed my fork at her. "Do. Not. I repeat, do not sleep with my brother. And especially not this weekend. We have a minor in the household to think about."

"Gabriel sleeps like a log," Willow countered and I shot her a disapproving look. When I glared at her, she sighed. "Fine, I won't sleep with him. God, I haven't gotten laid in so long, I am not even sure if my lady parts are even functioning anymore."

I rolled my eyes. Between the three of us, Willow got laid the most.

"What has it been?" I retorted dryly. "Like a week?"

Sailor and I haven't gotten laid in a long time. Way too long. I wasn't even sure I remembered how to perform the act.

"Like two months," Willow answered. My eyebrow shot up. That was a long time for her. Sailor and I shared glances, but she just shrugged her shoulders. Willow was the most confident among us with her sexuality. She liked to experiment and try anything once. Then if she didn't like it, she wouldn't do it again. Hence, no shortage of partners for her.

Maybe she had become more selective?

She was beautiful, in an exotic kind of way. Her deep chestnut hair shone with auburn highlights under the lights. Her petite frame, at five foot three, was even shorter than mine. Her mother was Portuguese and her father was French. She picked up the best of both worlds. She was blessed with beautiful ivory skin with light freckles across her nose and a slim body with curves in all the right places. But in my opinion, her best attribute was her smile. It blinded everyone around her.

Unfortunately, she didn't smile often.

"What happened with that umm..." I tried to recall the guy's name and failed. "That guy with benefits."

Sailor ripped off a piece of her bread and popped it in her mouth. "The fuck buddy," she added helpfully. Or not.

Just as Willow opened her mouth to answer, an unfamiliar deep voice interrupted. "Oh, I'm all for fuck buddies."

The three of our heads turned in unison to find a tall, broad figure in a dark Brioni suit. I blinked, unsure if I was seeing him right.

"Holy. Hotness."

I wasn't certain who muttered the words, Sailor or Willow, but I had to agree. My eyes traveled over a six-foot-four, or so, frame with solid, sculpted muscles packed onto every single hot inch of the powerful frame. His blond hair was shaved short on the sides, faded with an expert hand, showing off tattoos. Jesus fucking Christ. He was hot! I was fairly sure my mouth gaped, staring at the gorgeous man with pale blue eyes.

Wait a minute. *Those pale eyes!*

"Is this guy for real?" Willow whispered, though there was no chance the guy didn't hear it.

He grinned and somehow his whole face became even more gorgeous. Fucking scary if you asked me. Nobody should be that gorgeous.

"Yes, I'm for real," he proclaimed, displaying his brilliant white smile. His eyes traveled over Sailor, lingering on Willow for a moment and then ending on me. And they stayed on me. I kept waiting for him to say something, and when he didn't, I shifted in my seat uncomfortably.

"Can I help you?" I asked, my voice slightly agitated. Why in the fuck was the man just standing here? There was no mistaking who he was. He had to be Sasha Nikolaev. That kind of resemblance was not coincidental. God wouldn't create that many good-looking men and not make them related to each other.

After all, after looking up the Nikolaev men, I knew there were two brothers, one sister, and a half brother, Alexei Nikolaev.

If only that damn Milo hadn't wiped their record as I was doing my research, I would have learned a lot more than I know.

I cleared my throat. "Hello? I said, can I help you with something?" I snapped.

"As a matter of fact, you can help me." He leaned forward, and instinctively, I leaned further back. His wide smile didn't fool me. He was a shark, and just like that predator, he'd show you his teeth before he chomped you into tiny little pieces. "I'm Sasha Nikolaev, at your service."

I half expected him to bow and do one of those fancy hand gestures. I lifted my glass, brought it to my lips and took a sip to ensure

I didn't say something stupid. *Like if you don't get out of my personal space, I'm going to kill you.*

Yeah, saying something like that to a man who held connections with the mafia would not be wise.

"Oh, yes. Please service me," Willow muttered. "In the bedroom, in the kitchen, outside. Any-fucking-where," she added and I just about choked on my cocktail.

He ignored her comment, though the gleam in his eyes didn't escape me. But to his credit, he kept his gaze on me, those pale blue glaciers, matching his brothers, drilling into me.

"My brother over there." He tilted his head to the furthest balcony seat, his eyes never leaving me. "He's been devouring you. Well, at least his eyes have." He smirked.

Hesitantly, I followed his gaze, and so did Willow and Sailor. Alexei and Vasili Nikolaev sat there, their big frames seemingly taking up a quarter of the balcony space. Both men wore black. Vasili wore an Armani suit. Yes, I could tell the quality of suits; I grew up with brothers with extremely expensive tastes. Alexei, on the other hand, wore a plain black T-shirt and black cargo pants again, which probably cost more than my monthly salary. I had a feeling the man always wore black, which made his eyes uncharacteristically light.

Alexei's stoic expression met mine and I immediately wanted to fidget.

Those freakish, pale blue glaciers were too invasive. His gaze burned and cooled at the same time. It was like an icy shower on a hot day. I couldn't quite decide whether it made me feel good or not. Maybe both.

The three brothers shared the same eye color and same dangerous aura. Sasha Nikolaev might have smiled, but somehow, I knew he was just as psychotic as his brother Alexei. Or even Vasili for that matter. Except the eldest brother hid it the best.

Then why the other two brothers' impact on me was completely different from Alexei's, I had no idea.

"Jesus Christ, there are three of them?" Sailor whispered in an appalled voice, pulling me off the ledge. Alexei's stoic expression was a force to be reckoned with. I understood why she gaped at the men. I did the same. Two Nikolaev men were bad enough but three. I hope there wasn't another one lurking somewhere. Four would just be cruel to the women of Earth.

"He can't stop staring at you, and we'd like for you to join us," the guy announced, loud enough for the whole restaurant to hear him. "Your friends too."

My eyes flicked to the table again and my frown deepened. Which one was he talking about? It had to be Alexei, because the man's impassive mask still hadn't turned away from me.

"Isn't your brother married?" I asked, just in case he was talking about Vasili. Google Search was full of news on Vasili and his young wife. Yesterday, Vasili did all of the talking and his brother behaved like he couldn't stand me. It was fine by me.

"Not that one," Sasha blurted out. "The other one."

Wonderful! The psychotic one. Somehow I knew it was him. My skin heated with agitation. At least that was what I told myself. Alexei Nikolaev was my least favorite Nikolaev brother. There was just something so disturbing about him.

Why were they having dinner here anyhow? They should be going to the restaurant designated for criminals. Not ruin a good time for normal people like me. Okay, maybe I wasn't exactly normal, but fuck it. I was more normal than that cold man.

The irony was that I'd have to work with criminals to capture a criminal. Maybe I could put them all behind bars. But first, I'd use them for whatever they knew about the predator and then lock them all up.

I stabbed at my steak. "No, thank you."

"Why not? It could be fun," Willow piped up and my head snapped to her. She was eye-fucking Sasha, actual drool dripping off the side of her mouth. *Horny traitor!*

"Because I don't socialize with people I work with," I snapped at her. *Or might potentially put behind bars*, but I kept the last words to myself.

"Enjoy the rest of your evening," I added pointedly at Sasha, dismissing him. Without another word, I turned my eyes to my girl-friends, ignoring him as he stood there for another second.

"Oh, you and Alexei are going to be fun." He chuckled, then nodded at the girls. "Ladies."

He strode back to his table, while I fought the urge to glance towards it.

"He said something to the other dude," Sailor rasped in a hushed tone. "Are those tattoos on his face?"

The side of my cheek burned. I didn't have to look to know that Alexei was the one burning a hole into me.

"I think he is giving him shit," Willow added in a conspicuous tone. "I bet he decided to stir the pot. Ohh, the guy that was staring at you stood up." Tension seeped through me and I rolled my shoulders, trying to ease some of my tension. "He's walking. Oh fuck, he's coming this way."

I wanted to snap at Willow to stop giving me a blow-by-blow commentary on events that didn't concern me, but suddenly my mouth was so dry, the only thing I could do was swallow.

"Jesus, he looks pissed," Sailor muttered under her breath. "Or is that his resting bitch face?"

My heart thundered under my ribs and my hand trembled slightly as I brought a drink to my lips. I downed my entire glass, the alcohol burning my throat. I lowered the glass down onto the table a tad bit forcefully, just as Alexei Nikolaev passed by our table.

Not a word. Not even a glance.

Just a large, dark shadow for a millisecond as he walked by.

"Jesus! And you're working with him?" Willow questioned under her breath. "He is a scary motherfucker. Like a damn bulldozer," she muttered.

Once he was out of sight, I released a breath I didn't realize I was holding. It would have been almost better if I didn't look him up. Not that I found out a lot, but knowing these men had connections to the mafia rattled me.

"He scares you," Sailor stated matter-of-factly.

I wasn't certain that he scared me per se. More like rattled me. If the man would show an ounce of emotion or reaction, anything, I'd feel better. But he was so unmoving that I was convinced he was a psychopath disguised in black cargo pants and black T-shirt.

Okay, so maybe I was scared. I mean, who wouldn't be!

An audible gulp traveled through the air.

I leaned forward, and the two of them did the same, eager to hear what I had to say.

"He's just so… so—" I couldn't find the appropriate word and gave up. "So cold, you know. Like he doesn't have emotions or feel them. It's not normal to be so controlled." A strand of my hair fell over my eye and I tucked it behind my ear. "And he's connected to the mafia," I added quietly. The morbid curiosity we held back then was what got us into all that mess. "It rattles me. Last time we were around someone like that… well, you know."

Nobody knew about it but the three of us. Well, it was four, but one person was dead. Gabriel's mother. Just thinking back to that spring break sent hives throughout my body.

Sadness flashed in Sailor's eyes, while the fear I felt was reflected in Willow's gaze. There was guilt too. All three of us felt responsible for what happened in Florida. We thought we were invincible. Anya was there to watch over us. We should have watched over her too.

Instead, we partied hard and did stupid, reckless things.

"What is this case you're working on?" Sailor inquired in a low voice.

"I can't really say much about it," I muttered. "But the Nikolaev men are supposed to help me. Or I'm helping them. I'm not even sure."

"Vasili Nikolaev?" Willow and Sailor asked at the same time.

I nodded. "He's like a business tycoon," Sailor muttered.

"How do you know?" I asked dryly. "I never even heard of them until yesterday."

"That's because you obsess over finding the man who took your brother," Willow answered. "I think he also has connections in the entertainment industry."

These two knew me well. We have been inseparable since the first year of high school in Georgetown Day School. Though the entire world knew of Kingston's disappearance, I never spoke about what happened. Willow and Sailor knew how desperately I wanted to find who took him and where he ended up, but I could never utter those words of admission.

I didn't listen and led us right into the bad man's clutches.

Silence stretched. Memories flooded. No words were necessary.

"Aurora." A deep, accented voice had all three of us jumping in our seats. A tiny whimper escaped my mouth and my head snapped to the side to see Vasili Nikolaev standing at his full height, crowding our table, and he wasn't even seated. "My apologies, I didn't mean to scare you."

I inhaled a deep breath, my eyes connecting for a fraction of a second with Sailor and Willow. Slowly exhaling, I let my heart find its normal pace before answering.

"Mr. Nikolaev," I greeted him briefly. For some reason, I couldn't call him by his first name, as he clearly called me by mine.

His eyes traveled over my girlfriends, then returned to me. This man was perceptive and definitely not stupid. If he was stupid, he would have been behind bars a long time ago. The expression on Vasili's face betrayed nothing and I prayed all three of our faces did the same.

But who was I fooling. The three of us were never a match for brutality.

Not when we were eighteen, and not now. Even with my job at the FBI as a profiler, I didn't have a stomach for brutality. It was the reason I was fine with field work when it came to the predator. The predator never left a trail of blood, at least not anywhere that we could find it.

"Are you having a good visit?" His question was a perfectly normal one. Except there was nothing normal about the Nikolaev family.

"Yes." I cleared my throat, meeting his gaze. I'd be a fool not to sense the danger lurking under that polished suit. "Yes, thank you."

"My brother Alexei is looking forward to working with you." Admittedly, it wasn't exactly what I expected him to say. Especially considering how his brother acted around me.

I shifted uncomfortably, unsure how to reply to that comment. I couldn't quite force pleasant words out of my mouth. He'd know if I was lying. Besides, working with criminals wasn't exactly my forté.

"Have a nice dinner," Vasili concluded icily, sending me further into a spiraling panic.

I forced a smile on my face and noted from my periphery that Willow and Sailor did the same. Except they visibly paled.

"Thank you," I mumbled as the man strode off, taking most of the oxygen with him. I had no idea where his brother Sasha was.

If I got out of this alive, it'd be a miracle.

SEVEN
ALEXEI

A fter Friday's meeting in McGovan's office, I ran into Agent Ashford in Emeril's restaurant. As if she sensed me, her eyes darted around, but I was good at keeping to the shadows.

But she sensed me, and so did her brother.

And since then, I fought the need to stalk the young agent for twenty-four hours and failed. I blamed my brother for being a fucking idiot and approaching them in the restaurant. Sasha and I were closer in age than Vasili and I, but I swore Sasha acted like he was still twenty. Even in my twenties, I didn't act idiotically like that guy.

My thoughts shifted back to Agent Ashford at the restaurant yesterday. The moment my sight latched on to her, my muscles tightened and my fist closed around the glass of cognac I was nursing. I knew she'd look good in a dress. No amount of bulletproof vests, jeans, nor combat boots could hide that.

But the way she looked…

She glided through the restaurant with her girlfriends. The woman was fucking glowing. Every single pair of eyes traveled over her curvy body, and I wanted to grab my fork, then make my way around the restaurant to gouge their eyeballs out.

Ah fuck it! I'd kill them all. It was probably cleaner.

It wasn't normal, not that I ever claimed to be normal. This reaction to her was irritating and annoying.

Anger washed over me—at her—for causing such a reaction in me, and at myself for fucking noticing her. I didn't need this shit. Not today. Not tomorrow. Not ever.

She was a damn inconvenient distraction. Yet, I couldn't peel my eyes away from her. I couldn't stop thinking about her either.

The shimmering light pink dress she wore was tiny. Too goddamn short. It barely reached her mid-thighs, showing off her slim legs. Her dark hair was up in a fancy hairdo, exposing the skin on her neck, shoulders, and décolleté. I didn't need to touch her to know it would be soft.

And now here I was, stalking her.

The pressure in my chest was unfamiliar. From the moment this woman entered my life, my blood ran hotter than ever. My obsession crept up on me, the need to learn every single thing about her clawing at me.

So I dug up everything I could on her.

Twenty years ago, I ensured she got home safe. But since then, I kept my distance. If I lurked in her shadow, I'd attract trouble, so it was for the best. Though I'd check up on her—to ensure she was well and safe. Yes, her brothers took care of her, but I couldn't rest unless I looked her up every few months. I felt personally responsible for everything that happened to her twenty years ago. For causing her pain.

Now that she was in my world, no information was off-limits. I knew every single address Agent Ashford ever lived at, her social security number, names of her friends, how she liked her pasta, her coffee, and what shows she watched. Courtesy of her best friends. Agent Ashford didn't have a Pinterest account but her friends did. And they kept a board specific for her likes. So sue me, I stalked their Pinterest page.

Unfortunately, with every piece of information I learned about her, my obsession somehow tripped into overdrive.

Addicted to coffee.

No social media accounts.

No current relationship.

Two past serious boyfriends.

I might hunt them down and kill them. I was still debating it. Vasili wouldn't be happy if he got wind of it. He wouldn't though. I'd make it look like an accident.

And of course, there was the general public's known information.

Sister to the Billionaire Kings.

Daughter to Senator Ashford.

Four brothers.

One proclaimed dead.

Guilt was a bitter pill to swallow.

Just as Vasili kept trying to right his mother's sins, I kept trying to right Ivan's sins. I felt directly responsible for them.

I sat on the roof of Agent Ashford's building and watched her run the tenth lap around the outside gym, right alongside her brother. I'd just seen her last night, but the restlessness within me grew with each hour that passed since I'd seen her at the restaurant. I've been checking up on her on and off for years. But now that I've been in her presence, I didn't think I could ever let her go again.

Another lap. She was in good shape, and I hated that she did something so simple with someone else. I didn't give a fuck if he was her brother. Or her girlfriends in the apartment, or that little kid.

I wanted her to laugh only with me. Cry with me. Exercise with me. Eat with me. Breathe with me. And fuck me. Only me.

Heat crawled beneath my skin, though I was unsure whether it was this woman or the hot temperatures of the day.

The humid air of New Orleans was a welcome reprieve after living my teenage years in Siberia. Those cold days and frostbite settled into my bones and stayed there. If you asked me, the fires of hell were better than that freezing fucking hellhole. I'd pick burning over freezing any day.

I drummed my fingers on my thigh, keeping my hands busy. The need to keep any body part of mine busy was uncharacteristic for me. I could stand still for hours without twitching a muscle. And here I was fidgeting. *Fucking fidgeting!*

It was all her fault. This woman with a petite body, skin glistening with sweat. Her exercise shorts and tank top hugged her body like a second skin. I didn't like the impact she had on me. Especially considering the plan to use her to get to Igor and then to Ivan.

That club would require me putting hands on her body. Goddamn it! It made my groin twitch just to think about it. It was a stupid plan if I couldn't maintain my control.

Bad fucking timing for any emotion. I had to squash it.

I had always been immune to women's charms. Until now. Agent Ashford fueled my blood and all it took was an elevator ride to push me over the edge.

Fuck!

Not what I needed right now. I needed to keep a clear head. I had to ensure we got to Ivan and killed him, before he got his filthy hands on little Nikola. It would be all my fault and nothing in this world could right that sin.

I wasn't a good man, not even close.

My life consisted of a string of fucked-up things that made me numb. It made me the worst kind of villain. It was what Vasili's mother wanted. The ugly bitch wasn't satisfied only with destroying my mother. From the moment she kidnapped me and dumped me with various families, she kept coming back.

Over and over again. But it wasn't until that day, on my tenth birthday, that life became a living, walking nightmare. The day that kicked it all off. Not that days leading into it were all peaches and roses.

Thinking back, I thought that was the day I might have given up my innocence. An invisible noose wrapped around my neck, choking me as red images covered my vision.

Blood covered my hands. My clothes.

It was everywhere.

Splattered all over the living room. Lifeless eyes. Terror frozen on their faces. My adoptive family was dead. Again.

*Death always followed me. It was all **her** fault.*

Anguish gripped me, the need to fight and scream burning through my veins as I watched the cold, hard eyes of a woman claiming to be my mother. She'd shown up every two years, ripping me apart from my current family, leaving nobody alive and putting me with a new family. But this time, I was stronger. Slightly older than little boy. I was finally able to fight and defend myself.

I tried to protect my adoptive family. And failed. My adoptive sister. My adoptive mother and father. All dead. For loving me.

The scene in the room was grotesque, cold and lifeless. Their eyes blank, staring into a void of death. Gone forever.

Bitterness, hate, and rage swelled inside me at the woman who stood protected by her bodyguards. I hated them all. Wanted to kill them all. Make them pay for the suffering they caused.

It was hard to believe that not even an hour ago this room had burst with laughter, love, and warmth. This family had taken me in and treated me as their own. Loving me was their only mistake.

And because of this cruel woman, they paid the price in the worst way possible.

Yes, emotions could drive you to madness.

They made it hard to deal with life. So most of the time, I didn't feel any emotions. Not a single damn one. It worked best for me. In fact, I preferred it. Strong emotions only got you or your loved ones killed. And loss left gaping holes in your chest that were impossible to fill.

I breathed deep, tamping down the rage and sorrow that twisted around my gut. My heart raced, a slithering hate squeezing around it. Sweat broke across my brow, my palms clammy.

Lately, memories kept coming back. It was worse than ever. Tenfold worse. I knew what triggered the memories.

Isabella and Tatiana. Even Bianca Morrelli and retrieving her mother from the clutches of Benito King triggered them.

The semblance of a family started to form for me.

And one thing I knew for certain... It would cost everyone their lives, and I couldn't let that happen.

Goddamn it. I needed to get a grip.

Fuck. The. Memories.

I worked too hard to get to this stage in my life—where I had family and people I cared about.

Isabella. Her babies. Tatiana. My brothers. Even Cassio, Nico, and their gang.

Some people considered us bad men. Nothing was ever completely black and white in this world. I grew up seeing cruelty and evil as an everyday occurrence. Fighting and killing to survive. And not all those I killed growing up deserved to die.

Their deaths still haunted me. *Pashka. Ilya. Kostya.* Memories flooded through me. Their faces, their smiles, their deaths. The smiles were few and far between growing up in that world, but we had shared them. They had been my brothers… they were my family.

The burning spread across my torso, sweat dripping through the cuts. But it didn't compare to the burning in my chest.

Kostya's eyes widened, his blood spraying from his neck across my chest. I watched as he struggled, his hands clamping desperately over the gash. I stood in the ring next to Ilya as we watched our friend die. He stared into our eyes, knowing we had no choice.

Kill or be killed. It was our life.

I watched as his mouth moved. "It's okay." A whisper passed across his lips as the blood began to trickle from the corners of his lips.

The guilt ran red through me, just like the rivers of Egypt. It swallowed me whole. It didn't matter that it wasn't me who sliced his throat. I had made him weak. He fought me before he fought Ilya; I weakened him. Though I refused to finish him.

Watching my friend die a slow death was Ivan's punishment to me. For disobeying him. I had refused to finish Kostya, so he made Ilya and Kostya fight.

But Ilya could never hit the right artery to make death quick. Less painful. Instead he missed Kostya's carotid artery, so we watched him struggle. Fighting to live but knowing he'd die.

I should end his suffering. Slice the artery correctly so his suffering would end. My body shifted barely an inch, and Ivan's voice boomed over the ring.

"Touch him, Alexei, and you'll earn yourself another forty lashes."

The skin on my back itched, still raw from the last beating I earned. "You missed your chance, bastard."

My eyes found our captor. His evil smile spread across his face, thinking he'd taught me a lesson. Thinking that I'd follow his orders blindly. That I'd become one of his favorites as Igor had done. My eyes flashed to the boy no older than me sitting on the floor next to Ivan's chair like some obedient dog, a smile just as evil as his master's spread across his face. Because that's what he was to us... a master, someone who dictated our lives... our deaths.

My fists clenched. My ears buzzed. Hate boiled as Ivan's guards stood to the side, drinking their vodka and eating beef stroganoff, while none of us in the ring had had food since yesterday.

Kostya clung to life, his gurgling sounds the only thing I could focus on. His soul struggled to live. He was only a year older than me at twelve. Too young to die.

My eyes found Kostya's. The plea was there—the plea to end his suffering. To end his pain. The whole scene... heart wrenching. Though I wasn't sure that I had much of a heart left.

Two steps. One knife.

His hands fell from his neck as if accepting his fate. I slashed the blade across his carotid. The fatal blow. His blood soaked my hands and my forearm as I held his head.

We were children. Forced to take each other's lives in order to save our own. I watched as life drained from his eyes, until the frost of death covered them. I lifted my hand, sliding them over his lids, closing them.

He was dead.

He was free.

So many times I'd wondered if it wouldn't be better to let them kill me. So that I too could be free. But when the time came, I found myself desperate to survive.

Yet with each of the deaths I caused, something inside me died right along with them.

"Give him forty lashes," Ivan ordered, his voice hard. But he might as well have been on another planet. All my focus was on Kostya. "Twenty on the front and twenty on the back."

Twelve months. 365 days. 8,760 hours.

I turned eleven today.

Happy fucking birthday to me, celebrating with another death... another beating.

We'd all die here anyhow.

My memories sliced into my barely healed wounds. The scars on my skin were nothing to the scars inside me. Those tasted of copper, guilt, and hate. The kind that couldn't be healed.

Hollowness was so much better.

It fucking sucked to learn so early on we were no better than animals. We were all monsters. Our survival instinct kicked in and the need to live just as strong as it was for animals. Ivan counted on it. He used it against you, until you had to shut down every emotion or risk losing your mind with the consequences of your actions.

"What are you doing?" Sasha snuck up behind me. I was so out of it I didn't even hear him approach. Not good.

"Nothing."

"Looks like you are doing something," he added nonchalantly. Was he chewing gum? He really liked to fuck with me using those taunting words. "Stalking, by the looks of it. Looks like you have a thing for the FBI agent."

My jaw clenched. I loved Sasha but he was annoying as fuck. Loved to just talk out of his ass. Maybe I could pull his tongue out, so he'd be quiet for a year or two. Then I'd have it sewn back in. I knew how to preserve body parts. A sardonic breath left me.

Yes, I was a cruel motherfucker.

Fucking Ivan left more of a mark than he realized.

"Better get in her pants before she arrests you." He continued smirking like the asshole he was. "Otherwise, I'll bang her. Her girl-friends can join in too."

My molars grounded. "Why are you here?"

"Looking for you." He popped the gum in his mouth. I had to fight the urge to dig it out of his mouth and throw it off the building. Right along with him. "Bella wants you over for dinner. For some goddamn reason, she thought I had to deliver a verbal invitation."

"Delivered," I told him. "Now get lost."

He chuckled like I uttered a joke. "I bet you'd like me to get lost so you can stalk that pretty little thing all by yourself." God, I'd have to talk to Bella and warn her never to send Sasha to me. A fucking text would suffice.

When Sasha didn't move, I narrowed my eyes on him.

He just shrugged and continued, "Bianca and her obsessive, crazy-jealous husband are in New Orleans with their caravan of kiddos." He popped another bubble with his gum and my fist tightened. "I kind of want to see if Bianca wants me to kill him. Or maybe if she wants a change of scenery, so I could bang her." I almost wished Sasha would try it so Morrelli would have him shot. He probably wouldn't kill him, but he'd wound him so he could torture him for a long time for daring to touch his wife. And then there were Luca and Cassio—those two would kill him, revive him back to life, then kill him again. And repeat the process until the fucker would have to be saved by Vasili and me. "Anyhow, at least we know the food will be good. Bianca is cooking and that woman can cook. Bella can save lives, but her cooking puts people in the hospital."

My lips twitched, as they always did when it came to my sister. I regularly didn't smile. The scar on my lip made it look like a grimace, and it stung each time I moved my lips. But she was worth it. Since she entered my life, I felt the need to smile more. It scared me as much as it did Vasili to think of anyone in our world getting their hands on her. She was too soft.

Unlike Luciano's wife or Cassio's wife, Bella was too meek, too kind. Kind of like Nico's wife, except I saw firsthand that Bianca Morrelli was capable of pulling the trigger.

But Sasha had a point about our sister. Bella's cooking was medi-ocre. At best.

"So are you coming?" Sasha popped the gum again.

"If I say yes, will you get lost?" If not, I'd have to knock him out. I couldn't handle his mouth today. Or ever, for that matter.

"Maybe." He popped another bubble. I rose up to my full length. "Fine, fine. I'm getting lost," he grumbled. "So yes for dinner?"

"Yes."

"Okay, leaving you to your maniac stalking," he muttered. "You are just as psycho as that fucking Morrelli."

He was wrong. I was worse, but there was no sense in debating that shit with my brother. Sasha disappeared and my eyes returned to the dark-haired agent. Her brother said something and she threw her head back laughing so loud the sound traveled all the way to me.

I should find another woman for my plan. Going into the sex club with someone who made my blood run hotter than a volcano could harm us both if I lost my head. But my mind zeroed in on Aurora Ashford, and I knew it wouldn't ease up.

She deserved to be part of ending Ivan's life as much as I did.

I wouldn't take that away from her.

EIGHT
ALEXEI

I was the last one to arrive at Vasili's manor on the outskirts of New Orleans. He owned a hundred acres around it, affording him and his family privacy and protection. After the near-death experience Isabella went through at Tatiana's place a few years back, he bought extra land around his manor and padded the security with extra layers. Once Isabella told him she was pregnant, his protective instinct kicked into overdrive. Not that I could blame him.

I parked my Aston Martin, exited the car, and strode towards the back of the house. Hearing the tunes of Iggy Azalea travel through the air, I knew immediately Vasili let Isabella and Tatiana pick the music for the night. The fact I even knew it was Iggy Azalea was disturbing. I loved my sisters, but their taste in music fucking sucked.

The sun was slowly setting, and the lights already covered the large patio area. The hot July breeze swept across the yard, and I was glad we'd be mostly outside. Bella was quick to pick up that I preferred it hot. I never even turned on the AC in my own place. It only froze my bones and brought the memories of cold basements back.

Yeah, fuck that.

As I turned the corner, I found everyone there. Vasili, Sasha, Nico Morrelli, and Raphael Santos all stood together on the left side of the lawn while the women gathered on the right side of the patio. By the looks of it, the men had a lively discussion going. Nico had one of his boys on his shoulders, the little guy gripping his dad's hair with his small, chubby hands. If Nico wasn't careful, he'd end up with a big bald spot on his skull.

Vasili held his newborn girl who was fussing, probably due to her colic. Yeah, I knew too much about babies. I blamed it all on Isabella who insisted on telling me everything. Thank God she didn't share details of her sex life with me. Raphael, Isabella's other half brother, had our two-year-old nephew on his shoulders. Little Nikola loved danger and giggled each time Raphael pretended to almost drop him. I feared that little devil might become just like Sasha who at this very moment looked bored to fucking death. He lifted his wristwatch as if he was counting down to his exit.

My eyes darted to the right side where Tatiana, Isabella, Nico's mother, and Bianca sat chatting and laughing. Bianca held her other twin boy in her arms, while her blonde twins stood at the little play-ground in serious discussion, probably contemplating how to steal someone's car, jewelry, or stash of money.

Those two would be trouble, and with Luciano's son on their team, they might end up running the underworld. As if they sensed my thoughts, an identical set of blue eyes met mine and up-to-no-good grins spread across their small faces.

God help Nico when those two turned into teenagers.

"Hey, Uncle Alexei," they both greeted me, running over to me.

Everyone's eyes shifted my way and I nodded my greeting. Hannah pulled on my pant leg. I lowered down so the twins didn't have to crane their necks to look at me. For some reason, they decided to call me uncle and never felt uncomfortable around me.

Unlike their mother who always hesitated a bit. Not that I blamed her. She had good instincts. After the incident with her mother, she relaxed more around me, but she always kept herself guarded.

"Hey," I greeted both twins. Arianna pulled on my hand, urging me to lean closer.

"Want to know a secret?" she whispered.

"But you have to pay up first," Hannah added.

I cocked my eyebrow and Arianna, who was usually the shy one, offered an apologetic smile. "We need the money," she explained.

Nico was one of the richest men in the country. I was certain he gave them whatever they wanted.

"For?" I inquired curiously.

"To buy tools," Hannah explained. As if on cue, both of them glanced around to make sure nobody was listening. "We are going to break into Dad's safe."

Their eyes twinkled mischievously, extremely pleased with themselves. My lip twitched again. Definitely double trouble right here.

"In that case, give me the secret, and I'll give you the money." The girls were turning six soon, and already contemplated robbing their father. It was only right I supported them.

"How much?" Arianna whispered.

"How much do you want?" I asked.

"I didn't know you could say so many words," Hannah remarked. She was right, I usually kept my answers short.

"In a row," Arianna added.

"Want the money or not?" I challenged them, amused. Their eyes darted between each other and me while my mind filtered through the memory of the day my vocal cords were crushed.

Images flashing like a silent '20s film.

The calloused palm wrapped around my neck, gripping it so hard black dots swam in my vision.

I refused to give up, so I fought him, but his grip tightened. I'd be damned if I'd take death willingly. Yes, there had been nights I craved it, but now, when it came down to it, I wanted to fucking live.

Or maybe it was that I refused to let this asshole be the one to finally take me out.

I fought him. Letting my anger fuel my movements, I dug my fingers into his hand, clawing into his flesh. I'd rip it off his fucking bones if he didn't let up.

The devil grinned, his teeth rotten from all the fucking candy he liked to eat. Sweet treats given to those who obeyed and worshiped the man who held us captive or used as a method to torture those of us who refused. Having melted chocolate forced down your throat in some twisted form of waterboarding by a psychotic Willy Wonka would turn anyone off it.

Fuck him. Fuck Ivan.

The asshole above me smiled wider. He may have been almost thirty, but he fought like a boy my age, and I was half his age. His size was his only advantage against those of us younger than him. He thought beating boys so much younger was a victory.

I let all my rage out, ignoring the spots that built in my vision, almost blinding me to the man above me.

Anger flooded through me like hot lava, acidic and destructive.

He shoved the side of my face into the hard, compacted dirt floor of the fighting ring. So many boys had died here. Would my blank stare haunt someone like theirs haunted me?

Red overtook the black spots of my vision, pulling the rage to the forefront. I'd need it if I was to beat this motherfucker.

While my left hand remained on his wrist that was clutched at my neck, I put all my strength into my right arm and pushed a fist into his right kidney.

A yelp escaped him and his grip loosened just enough to give me an open window. Using my own body weight in his moment of hesitation, I shifted my legs beneath him, pushing him onto his side. My fist connected with his ribs, the crack of bones under my knuckles. It takes just over three thousand newtons of quick force to crack a rib.

I may not have gotten the same schooling as other kids, but I learned what I could about the human body. The right spots to strike to bring an attacker to their knees. The base of the neck, the kidneys, trachea, bladder, and of course the groin.

While I despised Ivan, he did give me the ability to learn what I could to become a killing machine. It was what he wanted us to become. Those of us he thought capable. Little did he know... he was creating his very own, personal grim reaper; because, in the end, I would be the one to take his life.

The asshole's grip faltered, and before he could get the bright idea to choke me again, I broke his right wrist.

"You fucking little bitch," he screamed, his body bent forward as he went down to his knees. Did he even realize he was the one screaming like a bitch?

From the corner of my eye, I saw someone throw a blade, but it didn't quite reach me. Whether it was purposely out of my reach or not, I needed it.

I jammed my knee into the devil's back, hoping it broke his spine, pushing him forward, and reached for the knife. The moment I grabbed the handle, he lifted his left arm, raised to attack, and I took advantage. Jamming the knife deep into his armpit, I severed the artery that pumped blood to his cold, black heart.

I watched as his eyes widened, pain crossing his expression. It wasn't enough. I would ensure today that Ivan's devil ceased to exist.

Pulling the blade free from the artery, a geyser of blood followed, and I smiled as I pressed the tip of the blade just at the base of his neck, parallel to his chin, jamming it straight in. His gurgling sounds echoed through the dimly lit room as everyone remained quiet at the sight before them.

One way or another, I'd fucking extinguish every single fucking one of them. I'd leave Ivan for last, so he could tremble in the dark. Like the coward he was.

The devil's soul drained from the asshole's ugly face, his black teeth exposed.

But that wasn't the most terrifying part.

It was that I felt nothing. Absolutely nothing.

Maybe I'd become a monster too.

It had taken more than a minute for the pain radiating from my throat to register. I knew he'd almost succeeded in crushing my windpipe.

For weeks after, I could barely speak without it causing pain. My vocal cords had been permanently damaged. But I found in the weeks of silence following… that I much rather preferred not speaking.

The girls whispering amongst themselves pulled me out of the memory. They debated back and forth, working on coming up with an amount they thought fair.

"Twenty dollars," they both answered in unison.

Damn little blackmailers. Both extended their hands.

"For each of us," Hannah added, tapping her foot impatiently.

I couldn't fucking wait until these two grew up. Nico would have to put the entire police force on the payroll to keep them out of jail. I pulled out my wallet and handed them each a twenty-dollar bill.

"Send me a picture with your dad's safe unlocked, and I'll give you a hundred dollars." Both of their eyes bulged out. "Each," I added.

"I can hack into Mom's phone," Arianna answered confidently. "I know her passcode," she added in a hushed tone. "So if you see a picture from her phone, that is us."

Jesus, maybe I should talk to Vasili and Bella about keeping my niece and nephew away from these two. They'd corrupt them and make them into criminals before they could say their first word.

"My secret," I reminded them.

They both shared a glance, then returned to look at me. "Mom is going to talk to you."

I frowned, debating whether I should be impressed or offended. "Did you just cheat me out of forty dollars?"

Arianna scoffed, an offended look in her eyes. "I would never," she vowed. "I'm gonna marry Nikola. I wouldn't cheat his family."

I cocked my eyebrow. Geez, last I heard she was marrying Matteo, Luciano's boy. Then I remembered. It was her sister who claimed she'd marry Matteo. Fuck if I knew. It was too much to keep up.

"Does Nikola know you're going to marry him?" I asked instead. She shrugged her little shoulders.

"Not yet. He is not very good at talking yet."

"Isn't he kind of too young for you?" I inquired curiously.

"Yeah, I guess I'll be a cougar," she answered, rolling her eyes. What did they teach kids in school these days? "I don't really like cougars, so maybe he can hurry up and outgrow me."

I shook my head at her weird logic. "So what does your mom want to talk to me about?"

Hannah shrugged, clearly done with this conversation. "About some bad Russian," she blurted. "Ivan the Great or something."

Did she mean Ivan Petrov? It couldn't be. There would be no point in time the two would have ever crossed paths.

"Ivan Petrov?" I asked. Uttering the name alone to the little kids sent disgust down my spine. No child should ever know that monster.

"No idea," they both answered, rolling their eyes.

Yeah, I definitely got ripped off. They owed me the next secret for free.

"Hey, brother." Isabella came up to us. Bianca, Tatiana, and Nico's mother were still in the same spot, discussing something vividly and laughing like crazy. Seeing their open window, the twins disbursed, right along with my money.

"Bella," I greeted her, then stood up to my full length. "How are you feeling?"

She only had her baby girl six weeks ago, but she was determined to behave like she was back to normal.

Back when she came to New Orleans to stay with Tatiana, Isabella patched up Sasha when he was shot. She took over our private clinic and took care of our men when they couldn't be taken to the hospital. It was a damn pain to explain gunshot wounds and police always got involved. So it worked out perfectly.

Of course, our private clinic wasn't as busy as emergency rooms, so Bella continued her studies. She liked to keep herself busy.

"Great." She beamed. "Bianca shared a recipe with me and bossed me around in the kitchen."

My eyes traveled back to Bianca who turned her head my way and waved, offering a small smile. Her dark hair and eyes often reminded me of my own sister. The two were similar in a lot of ways.

"Then at least we'll be fed," I stated matter-of-factly.

Bella chuckled softly. "Did you just crack a joke?"

It wasn't a joke but a fact. If Bella cooked, we'd be either in the hospital, starving, or packing up to go find a restaurant that could accommodate us all.

Pressing a smooch onto my cheek, she whispered into my ear. "Bianca wants to talk to you, but don't scare her."

Like I could even attempt to scare Bianca without having Nico up my ass.

"Sure." I glanced towards the group of men. "Does Nico know?"

Because Sasha wasn't joking when he said Morrelli was obsessive. Suddenly, I understood that obsession because there was a certain dark-haired FBI agent that seemed to have brought all that up in the span of two days. And at this very moment, that FBI agent was having dinner with her brother and her friends in her apartment.

Bella's eyes darted to the man standing next to her husband. Compared to us, Nico appeared like a clean-cut businessman. He hid his ruthless and obsessive nature well.

"I didn't ask her," she finally answered. "But I get a sense she hasn't told him about whatever she wants to talk to you about."

"That will go over well," I said wryly.

I knew how Vasili would act if Bella said something to another man rather than him. I knew how I would. And I damn well knew Nico would react the same way.

"Let me greet him. And at least give him a heads-up," I suggested. Bella nodded her head in agreement. Besides, I had an agent to work with and getting shot by Morrelli would interrupt those plans.

"Where is Adrian?" I asked, not seeing Tatiana's husband anywhere.

"He had some kind of security emergency. You just missed him." I nodded. He was a workaholic, so no surprise there.

I headed toward my brothers, Raphael, and Nico.

Nico was on vacation and Raphael came to visit his half sister. My full-blooded sister. That's right, the same womb made us full-blooded siblings. Raphael wasn't so fortunate.

"Another fucking hour and you'd have missed the whole event," Sasha muttered. "That busy stalking?"

I didn't bother answering him and instead flipped him the bird.

"Nico. Raphael." I leaned over and gave a high five to my two-year-old nephew. "Nikola, my man."

He smacked his little hand against my big palm. His speech was slightly delayed and he rarely uttered words. If one of the families that took care of me when I was a kid was to be believed, I had had the same problem. I spoke my first word well after my third birthday. I assured Bella little Nikola would be fine.

He grinned and my chest squeezed. He was so small and innocent, the worry that someone would get their hands on him, a constant worry in the back of my mind. Ivan's threat made that worry tenfold.

Why would anyone want kids? It was like having a heart attack on a daily basis.

I turned my attention to little Marietta and brushed my fingers across her chubby cheeks. She didn't even stir. Sleepyhead that one. When Nikola was that age, he'd wake up to a fly buzzing in the air. Not this one. She'd sleep through an invasion.

"Nico, your wife wants to talk to me," I told Morrelli, my eyes still on my niece. Man, what I wouldn't give to be able to sleep peacefully like that. I slept four hours a night at most. Memories always plagued me in the form of nightmares. I kept them at bay during the day, for the most part, but at night, they haunted me.

But no matter what, I'd ensure nothing disturbed my nephew's and niece's sleep. They wouldn't live through what I had, or even Vasili and Sasha. Every single person in this circle lived through some shit. We'd protect the little ones so they'd never experience that kind of shit.

"What about?" I sensed tension in his voice.

I met his gaze, the gray of the wolf. It wasn't the only reason they called him the Wolf.

"Ivan the Great according to your daughters," I muttered dryly. Though I suspected it might be Ivan Petrov she wanted to talk about but there was no sense in alarming Nico until I got my confirmation. "Will it be a problem?"

His eyes darted to his wife who was still laughing with Tatiana, Nico's mother, and Bella. Whatever they were talking about had all four of them on the verge of tears and holding their bellies.

"No, but I want to know what she says."

I nodded. I expected nothing less.

"Do we have all the information on Agent Ashford?" Vasili asked.

"I bet he has more than just information," Sasha blurted, smirking.

"You know her father is Senator Ashford. Rumors are he might run for president," I told Vasili, ignoring Sasha. "Her brothers are the Billionaire Kings."

"Get the fuck out," Sasha drawled, though he didn't sound terribly impressed. "The girl is from elite society and she settled for a government salary. I don't know if I should be impressed or disappointed. Maybe she's a nutcase like you, Alexei."

Cutting his tongue out sounded more and more appealing.

"Damn, that name rings a bell," Raphael added pensively. "Not the senator's political career. I think he had some business with my old man at one point. Though I know Byron. He and his brothers are tough in business, but everything they touch turns to gold. Byron helped me out on a few real estate transactions in Miami, though I'm sure he made out with a hefty profit."

"Maybe he was working on a campaign?" Vasili suggested.

"Senator Ashford is okay," Nico chimed in. "Though a manipulative bastard. You have to watch your back with that one." It didn't surprise me to hear it. Most politicians were like that. "I know her brothers," he continued. "I can introduce you. I never met Agent Ashford. I know they keep her out of the public eye, ever since—"

He didn't finish the sentence, but I knew what he meant.

"Ever since?" Sasha asked curiously.

"Ever since her brother was kidnapped," Nico answered, keeping his mask firmly in place. Nico knew about Kingston. This was something I never shared with Sasha and Vasili. It was my shameful secret to bear. "His sister was the witness."

"Fuck, that's rough," Vasili grumbled. "No wonder she joined the agency. Probably sees her brother in every single one of those abducted boys."

"The part that the world doesn't know," Nico continued, "is that Senator Ashford has a hard time keeping it in his pants. He has another son named after his old man, and another daughter. Davina Hayes, born in Texas."

"Well, their family sounds just as fucked up as ours," Sasha sneered. "When Alexei marries Agent Ashford, our family dynamic will go up a few notches and our family parties will beat your wedding, Nico."

"How about you worry about your own women, Sasha?" Vasili smirked. "Or are you scaring them with your BDSM shit?"

Sasha flipped him off.

"Not around the little ones," Nico taunted him, amusement on his face. "We don't want you to rub off on them."

"Oh, and you three bastards are so much better," he remarked back dryly.

"Her brothers have impressive Special Forces backgrounds. You know their empire better than anyone, Vasili," I continued, before Sasha could say another dumb thing. "They are powerful and have connections everywhere." That family was something and you couldn't help but admire them. Her brothers would tear down the world for each other and especially for their sister. I had no doubt Agent Ashford would do the same for them.

"We will have to tread carefully," Vasili commented. "We don't want to attract any unwanted attention if something happens to her or we have to get rid of her."

"Nobody is getting rid of her," I growled threateningly. "Or touching a single hair on her head."

The words escaped me before I thought better of it, cold and deadly. Fuck! My self-control was slipping. I felt it in every breath I took.

It was a mistake to show you cared too much. I never liked to show it, and I hadn't made such a mistake in a very long time. The lesson was fresh even after all these years.

Thick tension penetrated the air. Or maybe it was my barely functioning heart. I didn't know. One thing was for sure, the invasive silence stretched on.

Vasili raised an eyebrow but said nothing. Sasha smirked like the fucking idiot that he was.

Nico muttered something along the lines of, "It happens to us all."

Raphael just stared. Bastard! He was lucky he held my nephew; otherwise, I'd punch him.

"If you need help," Nico broke the tense silence. "You can use my resources."

Since he offered.

"I do," I said calmly. "I need you to keep her brothers occupied while I work with Agent Ashford."

"That'll be hard," Nico responded. "Her brothers have been all about their little sister. They'll ditch the U.S. president before they ditch their sister. But I'll definitely try."

A nod and that was set.

Two hours later, I'd done my quota for the day in terms of socializing. Heck, I'd done my quota for the year. I'd probably socialized more in the last year than I had in my entire life. I strode through the large family room and headed out when, as always, my eyes caught on the painting Isabella hung above the fireplace.

It was a 16-by-24 canvas of a weeping willow. I never understood why Isabella and Vasili liked the damn painting. It was bland and just boring. Tatiana even asked her once what the deal was with it. Isabella blushed crimson, then mumbled something about the beauty and peace of the tree. Her eyes fleeted to her husband as she answered and Vasili's smirk didn't escape me.

Who the fuck knew what those two did? Not that I cared to know.

I headed for the door when a soft voice called out behind me.

"Hey, Alexei. Can I talk to you, please?" It was Bianca's voice. I didn't need to turn around to know she was nervous. Everyone was always nervous around me.

I stopped and slowly turned around. I wasn't easy on the eyes and definitely didn't give out safe vibes. Bianca had gone through enough; she didn't need my scary ass to frighten her. Though she looked anything but frightened.

When I met her gaze, there was no reluctance in her eyes. Only that soft smile on her face, the one that made people usually do anything for her. Her husband in particular; she had him wrapped around her little finger.

"Bianca," I greeted her.

She stopped a few feet away from me and Nico's glance our way didn't escape me. God help the world if this woman ever decided to leave her husband. He'd hunt her down and drag her back, though by the looks of it, the two had no intention of leaving each other. It was hard not to notice the two always touched each other and how they tended to disappear.

I waited until she was comfortable enough to start talking. I was no good at small talk, so I stood still, waiting. Despite not being badass women, like Margaret Callahan liked to call herself and her cousin Áine, my sister and Bianca still fit in our world. Those two balanced our cruel world with a touch of softness.

Some might argue they didn't belong in our world, but I'd argue our world needed them.

"I heard that you might go after Ivan Petrov," she started, surprising me. Though I guessed correctly earlier. There weren't too many Ivans in our conversation topics. And Ivan the Great didn't count. Though I didn't know what she had to do with him. I waited for her to explain. "My grandpa's sister. She was the first payment in... in my family. My mother was named after her." Bianca's knuckles turned white. She hated anything to do with that goddamn Belles and Mobsters agreement. It cost her a mother. "The rumor was that she was married off to Ivan Petrov."

I frowned. I knew Ivan for a good part of my life. He never married.

"Who said that?" I questioned her.

She wrapped her arms around her small body. Nico would be coming our way any second because his wife's distress was his weakness.

Bianca swallowed. "My grandma heard a rumor. Not sure if there is merit to it," she muttered. "But if you go after him, I'd hoped—" She faltered just for a split second. "I'd hoped you'd kill him and bring her or her children home. To me."

And this was why our world needed Bella and Bianca.

"I'll check into it," I promised her. Though if her grandfather's sister indeed married Ivan, she was probably long dead. No woman could survive his brutality. Though, I'd never tell Bianca that.

A soft smile spread across her face. "Thank you," she exhaled, her eyes shining with gratitude. No wonder Morrelli fell for the woman.

She could melt the polar ice caps when she smiled.

t

NINE
AURORA

Ever since I ran into the Nikolaev men at the restaurant, tension filled my lungs and tightened my muscles. Deep down inside me, my gut warned me something was up. I could feel it dancing in the air, though I couldn't quite pinpoint what drove it.

And then there was the constant feeling of being watched. It was stupid; I knew it. But I couldn't shake it off. The hair on the back of my neck made the presence known. Byron could feel it too. It assured me that I wasn't crazy. Except, I couldn't even fathom who would even bother watching me.

My instinct warned me to be on guard. And when I doubted my instinct, I could rely on Byron's instinct.

Lunchtime was fast approaching. Byron wanted to have some alone time with me. Again. I loved my brother, but he could be smothering sometimes and having lunch alone with him was sure to start another form of grilling.

Now that he'd spent the weekend with me, he was able to study my worries and concerns and probably wanted to figure out how to make them all go away.

My gaze drifted to my guests in the living room. Willow, Sailor, and Gabriel played on the Xbox.

"Why don't we all go together and grab lunch?" I suggested. Yeah, so what, I was a tad bit sneaky. You had to be in order to survive older brothers.

Willow and Sailor glanced up. "What? Like now?"

"Well, it's lunchtime," I retorted dryly. "Isn't lunchtime when people have lunch?"

Willow stuck her tongue out. "Are you trying to be smart or a smartass?"

"Both."

"Mission accomplished." Sailor winked. "I think all three of us earned those badges."

"Besides, your brother already told us he plans on grilling you," Willow sneered. "You know how he is."

That was the problem. I did know how he was. "He wouldn't be so rude to deny you three coming," I tried one more time.

I knew they wanted to stay behind and play Xbox with Gabriel. Those two were damn addicts, a bad example for my godson. Here they were in New Orleans, and they were more concerned with an Xbox than sightseeing. "You guys have been playing the stupid game for the past two hours. It is Sunday, and we only have another day."

The three shared a look and then shook their heads. "Nah. We'll have lunch here."

"Traitors," I muttered, slightly annoyed.

I mentally prepared for a battle of words. Because Byron was good like that. Probably why people speculated he'd make it very far in politics. As much as you wanted to keep your mouth shut, he had a way of dragging an answer out of you and convincing you to do what he thought best.

It was probably why the *great* Senator Ashford always used Byron when he needed extra votes. Persuasive bastard! I loved him, but still, it wasn't right.

As we both headed towards my car, he spoke up, "I'm driving."

I rolled my eyes. "Byron, this is the twenty-first century. Women *can* drive, you know."

He shrugged his one shoulder, ignoring my sarcasm. "That is debatable. I'd like my stomach intact, thank you very much. Your constant braking makes me nauseous."

I shot him an annoyed look.

"I don't ride the brakes," I protested.

"Yes, you do."

"Asshole!" I muttered. "Where is my sidearm when I need it?"

He chuckled, unperturbed. "Keys, little sister," he demanded.

"I might take you to a food truck for lunch," I threatened half-heartedly, then threw the keys over the hood of the car, secretly hoping he'd miss them and they'd hit his handsome face.

No such luck.

I've learned the battles I could win with my brothers over my life-time. This wasn't one of them, so there was no sense in arguing with him who should drive. It would go on all night.

Byron opened the driver door and got behind the wheel as I got into the passenger seat.

He hadn't even started the car before he started pouncing. "How long have you been stalked?"

I exhaled, watching as he pulled away from the parking lot and into the traffic. My brother certainly didn't beat around the bush. Byron acted more like my father than our own father. I found comfort in the knowledge he did it with all his siblings, but he went slightly over-board with me. All my brothers did.

A sharp pain pierced through me thinking about Kingston. Would my brothers be so protective of me if they knew I was responsible for his disappearance? Or would they cut all their ties with me and hate me? Anxiety washed over me, my mind whirling with anguish and scenarios of being abandoned. I was trying so hard to fix it by catching this predator. It was my way of paying for my sins.

His hand shot out and grabbed mine, forcing my hand open. "Rora, you have to stop," he said in an exasperated tone. "This was the reason I didn't want you to work for the FBI. You take things too personally."

I yanked my hand back and lowered my eyes to find the crescent indentions from my fingernails in my skin.

"I don't know that I am being stalked," I retorted dryly, not commenting on his remark. "It just started this weekend. So it could be you."

He huffed. "Nobody smart would stalk me."

"Confident much?" I asked sarcastically.

He ignored me, his eyes focused on the road and the constant traffic that flowed in and out of the French Quarter.

"We should get you out of here," he suggested.

My head snapped to him. "I don't think so. I have a job to do, and I'm not leaving until the case is solved."

The predator was my case to resolve.

"What case?" he asked curiously, his posture relaxed but he didn't fool me. He was digging for information.

"Good try," I said dryly. "You can keep asking, but I'm not telling. I don't nose into your work. Don't nose into mine."

He chuckled softly. "How did my baby sister turn out so smart?"

"I had four brothers to—" My words faltered, realizing what I said. I had never stopped thinking about Kingston. His body was never found, and he was pronounced dead, but the hope in my chest was never extinguished.

It was still fresh as that day I burst through the door of my home, after running home from the zoo to find Winston lounging in the living room, smoking a cigarette. Byron was fifteen months older than Winston, and while our eldest brother did everything right, Winston rebelled at every stage of his life.

"Winston," I cried, my voice breathless and tears streaming down my face.

Nothing ever rattled Winston. Though that day, something about my voice rattled him to the core. All it took was one word. His name.

"What is it?" he demanded as he shot up straight on the couch, the cigarette in his hand forgotten.

Somewhere in the corner of my mind, I wondered why he wasn't at his practice. And I worried if our father saw him with the cigarette, he'd box his ears. But none of it seemed as urgent.

"Kingston," I wailed, my face wet and my eyes burning. "Bad men took my... my K-Kingston."

Events after that were a blur. The nanny came back, her face a teary mess. But Kingston wasn't with her.

My little fists pounded on the door. I wanted to go back out there. Winston's strong hands wrapped around me from behind, holding me back. "You're safe."

"My Kingston," I bawled, the first taste of fear something I'd never forget.

"Yes, Rora." It was the first and last time Winston called me that. "He's ours. We'll get him back. Byron will know what to do."

Not our father. Byron, who was still a kid, but to me he was a god.

Our nanny called Father. Then the police. Winston called Byron.

And the whole time I cried and remembered the bad man's words. "Sharing is caring."

My throat tightened painfully, while a shuddering breath barely found an airway or threatened to choke me.

My heart clenched, the unbearable ache that couldn't be healed instant. I'd rather break every single bone in my body than feel this heart-wrenching pain. I knew my brothers felt it too.

Though I was only five when Kingston was kidnapped, I never forgot him. None of us did! When I answered questions about my family, I always listed him, hoping he would find his way back to us.

The tense silence filled the car. I knew Byron hurt too. It was a sore subject for our family. Nobody ever talked about the fourth brother, but we all thought about him. He was ingrained into each breath we took.

"Maybe stay at a hotel once we all leave." Byron's voice was slightly strained. I reached out my hand and covered his fingers clutching the wheel, his knuckles white. I gently squeezed it in comfort. He might have been overbearing and overprotective, but he hurt too.

"I'll be fine," I told him. "I'm always extra cautious. I promise."

"I couldn't bear something happening to you, Rora." His voice was low and hoarse. The glance full of anguish he threw my way just about took my breath away. There was so much pain in his beautiful eyes. I wished I could take it all away and bear it for all my brothers.

Especially since it was my fault.

I swallowed hard. "Likewise," I rasped. "That's why I'm doing this." Then realizing I might have said too much and revealed my field work, I added, "I'm profiling men who could somehow have answers. If not for us, then other families."

He clenched his jaw. I knew it drove his dominant and controlling character crazy that I didn't just obey. But this was important to me. It felt like it would turn my life around, putting all my doubts about Kingston to rest. Whether we found him alive, as I hoped, or dead, as I dreaded.

"Then at least let me get someone to keep watch," he recommended, switching lanes. He masked his expression, and suddenly, he reminded me of Alexei Nikolaev. My brother rarely let his pain slip; he kept a tight rein on his emotions. Just like the man I just met.

"Let me think about it," I finally answered. The comparison of my brother to Alexei was ridiculous. Yet, I couldn't shake it off. Byron hid his pain behind high walls and an unapproachable demeanor. It made me wonder if Alexei did the same.

Or maybe he's just a psychotic and apathetic criminal, I added wryly.

My brother at least behaved humanly. People loved Byron's charisma and handsome looks. And he certainly wasn't all tattooed up. Yes, it was a good disguise because he was no less lethal. Though I bet Alexei Nikolaev sent people running just by looking their way. And if the guy smiled, everybody would be shitting their pants. His brother's smile was scary, I couldn't even imagine Alexei's smile.

Shoving the Nikolaev men out of my mind, I focused on my surroundings. We were almost at the restaurant, the Sazerac Bar. Supposedly they had a good lunch selection and Byron wanted to check it out. Even made a reservation all by himself, without the assistance of his secretary. The location of this restaurant was in the historical French Quarter, on the corner of St. Louis Street.

Once we arrived, he parked and we walked the block to the restaurant. The slow, melancholy sound of a lone trumpeter busking nearby carried on the air. Crowds of people meandered the streets, some laughing, some dancing, some already well on their way to a hangover. There was so much history in the city, yet most days it was overshadowed by tourists and chintzy ghost tours.

I pulled at my high ponytail, trying to calm the frizz that threatened, even though I had straightened it this morning. While Byron opted for one of his signature suits, I chose a short blue dress and white sandals. I wasn't sure how he wasn't dripping with sweat with the quickly rising temperatures and humidity. Humidity in New Orleans was a bitch, with a capital B.

Once we entered the restaurant, I congratulated myself for my choice in wardrobe. The restaurant was somewhere in between casual and formal. My eyes traveled over the large room and found myself relaxing. I liked the place. The ambiance of the restaurant reflected the livelihood of old New Orleans. The walls were painted in deep colors, decorated with old photographs. The low sounds of the trumpeter carried through the oversized, open windows. A large crystal chandelier dominated the room and the middle of the floor was left open.

A hostess greeted us with a ready smile, her eyes traveling over Byron. By now, I was used to it. He attracted female attention everywhere we went. He was tall, muscular, and good looking. It would seem that was enough when it came to him. And the fact his whole persona screamed wealth didn't hurt his chances either.

Ignoring her flirtatious smiles, I continued to survey the restaurant. The instant I spotted a familiar figure, I froze.

What. The. Fuck?

Suddenly, it felt like New Orleans was too small. Especially if I kept running into the Nikolaev men. It was like fucking déjà vu. Vasili was in his signature suit again, and Sasha in something resembling a suit but without the tie. Damn! Despite his shark smile, he was hot. Even I had to admit that.

Then I mentally prepared myself for the third brother.

I hesitantly shifted my gaze to Alexei. I didn't like to look at him.

Just a glance his way and I felt something cold and hot creep up my spine at the same time. Like damn icy hot. It couldn't be his tattoos that bothered me. His brother had obnoxious tattoos as well, not the same design but still plenty of tatts.

My eyes traveled over Alexei. Again, he wore a spotless black T-shirt, military cargo pants. My eyes glanced at his feet, and sure enough, his trademark combat boots. Like he expected to go into a battle at any moment. I was beginning to believe it was his signature outfit.

I'd laugh if he didn't make me so damn uncomfortable. Yet, I couldn't resist locking eyes with him. Call it a morbid curiosity. As if he could read me like an open book, his gaze flickered with something akin to dry amusement. Or maybe I was misreading him completely. It could be a threat, for all I knew.

Our eyes locked, and if a bomb exploded next to me, I feared I wouldn't be able to look away. It was as if he kept me captive. It felt like drowning in the coldest ocean, yet I wasn't cold. Probably some reverse psychology shit, though the man barely spoke two words to me.

A memory flickered in the back of my mind, nudging me to remember. It was right there, and I furrowed my eyebrows, focusing on it. It was just…

I froze as booming laughter had me snapping my eyes at the rest of the group Alexei sat with. Damn it! Just like that, the memory escaped me. It vanished into thin air. Maybe it wasn't even a memory.

Alexei never looked away from me, unmoved by anyone around us. He literally had to take all the oxygen in the room because I could hardly breathe. Suddenly, I wished for a glass of hard liquor. And I hadn't touched anything but wine or beer since my high school graduation trip in Miami.

God, this man was too apathetic. Too dark. Too deadly. And my boss wanted me to work with him and his brother.

Jesus Christ!

I'd probably end up dead. My brothers would be pissed.

Forcing my gaze to shift to the large group seated at his table, I studied the men, women, and children, laughing and eating. It was a casual, family-like atmosphere. The booth was extended by two tables to accommodate them all. Every single one of the men seated at that table was drop-dead gorgeous. Maybe it was good that Willow didn't come. She'd drool all over them and probably land herself on one of their laps.

The men sat on the extended part of the table, while women and children were tucked into the booth. Almost as if they were protected, which in itself was ridiculous since someone could get to them through the large windows that were cracked open.

"This way." The hostess pointed, and both my brother and I followed. Byron right behind me, I purposely kept my eyes away from *the* table. I hadn't exactly admitted to my brother that I had been in the field since moving to New Orleans. He'd blow a gasket.

Overprotective brothers were a major pain in my ass.

I moved down the path following the hostess. When I turned around to ask my brother a question, he wasn't behind me. My eyes sought him out and I found him standing by the table with the Nikolaev men.

"For Pete's sake," I muttered under my breath.

He was exactly where I didn't want him to be.

TEN
AURORA

I watched as he shook hands with a dark-haired man I'd never seen. Though something about him seemed familiar.

Annoyed at my brother, I stopped and waited. It wasn't surprising he ran into someone he knew. He always did. Probably the result of his extensive career. I just wished today wasn't that day.

"Rora, come here," Byron called out. "I want to introduce you." I frowned, shaking my head lightly. I already knew how this would end up. "Come on, sis."

I glanced at the hostess with an apologetic look. "We'll be right back," I mumbled.

I took several steps back, never removing my eyes from my brother. I knew he wasn't an idiot and could see me glaring. For once couldn't he just ignore his acquaintances?

As soon as I was within his reach, he took my elbow and gently squeezed, pulling me next to him.

"Nico, Raphael," Byron said, a proud look on his face. "This is my little sister."

I switched to a polite smile. You'd never guess I was a politician's daughter as much as I hated socializing with strangers. My father was great at schmoozing. So were my brothers. I detested it.

Byron's gaze returned to me. "Remember Nico Morrelli." I froze at the name. I knew the name. Anyone who ever lived in the D.C. area was familiar with Nico Morrelli and the underworld he and his friends ran. My eyes slowly traced to the man Byron just introduced me to. He was younger than I thought. "He supported Dad's campaigns."

And a major strike against him. I didn't know he was Father's supporter. Father probably danced to Nico Morrelli's tunes. Father was as much of a manipulator as the mobsters. And make no mistake, this guy was a mobster. A big one. And as such, he was exactly what my father needed.

"Mr. Morrelli," I greeted him tightly.

Unlike my brothers, I avoided our father's gatherings like my life depended on it, and I certainly avoided criminals.

"It doesn't look like she remembers you, Nico," Sasha interjected, leaning back into his chair with an arrogant smile on his face. "Do you remember me?"

Before I could think of a smartass comeback, my brother answered on my behalf.

"She probably doesn't," Byron told him. The way he studied Sasha told me he was evaluating him, trying to decide whether he was a threat or not. Just what I needed. "Don't take it personally. Or do, it doesn't really matter."

"My wounded heart," Sasha sneered.

I had to bite my tongue to stop something completely inappropriate from slipping through my lips.

"Nice to meet you," I told Nico, lying like a good politician's daughter, and extended my hand. All the while, I ignored the Nikolaev men, scared my brother would pick up on something. Anything.

And then, he'd get McGovan to take me off the case. Or even worse, fire me.

"You as well, Agent Ashford," Nico replied, his voice measured and his smile cold. "My wife, Bianca, and our children."

Jesus. How did he know I was an agent?

I didn't need a genius IQ to know Morrelli realized I didn't like him. And the word was that Nico Morrelli had a genius IQ. Too bad he used it for his criminal activities.

Keeping my eyes leveled on him, I could see how he'd connect with high-ranking politicians in D.C. He had the looks and the charisma. Just like my own brother Byron. My father turned a blind eye to men like that. Though I never understood why.

Scratch that. I knew why. For the same reason he married my mother. He wanted an influx of funds and criminals had plenty of it. They'd give him campaign money and he'd grant them favors that could get their businesses going.

Round and round we go.

Slowly, my eyes traveled over to his family. A beautiful wife who eyed me curiously and two sets of twins. My eyebrows shot up. Twin girls and twin boys. Wow, he'd been busy. I kept my expression neutral as my eyes darted over Vasili, Sasha, and Alexei Nikolaev.

I guess criminals hung out together.

"Do you remember the Santos family?" my brother asked, stopping my train of thought and I instantly froze. "This is Raphael Santos, we've had a few business dealings." My feigned smile fell and my eyes traveled to the man seated across the table from Nico Morrelli. My heart thundered against my ribs, threatening to crack them.

Thank God Sailor and Gabriel didn't come! I kept whispering in my mind. *Thank God Sailor and Gabriel didn't come!*

I shook my head, swallowing hard. He didn't look familiar, but I could see resemblance to little Gabriel. Oh my freaking God!

"That's right," Raphael said, his eyes studying me. "I seemed to recall your father and my father worked out a deal. You and your girlfriends broke into my father's home during your spring break." I swallowed hard, my heart drumming so hard, I was sure my ribs would crack. "Don't worry, it happens more than you think," Raphael added teasingly, unaware of the turmoil going on inside me.

"Yeah, I was pissed that Dad was called. It should have been me," Byron grumbled.

Usually Byron took responsibility for me. But that one time, Father was called. I kept my breaths even, careful not to reveal the unrest inside me. I had plenty of practice hiding behind my masks too. Alexei wasn't the only expert here.

"My sister went through a reckless and rebellious stage," Byron said, his arms coming around me. I narrowed my eyes on Byron. Jackass! I loved him but he was a jackass for saying something like that in front of strangers. "Her spring break was a tad bit wilder than normal. The ocean wasn't enough, so Aurora and her friends broke into a house and went skinny-dipping in their pool during the spring break."

A soft chuckle sounded around the table, and I bit the inside of my cheek, tasting copper. If only Byron knew what the fuck happened that week. There were two key incidents in my entire life that changed me. The first one was the disappearance of my brother. The second one was spring break. That one altered four lives—Sailor's and her sister's, Willow's, and mine.

"I'm afraid I don't remember," I answered tightly, my voice snappy. "Spring break was a long time ago."

That particular spring break seemed like a different lifetime. My best friends and I were buzzed pretty much every day during that week. I remembered our reckless stupidity, certain events were fuzzy until we woke up in the police station on the last day of our vacation. Willow, Sailor, Anya, and I were still in bathing suits, wrapped in beach towels. Anya got into her own shit and we followed. We got in so much shit. Dad had to bail us out.

Of course my brothers knew only the short story. The one my father shared. He made it into an entertaining rendezvous. If Byron came for us or knew what happened, he would have murdered the old Santos, and he would have never broadcast it like it was the most entertaining story of the year.

But then, I'd have another brother's blood on my hands.

I purposely ignored looking at Raphael Santos and the Nikolaev men.

"Nice meeting you all," I attempted to cut it short. "Come on, Byron." I tugged his hand, but he wouldn't bulge. "The hostess is waiting for us."

My eyes darted behind me. And sure enough, she stood, patiently waiting for us.

"Why don't you join us?" My eyes snapped to Sasha, glaring at him for daring to suggest it. "You refused us yesterday. It would be rude to do it again today." He grinned and I wanted to smack that smile off his face. "After all, we'll be working together." I narrowed my eyes on him. He had to be the most annoying Nikolaev man. And with the biggest mouth. If he thought he would make me do anything, he had another thing coming. "This is my sister-in-law, Isabella, and her kids."

I acknowledged the women with a nod.

"We have plans," I answered, trying to keep my tone polite. Then I turned my head to Byron. "We should get going."

I was an FBI agent. I couldn't sit at the same table as criminals. And certainly not around a member of the Santos cartel.

Byron cocked his eyebrow. "What is this I'm hearing? You are working with the Nikolaev family?"

Of course he'd hear that. He didn't hear how I indicated we had plans or that we should get going. He only heard I'd be working with the Nikolaev men. Were all men this dense?

"Let's join them," Byron stated, his demeanor clearly portraying he always got his way. If I could strangle him right now, I totally would. "I want to hear more about this arrangement you have going."

"We were going to—"

"Rora," he warned lightly, the overbearing brother I came to relish and dread coming out full force. "I want you to know a few people here so I'm not worried about your stalker."

I mentally slapped my forehead. "You have a stalker?" I wasn't sure who asked, but I kept my face frozen with a smile.

"No, I don't," I snapped. "Byron, we—"

"Rora?" Byron didn't drop things. He was the most persistent human being on this planet. "Don't think I didn't notice you left my question unanswered."

I swallowed, my eyes flashing with annoyance. I could murder Sasha and his big mouth.

Casually shrugging one shoulder, I pretended to be interested in the hostess's motions who brought over two extra chairs for us to join the group.

"It wasn't of my choosing," I told him dryly, answering his question about me working with the Nikolaev men. "I don't have a tendency to work with criminals."

The hostess who was putting one chair next to Alexei suddenly dropped it, emphasizing my proclamation. She quickly got herself together and went to place the other chair next to Raphael. Which one of the two was the greater of two evils?

"This will be fun," Sasha announced, grinning like an idiot. "Don't worry, Aurora. Criminals don't bite." My spine could have snapped with how tense I was. "Much," he added.

"Can I talk to you for a moment?" I asked my brother, ignoring Sasha and the rest of the table. "In private," I added, agitation clear in my voice.

Not bothering to wait for him, I left the table without another glance while he muttered some apologies. I moved through the restaurant when I felt a hand grazing my ass. It was barely a touch and my head snapped towards the man seated at the table. He was talking to a woman at his table, his eyes never even glancing my way.

I must have imagined it, I thought to myself.

Though I was certain I felt something. Shrugging my one shoulder, I continued on when I heard a woman's shriek and the clattering of silverware. I turned around just in time to see plates smashing against the fancy, polished floor.

My heart leapt into my throat, my pulse jump-started, and adrenaline rushed through my veins. I watched with wide eyes as Alexei yanked the man by grabbing the back of his neck, slamming his face on the table.

The woman who sat with the poor man scrambled to flee the table, while others watched with wide eyes full of horror.

Jesus Christ!

As if in slow motion, I saw everything unfold through a lens as Alexei's tattooed hand wrapped around the man's neck, choking the living daylights out of him. My eyes shifted to Alexei and his face was just as unmoving as ever. Not a single emotion on his face.

He might as well have been watching a boring TV show as he lifted weights. No rage. No indignation. No flicker of emotion as he lifted the man's head and slammed it down again with a loud thud, the table shaking.

My breath hitched in my lungs as my heart raced, making it hard to breathe.

My eyes darted to my brother. Surely, he'd see this bunch was crazy and now we'd go. But Byron's hands were deep in his pockets, his expensive suit immaculate and the expression on his face resembling entertainment.

"Byron," I cried out. My brother's eyes that reminded me so much of our father flashed to my face and he smiled. Actually smiled!

"All good, Rora," he drawled. "It was either him or me. Nobody touches my sister and gets away with it."

My gaze returned to Alexei who showed no signs of stopping. The scariest part of this whole scene was his expression. Or lack of it.

The man is psychotic.

It totally freaked me out. There couldn't be any other explanation. And I'd have to work with him on locating a predator. My boss had thrown me to the fucking wolves.

I took a step forward. Enough was enough.

"Stop!" I demanded in a calm voice, though my heart beat frantically. I couldn't be found amidst a violent crime. It would ruin my career. "Stop, right now."

And just like that, Alexei's movement paused, his hand holding the man's head against the table. I held my breath, waiting for his next move. I sensed there would be.

"Run." One word. Emotionless. His tone even. And fuck, I wanted to run. But the words weren't directed at me.

Not this time.

"Run, Aurora! Run and don't look back," Kingston yelled, the panic in his voice matching the one inside me.

But I didn't want to leave him behind. I couldn't leave him behind me.

My Kingston.

"*I don't want to go alone,*" *I cried, fear clawing at me. In my head I screamed for the bad men to leave us alone. He was my brother. My family. Though I didn't hear the sound of my own voice—whether it was from my loud, pounding heart buzzing in my ears or because my voice was soundless.*

"*Don't worry, little girl.*" *The scary man took steps towards me, his smile twisting me on the inside.* "*Sharing is caring.*"

"*Leave her alone,*" *Kingston demanded, his little voice growling. Like a little wolf he sometimes pretended to be.* "*Run, Rora!*" *he demanded, his voice stronger and meaner than I ever heard before.*

My eyes fleeted to a man. A stranger with blue eyes. I couldn't see him clearly, his face blurry in my mind. But I knew without a doubt his eyes were light blue.

Full of pain and sorrow.

I blinked and the memory faded away.

"Kingston," I whispered, my mind still in the past.

Alexei's eyes, those freakish pale glaciers, lifted and connected with mine. No, they couldn't be the same eyes. There was no pain and sorrow in his blue eyes. Only an unhinged expression. Psychotic didn't even begin to describe this man.

My eyes fleeted to the man with the smashed face. His nose was bloody, likely broken. I was sure tomorrow his entire face would be black and blue. I glanced at my brother who seemed unperturbed, then to the table with Alexei's friends and family. The men sat back, watching the entire scene with a bored expression on their faces. The women whispered among themselves, then glanced outside every so often. Not a single child in that group cried. In fact, I swore they seemed bored with the whole thing too.

The man who had the unfortunate idea to touch my ass stumbled to his feet and ran out of the restaurant. Alexei's eyes followed him and I got the strangest feeling he'd hunt him down. Call it my sixth sense.

Taking a deep breath to calm my racing heart, I focused on my brother. This had to be a nightmare. A freaking horror movie.

"Byron. Outside. Now." My voice sounded amazingly calm compared to my frazzled emotions.

This time Byron moved, though casually, and followed right behind me. My nerves teetered on the edge. It felt like every single pair of eyes in the restaurant was on me as I exited. It was ridiculous, of course. They were probably staring at the lunatic back there who'd remained in the restaurant. Freaking psychotic caveman among civilized people.

Why in the hell did nobody call the cops? *Not a single staff member moved*, I realized.

"Who owns this place?" I asked out of the blue, the second we stepped outside.

"How in the fuck should I know, Rora?" I hated and loved when he called me by that nickname. Byron was the only person in the entire world who called me Rora. Well, aside from the brother who was no longer here.

Inhaling deeply, I glared at him, trying to rein in my temper. And failing.

"What the fuck, brother?" I snapped.

ELEVEN
ALEXEI

I sat back in my spot. I didn't need to look up to notice Vasili's knowing smirk. Nico's cocked eyebrow. Bella's concerned frown. Sasha's stupid grin.

I didn't bother saying anything. I didn't care for pointless social gatherings. I hung out with my niece and nephew frequently. But not in social settings. I didn't need chitchat, even if it was with people I cared about.

"Well, that escalated quickly," Sasha announced, breaking the silence that not even the little ones dared to interrupt. "I bet it was the only reason Alexei agreed to join us. His stalkerish ass knew our little FBI agent would have lunch here."

One of these days, I'd punch Sasha so hard, he wouldn't be able to talk for days. And the moment he started getting better, I'd punch him again. It would be the equivalent of a normal person's vacation not to hear his fucking mouth for a week straight.

"Vasili owns the bar," Bella immediately came to my defense. Not that I needed defending. "We always come here to eat."

Except I usually didn't bother joining them. Sasha's assumption was right. It was the only reason I came. I did my quota for socializing yesterday with dinner. And the night before with Vasili and Sasha. Fuck, it was more than my quota for the quarter.

"What the fuck, brother?" Agent Ashford's voice traveled through the cracked window. She sounded pissed, though somehow she managed to keep her voice soft. I wondered if she ever screamed.

Not that I cared much, I lied to myself.

"Be specific, Rora." Byron Ashford's voice was cool, and I had to admit, it surprised me he wasn't more uptight. And his friendship with Nico and Raphael told me there was more to him than meets the eye.

"First, goddamn you. I cannot sit and have lunch with criminals." If she moved just slightly, we'd be able to see her through the large window, but then she'd probably see that it was cracked open. "It would ruin my career."

"Don't exaggerate. Just because you eat with them, doesn't mean *you* are a criminal."

"You know very well appearances are everything," she hissed. "And secondly, tell me you are not schmoozing with the Morrellis. Or those criminals down in Florida. Father did enough of selling us out, and his soul for politics. Tell me you won't do what *he* did."

The comment was odd, but not off the mark. It was her father who brought Ivan to their doorstep. If he wouldn't have been so power hungry, the Ashford family would have never come to Ivan's attention.

It didn't escape me that everyone at the table was shamelessly eavesdropping on the conversation too.

"Schmoozing?" I'd have to agree with her brother. It was an odd word to use when describing dealings with us. "I don't schmooze. And you didn't mind the criminal when you broke into his house."

"First of all, I was drunk. Just turned eighteen. You've done worse."

"But I never got caught. Big difference."

"Asshole," she cursed her brother.

"Illegal underage drinking," her brother retorted dryly. "Breaking and entering. Those were some serious offenses, Rora."

"I did my community service. All four of us did." I couldn't picture Agent Ashford breaking a law. "For the whole goddamn summer. We paid our dues. And don't turn this on me. Are you or are you not doing shit with the Morrellis and Santoses?"

"Aurora, there are many shades of gray in the world."

"Don't fucking start with shades of gray and criminals. You are either a criminal or you are not. There is no in-between."

If Agent Ashford didn't believe in shades of gray, I'd be tar-black evil in her book. I could already see it. Agent Ashford and I would work *great* together. I wouldn't be surprised if she tried to lock me up.

"Yes, there is," her brother protested. "There is always another criminal to take the spot of another who is even worse. So you opt for the lesser evil." She snorted so loud, we could hear it from our spot. "I'll never apologize for keeping us safe. Our family, Rora."

In a different world and under different circumstances, I suspected I could see eye to eye with Byron Ashford.

"Not a single day goes by where I don't worry about something happening to you," her brother growled. "Why do you think your brothers and I build all this shit? Not for our father. So we can keep you and each other safe."

"But—"

"Rora, if you are looking for me to say I'm sorry for dealing with them, you'll wait a long time." Bianca and Bella gasped softly. "I'll deal with the criminals as easily as kill them. Nico Morrelli is a lot better than his father, so I opted to deal with him. The same is true with Raphael. And as long as they don't threaten you or our family, I'll deal with them. And you will too."

"Do you even hear yourself, Byron?" Agent Ashford's voice shook, though it wasn't from fear. I knew her brother would never hurt her, but I still had to fight the urge to go beat him so he'd stop upsetting her. "Dealing with them will bring trouble to our doorstep," she continued. "Did you see what just happened? Psychotic, I tell you. Dad dealt with them and look what—" Her voice broke and it was a fucking stab straight to my heart. "Why do you think all that fucking shit happened? He made deals with the wrong devil. At our cost. At Kingston's cost."

"I'm not him, Rora. And you know that. He did it for his own benefit. His own advancement. I'm doing it for us. Because I'll be damned if I let another sibling get taken. And you know our mother's connection to the Kingpins keeps our one foot in that world."

My eyes shot to Nico, wondering if he knew. The surprise across his expression told me he didn't know, and that was a rarity. Raphael's and Vasili's expressions told me they didn't know it either.

"How in the fuck didn't we know that the Ashfords had a connection to the Kingpins of the Syndicate?" Vasili hissed under his breath. Yes, that was a crucial piece of information that I didn't share with him. However, it had no relevance here.

"Sis, do you trust me?"

A heavy sigh followed.

"I do, Byron." The pain in her voice gutted me. "I just don't know if I can live with myself if something bad happens again."

"I've got this," he assured her. "I'll keep us safe, from everyone. And Father's enemies can go fuck themselves."

Her soft chuckle traveled over the breeze. Byron Ashford would be busy for as long as his father was alive because that bastard dealt with shady motherfuckers.

"If people only knew what a foul mouth you have, brother," she mused.

This time he chuckled right along with her.

"Okay, Miss FBI. Tell me what the deal is with you working with the Nikolaev men."

Silence stretched. Three seconds and then an exhale.

"It's confidential."

"You are in the field, aren't you?"

"No." Even without seeing her, I could hear the hesitancy in her voice.

"Liar."

"You keep us safe your way. I'll do it mine," she argued, sounding too defensive.

"Aurora, you've got to—"

"Don't tell me what I have to do," she retorted back. "I'm a grown woman and I'm doing my job."

"Your job is not to be out in the field."

She scoffed. "Because you say so?" she challenged.

"You just gave me a lecture on dealing with criminals and now you'll go into the field with one?"

"Who said I'm going into the field with him?" she barked out. She didn't know it yet, but we'd be going into the field together. "I certainly didn't. You better not be hacking into their database, Byron." Oh, so her dear brother did break laws. I couldn't fault him for it though, because he did it to protect her. "And now that it's convenient for your cause, you'll agree with my assessment of a psychotic criminal, huh?" she scoffed. "All of them are psychotic in one way or another, I assure you. Just because some of them are hiding it better than Alexei Nikolaev, it doesn't mean they are any less brutal or crazy. So if you are dealing with Morrellis and Santoses, I'll deal with the Nikolaevs and you'll stay out of my goddamn way."

Okay, so not exactly flattery, but why did I get so goddamn hard hearing her words? Agent Ashford had a backbone.

A heartbeat of silence and then Byron's deep laugh broke through the tension.

"You did your homework," her brother commended her. "I taught you well. Go into it with eyes wide open. I'm proud of you, Rora."

"Whatever. Flattery will get you nowhere," she mumbled. "I'm going home. I kind of lost my appetite seeing all that shit. Go schmooze, brother. I'm going to hang out with the girls."

"Come on—" He tried to sooth her. Those two cared about each other. I'd bet she was close with all her siblings.

"See you later."

A string of his curses followed. "I'm coming with you, Rora. What kind of brother do you take me for? To let you go home alone after this."

"Don't worry, I can shoot. And if that psychotic moron inside didn't go bananas, I could have handled grabby hands myself. Go catch up with your buddies. God forbid they think you bailed on them."

"They'll live. My sister might not with her smart mouth."

A smack and a soft chuckle followed.

"At least I have a smart mouth. Unlike this brother of mine."

"Come on, let's go home. I'll fix you a peanut butter and jelly sandwich. It is much fancier than anything this place has. Maybe the girls and I will even convince you to play on the Xbox."

Her snort was loud. "Fat chance."

Both of their laughter trailed off.

Not wasting any time, I stood up and shoved my hands into my cargo pockets. "Nico, I'll need information on her mother and brothers," I told him and left the table without another word.

After all, the reason I came to this lunch just left.

Two hours later, I was in the basement of the Sazerac Bar. We hadn't had anyone in our soundproof, interrogation rooms here for a few years now. Not since that jackass tried to slip a roofie into Isabella's drink way back when.

I walked down the dimly lit hallway. Centuries ago, these hallways were used for smuggling. Today, they were used for torture and the disposal of bodies. Stopping in front of the metal door, I keyed in my passcode and stepped inside.

The fool that dared to grab Aurora's ass was tied up in chains, hanging off the ceiling and waiting for me. That familiar, cold calm washed over me, just as it did every time I executed men.

Killing him shouldn't feel any different than any other man who wronged me.

Yet, it did.

I knew it would, because I was doing it for Agent Ashford. Because he dared to put his filthy hands on her ass.

He began to struggle when he saw me, chains rattling filled the room. I knew I'd go hunting when I told him to run. I was going to toy with him for a few days and teach him a lesson.

But then I did my homework. Nico's people pulled the information and found out what this asshole did for entertainment. To little girls and young women. There was nothing that would save him now.

My knuckles tightened, that familiar rage flooding through me like a poison that I'd grown immune to, but it still impacted me.

I went to the stainless steel table, full of pristine torture tools. I eyed the variety of tools, deciding on the best one for this sick mother-fucker who liked to stick his dick where it didn't belong.

The moment I picked up the vegetable peeler that could slice one's skin as easily as peeling a carrot, the child molester gave a muffled groan under his gag. It made me sick to my stomach to think how many innocent girls whimpered when he tortured them. Raped them.

I turned around slowly, walked over to him and gave him one of my rare smiles. The skin over my lip pulled, the sting a dull pain that I tried to avoid, but at this moment, it was worth it.

"This will hurt just a little."

TWELVE
AURORA

The second Byron and I returned, Sailor and Willow knew something was up. *Later,* I mouthed so they said nothing. The thought of any member of the Santos family being in the same city as Gabriel was terrifying.

It was five in the afternoon when Byron offered to take Gabriel on one of the children's ghost tours. Sailor, Willow, and I only had to share a look before deciding to stay behind. It would give us time to talk without Byron around.

I knew it didn't escape my brother, because on his way out he warned all three of us to stay out of trouble.

"What happened?" Willow blurted out the moment the two were gone.

Even now, five hours later, my heartbeat sped up remembering running into the ruthless mobsters. Though from all the shit that happened, the fear of Raphael Santos being so close to Gabriel was the scariest.

"We ran into the Nikolaev men, again," I muttered, trying to ease them into it.

"Ah, damn," Willow complained. "I wanted to see that hotness one more time. Maybe to fuel my orgasms for the next five years."

I scoffed. "That is kind of a stretch."

She shrugged. "I don't think so. That kind of hotness melts your brain, heart, and coochie." I rolled my eyes at her exaggeration, but it didn't stop her from elaborating. "Your brothers are fucking hot. But they are more like clean-cut hot and filthy as fuck in the bedroom."

"Willow, I'm not even gonna ask," I muttered. That sounded dangerously close to an admission of testing out one of my brothers in the bedroom. "I don't want to know."

"Oh, I didn't have sex with any of your brothers," she quickly assured me. "Just trying to make a point. Anyhow, as I was saying. Your brothers are probably filthy in the bedroom. But these tattooed guys..." She waved her hand, attempting to cool her flushed cheeks. Horny woman. "You just know these tattooed guys are fucking hot in the bedroom. Guaranteed."

Sailor and I chuckled. "No refund needed," Sailor giggled. "I mean, really, Aurora. Have you ever seen men so hot?" I shook my head. If I said yes, they'd know I lied.

I inhaled deeply, then exhaled. I decided not to say anything about Alexei going all ballistic on the guy who grabbed my ass. Instead, I focused on the most important issue at hand.

"I ran into Raphael Santos," I muttered and both my girlfriends gasped, their eyes widening with shock.

And just like that, all thoughts of filthy sex and hot, tattooed men evaporated.

Silence stretched as I waited for them to get their shock under control.

"Did he recognize you?" Sailor blurted out.

I shook my head. "He just seems to know we broke into his father's house."

"Was his father there?" Willow whispered, though there was nobody else in the apartment.

"No. Remember, he was shot dead. Raphael was there with the Nikolaev men and Nico Morrelli." Neither one of them recognized Nico Morrelli as a mobster who ran the D.C. and Maryland underworld. The only reason I knew that fact was because of who my father was.

"You think he knows what happened?" Willow asked.

"I don't know," I rasped.

"Thank God we didn't go with you," Sailor muttered. I nodded, a lump in my throat. It was only on the way home that it sunk in how much Gabriel looked like Santos. His dark hair, dark blue eyes, his olive skin tone.

"Is it smart that Gabriel is roaming the city with Byron?" Willow questioned.

"None of those men strike me as men who would take ghost tours," I justified. "If they happen to see him with Byron, they'll assume Gabriel is his. They look similar enough."

It wasn't far-fetched. Just like Gabriel, Byron had olive skin tone.

Anya's pleas for the old Santos to stop still shattered the three of us. As we huddled in the corner, Anya paid for it. At that time we didn't know that the two of them hooked up in one of the nightclubs we snuck into a few days earlier.

The taste of freedom that week wasn't worth the end result.

THIRTEEN
ALEXEI

I read the report Nico emailed me.

It was no wonder Byron Ashford knew Santos and Morrelli. He often worked with them, but Byron and his brothers kept to egal businesses, which was smart. Real estate tycoons, technology ycoons, hotels. You name it; they had it. It seemed the Ashford family had the Midas touch. Their empire stretched over every inch of this earth and touched almost everything, if you included their illegitimate brother and sister.

Though there was one little piece that surprised me. The three brothers had a small exclusive security company that extracted the kidnapped. And they did it pro bono.

And then there was the information on their mother. It was what hocked everyone else the most. She was the sister of Gio DiLustro who ran the New York Kingpins of the Syndicate. Gio's brother ran the Syndicate in Chicago and Philadelphia. Gio DiLustro worked different llegal businesses and avenues from Cassio King, so the two had no quarrels. Gio's son, Basilio DiLustro, expanded their empire to legal dealings.

Either way, her mother was killed by one of the other Syndicate gangs. The culprit was never identified. It could have been the Irish. Or the Russians. The sister of the Irish head, Liam Brennan, got shot around the same time. The coincidence was suspect.

I continued through the report, though there were no other surprises. The three brothers fussed over their youngest sibling and often checked on her. Frequent calls and texts, no matter where they were in the world. They ran billion-dollar global empires, yet Aurora opted for a low-paying, government job despite her connections and wealth.

And then there was the youngest brother.

Kingston Ashford. Aged ten. Kidnapped during a visit to the Washington zoo. The only witness, his five-year-old sister. Twenty years ago. But then, I knew that as well.

"That prissy prick has messed with me for the last time," Ivan hissed, pissed off he didn't get his way. He was always like that when someone stood up to him. Unfortunately for Ashford, he took Ivan's money and then backed out of their deal.

The local governor refused to approve the purchase of two hundred acres in Virginia to Ivan, along with a permit. Instead he sold it to the Cassidy Enterprise and got himself a kickback. Turned out Morrelli offered him a better kickback than stingy Ivan Petrov.

I watched the fifty-something-year-old nanny walk out of the million-dollar mansion along with two kids. A little girl with dark curls skipped from one foot to another, her curls bouncing with each movement. Even from here, I could see she brimmed with energy and her smile lit up her whole face. Despite her fancy red coat with black bows for buttons, she acted wild, with no regard for her fancy clothes.

Fearless, she came up to the gate where I lurked. I caught a whiff of chocolate and my stomach rumbled. I hadn't eaten in over twenty-four hours.

If I didn't see this one through, I wouldn't live long enough to turn eighteen, despite being just a few months shy from turning the legal age. I was so close to getting out, Ivan promised he'd tell me who my family was... and let me go. Though Ivan had told plenty of lies over the years and deep down I already sensed the truth.

He never let anyone out.

"Hurry, hurry," she giggled, her light voice traveling through the breeze. The girl couldn't have been more than five. Six tops.

"Rora, stop." The boy who had to be her brother yelled after her. They resembled each other. "You're going to get run over," he warned her.

She giggled, twirling around on the immaculate lawn. "I'm invi-ci-ble." She sounded out the word, her small voice beaming with pride.

In my entire life, I couldn't ever remember feeling that much pride. Or happiness. Her brother ran towards his sister and grabbed her hand, gently tugging it.

"Stay with me, Rora," he reprimanded her.

She lifted her face, trustingly, to her big brother, offering him a big smile. "Always."

Her big brother fondly tugged on her pigtail and a giggle bubbled on her lips.

I followed them for five blocks, until they strode into the zoo. It was then that little Rora got wild. She tugged her little hand free and ran circles around her brother and nanny.

"Lion," she squealed, smiling widely. "Here, come here. Bears!"

Her enthusiasm earned her smiles from strangers. I couldn't blame them. There was a warmth about her that was captivating. I hoped nobody squashed that about her. Then I winced, remembering why I was here.

I shouldn't shatter that happiness. It was a rare thing these days to see. At least for me it was, and as dumb as it sounded, I wanted to bottle it and preserve it. I thought back to the last time I felt anything remotely close to being happy. It was before my tenth birthday.

It wasn't exactly happiness, but it felt close to it. I wasn't their son. I called them tetya and dyadya. Aunt and uncle. Of course, they were neither. Just poor souls who took money they needed to survive, but at least they treated me kindly. They fed me, clothed me, and sent me to school.

Shame and guilt slithered through me. It was because of me that their lives were cut short. And now, I was dangerously close to destroying another family. Fuck, I didn't want to do it. But I wanted to

127

know the names of my parents. Cut ties with Ivan. I was so damn close to freedom I could almost taste it.

Ivan didn't tolerate disobedience from his soldiers. Or whatever the fuck we were. His soldiers. His whores. His thieves. His killers.

Another loud giggle sounded and my attention was back on the little girl. Her dark hair was a wild mess by now, but her eyes shone like diamonds.

"Oh my gosh." She beamed, her cheeks rosy from the cold.

With each minute, little Rora became braver and braver.

"Rora, stay close!" her brother called out. He cared about his little sister. His eyes constantly sought her out. I didn't know much about the governor's family, but in the past week as I watched them, I could tell all of the siblings were close. The father was rarely around though.

Twenty minutes later, as the boy stared wide-eyed at the elephants, little Rora took a step back. Another. And another.

Since the boy was with the nanny, I followed the little girl. To ensure nothing happened to her. She made it all the way to the corner of the little water pool area. She wanted to see the hippos.

This area was empty. Either nobody cared about hippos or the elephants stole the show.

One of the hippos opened his mouth and a loud honk, followed up by a grunt, traveled through the air.

She turned her head to me, her dark eyes shining with happiness. Her hand reached for my sleeve, uncaring that my shirt was old and dirty.

"Did you see it?" she exclaimed excitedly. I nodded, my lip tugging up. It was the first time in so many years that anything resembling a smile curved my lips.

"You like hippos too?" she chirped, her whole face beaming like a lightbulb.

"I do."

She shuffled a step over, standing right next to me. "Kingston likes elephants," she confided softly. "But hippos are my favorite."

"Why?" I asked her, suddenly curious. Personally, I would have picked elephants too.

The brightest smile lit up her face. Like a Christmas tree on a cold and sunny December day. And then she started singing.

"I want a hippopotamus for Christmas
Only a hippopotamus will do."

I blinked. What was she doing?

Suddenly she stopped and her face fell. "You don't know the song," she mumbled sadly, and for some reason, her sorrow hit me right in the chest.

"Sorry." It was stupid. I apologized to a little girl for making her sad, yet I've killed more men than I cared to remember. And I was about to shatter her world.

Her small hand came to mine and she slipped her fingers into my big hand.

"It's okay," she whispered, comforting me. Nobody had attempted to comfort me in such a long time, I couldn't quite remember ever feeling this warmth in my soul. "I can teach you."

I had to get her out of here. I had to get them all out of here.

"Rora." Her brother's voice traveled over the air. The panic in his voice had the little girl snapping her head in his direction. He stood on the other side of the pool pathway, Ivan Petrov and his minion approaching from behind, like a dark cloud that would destroy him and his family. It took no time and Ivan was by the boy. Towering over him, Ivan yanked him by his hair and a small whimper filled the air.

Me and the hippos forgotten, Rora ran towards her brother.

"No, Rora!" he yelled at his little sister.

Her steps faltered and she came to a stop. Staring at her brother, her chest rose and fell with each breath.

"Run, Aurora. Run and don't look back!"

I should grab her and run her home. Ivan would destroy this little girl, her innocence. There was no coming back from someone like Ivan Petrov. I knew it firsthand.

"I don't want to go alone," she whimpered, her eyes wide with fear.

"Don't worry, little girl." Ivan took steps towards her, smiling menacingly at her. "Sharing is caring." He'd make both of their lives a

living nightmare. Ivan didn't do forgiveness. He'd make their father pay for denying him. "I came for you but we can take your brother too... sharing both of you will be fun, da?"

"Leave her alone," her brother shouted, pushing against one of Ivan's minions. I was one of his minions too. And it made me sick to my stomach, seeing two innocents destroyed right in front of my eyes. "Run, Rora!" her brother screamed at the top of his lungs, his demand clear.

Swallowing hard, her eyes looking my way. So much fear. I gave her a barely noticeable nod, and she took off in a sprint.

I went after her. "Get her," Ivan ordered in Russian, assuming I was after her to bring her back.

Fuck that! I ran with her all the way home. Her little legs carried her fast. I couldn't believe she remembered her way home, but she did. Once she was safely inside her mansion, I left and never looked back.

I had destroyed her life before it began. And the realization hit me like a tsunami. *I'll never have her.* Not in this life. Not in the next. She'd destroy me if she knew what I did, and I wouldn't stop her.

Nico knew her brother. After all, he went back with me to Moscow, along with Cassio and the crew ten years ago. You didn't forget shit like that, no matter how drunk we got while we waited for our flight out of that godforsaken country.

Something inside me hardened to rock-solid ice. And there wasn't much softness left.

My phone rang, stopping my memories. Glancing at it, Raphael's name flashed on the screen. Why in the fuck would he call me? The only thing we had in common was Isabella and we never discussed her. Needless to say, he rarely called.

I pushed the answer button. "Yes."

"Do you ever greet people any other way?" Raphael's tone dripped with sarcasm.

"What do you want?" I asked, already bored and annoyed with this conversation, and it hadn't even started. "Different enough?"

Raphael mumbled something under his breath. I was pretty sure he called me a *psicópata frio,* a cold psycho in Spanish. I didn't bother commenting. I'd been called worse, and he wasn't far from the truth.

"Byron Ashford called me," Raphael continued. My interest piqued, but I remained silent. "He asked if you and your brothers could keep an eye on his little sister."

It was convenient to get approval of the big brother to stalk Aurora. But it would be nobody's job but mine. If my brothers tried to do anything with the young agent, I'd slice them alive. She was mine to watch and keep safe. Though I'd never have her, I'd be sure to atone for my sins. I'd ensure I kept her safe.

"I figured I better start with you since you went ballistic in the restaurant," he added.

Whatever. It was none of his business. I could sense Aurora didn't like Raphael. She stiffened the moment his name was uttered. Though it was curious that Byron asked us to watch over her. He knew who we were, yet he didn't hesitate to ask for a favor. Though he would reverse that ask within milliseconds if he knew what happened twenty years ago.

Too fucking late.

"Are you there?" Raphael called out.

"I'll keep an eye." *Click.*

I ended the call and glanced at the time. No sense in saying anything else. I intended to keep an eye on her regardless.

Speaking of the FBI agent. She should be here in half an hour.

I strode through the compound and headed for Vasili's office. The beautiful agent would be escorted here, and though I knew Vasili only had eyes for Isabella, something inside of me objected to leaving Aurora alone with Vasili.

"Alexei," Vasili greeted me. I hadn't seen him since yesterday.

"Brother."

"Did Nico's information reveal anything else?" Only that I led the lambs to the wolf.

"No."

This was my cross to bear, and I'd pay for my sins. I had to wonder though if Agent Ashford's obsession with the child predator was related to what had happened that day. She'd remember me eventually. Of that I was certain.

"You want to talk?" My eyes locked on my oldest brother. Sasha and I were closer in age, me being the youngest. But my experiences made me more relatable to Vasili. Sasha was too impulsive, too free.

"No." Talking wouldn't do me any good. And I knew my brother. If he felt his family was threatened, it wouldn't bode well for Agent Ashford.

"You seem quite taken with Agent Ashford," Vasili continued casually like I didn't just tell him I didn't want to talk about it.

The icy silence stretched. I was fine with it. Unfortunately, so was Vasili. I didn't bother looking at my brother, my eyes locked on the door that would bring in my obsession. A petite dark-haired agent who thought me a psychopath.

"Will taking her to the club be a problem?" My cock jerked at the thought. Truthfully, I couldn't wait to take her there. I was intrigued to see her reaction. Fuck, now I was rock hard. I gritted my teeth and willed myself to think of something else. "Maybe I should take her?" Vasili suggested.

My eyes snapped his way and a low growl sounded in my throat. "Over my dead body."

Vasili raised one eyebrow, not accustomed to being told no.

"*You* even think about it, I'll break your hands and legs," I said coldly. "Nobody goes around her but me," I warned, my voice frigid. Brother or no brother, he touched her and he was dead.

A knowing smirk played around Vasili's lips. Fucker was egging me on.

"Well, fuck me," he muttered under his breath, amused.

"I'd rather not," I told him dryly.

"So what's your plan?" he asked. "And how does the pretty agent work into it?"

"Vasili."

"Yeah?"

"I got this. Aurora is mine." Fuck, I called her mine. I might as well go all the way. "Comment on her appearance again and I'll gouge your eyes out."

A deep chuckle vibrated through the room. Taunting asshole! He opened his mouth to say something but luckily his intercom buzzed.

"Agent Ashford is on her way. She refused to turn in her weapon."

My lip quirked up. I wasn't surprised. The next minute, the beautiful agent was led in by one of Vasili's men.

"Mr. Nikolaev," she greeted him with a pissed-off look on her face. "Let's set some rules, shall we?" She didn't wait for either one of us to answer before she continued, "I do not work for you." She narrowed her eyes on both of us. "Next time you want to see me, get your fucking ass to my office. You know, that same one where you showed your face last Friday." Fuck, her mouth was giving me a serious hard-on. "And in case your old ass cannot remember the address, I will be more than happy to drop a pin into your phone, so you don't get lost."

Fuck! Was this love or fucking what? It was when she spit fire that I wanted to fill her sassy mouth with my cock and thrust into it, as she watched me with reverence in her eyes.

"You'll need to disarm, Agent Ashford," Vasili announced, ignoring her other comments.

She scoffed. "I don't think so. Considering who you are, I'll keep my weapon on me."

"I don't give a fuck who you think I am," Vasili told her in his voice that usually scared the shit out of people. Not Agent Ashford. If she was scared, she hid it well. "My children are in the house, and I won't have a stranger with a gun in my home."

I found the interaction between my brother and the FBI agent entertaining. In fact, it was the most entertainment I'd gotten in years.

"*You* wanted this meeting in *your* home," she reminded him, keeping her cool. "I'm keeping my weapon. If you are scared or worried, let's take this meeting elsewhere."

Vasili's eyes flashed with annoyance and an underlying hint of admiration. This woman was something, and I knew deep down, Vasili liked her strength. He admired her brother too.

As if on cue, little Nikola wobbled into the room. Agent Ashford's eyes darted to the little man and her expression softened. Though Vasili's posture tensed and one wrong move could cost the beautiful FBI agent her life.

I shifted slightly. Vasili never made rash decisions. But when it came to his wife and children, he'd kill without a second thought or remorse. In his book, it was better to be safe than sorry. I'd regularly agree but we needed Agent Ashford to get to Ivan.

And she was mine.

My brother and I watched in amazement as Nikola's eyes darted to the young woman and then wobbled to her with a big grin. The kid never went to strangers. Ever! His chubby little hands came to her knee. She shifted so her sidearm was on the opposite side, out of Nikola's reach and lowered down.

"Hey, buddy," she greeted him, smiling. "What's your name?"

"Nikola." Vasili and I shared a fleeting glance. He spoke. And to a stranger. "Up."

Agent Ashford chuckled. "Bossy little thing, aren't you?"

"Up."

Jesus Christ. Three words in a span of ten seconds. The agent's eyes rose to meet Vasili's gaze. "Yours?"

Vasili nodded. My brother was good at hiding his emotions, but I could tell it bothered him that his son spoke to a mere stranger. Nikola said more words to her in less than a minute than he did to his parents the entire month.

"If I pick you up," she murmured softly to my nephew, "I won't be able to see how big you are."

Nikola tilted his head as if he was thinking about it. "And you are such a big boy."

She must have won him over because little Nikola grinned, nodding eagerly. Surprisingly, Agent Ashford had a way with children. It had to have something to do with her friend's kid. The background check had revealed she was his godmother.

"Okay, Nikola," Vasili interrupted their session. "Come here."

A soft smile spread on Aurora's lips, reminding me of the little girl from twenty years ago. She winked at the little boy and nudged him gently towards his father. Then rose to her full height once Nikola wobbled over to Vasili.

"With all due respect, Mr. Nikolaev," she started, keeping her voice soft, as if she worried about upsetting his son. But her eyes were firm on Vasili and me. "This is work, and I'll keep my weapon on. It is nonnegotiable." Her dark eyes glanced my way for a fraction of a second, wariness in them. I bet she recalled the way I beat the man down who dared touch her ass yesterday. Her brows furrowed, yet her eyes remained on me. "As I walked through the compound, there were at least ten guards I passed who carried their firearms. So forgive me for being a tad bit hesitant to leave myself defenseless." Tick. Tock. Tick. Tock. There was no mistaking that the jab was for me. "Especially considering your reputation."

Girl had some balls, I'd give her that. Maybe that was the reason she appealed to me so much. Women usually wanted me to fuck them, choke them, make them come, but in all of them, there was an underlying fear.

In Aurora, I sensed the hesitancy but no fear.

My sister's chuckle sounded behind her and Agent Ashford whirled around, coming face-to-face with Isabella.

"You are absolutely right," my sister agreed with the agent. "And I see you keep your weapon secured. That is all I ask. Little Nikola tends to grab everything." Agent Ashford kept her eyes on her, nodding lightly. "I'm Isabella Nikolaev. We saw each other for a fraction of a second yesterday," she continued, extending her hand to Aurora. "I know my husband can be a stubborn ass, but it's all for the little ones' safety."

Aurora accepted Isabella's hand. "Aurora Ashford."

"Hmmm, Ashford, Ashford," Isabella murmured. "Why does that sound familiar?"

Agent Ashford shrugged her one shoulder. "It's a common last name."

"Her father is Senator Ashford," Vasili explained at the same time, lifting little Nikola onto his shoulders. "Speculations are he might be our president one day."

"Ah." Isabella glanced back and forth between her husband and Agent Ashford. Annoyance flashed across Aurora's expression but she quickly masked it, then looked straight at my brother.

"Why don't we get straight to the point?" she commenced. "I have a long day ahead of me and you are wasting my time."

Isabella stifled her laugh, her eyes shining with amusement. Usually, people just had to look at Vasili or me, and they shit their pants. Not Agent Ashford. She'd be good for what we had to do to get closer to Ivan.

"There is a way to get closer to the person we believe is responsible for kidnappings," Vasili explained while I observed them.

"And where is the suspect?"

I gave her kudos for trying, but she wouldn't get any info. Not until that motherfucker was dead without any chance of resurrection. She had the resources and I had the knowledge to get to him. So we'd have to work together to get him.

"You'll know when you get there." Vasili didn't miss a beat.

"Okay, so what is this way, then?" she asked, an annoyance in her dark eyes. Vasili's eyes darted to me.

This ought to go well.

FOURTEEN
AURORA

To say I was annoyed was an understatement.

First, I arrived at work late after dropping off the girls and my brother at the airport. Then McGovan pretty much greeted me with the order to follow the Nikolaev lead. Now, I was standing before two of the most powerful men in New Orleans and Isabella Nikolaev... formerly Isabella Taylor. Color me surprised when I learned she was the ex-girlfriend of rock star Ryan Johnson, and one of the best surgeons in her field.

And to top it all off, Jackson got reassigned to another case, in a different field office. Way to leave me hanging.

"I'm all ears," I added dryly. "But please do speed up. I have a case to solve."

Isabella chuckled. "Oh, I like you. I'm going to grab Nikola, because I have a feeling this is not appropriate for the little one's ears."

"Probably a good idea," Aurora muttered.

Isabella strode to her husband taking Nikola into her arms. And suddenly the giant motherfucker looked like a big teddy bear. When Vasili looked at his wife, his entire face transformed. I had never seen anything like it before.

As I watched mesmerized, Isabella and Nikola walked by me, and the little dude who looked like a spitting image of his father grinned at me.

"Bye." He waved his chubby little hand. Unlike his father, the boy was adorable. His mother shot Nikola a weird look, then glanced at me. She looked back to Nikola, shaking her head as if surprised by something.

"It was great meeting you," she said as she strode from the room.

"You too."

I waited for the door to shut behind her before I returned my eyes to the two men in the room. The way Alexei watched me made me want to fidget, and I refused to show how he rattled me. In fact, I tried to avoid looking at him. I really did. But my stupid eyes kept going back to him, like he was some kind of magnet. He was unlike any other man I had ever seen. Covered in tattoos, as if he purposely hid himself. Though it didn't make sense since the tattoos would have made most people give him a double take.

It certainly made me look at him twice.

I couldn't stop my eyes from giving him a once-over. He wore his signature wardrobe again. And for some reason, I really wanted to know whether that man's whole body was covered in tattoos. I regularly hated tattoos; they reminded me of a memory from a long time ago.

Sharing is caring. Fear crept into the dark corners of my mind. It was cold and suffocating. My pulse sped up and bitter fear wrapped around my throat. It cut off my fucking breath.

I forced my eyes closed, scared these two men would see something in my eyes. I inhaled deeply, then slowly exhaled. I heard people claim it helped. It made me more agitated than calm. But I guess it was better than nothing. I forced my eyes open to find pale, arctic blue eyes staring at me.

"Okay, let's get this started, so I can get out of here," I snapped annoyed. The worst part was that I was annoyed at myself. I didn't want to show these men my weaknesses.

My eyes glanced at Alexei again. I couldn't stop it any more than I could stop breathing. This man was a force of nature with an undercurrent of something raw and dangerous. Yet, the idiotic part of me deep down found him fascinating.

Not attractive; just fascinating.

"There is a club called Eve's Apple," Alexei broke the silence. "It's a sex club."

My eyebrows shot up. Okay, his comment blindsided me a bit. I wasn't expecting a sex club.

"What an original club name," I scoffed, my tone slightly breathless. I didn't like the direction this was going. I wasn't a prude, but I wasn't wild either. Willow was always the wildest one of our trio. "Zero points for originality," I added, seemingly unaffected while my insides burned.

From frustration, I told myself.

He ignored my comment. I knew he noticed my reaction to his words. Nobody had to warn me that this man noticed everything. And I meant *everything*. From a slightly hitched breath to a twitch in my eye from all this goddamn stress.

"There is a member of that club who can get us closer to the predator," he added in that icy tone of his. Jesus, if I ever had a fever, I'd just search this man out and have him talk to me. That would cool me off for all eternity.

"Okay." My instinct was warning me that he wasn't telling me everything. "Can we call him?"

"It's not as simple as that."

Of course. It never was.

"How about you stop beating around the bush and just tell me what the deal is?" I asked exasperated. At this rate both of my eyeballs would be twitching.

"The only way to enter the club is as a couple." My eyes widened, but I said nothing. "The two of us will go undercover."

"Two of us?" I repeated stupidly, as my eyes ping-ponged between Vasili and Alexei.

"Yes, you and Alexei," Vasili clarified. "He sure as hell isn't going to pretend to be a couple with me."

I narrowed my eyes on both of them, watching them warily. *Jackass!*

"And if I was a guy, what would your plan have been?" I asked, my hands on my hips as I glared at them.

Vasili shrugged. "We'd dress you as a girl," he grumbled, like it was self-explanatory. And for the life of me, I couldn't tell if he was serious or not.

"You must be joking," I objected dryly. This had to be some kind of test.

"No." Alexei Nikolaev was pissing me off. No clarification, no explanation. Nothing. Just *no*. And that was it.

"Why don't you just give me the address of the club and I'll get a warrant?" I reasoned. "We can question them until we get the information that will get us closer to this predator."

"It doesn't work that way."

Tension creeped up my spine and my shoulders tightened. This couldn't be happening. The idea was ludicrous. I rolled my neck, attempting to loosen some tension. Alexei took three large strides to the little minibar and calmly poured himself a drink.

"Drink?" he offered.

"You wish," I snapped. "So you can get me drunk and drag me to some freak show." I knew I wasn't behaving reasonably, but what did he expect? Dropping something like that and expecting me to be cool about it. "Anyway, I'm on duty," I added.

Besides, images I didn't want to remember from a long time ago flashed through my mind, like a horror movie. Seeing what happened to Anya scarred Sailor, Willow, and me. It would have damaged any eighteen-year-old.

I never understood why Anya recommended we break into the old Santos's house. And took us with her, three idiot teenagers. It was something Sailor kept asking her—over and over again. The three of us were going to report him to the police, but then Anya freaked out.

She went crazy, babbling it was consensual. I thought she was scared because the man was the head of a cartel in Miami. I assured her my brothers would keep us safe; we just had to tell them. She wouldn't hear of it and threatened to kill herself.

Cold sweat trickled down my back at those horrid memories and I pushed them back down into a deep, dark hole.

"Suit yourself," Alexei replied coolly, and strangely enough, it pulled me back into the light and matter at hand. Sex club.

"Give me the address, and I'll go with someone else," I reasoned. I'd beg Jackson on my knees to come back for a day. Anyone would be better than Alexei.

Alexei's glass paused an inch from his lips before he replied, "No."

Again, no explanation. God, I never liked to judge a person without knowing them, but I really didn't like him. His voice was worse than a cold shower. It grated on my nerves.

"And why not?" I challenged him.

His eyes didn't flicker. No expression passed his face. Just like when he beat the guy at the restaurant.

"I mean, do you even have sex?" I blurted out stupidly. "I thought your kind gets off on killing people."

His inked fingers curled around his glass, and for a fraction of a second, I thought his grip tightened. *Interesting.* My eyes flicked to his glacier blues, but his expression was blank, and I returned my gaze to his fingers. They no longer gripped the glass. Maybe I imagined it.

My eyes lingered on his hand, holding the glass, studying for any sign of anger. Nothing. Though the strength he held didn't escape me. And despite the tattoos, his fingers were beautiful. Big. Strong.

"I have sex," he answered.

I blinked confused while warmth rushed to the pit of my stomach and spread through me like wildfire. I inhaled slowly. Released it. My skin came to life. It buzzed with a dark sin and elusive timbre.

A shiver ghosted through me, and I marveled at the odd reaction. I had never experienced a reaction like this to another human being.

"Do you?" His gaze flicked with something heavy and emotionless. His voice was professional and disinterested, a cold tenor of it freezing me to the bones, but the meaning behind them set me ablaze.

Jesus Christ! The man would fuck up my body temperature.

And I was supposed to go to a sex club with him. Yeah, I didn't think so. My ass would freeze being too close to him. And if he touched me, I'd turn into an ice statue. Or maybe he'd burn me alive because the blue flames that lurked in his eyes burned hotter than any normal fire.

"There has to be another way," I tried another approach. "Maybe we can go undercover as some of the staff."

I held my breath for his answer, but it never came. I sighed. This man was difficult; I knew it without a doubt. And the reaction I had around him was the most disturbing of all.

"Listen, going undercover with you will never work. I have a partner," I told him. Was I stretching it a bit? Yes, but he didn't know that. "Usually, my partner and I are on the same wavelength. It will be believable with him."

Yuck, just thinking about Jackson touching me made me uncomfortable. Besides, he was married, so that would be a problem. Yet, somehow he felt like a safer option than this guy.

"Your partner has been reassigned." My eyebrows shot up. How did he know that? I only found out an hour ago.

Our gazes locked. A shiver ghosted through me and an audible gulp sounded in the room. It was mine.

Sex club and Alexei Nikolaev in the same sentence was a bad idea. Never mind attending the actual sex club. This man had bad news written all over him. I mean, just look at the ink. Who in the fucking hell tattooed their face? Certainly nobody I knew.

Hell, men I dated didn't ink any part of their skin. They were clean cut.

Yet, none of them ever impacted me like Alexei. His stance oozed power and confidence. He knew he'd get his way and I resented it. He was overwhelmingly big. Too tall. Too bulky. Too something that just didn't work for me.

My eyes traveled over his wide shoulders. He wore a black T-shirt again. It fit him like a second skin. This time instead of back cargo pants, he wore black jeans. Reluctantly, I had to admit he looked good in jeans. They molded to his toned body. His muscled arms covered in ink would probably overpower most men on this earth, never mind little old me. I worked out, jogged almost daily. Yet, I knew without a doubt, there was no chance of overpowering this guy. Even with a weapon on me, I couldn't beat him. If he wanted me dead, I'd be dead.

And I'm supposed to go to a freaking sex club with him. No way. No how. I'd end up dead, never to be heard from again. A statistic. My brother didn't save me so I'd end up on another chopping block.

"So what do you expect to happen at this sex club?" I breathed. My imagination was in overdrive. I'd never been, though I heard plenty about them.

"We'll pretend to be a couple and get invited to another event that will get us closer to our target."

Okay, it was a better explanation than I expected. "And we'll just —" I swallowed hard, unable to utter the words. "Just question people."

"No, we'll pretend to be a couple and participate."

My eyebrows shot up. "Participate?" I rasped, my voice barely above a whisper. "In sexual activities." When he didn't answer, I added, "I don't know about you, but I am definitely not having sex with strangers."

A shadow passed his face, but it was so fleeting, I wasn't sure if maybe my mind was playing tricks on me.

"It's a couple's sex club," he said icily, like that explained it all. "Couples have sex in it, not strangers."

I gulped. Maybe gasped too, while my heart went into some kind of overdrive. "Have sex with you?"

Why is my voice so goddamn shaky?

"If it comes to that." Alexei might as well be discussing weather.

"I don't get paid enough for this shit," I muttered, pushing both my hands through my hair.

What if I never came back? The Nikolaev men were criminals. On the FBI's radar but always skimming around it. And now they found a way to get the FBI to work with them. No, not with them. For them.

There was no code or trust among criminals. They'd dispose of me when they were done with me.

His gaze caught mine, emotionless, as if he was looking straight through me and my heart turned cold in my chest. This man might as well be cut from a cold stone. He was blessed with the face of Adonis, but none of that mattered when he left a trail of ice and death in its wake.

A killer. He had ties to the Irish mafia, Bratva, and Italians. Every criminal organization on this planet that was on the FBI's radar worked with Alexei Nikolaev. He was their go-to man when all else failed. Of course, there was no evidence to support that theory either.

Thanks, Milo, I thought dryly.

"You never answered," he remarked dryly. I blinked, confused about what he was asking. "Do you have sex?"

My skin flared. *At his rudeness,* I told myself. My eyes darted to his brother who for some reason remained quiet the entire time, observing his brother and me.

Frustration flickered in my chest that I would find myself in this situation.

"You're not my type," I replied dryly.

Women probably swooned all over him, until caught under that cold expression. I'd easily consider him one of the most handsome men I had ever met. If not for those eyes. Blue. Heartless. Colder than the Arctic. His gaze alone was enough to send you running. But there was something hiding in those glacial depths. Deep, deep in the darkness where only monsters lurked.

"Be ready." His cold voice sent a trail of ice through my veins.

I blinked in confusion. His conversation skills would give me whiplash.

"For what?" I cursed my voice. It came out too breathless. Too unsure. Too shaky.

Goddamn him.

"My call."

Getting some of my senses back, I cocked an eyebrow. "I haven't agreed to your ridiculous plan."

"You will."

My cheeks flared hot with frustration. "You don't know that," I snapped. "You and sex club in the same sentence is bad news. Never mind anything else. I'm not—" My words stammered. "I'm not doing any sex shit with you." I thought I said it rather convincingly.

"Don't worry, I'll go easy on you," he retorted, his voice leveled.

What. The. Fuck?

I must have misheard him. My eyes fleeted to his brother who now had an amused expression on his face.

"I'm not worried," I snapped back in a taunting voice and a feigned smile on my face. "Because when I lock your ass up, I'll be sure *not* to go easy on you."

"I'm counting on it, kroshka." A deep timbre in his voice came to the surface, and it could possibly be the only thing this man had going for him.

Mentally, I made a note to look up what kroshka meant.

"I don't want to do it," I hissed.

"Yes, you do." His sharp jawline flexed, and I realized he was pissed off. I almost missed it. "You want to catch this predator, as if your life depends on it."

It did. One piece of information I never shared with anyone else was that the MO of all these kidnappings matched my brother's. Except, there was a witness. Me.

I wanted to atone for my sins.

Glaring at this man, I hated that he could read me that well. "When I catch him, you will be next," I promised, then whirled around to depart.

A cold shiver prickled at my neck, and a familiar feeling washed over me. Like someone stared at me, burning a hole into me. The same feeling I had all weekend. Ever since I met him.

A wave of uneasiness swelled in my chest. This man wasn't right. *Psychotic*, the word kept playing in my mind.

I glanced over my shoulder, my fingers curling around the handle of the door.

"And, Mr. Nikolaev—" I started.

"Alexei," he cut me off. "Call me Alexei," he demanded. "After all, we're going to a sex club as a couple."

Fucking lunatic.

"Stop following me," I seethed, then rushed out of there before losing my cool and doing something that could cost me my job.

Or worse, my life.

FIFTEEN
ALEXEI

The door shut forcefully after Agent Ashford stormed out and silence lingered. I had no intention of breaking it. I sensed Vasili was agitated, though I was unsure whether it was with me or the woman who just told us both off.

Well, fuck him.

"Are you purposely trying to piss her off, Alexei?" Vasili finally broke the silence.

I shrugged my one shoulder. It must have been a form of self-destruction, but I loved seeing the fire flare up in the girl's gaze when riled up. It was a special brand of adrenaline I didn't know existed until I met her.

Vasili's deep sigh followed the silence.

"I trust you know what you are doing," Vasili finally said. *Maybe.* "You are not as impulsive as Sasha." Unlike any other time, I had no goddamn clue what I was doing when it came to the agent. Around her, I kept tripping up. When she was in my vicinity, she was all I could focus on. She was my walking temptation.

That petite, curvy body of hers. Her scent. Her dark chocolate eyes. Her thick, dark mane.

Vasili watched me, waiting for me to comment.

147

"Jesus fucking Christ," he muttered, rubbing his jaw and amusement in his expression. "You have a hard-on for her." Tension rolled through me because I knew what was coming next. "Maybe you should seriously consider either Sasha or I taking the agent to the club?"

"Brothers or no, I'd kill you both." The threat escaped me, calm and deadly. The thought of Vasili or Sasha in the club with Aurora, their hands on her made me want to go on a murder spree. The pulse in my temple throbbed. It fucking throbbed and rage slithered through my veins.

Fucking great. In the few days since meeting her, I tripped multiple times. Like she was my personal ticking time bomb. My eldest brother watched me, then let out an amused breath.

"This should be fucking fun to watch," he muttered.

"Then watch," I said. "But don't you fucking dare touch her. Ever. Even if she points a gun to my head. You. Do. Not. Touch. Her."

His eyebrow shot up in surprise. Yeah, it was a surprise, but I owed her that much. Before Agent Ashford, I never threatened my brother, and I'd never put anyone before my family. But she was different. I owed her.

"You anticipate ending up in Russia with her?" Vasili steered the topic away from the young woman. It was probably safer for all of us.

"Da." *Yes.* Russia was Ivan's territory and where he felt the safest. "If things go according to plan at the club and Igor takes the bait…" I had no doubt he would. He never liked being second best—not in a fight, not in bed. And he was always second. "You and Sasha can track my movements. Be in Russia, as close as possible. I don't want to see a scratch on her."

We both knew who *her* was.

Vasili shook his head. "I don't like sending you back to him."

I didn't fucking like it either, especially not with Agent Ashford. But it was our best chance.

"You and Sasha just be there."

"Bella will have my balls if something happens to you," Vasili grumbled and the picture of my petite sister having that effect on Vasili, who was built as big as I, was comical at best.

"Don't tell her until it's over."

Without another word, Vasili moved toward the door, then stopped. "Another threatening message came in."

He pulled out his phone and my phone beeped the next second. Without a word, I slid it open.

Nikola for Alexei's sins.

Ivan's threat lingered in the air. Vasili shut the door behind him, leaving me alone with my fucked-up past.

When I walked away from Ivan, he lost my skill set. He considered me his asset, the one he groomed and nurtured. *Nurtured.* I had to scoff at that. But I really fucked him up badly when I went back ten years ago and took another piece of precious cargo from him.

Kingston Ashford, Aurora's brother.

Now he wanted the debt paid.

I fucked up. I knew I did the moment I set foot on Russian soil.

Fucking pride. Yet, how would one admit to being the one to lead Ivan to an innocent little boy and girl? The shame ran deep. I saved myself at their expense. It wasn't right.

Now, I came back to right the wrong. To save him. The little boy who saved his sister, Rora. To uphold the promise given to a little girl.

I might have built a name for myself now and could afford the nice things in life, but nothing could erase who I was. A monster dressed like a gentleman. I'd done unimaginable things. Unforgivable things. Though until that winter day in the zoo, I comforted myself that all those I killed, all the havoc I caused, was on bad men. The men who didn't even deserve death.

But that day in the zoo I crossed the line.

I should have never led Ivan to them. I should have sent them a warning. It was their father who ripped him off, not his children. But I learned a hard lesson throughout my life; it was usually the children who paid for their parents' sins.

The cold wind wrapped around me. Winters in Siberia were no joke. And after years of staying away from this godforsaken country, the cold quickly seeped through my bloodstream and straight to my bone marrow. Fuck, when I got old, I was certain I'd have arthritis or some shit.

Courtesy of Ivan fucking Petrov.

I lurked in the dark, right outside Ivan's known location. The compound. It was where he kept his boys. It was where I hoped to find the boy who I owed so much to.

In all my years, I never thought I'd hate myself so much, but since that day ten years ago, self-hatred consumed me.

I had been in this country for the past five days, stalking Ivan's men and the surrounding area. What worried me was that I hadn't seen any boys or the men Ivan had used during my confinement here. Usually, he gave them an hour per day outside, regardless of the freezing temperatures.

My breath clouded the freezing air in front of me. I stood still in my hideout in subzero temperatures, watching the Belgian Malinois prowling through the snow, circling the property. Every so often, one of them stopped about twenty feet from me.

I recognized her. The dog I called my own. Puma, I named her. Not a very original name, yet it was the first living thing that loved me unconditionally. Blindly even. I'd helped bring the litter of her mother's into this world. Somehow she was the only one I connected with.

Bright lights from the house illuminated the immediate yard, and I could see Puma inching closer and closer to me with each parameter around the house. Until she was right in front of me.

Her tail wagged, and before I could send her away, she plowed into me. Despite the blanket of snow on my back, it was the best welcome ever.

"Kotyonok," I whispered, as she licked my face. It was a pet name I used for Puma, because she was like a cat. She opened her muzzle, getting ready to bark happily and I gently wrapped my hands around it. "Shhh."

I ran my hand through her fur, hugging her tightly. "God, I fucking missed you."

Another lick to my face. It must have meant she missed me too. My heart squeezed in my chest that I left her behind. Ivan and his men weren't any better towards the animals than they were the boys.

"I'm going to get you out," I rasped, guilt clawing at my chest. I fucked up so many things. "You and me. And we'll save the little boy. Maybe all the boys."

It had been ten years. Ten fucking years.

Except, he was no longer little. I wasn't even sure he was alive. Not many boys survived into adulthood under Ivan.

But the world had changed; I had changed. I managed to make a life for myself and build up my own wealth. After I abandoned Ivan, I roamed the States for years before I ran into Cassio. Turning over a new leaf and living on the right side of the law wasn't an option for me. All I had was my first name and date of birth. No money. No resources. Nothing.

So I did small, odd jobs for different gangs, but never stayed in the same place for long. Ivan had put a price on my head; he wanted me back under his control. When I made the connection with Cassio, Ivan backed off. Though he still lingered in the shadows, waiting for the right opportunity to strike.

It wasn't until this year that I finally had resources and a way to penetrate Ivan's establishment to come back for the boy. The one with dark hair and dark eyes, just like his sister's.

My cell phone in my pocket buzzed and I dug it out, while Puma refused to leave my side. I worried they'd realize she was missing, but I didn't want to send her back into their den.

It was a text from Luca.

> Yo. Where are you?

I rolled my eyes. Luca probably wanted to go hunting for someone and place a bet who'd get him first. I readied to put the phone away, when another message from him came in.

> We just blew up a compound in Turkey.

I cocked an eyebrow. He must have been bragging. It was their third attack on the compounds in Turkey, and it had all started last May.

Another message came in and this one was from Cassio. I didn't realize Luca made it a group chat.

> Any places in Russia that are safe for women who have been trafficked?

Fuck.

It was the worst place and time to bring them to Russia. Even worse would be to connect them to me. For months now, Cassio and Luca had made it their business to save women from trafficking. Initially, I thought it was their way to say "fuck you" to Benito King, but now I wasn't so sure.

I debated whether to ignore the message, but if they were saving someone, I couldn't just pretend I didn't see it.

> Don't bring them to Russia.

I typed fast.

> Shitstorm coming. I have secured a place in Portugal.

Though I meant it for whoever I would save from this frozen hell on earth.

Bubbles appeared.

> Fuck, will you need saving?

Of course it was Luca, the little shit. I probably would need saving, but I wasn't worried about me. I wanted to right the wrong and save as many as I could in this process.

> Take them to Portugal.

I quickly typed in the address. Then added:

> If you can show up here by tomorrow, then fine. Going into Ivan's compound.

Bubbles showed up again.

> Fuck, Alexei. Wait for us.

It was Cassio. He was the sound of reason among his friends.

> Don't hog all of the fun, cold Russian bastard.

Of course, that would be Luca.

> Wait for us.

It was wiser that I waited for them, but my resources indicated Ivan would be back the day after tomorrow, and then this place would be a fortress.

> Tomorrow.

I had to atone for my sins. Save him at all costs. There hadn't been a day that went by where I didn't think about the little girl who slipped her hand into mine to offer comfort and the terror on the little boy's face whose only concern was to save his little sister.

> Drop your goddamn location pin.

It was Cassio.

> So we can find your ass.

> Stop talking about his ass, Cassio.

God, Luca could drive a saint to drink.

Not the image I need in my head.

Fuck both of you, asses.

Fucking Luca.
I dropped the pin. And another message beeped. This one from Cassio.

Shit, man. You couldn't have picked out a better place. Fucking Siberia?

Luca's message came in next.

Fuck, I'm on R&R. Siberia will freeze my balls this time of year.

I didn't have time for this shit.

Didn't ask you to come. And what balls, Luca? You got peanuts.

The next day, I had never been more grateful for Luca's peanuts. Carrying a battered body over my shoulder, I fought Ivan's men.

"Blyat," I cursed as I emptied the clip of my gun into another round of men. I killed five, ten more showed up. The battered body of the boy needed medical attention; otherwise he'd die within the next hour.

I rounded up the other boys and directed them to wait for me in the library of this fucking castle. Ivan had a dungeon for those that were used for sex, a housing section for his minions, and a luxurious castle for himself. If I got out of this alive, I'd blow up the whole motherfucking place.

Kingston's body started convulsing, and immediately, I lowered him onto the floor, ignoring the pain in my shoulder and torso. Some motherfucker threw his knife at me, like some goddamn acrobat using me for a target practice. I shot him dead, though not before the knife lodged itself into my torso.

I held Kingston's head, his dark hair dull and dirty.

"Don't you fucking die on me," I gritted, my voice shaking. "I made a promise."

Kingston's eyes rolled back in his head, blood running down his nose and mouth. I've seen men die enough times to know he was slipping.

More of Ivan's men burst through the door. I ejected the magazine of the gun and shoved a new magazine into it. It was my last one. Fuck!

My one hand on Kingston, I held him up so he wouldn't choke on his own blood, while I shot with my other. One. Two. Three... I had only enough to kill ten men. Then we'd both die.

The sounds of the bullets neared. They weren't mine. A man I hadn't shot, fell. Then another.

"Fuck, I told you to wait." Cassio came behind the man who fell to the ground at his feet, moaning and clutching his stomach. As if that would save him from bleeding out. Cassio pointed the gun to his head and pulled the trigger.

Nico, Luca, Luciano, and Alessio were right behind him.

"He just wanted to hoard all the fun for himself," Luciano retorted dryly.

"Alexei, tell us what we need to do," Nico growled. "So we can get out of here and get whoever we need out."

Kingston's body started convulsing again as I hovered over him, shoving my finger into Kingston's mouth.

"There are boys in the library," I told them. "Get them out. I have a place in Moscow. Take whoever you can there."

Without hesitation Nico, Alessio, and Luciano took off, while Luca and Cassio stayed behind.

"Buddy, I don't think he'll make it," Luca muttered. Just as the last word slipped through his lips, Kingston's body went limp.

"No," I hissed. "Don't you fucking dare."

I started CPR. Chest compressions. Mouth-to-mouth. Chest compressions. Mouth-to-mouth.

It was the first time in a very long time that I felt desperation welling in my chest, fear on my tongue. Broken promises.

It took Cassio, Luca, and me three hours to blow Ivan's place to dust. Getting rid of the memories wasn't as easy. In fact, it was impossible.

Hours later, I stared at my empty glass, while seated in a chair that faced the window and the door. The boys we were able to save were in bad shape. Some physically, but all were fucked up mentally.

"Fuck." Luca shoved his hand through his hair. "I need more of this cheap liquor to forget that shit."

Those images weren't forgettable. They stayed with you for the rest of your life.

"How did you know about the boys?" Alessio rasped, his hand shaking as he brought his glass to his lips.

I was one of those boys, I thought silently. "A tip," I answered instead.

Cassio's eyes drilled into the side of my cheek, which told me he didn't believe me. Especially since he heard one of the guards say how he should have known it was me who took Puma. As if she sensed my thoughts, my dog pushed her muzzle against my leg and laid her head on my thigh.

Fuck, I felt old. So goddamn old.

Nico strode over to us, filling all of our glasses. "You did the right thing, Alexei," he grumbled. "To save those boys." My throat burned from cheap liquor and emotions I had long learned to ignore. "I'm sorry we couldn't save them all."

Me too, I wanted to say. But my throat was too tight, memories of promises given to the little girl with dark brown eyes.

"Let's form a pact," Luca suggested grimly, his face serious which was a rare occurrence. "To always have each other's back. Always fight together."

"I'll drink to that," Cassio agreed, and the rest of them followed. I did too, though my voice failed me.

"Our blood family might fail us," Alessio said, his jaw clenching

with anger. It didn't take a genius to know he was thinking about his own father. "But we won't fail each other."

"Fuck blood. We watch each other's backs," Nico agreed. "No matter where and when, we look out for our own."

"Agreed." Luciano downed his drink. "And we'll all become filthy rich, so we'll have resources and funds to eliminate the ones who fuck with us."

Luciano had the right mindset. It was money and resources, combined with our trusting of each other, that would make us powerful and invincible. And trust was hard to find when you grew up the way I did.

Though I must have some hope still left in my heart because I raised the glass.

"Let's drink to that," I said coarsely, while my heart clenched in my chest for the little girl with dark hair and soft eyes.

The door of Vasili's office swung open, shutting down memory lane. Sasha strode in with his stupid grin.

"Are you daydreaming about our little agent that just stormed out of here?" God, his mouth would be the death of me. Or him. I hoped it was him.

"She isn't our little agent," I said icily. "She's my agent."

With that, I left him staring after me in Vasili's office. Let our big brother deal with his dumb ass.

I searched for a sex club named *Eve's Apple*. I couldn't find any record of it.

Then I searched for any sex club in New Orleans. To my surprise, there were way too many. It was how I found myself in this wretched club, before their business hours. I pretended to be searching for a job, but the moment I met the owner, my instincts told me this was the wrong club. I had no basis for that conclusion, but I was certain he wasn't the man Alexei referred to.

"You can come any time," the owner of a sex club called Venus and Mars offered. Yeah, the name was also very original. It would seem all the sex clubs had corny names.

"So generous," I mused, grabbing my purse and heading out the door. Mr. Starkov, the owner of Venus and Mars, followed me out of the club and into the humid New Orleans air. It was barely six in the evening and I came early on purpose, not wanting to be caught in the sex club when all the action started.

I stepped outside the door and offered him a polite smile.

"Thank you for the job offer." Not that I would ever take it. He wanted me to be his cage dancer. He was out of his goddamn mind.

He grabbed my wrist as I turned to leave. "Can I take you to dinner?" I furrowed my brow at the sudden offer. I feigned interest for a job, not a date. He smiled, though somehow it creeped me out more than charmed me. He wasn't a bad-looking guy, but something about him just rubbed me the wrong way.

"Ah, thank you," I faked being flattered. "The truth is that I have something else going on tonight."

He still wouldn't let go of my wrist. "Take me with you."

Desperation never looked good on a man. On this one, it was particularly unattractive. The way he watched me had alarms blasting in the back of my mind. Suddenly, I was painfully aware of how vulnerable I was. Nobody knew where I was or that I've been going down the sex clubs, using the process of elimination to find the club Alexei mentioned.

My eyes studied him and every single fiber of me stilled. There was something unsettling about Mr. Starkov. I couldn't quite pinpoint it, but I didn't like him.

I tugged on my wrist, trying not to make a scene but he refused to let go. From the corner of my eye, I caught movement down the street.

"You have been toying with me," Mr. Starkov hissed, suddenly looking very unattractive. "Now we're gonna play."

Stupid, I cursed myself. I was so goddamn stupid. The number one rule was never to go in the field alone. I attempted to jerk my arm away from him, but his grip was firm. I opened my mouth to tell him off when a familiar cold voice reached me.

"Let. Her. Go." The ice lacing Alexei's voice chilled the blood in my veins and my heart stalled. "Or I'll rid you of your fingers and hands."

I turned my head in his direction, no longer worried about the threat in the form of Mr. Starkov. If the restaurant incident was any indication, Alexei would break this man's hand unless he let go of me. Or cut them off as he threatened to do.

Sure enough, Alexei wasn't looking at me. His threatening gaze was entirely focused on the clingy Starkov. And just like that, Starkov let go of my wrist, and I rubbed it with my other hand.

"E-easy, buddy," Starkov stammered. *Buddy?* Was Starkov an

idiot? Alexei Nikolaev was anything but a buddy. "I was just finishing up an interview with your girlfriend."

Alexei didn't correct Starkov of his assumption. Neither did I.

The intensity in his eyes was volatile and dark, all his focus on Starkov who took a step back away from me. And another. Until he scurried back into the building.

Left alone with Alexei, while the buzz of New Orleans chattered in the distance, all I could do was stare at him. His hands were tucked in his cargo pockets, not a speck of dust on his clothing. He wore all black again. No surprise there, though he should really put some color in his wardrobe.

Like blue. It would accentuate his eyes even more. Then I'd immediately shook the dumb thought off.

I held my breath as I waited for him to say something. Anything. But the stoic man remained quiet. Jesus, he frustrated me. I was thankful he showed up at the right time, but he didn't have to act like an asshole now.

"Thank you." I finally broke the silence between us. I tried to pass him, but he stepped in front of me, blocking my path. I met his gaze head-on and sighed. "What?" I asked in an agitated tone.

"You won't find it this way." His tone was smooth, calm and final.

Okay, so he didn't take my warning about stalking seriously. No surprise there.

"I'm not going into that Eve's club blindly," I finally said. I hated feeling vulnerable. He expected me to just follow him without any regard for my own safety. A small noise of frustration escaped me and I wanted to growl. "You have to give me something."

My heart stalled, the words taking a whole different meaning. Shit, he flustered me. And not in a good way.

"Fine," he replied and I looked at him in surprise. I didn't expect him to cave in. If anything, maybe take me into a dark corner and kill me. "Let's go to my place," he added. Ah, and there it was. He wanted to kill me. I shook my head, keeping my breathing even. "It's too open here."

Yes, his reason made sense, but hell if I'd willingly go into a killer's basement. Or house. Wherever the fuck he slept.

"We can sit in my car," I suggested and immediately realized my mistake. I took an Uber here. *Fuck.*

"Fine." He turned around and started walking away, while I debated what to do. I suggested a car, so backpedaling wouldn't be wise. He stopped, glanced over his shoulder and cocked an eyebrow.

"I took an Uber here," I admitted with a heavy sigh.

He didn't miss a beat. "My car, then."

I hesitated for another moment and then followed with a sigh.

Curiosity killed the cat. Or the agent.

I walked down Bourbon Street, struggling to keep up with him in my heels. I hated wearing high heels. They were impractical and killer on your feet. Of course, Alexei wouldn't be a gentleman and wait for me. I watched his broad shoulders as I followed him. He was by far the biggest man I'd ever known. He and his brothers must have eaten a boatload of spinach growing up. It had to be the only explanation for their size.

I wonder if their penis size matched their physique, I mused and my lips curved into a smile. It would be funny as shit to see them naked with a tiny penis against such a large body.

"Something funny?" My eyes snapped up and caught him eyeing me. My face heated. No way I'd admit to him what I'd been thinking. Yeah, that would make things awkward.

"No. How far is your car?"

He tilted his chin to a Mercedes Benz G-Class.

"Nice car," I muttered. "G-Class?" I drove a gas-efficient Honda. Yes, my family had money, but there was no need to flaunt it. He cocked his eyebrow, as if he was impressed I knew vehicles. "My brothers are into cars," I explained.

Without a word, he opened the passenger door. I didn't want to hassle with parking downtown, hence taking Uber. At this moment, I regretted it.

"You make me disappear," I warned him, glancing around, "and my brothers will hunt you down."

His eyes remained impassive, but he gave his head the most subtle shake. Like my words amused him.

"Good to know," he said in an unemotional tone.

I ignored his stare and slid into the passenger seat. The door shut firmly behind me and he came around to the driver's seat, then shut his own door. He started the car and put it into drive.

"What are you doing?" I asked him, alarmed.

"Driving."

"We were going to sit in the car and talk," I muttered, suddenly feeling stupid for getting into a criminal's vehicle. Wasn't that covered in the beginner's class? Jesus Christ, I had to be the worst agent to walk this earth.

"We'll talk while I drive." His words said nothing.

"While you drive me to—" I left the sentence open-ended.

"Home." Okay, home was good but the question was whose home. My arm rested on the console and I tried hard not to move it. The urge to fidget was strong.

"Mine?" I breathed the question. "My home?"

His arm brushed mine, and I shifted barely an inch, avoiding another accidental touch. Noticing my movement, his eyes swept over me. It wasn't a quick glance, but more lazy and slow. As if he was reading all my secrets. Goosebumps broke over my skin and my fingers curled over the edge of the console.

"Nervous?" he asked, his eyes returning to the road. He was no longer looking at me, yet I felt the weight of his gaze.

I swallowed hard, then shook my head.

"Yes, your home," he answered my earlier question.

Thank God! The air in the car was thick, his large body somehow making the large Mercedes seem too small. I watched his movements as he drove, shifting smoothly, which was surprising for such a large man. I had a feeling he was invisible when he wanted to be.

Duh!

He was certainly invisible when he stalked me, so no surprise he knew where I lived. I inhaled deeply, the scent of his cologne and the leather invading every inch of my lungs. It wasn't a cologne I recognized, but it fit him. It was exotic, spicy and strong, but not too strong to overwhelm all your senses.

"So about this club," I started, hoping to regain some control of this situation. "And the man we are going after. I want to know everything."

The corner of his lip tugged up. Wonderful, I amused him. "Everything, huh?"

I blew a piece of my hair out of my face. "Yes, everything. You are asking me to trust you blindly, and I can't do that."

"Why not?" He couldn't be seriously asking that question.

"The list is pretty long," I scoffed.

"We have time," he said coldly.

"First, you're a criminal," I started, eyeing him for any signs. "Second, you're not my partner. Third, I need a plan so I can organize my life. Ensure I don't have anything going on the days that you drag me to God knows where."

"Have a date?" he mused and my mouth just about dropped. Did he just crack a joke? His face was impassive, so it was hard to tell.

"No, I don't," I sighed. With this man it was whiplash from one minute to the next. "My brothers like to check on me. My girlfriends like to check on me too, though they are not as crazy as my brothers. And they'll freak out if I'm not available when they assume I'm relaxing at home." He cocked one eyebrow, and I felt the need to quickly explain. "Trust me, they'll have the entire force and their security company hunting for me. The last place I want them to find me is in a sex club. With you." I let the words sink and then continued, "So I need the place and time for the event, you know."

Alexei didn't miss a beat.

"It is an underground sex club." Well, that explained why I couldn't find it. Goddamn it!

"Where is it?" I questioned him.

"The location is different every time."

I rolled my eyes, annoyed. "Well, is there a pattern?"

"No."

Of course not. I watched his hands firmly on the steering wheel. "Okay, when will the event take place?"

"The date isn't set yet."

I let out a frustrated breath. "You've got to work with me," I huffed, annoyed at this stoic man. "Didn't you just hear me tell you that my brothers will go ballistic if they happen to call one night and I'm nowhere around."

I'd admit that it sounded like my brothers were controlling my life. They didn't; not in that sense. But they worried about me a tad bit too much. I didn't freak out when they took an hour to respond. My brothers did.

"They sound like good brothers," he commented. "They're doing their job."

My eyebrows shot up. "One time, I was an hour late getting home from a boyfriend's house, and they destroyed his front door." It was right before my twenty-first birthday. When I didn't come home on time, Winston and Royce showed up with security and some of their ex-SEAL buddies, busted through the front door, and scared the living daylights out of his family. "What do you think will happen if I don't respond to their texts for several hours?"

Alexei shrugged, apathy on his face. "Jesus, I hope you never have daughters," I muttered. "I have a feeling you'll be worse than my brothers. Actually, I'm pretty sure you'll be obsessive over your sons and daughters."

He didn't react but his knuckles tightened around the wheel. Did I say something wrong? Regret instantly flooded me. I didn't like to upset people.

"Who are we trying to get close to?" I attempted to steer the conversation back to the sex club and maybe take his mind off his future children.

He side-eyed me, as if he was considering how much to tell me. "A guy named Igor owns the club."

"Does Igor have a last name?" I questioned. He was rather stingy with information.

"No."

Dammit. Didn't he know there were millions of Igors on this planet?

"Okay, and he will lead us to whom?" His clipped responses were agitating me, and I tried hard not to lose my cool.

"Ivan Petrov."

My heart skidded to a halt. The FBI ghost criminal and the reason Alexei was on their radar. Until Milo wiped out Alexei's record.

"You know him?" I asked, trying to subdue the tremble in my voice.

"Yes."

"How well?" I put effort into keeping my voice steady while my nerves danced under my skin. I waited three heartbeats. "Your friend."

"Definitely not."

I sighed, running a hand through my hair and sank back into the seat.

"How does he look?" From all the questions, it wasn't the best one, but the appearance was all I remembered from Kingston's kidnapper. My eyes returned to Alexei's hands and remained there.

"Ugly." His short answer didn't surprise me.

What surprised me was a memory that flickered in my mind but faded too fast.

A boy's hand that held mine.

SEVENTEEN
ALEXEI

I t had been two days since I talked to Agent Ashford. I hacked into her building's security cameras to see her, just to get a glimpse. I checked on her a few times throughout the day. It was only when I confirmed her safety that I could finally continue with my day.

I fucking hated that this fear was ingrained into me. The Nikolaev bitch ensured I was just as fucked up in the head as I was physically. She'd given me something to cherish, then took it away. Over and over again. It didn't matter what it was.

Family. Toy. Pet. It was always taken away.

And now, all that paranoia was focused on the young woman. This obsession with her wasn't healthy. I knew it as surely as I knew the moon would rise each night.

I even contemplated getting a dog. Maybe it'd split the obsession between the two living things. I hadn't had another dog since I got Puma out of Russia. She had a good five years with me and then died of old age, peacefully. Just as her whole life should have been.

Though it was another loss.

Maybe when all this shit was over with Ivan, I'd get a dog. There'd be no judgment there and dogs were excellent listeners. They never repeated the shit you confessed to them. And God knew, I had some fucked-up shit to confess.

I stood in front of the elevator in Aurora's building. Pushing the button, I waited for the door to open. Seeing her through cameras was all well, but it didn't compare to the high of seeing her in person. And her chocolate scent... I fucking loved it. My car still smelled like her from two days ago, and I forbid anyone from touching it.

Lavender calmed normal people. Aurora's scent calmed me.

As I took the elevator up to Aurora's apartment, I readied for the tension that was always there between us. Sexual tension along with animosity. Possibly loathing.

My chest tightened.

I deserved her loathing. Eventually, she'd remember I was the boy from the zoo. She'd realize I betrayed her. After her father backed out of his deal with Ivan, I had been studying the Ashford family's routines —school time, practice time, bedtime. I was there when the family woke up and when they went to bed. I knew they'd go to the zoo that day. The nanny who happened to be sleeping with their father shared it with another nanny.

It was me who told Ivan about the open window we'd have. I led him to her and her brother. A little girl who offered me the first glimpse at kindness in a long time. And I burned it all to ashes.

Maybe it was the reason I couldn't stop stalking her. My fucked-up brain thought of it as a way to atone for my sins against her and her brother. So I was overcompensating the only way I knew how.

By watching her.

She was my responsibility. And when I saw that prick Starkov grip Agent Ashford's wrist, I almost lost my shit. Again. I came to a conclusion that I fucking hated any man touching her.

Because she's mine, my mind whispered.

I buried the words somewhere deep down in my soul, hiding them from the world. Fighting the urge to tattoo them onto my skin. If people knew she was mine, someone would surely come and take her from me.

Fear still lurked underneath my skin. As cold as the winters in

Siberia. I realized I might be losing my grip on shit when I went back and taught Starkov a lesson. I knew Agent Ashford wouldn't take it kindly to me beating him up in broad daylight or in front of her. So I found him in the middle of the night—harassing another woman.

And taught him a lesson.

The knowledge he'd never hurt another woman soothed me. For now.

Thanks to my stalking, I knew she dug for information on Igor and Ivan. When I mentioned Ivan's name, the flicker of recognition in her eyes didn't escape me. She had heard the name before. Not surprising considering he was on the FBI's radar, but I had to wonder if she heard his name anywhere else.

I let out a frustrated breath as I stood in front of her apartment door. I should back off, let her go to the club with her partner. It would have been the right thing to do. He was only unavailable because I made it so.

Yet, I couldn't let her go.

I wanted to be there when she finally got her justice. And I wanted her there when I got my justice. But somehow hers took priority.

It had been days since I laid eyes on her again and nothing would ever be the same. My obsession ran deeper with each breath I took. It wasn't healthy. It wasn't right. Yet the more I told myself I couldn't have her, the more I wanted her. I had never wanted anything as much as I wanted her.

It was like I was an addict that needed another fix. With each glimpse of her, she fed my addiction, and I feared any moment I'd reach a point of no return. Quite possibly, I was there already.

I raised my hand to knock on her door and my hand trembled. It fucking trembled. A cold sweat broke out across my skin, and I stood there with my hand hovering in the air. Fuck, I had to shake this off. I wanted her so badly, it was fucking with my mind.

My hand curled into a tightened fist. *Bang. Bang. Bang.* I banged on the door like a madman.

The door swung open the next second, and I came face-to-face with my obsession. Instantly, my heart stalled and a calm washed over me with her scent. *Chocolate.* Her unique scent and the sight of her had my shoulders relaxing.

Jesus, the impact this woman had on me wasn't right.

"What the fuck are you doing here?" she snapped, annoyed. I let out a sardonic breath, my lips twitching. She was certainly happy to see me. Or not. "Did I invite you and forget?"

Instantly any thoughts of doing the right thing evaporated. Fuck. That. Shit. With her mouth, she'd get herself killed if she went after Igor and Ivan alone. She was mine to protect and nobody would steal her from me. She was within my reach, and I'd keep her that way, even if I had to handcuff her to my wrist and throw away the key.

I lifted up the package I held. I got her an entire outfit. First time ever I bought a fucking dress and shoes for a woman.

"What?" Her eyebrow shot up, annoyance still clear on her face. "Please tell me you didn't come here to show off your shopping skills."

I shoved it into her chest. "It's for you," I told her. "We are going out tonight."

She tucked a strand of her dark hair behind her ear. "I already told you before. You're not my type," she said sarcastically and a corner of my lips lifted. *Yet,* I added mentally. "Besides, I'm not in the mood for company."

Her cheeks flushed and her lips slightly parted. Little liar. She felt this sizzling attraction too. She had to; otherwise, it made me a pathetic, obsessive psychopath and I refused to be that. Not with her. She made me *feel. Want.*

"The club event is tonight," I added, sidestepping her and entering her apartment without an invitation. It didn't take a genius to see she didn't want to invite me in. When I brought her home the other day, she emphasized that I was only dropping her off in front of her building. The smart agent didn't even question how I knew where she lived. She just shot me a warning glare and slammed the car door in my face.

She probably would have slammed the door of her apartment too if I wasn't already inside it.

A deep sigh sounded behind me and I heard the door click shut.

"By all means, come in," she muttered exasperated. I glanced over my shoulder to find her leaning against her door and her eyes on… my ass. *Interesting.*

"What are you wearing?" she muttered, her eyes traveling over me.

"A suit."

When she looked up and our eyes met, a flicker passed through her dark gaze. Usually people were an open book. Women especially. Not my little agent. Her thoughts were her own, and as idiotic as it sounded, I wanted to own them too.

I wanted to own all of her.

Her body. Her thoughts. Her heart. Her soul.

Every goddamn thing.

Electricity danced between us, her expression dark and tempting. It was ironic because for all her dark hair and eyes, she was my light in this world. And despite my light coloring, I was the very definition of darkness.

She licked her lips, and I slipped my hands in my pockets or risked reaching out to touch her. I wanted to touch every single inch of her. Lick her everywhere. She'd be my own personal dessert.

I watched her neck, her pulse throbbing visibly. Did I make her nervous? It was hard to tell. She didn't think twice about talking back to me, despite my rough appearance. Despite my criminal activities, which she'd clearly dug up.

A shuddering breath left her, her eyes locked on my lips. Her tongue swept over her lower lip and all the blood in my body shot to my groin. Someone had to be laughing at me up there. A little five-foot-six FBI agent became intertwined in every single part of my being.

I. Am. So. Fucked.

My eyes roamed over her petite frame. She was barefoot, her toes painted in the perfect French manicure. She was a perfect mixture of badass and elegant. My gaze traveled up her slim legs to her torso. She wore the shortest pair of white shorts I had ever seen on a woman. And Tatiana and Isabella pushed the limits, so I've seen short. Combined with a pink tank top, her slim shoulders and arms on full display, I had images of her naked in my king-size bed flashing through my mind. God, what I would do to her if she was tied to my bed.

Fuck, it's going to be a long night.

I wanted her body bent over the couch, so I could ram into her and fuck her into oblivion. As if she could read my thoughts, her little claws dug into her palms. Maybe she fought the urge to touch me, just as I fought the urge to touch her.

Except she'd never be allowed to touch me. As much as I wanted her to. There was a reason I covered my body in ink. It was better than letting the world see the scars that marred most of me.

Pinkish. Rough. Ugly.

There was only so much healing your skin could do until it was permanently damaged. And my brand of damage ran deep.

"Kroshka." *Baby girl.* She had always been my girl. The girl who saved me with a single gesture of kindness. She'd never forgive me once she learned. I knew I wouldn't forgive someone for hurting my siblings. "Only good girls get to touch." My voice came out rough; my accent pronounced. After all, I spent the first sixteen years of my life in Russia. Though I didn't consider myself Russian.

A sharp gasp broke the tense silence swimming between us, and something in her eyes flashed so feral I had to clench my teeth to fight this need brimming through my veins.

To make her *mine*. To fuck her until she remembered nothing but *me*. I'd be her entire world and she'd be mine.

Why did I tell her that only good girls could touch me when in fact nobody could? No fucking idea. Maybe I liked to rile her up. Or I liked to taunt myself with something I'd never have.

She got herself together and an undignified scoff slipped through her lips. "You wish," she spat back in a husky voice. "I wouldn't touch you if you were the last man on this planet."

Ouch.

Her eyes filled with defiance and bitter amusement filled me. The little agent could deny all she pleased, but she *wanted* to touch me. My stomach tightened in distaste for what she would find if I ever allowed her to get that far. She'd be disgusted.

Contempt at the fucking fate that made my life a living hell spread like wildfire in my chest. I had learned a long time ago wishes were for naught. Just a waste of time.

I survived. Period. Nothing more; nothing less.

But now, seeing the woman who made my chest actually hurt when she looked at me, I cursed all the saints for fucking me up. Because when it came to her, a visceral need formed and hunger roared in my ears and through my veins.

To give her everything she needed. And take everything I craved from her.

Except I knew what would come out of it if I went that far.

Distaste. Pity. Disgust.

"Get dressed," I told her, gritting my teeth. I had to get a grip around this woman. "We have an hour to get there."

She shrugged her slim, tan shoulder and disappeared into her bedroom. For a moment I stared at the door, burning a hole through it as if it would magically turn into glass so I could see her changing.

Too deep, I kept warning myself. It wouldn't end well. Did I try to stop it though? Fuck no.

Trying not to picture Aurora changing, my eyes shifted over her furniture. In that regard, my FBI agent was similar to me. She was a minimalist. No pictures. No knickknacks. No personal effects sitting around except for a screensaver-locked laptop on the coffee table and a *Star Wars* movie disk.

Weird, she didn't strike me as a *Star Wars* fanatic. But then I remembered, it was her brother's. Agent Ashford preferred *Lord of the Rings*. The little benefits of stalking and monitoring my little agent, as morally questionable as that was.

The place was polished, just as I would expect from someone who was born into a prestigious family. A slick tan couch with white cushions, matching white side tables with lamps, and a low coffee table. A large flat-screen TV hung on the wall with a game console sitting on a shelf.

The bedroom door opened and Aurora walked into the living room, taking all the oxygen in the apartment.

Blyat! *Fuck!*

She looked hot as fuck, with the sweetest body I had ever seen. Drop-dead gorgeous. Dressed in red, she was the definition of sin. Sexy. This woman should always wear red. I debated whether there was any possible way I could patent the color and reserve it only for her.

My eyes roamed over her body. The dress hugged her luscious curves, giving me a glimpse of her breasts. Her tits pushed against the corset of her dress. The red pumps made her legs look even longer, her skin luminescent under the soft light of her apartment.

Suddenly, I regretted going to the club and letting anyone see her like this.

EIGHTEEN
ALEXEI

"**W**e didn't even practice." Aurora's voice trembled; so did her hand as she smoothed her dress down her torso for the hundredth time. "Are you sure there isn't a better way?"

This was the only way. Igor would lead us to Ivan. The need to prove himself to Ivan was ingrained into him. And the temptation to bring to Ivan the girl I didn't would help him earn extra brownie points. Little fucking shit.

"Yes."

I'd never let anything happen to her, but I suspected it was the part about possibly having to perform that got her all riled up. It was ironic really. It was the only part I looked forward to. Yes, the circumstances weren't ideal, but it was certainly a perk. At least for me.

There was an air of vulnerability about her as she wrapped her arms around her waist. Like she was protecting herself.

I couldn't help but admire her. She portrayed strength even when nervous. There weren't too many women who'd be brave enough to follow through with this. Though the final act was yet to happen.

Her gaze kept fleeting my way as if she studied me. It was clear I wasn't her type. If her ex-boyfriends were anything to go by, she liked clean-cut guys. I was far away from clean cut.

Her ankle gave out, and I instinctively wrapped my hand around her upper arm, catching her. The softness of her skin registered immediately. Flawless and smooth. I could almost imagine how good she'd feel against me.

She stared at where my fingers clutched her bare skin, then her dark eyes flickered to my face. Careful not to betray how much I loved the feel of her skin under my palms, I slowly let go.

Her delicate neck bobbed as she swallowed. "Thanks."

I nodded, then we continued walking and I ensured my steps were slower to accommodate her. In no time, we stood in front of the discrete black door.

Glancing her way, I gave her another chance to bail out. A jerky nod and I knocked on the door.

One. Two. Three.

"One more," she murmured, her voice hoarse. I raised my eyebrow in question. "Three's bad luck."

Her explanation made no sense. But I knocked one more time to appease her.

The door swung open and Irena stood in front of us in her signature black dress. She had been hinting for a while that she'd be interested in entertaining me sexually. She'd even been willing to do hard-core shit with Sasha. I'd rather cut my dick off than take her up on it. Apparently so would Sasha because he avoided her like the plague.

Voyeurism wasn't my thing. Even if it was, I'd never bother with someone who willingly attached themselves to Igor. And I knew how deep she was in with Igor. I made it my business to know, though the little weasel was good at hiding.

Aware of Aurora's eyes on me, studying me, I slid my hand to her lower back and nudged her in. If she changed her mind, I knew there'd be nothing to make her take that step. I certainly wouldn't force her.

Aurora moved forward, her steps slightly hesitant. Once inside, her sharp gaze studied her surroundings. *Smart.*

"Welcome to the Eve's Apple," Irena greeted, smiling at us like she scored big-time.

Urging Aurora forward, we made our way down the hallway and to the large bar.

"Drink?" I asked her. She nodded, and as we sat down on the barstools, I signaled the bartender.

"Vodka spritz for the lady and cognac for me."

The moment our drinks landed in front of us, Aurora downed hers. Her eyes were like a deer in headlights, glancing all around. I leaned closer to her ear, to give an appearance of lovers whispering to each other.

Potentially discussing other partners.

She'd never get another partner. I'd rip him to pieces. She was mine. I should have admitted days ago or the moment she stepped into the elevator that I was fucked.

But I didn't.

"No eye contact," I told her, my lips brushing her earlobe. "Otherwise, it's an invitation."

And their death, I added silently.

To my satisfaction, her eyes returned to me.

"Jesus, Mary, and Joseph," she muttered. And she gulped down another drink. I felt his presence before I saw him.

"Alexei Nikolaev." I fucking hated Igor. And the moment his filthy hand landed on Aurora's shoulder, I wanted to slice it off.

"Get your hands off her," I told Igor in Russian, keeping my voice low. He immediately obeyed, knowing full well the killer that I could be.

"Are you enjoying the club?" Igor drawled, his eyes on Agent Ashford. Fuck, I was so tempted to rid him of his eyeballs. Fucker didn't need them to get us to Ivan.

"It's great," Aurora answered, forcing a smile.

"Introduce us, Alexei." He was getting closer and closer to losing his eyesight.

"Aurora. Igor." Goddamn fucker. I didn't want him to know anything about her.

I placed my hand on her thigh, ensuring Igor understood she wasn't available. Fucker didn't get lost.

"Would you like a tour, Aurora?" Igor offered, his eyes never leaving her.

"Ah, thank you. Alexei already offered." She actually offered him a sweet smile while her hand covered mine, patting it awkwardly. As fucked up as it was, it made me want to chuckle. I couldn't even remember the last time I had that feeling.

She turned her head and focused on me.

"I have a VIP room ready for you," Igor added.

"Do svidaniya." Dismissing him, I focused on the woman next to me. She was attracting too many glances from other men. The sooner I got her out of the open view, the better.

When Igor was completely out of earshot, she leaned slightly over and whispered, "Is that the guy?"

"Da."

A group of men crowded the bar, their eyes devouring my date like she was a rare delicacy. She was, but not for them.

"VIP room. Now," I barked.

I guided her to our VIP suite and it wasn't until the door clicked behind us that the red murder haze finally receded. This room was pretty standard, though it appeared my date wasn't accustomed to it.

Her eyes lingered on the St. Andrew's cross mounted to one wall, and it was clear she was appalled. Her gaze flickered to me in exasperation.

"Don't even fucking think about it," she warned. A slight tremble to her voice didn't escape me.

"Relax." Hard-core shit was Sasha's thing.

I strode to the only chair in the room and sat myself down. It'd be a long night if she couldn't relax. And the way she looked right now, she was anything but relaxed. Her eyes darted all around, back and forth, watching me like I was her enemy.

I wasn't her enemy but maybe her instincts weren't far off.

"Sit," I ordered her.

Her eyes darted around and came back to me. "Where?"

I should be sorry to put her in such a situation. Yet, I couldn't muster the will for it. I liked the idea of having her sit in my lap.

Like a wild animal, she took a step closer to me. And another one. Then she turned around and sat down stiffly onto my lap. Igor was watching us, but she didn't need that pointed out. She was a ball of nerves as it was.

"He's watching," she mumbled, barely moving her mouth.

"Da."

Placing my hands on her waist, I held her still. She hadn't realized it but each time she moved, her ass grazed against my groin. There was only so much torture I could endure. My hands slid down her waist and to her thighs.

Her eyes glued on the screen, her breathing hitched and her lips parted. I wasn't even sure she was aware of it. She kept shifting, her skin flushed. She watched the show out there; I just watched her.

She moved again, her ass grinding against my hard groin and she froze. Her eyes flared to my face. There was something warm and beautiful in her eyes, like a lifeline I never knew I needed.

I didn't want to scare her. Me wanting her wasn't part of the deal. But fuck, I wanted her. Unlike anything or anyone before her. It was a depraved kind of hunger for her. An obsession that a single touch with her would fuel for the rest of my days.

Since the day she walked back into my life, I'd dreamed of her, fantasized of her and obsessed over her.

Her tongue swept over her ruby-red lips and lust crossed her expression. For me? I wasn't sure but my control snapped. All the blood rushed to my groin and my brain stopped functioning.

I stood up, my hand gripping her hips and pressed her hands against the window. Bending her over, her palms braced against the glass, my hands pushed her red dress up, baring her ass to my view. The woman wore the tiniest string I had ever seen. I pressed my body against hers so she could feel my cock against the soft curve of her ass.

Pressing my lips to her fragile neck, I enjoyed her soft skin, the racing pulse beneath my mouth. Licking the skin over her collarbone, I brought my palms to her round ass.

This wasn't for the show. This was for me.

Yes, I was a bastard, but I fucking wanted her. And the scent of her arousal told me she wanted me too. At least at this very moment.

"Ready?" I asked. A small whimper escaped her mouth, her breathing labored.

She glanced over her shoulder, our eyes connecting. Those deep, warm brown eyes. The color of chocolate. She smelled like chocolate too.

"Ready, kroshka?" It was her last chance to stop me.

"Y-yes." Her voice was breathy, her lips pouty red, and her eyes hazed with lust. Fuck if I knew whether it was for me or what she saw that threesome couple do.

The petite, dark-haired FBI agent was full of surprises. I shouldn't take it too far. Everything that touched me ended up broken. Everything I touched ended up ruined. Filthy.

But unless we played this right, Igor would rat us out and our ticket to Ivan would go to fucking hell. The way he leered at her pissed me off. It sent cold fury down my spine and made me want to murder him.

Aurora was *mine*. Her breasts. Her ass. Her pussy. All fucking mine. Her mouth, though, wouldn't be. Regardless how much I wanted to own and taste every inch of her.

I didn't kiss. Period.

I reached around and parted her thighs, pushing the flimsy material aside and sliding my finger past her folds. She was soaked. So fucking wet that my fingers were drenched within seconds.

God help me, but she was intoxicating and maddening at the same fucking time. Unlike anyone I had ever met before.

Even her arousal smelled like chocolate, like a drug you inhaled and it forever remained in your system. I pushed my fingers deeper in and her pussy clenched around my fingers. Her head fell backwards, her eyes watching me over her shoulder, through her heavy eyelids and her cheeks flushed.

With my free hand, I fisted her hair and tugged it backwards, aware others from the club were watching. Except they could barely see, only the outline of us because I dimmed the lights just right to ensure they couldn't see us clearly.

Her pussy kept clenching around my fingers, eager for more as I thrust my fingers in and out. Her moans grew louder, her ass pushing against me. Then without warning, I removed my fingers and brought them to her mouth. Without my asking, her lips parted and she sucked them clean.

Fucking beautiful!

Still gripping her hair with one hand, I unbuckled my pants, pushed her thong aside, then slid my rock-hard cock along her hot folds, then slammed into her. She was tight, her pussy clenching around my cock like a stronghold. Her moans vibrated straight to my chest as I fucked her hard. For the past two weeks, ever since she opened her sassy, smart mouth, this was all I wanted, and it was better than I envisioned.

She felt like heaven. My own personal heaven that I had no right to, but I stole a taste of it anyhow. All my control disintegrated as I fucked her hard and relentless. She matched each one of my thrusts with a whimper.

I worried I'd break her, forcing myself to ease up when her low warning growl spurred me on.

"More." I was more than happy to oblige, picking up my pace and pounding into her mercilessly. Her soft moans turned into gasping, urgent cries. She was close. I felt it as if it was my own orgasm. I turned her head, so I could see her face as she shattered with pleasure. For me.

Her dark eyes glazed with desire, her mouth parted, and I fucked her faster and deeper until I felt her fall apart, her pussy milking me for all I had. She was fucking gorgeous.

A shudder rippled down my spine and I blew my load right into her tight, hot pussy, and the most powerful orgasm of my life cut through me.

Fuck. Me.

Her body slumped back into me as if she sought out comfort from me. Little did she know, I only brought havoc. Never comfort.

I used my hand to turn her head towards me, and for the first time in my life, I was tempted to kiss a woman. Not just a woman; this woman.

She must have felt the same urge, because her eyes lingered on my mouth.

I was fucked. So fucked!

NINETEEN
AURORA

T he entire time we made our way to the door of Eve's Apple I had complained that there had to be a better way to find the man who would lead us to Ivan Petrov, that Alexei and I hadn't even had a chance to rehearse what we would need to do, to say.

Although, no amount of rehearsal could have prepared me for this. For the way he made me feel. The way my body responded to him.

It was explosive. Like fireworks in the darkness. Beautiful, thrilling, and scary.

Yet, amazing.

I couldn't move. My whole body was frozen against the glass.

My muscles quivered after he had delivered the most intense sex of my life. The best sex of my life. And it happened with a criminal. Though my pussy didn't discriminate. And at this very moment, neither did my brain because I liked the way he felt inside me.

Somehow it didn't surprise me that Alexei fucked rough. I should be freaking out that I went so far with a complete stranger, and in a damn sex club, but the only thing I could muster the energy for was to lean back into him.

Glancing over my shoulder, my eyes lingered on his lips. I wanted to taste him. Trace his mouth with my tongue. His scar didn't repel me. In fact, it added to his appeal.

My heart thundered, and suddenly, heat shot straight to my core. Again. He just fucked the living daylights out of me, and I was ready for round two. He smelled so good, his muscles hard against my back.

My pulse rang in my ear, desire fluttering through my veins. I barely shifted an inch backwards, the pull strong. I needed more. So much more from him.

Something flashed through his eyes as I leaned further back, barely another inch.

"No kissing." His voice, deep and guttural, shattered the moment, freezing my heart and soul. He certainly knew how to make a woman feel cheap.

I held my breath. He was still inside me, but he might as well be on another planet. I didn't care to ponder why the rejection bothered me. It wasn't as if I cared about the man. I didn't even particularly like him.

Something wet slid down my inner thigh and the fire in my veins turned to ice. We had unprotected sex.

Fuck! Fuck! Fuck!

I lost my head and let him fuck me without a condom. I had *never* had sex without a condom. Ever. Regardless that I was on the pill.

My whole body tensed, which he must have felt because his eyes searched out mine.

"Please tell me you're clean," I hissed under my breath. "You didn't use a condom."

God, I was such an idiot. How could I let it get so far?

"Don't worry, kroshka." His gaze darkened, and I couldn't tell whether it was in anger or something else. "I'm clean."

TWENTY
ALEXEI

I gritted my teeth.

Aurora was the hottest woman I had ever seen or touched. High, smooth cheekbones, dark eyelashes, pouty mouth. Her scent was my own personal flavor of heaven. And the way her eyes glazed over and her olive-toned skin flushed with desire for me was intoxicating.

It made things move deep in my chest, and I didn't care to evaluate it.

"Please tell me you're clean." It was hard to miss the regret in her voice. "You didn't use a condom."

I let out a breath and swept my gaze over her face. I could point out to her that she didn't ask for a condom either, but I didn't trust myself not to lose my shit if she came back with another sassy comment.

Besides, that word. *Clean.* I was anything but clean. No, I didn't have any sexually transmitted diseases. But I had been used so many times that clean was the worst way to describe me. Physical pain, mental anguish, humiliation, and degradation. Hopelessness. *Been there way too many times.*

Igor was always willing, I fucking hated it. Though Ivan's women and men seemed to prefer blue eyes to Igor's dark pools.

185

The memories left an acrid taste in my mouth.

"Don't worry, kroshka," I told her, keeping my voice icy. "I'm clean."

Anger flashed in her dark eyes, and it hit me all wrong. I knew it was me who ruined the moment the second I uttered the words.

No kissing.

It was the only hard rule I had when it came to sex. I hadn't experienced kissing in twenty years and just the memory of the last kiss had bile rising in my throat. It took years to undo the damage the abuse under Ivan caused, now when I had sex, it was my choice, and just for the release.

I hated the feeling of being pulled back into time, but as of lately, it seemed I couldn't escape the past, and it was doing its damndest to catch up with me. The memory slammed into me like a hurricane against the shores.

Drip. Drip. Drip.

The sound of water dripping pulled me from the drug-induced haze.

My eyes flickered open to the bars above me. A makeshift viewing gallery that allowed the spectators above to have a clear view.

"For better viewing," Ivan gloated.

I jerked my arms, but the cold, metal shackles kept them outstretched as did the ones clasped around my ankles. The springs of the bed protested beneath me. The drugs in my system were beginning to wear off, and I knew what was coming.

It was Friday night and Ivan's customers were back. I had hoped tonight they'd choose Igor, but hope was for fools, and tonight I was the biggest fool of all.

I wanted to rage, bellow, and fight. I wanted to kill. Anything but endure another man or woman who wanted to kiss me. Moan into my mouth. Touch me.

My wrists jerked against the chains, hoping one would break, desperate to set myself free. If only I'd set one hand free, I could fight. The last customer ended up with a cracked skull.

All these years of doing what was necessary to survive. I couldn't do it any longer. I was seventeen. It was time to find my moment of escape or die trying. I'd been preparing, waiting for the right moment to make my move. To leave this godforsaken place.

I was tired of the cold. Tired of surviving. All I wanted was to live. Free of the constraints. My eyes found Ivan and Igor standing at the top, peering through the bars; one with dollar bills in his eyes, and the other with envy as he licked his lips.

Igor loved this. He enjoyed the nights he was chosen to do this. Men... women... he didn't care. So many nights he spent watching bodies writhe against each other, while I closed my eyes and ignored the sounds, finding reprieve somewhere deep in my mind.

The sound of light footsteps brought my eyes to two women strolling towards me. Each step brought them closer to me and sweat formed on my brow. Both wore long gowns, one of white silk, the other black as night.

Lust and desire danced in their eyes, as they took in my naked form. The one in white came to my side, her light brown eyes taking in my body as her fingers danced lightly across my chest and abs.

Both took their time, touching me, enjoying what they'd paid for. My muscles shook, and again I thrashed against my restraints. They both smiled at my attempts, laughing lightly as they began brushing their hands along my body once more.

"I think I'll enjoy my time with you," the one in black remarked.

The woman in white leaned forward, her tongue sliding across my cheek. The overpowering smell of her flowery perfume made my stomach churn. Her mouth brushed along mine and every fiber inside of me tensed.

The hands of the other woman took my penis into her palm, stroking it as she moaned. I couldn't stop my body from reacting any more than I could stop a raging blizzard. I hated myself for it. I didn't want this to happen. It did nothing for me, yet my body still reacted, my penis growing firmer with each stroke.

The woman in white forced her tongue between my lips. I may not have been able to control how my body reacted, but I could control this. I opened my mouth slightly, allowing her to believe that I gave in to her. The moment her tongue slipped into my mouth, I bit down. The coppery tang of her blood flooded my mouth, and she screamed, jerking back.

I smiled as I spit the blood at the woman still standing towards the end of the bed. She moved quickly out of the way.

A blow came suddenly. I couldn't tell where it came from as my head jerked backwards. Two guards came in, ushering the woman with half her tongue hanging on by a thread out of the room. Another blow landed, and I didn't mind. I'd rather take the beating than the alternative that stood at the end of the bed.

Light brown eyes met mine, and I was surprised to find eagerness in them.

"Now I have you all to myself," she breathed, her voice hoarse, like she smoked a pack of Belomorkanal a day.

I waited, unmoving. Every muscle tense.

Given the chance, I'd bite her too.

But she was smarter. Her eyes darted somewhere behind me, and I heard footsteps approach before someone gripped my head while another set of big hands pried open my mouth. A twisted version of a horse bit slipped into my mouth, not allowing me to bite down as a strap was tightened around the back of my head.

The woman mounted my hips. She was slick, rubbing all over me and causing friction. My fucking dick responded, the weight of it growing with each second.

She moaned, speeding up her movement, and I wanted to cut my dick off.

"You're big," she panted. Her hands roamed my skin, slick from a cold sweat. She moved against me, pumping up and down, harder and faster. I could feel my body reacting, that hated, familiar tingle starting in my toes, rushing through my body.

I didn't want to come. Didn't want to give her the satisfaction that she could get me off, but my fucking body refused to listen.

And then her face hovered above me, twisted with her impending orgasm. Her lips ran along my own, the bit spreading my mouth restricting me from reacting. I struggled against the restraints as she dipped her tongue into my open mouth. Kissing me vigorously while I was forced to allow it. I gagged as her tongue slid into my mouth again. She didn't care.

Lifting a knife I hadn't seen before, she slashed the side of my lip and blood gushed, filling my mouth. Gagging me.

The cries of her orgasm followed, her hips straddling me, riding the wave. She slid off before grabbing my dick and stroking it until my own body finished.

"Now, you'll always remember this," she said, still breathing heavily. "You'll always remember me."

I blinked the memories away, all of them disintegrating into the back of my mind. The scar on my lip a daily reminder.

The past may be catching up to me, but I refused to fall victim to it.

I was so fucked up. So fucking broken and I dared touching something so good. So innocent. My eyes met dark chocolate ones, and in them I found peace.

Though she didn't find the same thing in mine.

Aurora turned away from me, as if she couldn't stand the sight of me. Not that I blamed her.

It was on the tip of my tongue to tell her it wasn't her. It was me. It sounded cliché, but in this instance, it was the goddamn truth. But giving her the reason behind it was not an option. I didn't want her pity.

We were interrupted by the door opening behind us and Igor's voice.

"I want to invite both of you to my place."

Aurora tensed in front of me. I slid out of her, my hands on her hips, pulling her dress down. She struggled to fix her flimsy panties, and I instinctively blocked her body with mine, as I tucked myself in.

My hand snaked around her waist and I tucked her closer to me. I didn't want Igor to get any ideas. She was with me and only with me.

Igor smiled, his eyes hungry on Aurora. I fucking hated it. That voyeuristic motherfucker. I hated anyone seeing my woman as I fucked her. She was mine and mine alone.

Igor leisurely took several steps towards us and my hand tightened around her waist, pulling her closer to me.

Her dark eyes shifted my way, her eyebrow lifting in a silent question. When I said nothing, she returned her attention to Igor.

"We'd love to," she told him, though her muscles were tense against me. "Right, Alexei?" she added in a sultry tone, those pouty red lips curved into a seductive smile.

"Da," I said dryly when I actually wanted to tell Igor to go fuck himself and snap his neck. But I knew how much was at stake here if we didn't get to Ivan. The message was clear. He was after the Nikolaev family and my nephew would be the one to pay for my sins if I failed.

We had to get to him before he got to us.

"Odlicno." *Great.* He rubbed his hands together, a gleam in his eyes.

I fucking hated Igor's guts. The term womanizer and slimebag took a whole new meaning with that fucker. He'd smile in your face and stab you in the back without a second thought. He volunteered to hold me still all those years ago. Jerked off right above my head as he watched that woman fuck me.

It was the reason he worked so well with Ivan. We were a similar age, but unlike Igor, I never enjoyed Ivan's fucked-up shit. Regardless if I was at the receiving end of it or the giving end of it.

"Let's go," Igor drawled, his eyes not even bothering to look my way. "You can come with me, Aurora."

"Ona moya," I warned in a low, threatening tone. *She's mine.* There was no need to say anything else. If he touched her, I'd make him regret ever surviving this long.

"Tvoya." *Yours.* Igor's voice shattered through the memories, a stupid, ugly smile on his face.

He nodded, surprise in his eyes. I had never laid claim on anyone or anything. I learned within the first decade of my life that forming an attachment always ended in loss. In their death. A familiar cold sensation slithered up my spine, and invisible hands squeezed my neck tighter and tighter.

I didn't give a shit that Igor now knew I had a weakness. He could hold this over my head; except, he knew how brutal I could be. And if he dared to touch her with his pinky finger, I'd destroy everything in his life. His wealth. His clubs. His so-called friends. And leave him for last, so he could wait for his end in agony.

I'd fight for this woman. I'd burn the whole world down. And at the end if she demanded my life in payment for her brother, she'd get it.

It was hers anyhow.

All my broken pieces. My fragmented heart. My fucked-up soul. The haunted memories that made it impossible to move on.

No matter how hard I worked to suppress the memories into the dark recesses of my mind, they always came back. Plagued me in my dreams. Plagued me in the daylight.

Physical scars on my body matched the mental ones. My flesh marred just as much as my mind. Except, I couldn't hide my mental scars with ink, like I had my body.

TWENTY-ONE
AURORA

I sensed the strain in the air, the oxygen surrounding Alexei thin and frigid. Tension rolled off him and his shoulders pulled tight. The lighting was dim, but I swore his skin paled slightly under all that ink.

Igor turned around, fully expecting us to follow him, and I glanced at Alexei who remained glued to his spot.

Without thinking, I reached for his hand and slipped my fingers between his, then squeezed. Yes, he pissed me off and humiliated me with his behavior, but every cell in my body protested at seeing him suffer. There was clearly something wrong, and I wanted to help him.

"Are you alright?" I whispered under my breath, watching him with worry.

His eyes lowered to where my hand held his and I followed his gaze. An awareness tickled in the back of my mind as I watched our hands connected. An image flashed behind my eyes. His inked hand over a little one.

A feeling overwhelmed me that I'd held hands with him before. It was ridiculous though. Yet I couldn't shake the conviction. Before I could further ponder on it, Alexei's answer pushed it temporarily out of my mind.

"I'm fine." He didn't look at my face, his voice emotionless. I waited for a heartbeat and then exhaled slowly. It wasn't as if I could press him further here. Besides, it wasn't as if we trusted each other. Yes, I had his cum running down my inner thigh, but it didn't make us intimate.

"Let's go," he said, his voice frigid and low.

We walked out of the VIP room; his hand still connected with mine. Honestly, I was surprised he didn't slice the connection because it almost felt like he disliked the idea of touching me. My heels clacked against the marble floor, our steps in sync and hurried.

And the entire time, our encounter played through my mind. I didn't expect to get turned on by the sight of what was going on in this club. Voyeurism wasn't my thing and usually shifted my memories back to Anya. Though something about Alexei, focusing on him and his strength, kept me with him. I knew he wouldn't let anyone touch me or hurt me. And I knew he'd never force me to do something I didn't like.

Was it the first ounce of trust that I gave him? I didn't know, but I knew there'd be nobody else that I would have done this with. He made me feel safe and so damn good. Until he said no kissing, but even those two little words didn't diminish the pleasure I just experienced.

We followed the path through the dark hallway, my heels clacking against the marble, and I noticed Igor was already out of sight.

"Where is he?" I asked in a hushed tone.

"Outside."

I really wished Alexei didn't resort back to one-word answers. They grated on my nerves. But I kept my mouth and temper under control.

As we walked down the corridor in silence, the initial disappointment flooded me. *No kissing.* Why did he insist on no kissing? I sensed his rule of no kissing went beyond what happened here. A rush of confusing feelings swirled in my chest.

Maybe it was for the better; otherwise, I might lose my head completely.

Leading us out the door, my stomach clenched with nerves. I didn't like this. Igor invited us to his place and then disappeared. The humid evening air hit me, and as it had numerous times before, suddenly made me feel as if I were suffocating. The thickness covered us like a damp wool blanket in a heat wave.

"It's so fucking hot," I muttered. "My makeup will melt."

"Ah, there you are, lovebirds." Igor's voice had me whipping my head to the right and found the creep lingering in the dark. Every single piece of hair on my body stood up spotting the man lurking in the dark, and I stepped closer to Alexei. Hurt pride or not, I knew I was safer with the iceman than the creepy man.

"Igor." Alexei's voice was like a whip.

"My car will take us," Igor announced, ignoring Alexei's cold demeanor. He barely tilted his chin behind him where a limo sat.

The meaning of his words sank and I tensed. "Why can't we follow you in Alexei's car?" I rasped.

Igor chuckled like I just uttered the funniest joke. "He can't follow unless he has a Batmobile that can fly."

I threw a side glance at Alexei, but his face was impossible to read. A cold mask. It wasn't wise to get into the car with him, leaving us vulnerable. I didn't trust Igor and this felt like going into the trap blindly, without anyone else knowing where I was. I didn't have my phone on me. Nor my sidearm. Nothing.

Just a stupid snug dress and a pair of heels that made me feel more like a hooker than an undercover agent.

Alexei squeezed my hand and my eyes shot down. I had been clutching his hand so hard, my nails dug into his skin. I forced myself to loosen my grip, but left my hand in his. I didn't trust myself not to start fidgeting.

Apparently, Alexei was better at the undercover shit than I was.

Another squeeze of his hand and a silent sigh slipped through my lips.

"I have a bag in my car," Alexei told Igor.

Igor nodded as if he expected that. "I'll have my man retrieve it."

Alexei didn't miss a beat. "Nyet. Nobody touches my car."

I cocked my eyebrow. It would seem Alexei wasn't the sharing type. Unless he had something in the car he didn't want Igor to see. Preferably a weapon. When we left my place, we got into the Aston Martin and came straight here.

"Go get your bag, Alexei," Igor drawled, his gaze stripping me naked. "I'll keep your lady safe."

My spine went rigid, but I kept my mouth shut. I didn't want to ruin our chances at getting Ivan.

"She'll come with me," Alexei said icily. His voice was nonnegotiable. I knew it well by now.

I swallowed hard, my eyes fleeting to Alexei.

"My two guys will escort you to your car and ensure you don't bring unwanted things," Igor told him.

A jerky nod, no words. While I was certain I looked like a deer in headlights, Alexei's pulse didn't even skip a beat.

Igor chuckled like he won, then turned around, nodding at someone. My eyes shifted to the dark corner, and I realized he had reinforcements standing there. Jerk!

Two men went into motion, and without any words, we strode to Alexei's sleek Aston Martin with Igor's bodyguards right behind us.

Clack. Clack. Clack.

My ankle almost gave out but Alexei's hand wrapped around me for support and remained around my waist as we continued our journey down the dark alley. So appropriate our evening would end the way it started. With me wobbly on my feet.

I kept sneaking glances at Alexei. I wished the bodyguards would have driven with Igor, so it'd give us a few minutes to discuss this strategy and the next steps. But beggars can't be choosers, I guess.

We went straight to the trunk, where once popped open, Alexei grabbed a large duffle bag and shut the trunk.

"Wait."

An order came from behind us and I froze, my eyes snapping to the bodyguard. Alexei must have anticipated it because he handed him the bag without prompting. The bodyguard grabbed the bag and slammed it against the hood of Alexei's trunk.

"Hey, watch it!" I reprimanded him. The bodyguard cocked his eyebrow, like he didn't understand what he did wrong. "That car is Alexei's second-favorite thing," I clarified, rolling my eyes. I had to play my part, right?

"What's his first?" the bodyguard asked me intrigued.

"Me, duh," I retorted dryly.

Amusement flashed in the bodyguard's eyes, but he didn't say anything. He unzipped the duffle bag, dug through it, then zipped it back up and returned it to Alexei. Throwing it over his shoulder, Alexei nudged me back to the car, and to my surprise, he took my hand.

"No weapons," he retorted to his boss over his earpiece. "Just clothes and a first aid kit."

Interesting. So they expected Alexei to bring along weapons.

As if on cue, a black limo drove up to us and came to a stop. The second bodyguard rushed to the car to open the door. The other remained behind us, like a dark cloud warning he'd kill us in a heart-beat. Though I was inclined to think he'd have a hard time beating Alexei.

Jesus, Mary, and Joseph! Am I boasting? I pondered.

"Let's go," the bodyguard grumbled.

He was going to make us get into the car willingly or not. I didn't expect it to escalate so fast. Yes, Alexei indicated the goal was to draw an invitation out of Igor, but not on the same night. When I accepted Igor's invitation, I didn't think he literally meant he was inviting us *now*.

Igor's head peeked from the car, his eyes lingering on my legs. I hadn't realized I shifted my body back, until I was pressed against Alexei.

"Ladies first," Igor purred, sending all kinds of wrong goose bumps down my spine. Every warning bell in my body warned me it was a bad idea, leaving me glued to my spot. This was what parents warned you about when you were a little girl.

Do. Not. Get. In. The. Car.

There would be no candy in there. Only pain and suffering. My heart drummed against the rib cage, and each breath I took was shaky. Alexei's hand slipped out of mine, and he placed his palm on the small of my back, urging me forward.

I turned my face to him, searching for any assurance. Something resembling a smile touched his face, like he tried his damndest to assure me. And like a fool, I trusted him. A criminal that was on the FBI's radar. But for some reason I did.

Taking slow steps towards the vehicle, Alexei followed right behind me. Ignoring Igor's hand to assist me, I slid into the car, ensuring I didn't flash Igor. That guy wouldn't need too much prompting to do something. There was something evil lurking underneath that civil smile and that ugly-ass striped suit. Alexei came in right behind me, the two of us seated opposite of Igor.

The door shut, and suddenly, it felt like the walls were closing in on us. My fingers tugged on the hem of my short dress, and I immediately shoved them under my thighs to stop myself from fidgeting. I was a fucking FBI agent and the F didn't fucking stand for fidgeting.

Alexei's strong thigh pushed against mine as he manspread next to me and I realized my legs were shaking. Instantly, I stilled and his hand came to my thigh, resting there, his strength seeping into me.

It didn't escape me that Igor's eyes lingered on Alexei's hand on my thigh. Something flashed in his eyes. Something dark. Something cruel. I didn't like it. The urge to start shaking my legs felt as strong as the need to breathe. Yet, I knew showing any weakness to Igor would be a fatal mistake. So instead, I lowered my eyes studying Alexei's ink and focused on the warmth his palm seeped through my thin dress.

There was so much ink on his hand, I couldn't quite distinguish what it was. But on his fingers there were symbols. Or letters. My hands were still tucked under my thighs, my fingers itched to touch him. Trace the ink over his skin. He had been inside me, yet I didn't get to touch one single piece of him.

I glanced out the window, the city of New Orleans a blur as we pulled onto the highway.

This would be a long night.

TWENTY-TWO
ALEXEI

A fter a two-hour drive and a helicopter ride, we landed on the roof of a building. We were still in the States. Though it was anyone's guess for how long. I had my suspicions that we'd end up in Russia.

Thank fuck it was summer here. Just thinking about Russia made my balls freeze. Put me in any hellhole. In the desert without water. Any-fucking-where, just not goddamn Russia.

Ironically, the only thing that kept me on the sane side of things was Aurora's subtle chocolate scent, her small smiles that lit me up inside. I ate that shit up like my life depended on it. I'd need it to ensure I'd keep us alive. Keep *her* alive. As long as she lived through this, that was all that mattered.

"I gave you two lovebirds a whole suite." Igor pushed the door of the penthouse open. He acted like he gave us keys to the kingdom; when I knew very well the fucker would be watching us. He took voyeurism to a whole new level.

Aurora and I strode into the hotel room, the door shutting behind us with a firm click. Then another click. He locked us in. Fucking asshole. Aurora glanced at the door, her eyes fleeting my way, then back to the door. We kept our words to a minimum since we left the club. She was holding up rather well, all things considered.

Kicking off her heels and turning her attention to the suite, a deep sigh left her as she strode further into the room.

"At least we got the penthouse suite," she muttered, rolling her shoulders. "Igor isn't a cheapo; though he's definitely a creepo."

She glanced over her right shoulder, those almond-shaped eyes meeting mine. She cocked her eyebrow as if waiting for me to agree or disagree. When I said nothing, she turned around again.

Lingering for a moment, in the middle of the hotel room, her gaze surveyed every corner of it. I could tell the moment she spotted the cameras. Her shoulders slightly tensed, her guard back up.

I knew he'd have cameras wherever he put us. Igor the creepo, as she eloquently called him, would be watching us until he was convinced there was nothing beyond me fucking this woman and wanting to take her to the most notorious club in Russia where everything and anything goes—voluntarily and involuntarily.

Except there was more. A lot more. And once it unraveled, I didn't doubt that Aurora would make it her mission to lock me up. Or kill me. And I wouldn't stop her. I deserved all the wrath she'd dish my way.

I headed for the large bathroom. I knew she'd follow me. The little agent was a curious and demanding little thing.

It didn't escape me how she demanded I go faster and rougher when I fucked her at the club. It turned out the little agent wasn't shy in the bedroom at all, and I fucking loved it. Until we both reached our climax and she wanted affection. To be intimate.

I hated that I wasn't wired for it. I hated that I lacked the capacity to give her what she needed. It made me feel inadequate.

Frustrated at myself, I stopped in the middle of the bathroom, mirrors decorating each wall of it, and her little body promptly ran into the back of me.

"Shit, sorry," she muttered, her palms pressing against my back. For the briefest moment, I marveled at the warmth of her touch. I never particularly cared for a woman's touch, yet somehow I craved hers.

I slowly turned around, coming face-to-face with her, and her hands fell down to her sides.

"Shut the door," I ordered her.

She did it without protest. I watched her back, her red dress hugging her curves. She had the most magnificent, sweetest ass I had ever seen. Round and perfect. I wanted to grab a handful of it and squeeze it, bend her over and pound into her. Again and again. But it was two in the morning and Aurora looked tired.

I should have known from the moment I spotted her in the elevator, she'd become my prey. My craving. The pull was instant. The innocent FBI agent had no idea what was coming her way.

Guilt clawed at me for not being upfront with her. Especially when she obeyed without questioning me. The club was just the beginning, the easiest piece.

She returned back to stand in front of me, her eyes surveying the bathroom. She was checking for cameras.

"Bathrooms are not wired," I told her, placing down my duffle bag onto the large marble counter.

"How do you know?" she whispered, leaning an inch closer toward me.

Her eyes locked on me, waiting. For what, I didn't know. Reassurances and words weren't my thing.

When I didn't answer, she sighed.

"Fine. I agree with you; I don't see any cameras here. So now what? Want to sleep in the bathroom?" She wrinkled her nose, her eyes darting around the room. "It will be uncomfortable as fuck."

"No sleeping in the bathroom. The expectation is that club activities will continue."

Her head whipped around.

"W-what?" she stammered, her eyes widening. "More sex?" I nodded. "Whose expectation?"

She didn't sound happy about it. Not that I could blame her. It wasn't like I had much to offer her in that department. I wanted to fuck her tied up and gagged. On all fours, her ass up in the air and face-down. It wasn't hard-core BDSM. That was more up Sasha's alley, but my methods were a far cry from lovemaking.

My experience twisted me into one fucked-up being.

"Don't stress about it," I told her before I gave in to my more carnal urges and fucked her right here against the cold tile.

"What?" she hissed. "You can't drop a bomb like this and then say *'don't stress about it.'*" She pushed her hand into her hair. "I won't be able to sleep after hearing something like that. Man, this is fucking bullshit," she muttered. "I'm all for busting this guy, but I never signed up for whoring myself. And to top it all off, being watched while being fucked." Her fingers tugged on her silky strands.

My eyes traveled down her curves and my cock throbbed. I fucked her mere hours ago, and I was hard for her already, my dick straining against my zipper. I could fuck her all night and all day, and still not have enough.

"Fine," she exhaled, a string of curses slipping through her pouty red lips. "I seriously need a raise for this shit. But since we got this far, we might as well go all the way." She reached to her side, struggling with the zipper. "This field work is not all it's cracked up to be," she muttered. "But here I am, taking my clothes off." Then as if she worried I'd pounce on her, she added, "I'm just taking the damn dress off. I can't wear it for another second. Next time, get me something loose. I hate tight clothes."

She yanked on the zipper, left and right. Up and down. It wouldn't budge, and with each passing second, she became more agitated with it. And all the while, she muttered to herself.

"Let me help you." I reached for the zipper, covering her hand, and she instantly stilled. Her eyes zeroed in on my hand, and I watched her graceful neck bob as she swallowed. My cock throbbed harder.

The impact this woman had on me. I should have squashed it. Killed it. Instead, I let it fester, and now, she was a full-blown obsession. My cock nor my heart no longer cared what was good for her nor me. It just wanted her.

She slowly pulled her hand from beneath mine, then lifted it above her head to allow me to unzip her. Another tiny bit of trust. I didn't deserve it.

It would shatter. Very soon.

The sound of the zipper cracked the silence in the bathroom. She let the dress slide down her body, leaving her only in her lacy panties. The red dress pooled around her ankles, baring her sun-kissed skin. She was so beautiful; it actually hurt to look at her. Though I didn't think it was her outer beauty that appealed to me. It was her soul.

Despite the shitty way I treated her at the club, she still worried whether I was okay. That caring little girl from the zoo was still there. And as she slipped her hand into mine, just as she had twenty years ago, I mourned the impending loss.

There wasn't a single ounce of doubt that she'd walk away from me once she learned the truth. If she didn't kill me first.

We faced each other, her eyes locked on me. Wide and innocent. Guarded and trusting at the same time. She didn't cower; she didn't look away in embarrassment.

Brave little woman.

"What do you want to do now?" Her tone was husky, her breathing hitched.

I want to fuck you, hear you scream, until your throat is raw.

It was fucked up that I didn't care to do it knowing that the second we step back into the room, we'd be watched. I wanted to get my fill of her—to fill the void for the rest of my life. However long or short it might be. I was on borrowed time with her. Albeit, I didn't want Igor to see the way Aurora's skin flushed when she was turned on or hear the noises she made. Fuck, those noises alone could get me to spill in my pants, and I'd store those sounds deep in my memory for the cold days ahead without her in my life.

A faint buzzing and click sounded outside the bathroom and Aurora's head whipped, staring at the door. She held her breath for two heartbeats, then returned her eyes to me.

"Did you hear that?" she whispered.

"He turned on the cameras." I kept my voice low.

I watched her graceful neck move as she gulped.

"I guess he's ready for some action," she rasped. "Doesn't that man sleep?"

There was no point in telling her that we survived most of our lives on three hours of sleep. It was probably how his voyeurism came about. If you slept, you were vulnerable. If you were awake, you kept watch. Unfortunately, the only thing to watch was the fighting and fucking since our room had only one large window. Overlooking the makeshift ring.

I didn't want him watching Aurora being fucked. Back at the club, the light setting was low, and I ensured to take her in the way she was mostly shielded. But here, in the penthouse suite, she'd be visible from one of those cameras. I could only shield her with my body from one, max two cameras. But the bathroom didn't have cameras.

My eyes settled on her, devouring her like a dying man.

Christ, she was gorgeous. I'd seen my share of women's bodies but none of them compared to hers. Her skin was soft like silk, her body firm and strong. She was an odd mixture of strong and vulnerable.

Her chest rose and fell with every breath, staring at me with those big, dark eyes.

"Y-you are freaking me out," she stammered, flush coloring her chest. "The way you're staring at me."

"Ty prekrasnyy, kroshka." *You are beautiful, baby.* My voice was thick with gravel. Her beauty shone in her dark eyes, in her soft touch. She was so close to me I could smell her sweet arousal.

I shouldn't do it. I'd break her. Ruin her.

Too late.

TWENTY-THREE
AURORA

This was insanity.

We stood in the bathroom, my breathing hitched. My heart drummed against my ribs while my mind raced with all the events that happened over the last two weeks. And especially with what happened at the sex club.

I could blame it all on the club, the atmosphere, the case. But the truth was I wanted it. Alexei asked permission before he fucked me, and I gave it.

Freely. Eagerly.

I wanted him, craved him even. If someone had tried to stop us, I would have been tempted to kill them. And while Alexei's expression wasn't exactly euphoric, it was the first time I saw any kind of emotion pass his face.

Except that he didn't offer affection after sex. He enjoyed fucking me, but it was as if he wanted to remain removed from it. I couldn't understand it.

"I'm going to shower," I choked out, my insides quivering with something I didn't care to evaluate. Maybe the issue was that I haven't had sex in so long. Though I didn't think so. "Alone," I clarified quickly in case it sounded like an invitation.

The corner of his lips tugged up into some kind of a half-smile. Did the man ever smile? I was so wrapped up with the unexpected pleasure at the club that I missed how he looked when he came. He didn't make a sound, but I knew he finished because I'd felt his cum leak out of me.

He turned to his duffle bag and pulled out a T-shirt, undergarments, and shorts along with a small toiletry bag, then handed them to me. They looked too small to be his.

"For you," he grunted. I reached for it and eyed it suspiciously. The T-shirt was my size. So were the shorts and panties. I unzipped the toiletry bag and gasped. The Redken-brand shampoo and Laura Mercier body wash I used inside. As twisted as this whole situation was, something about his gesture made me warm inside. "Stalker," I breathed, though there was no merit or anger in my voice.

He didn't seem worried about my accusation. It wasn't the first time I called him out on it.

"Take your shower."

He left the bathroom, shutting the door behind him with a soft click. I had to get my head on straight and stop losing it over him. I started the shower, waiting for the water to warm before I stepped in and washed away the events of the day. I hoped it would clear my mind too.

Twenty minutes later, I strode out of the bathroom to find Alexei seated on the lounge chair reading a book. He had discarded the suit jacket and rolled up the sleeves, his inked forearms on display. My eyes flicked to the book title he held. *Voyeurism.* My eyebrows rose.

"Interesting reading material," I commented. Our eyes connected and he shrugged his shoulders.

Placing the book on the little coffee table, he stood up and I watched his broad back disappear into the bathroom. It didn't take long to hear the shower come on. For a few moments, I stood in my spot unsure whether I should just slide between the sheets or sit down to wait for Alexei to be done with his shower. And all the while I was painfully aware of being watched.

I opted for the bed. Fatigue was heavy in my bones, and I needed to get some rest so I could keep my wits about me. Especially with the creeper Igor. I slid between the sheets and lay in bed, listening to the constant run of the water in the shower. I was tired, yet unable to sleep. Images of Alexei in the shower played in my mind. The way water would trickle down his body, or the way he'd slide his hands over his skin to wash himself.

It was wrong to picture it. Yet, I couldn't stop it. Any more than I could stop rain from falling. Or the sun from shining. This *thing*, whatever it was, would end in catastrophe. I was an FBI agent. He was a criminal. I wondered what my boss would say if he knew how tonight's event unfolded. Though McGovan hadn't seemed worried about the methods or plans to find the predator. He just wanted the case resolved —by any means necessary.

The shower shut off and the bathroom got quiet. I held my breath as I listened for any movement in the bathroom, yet I didn't hear any. But then I had a feeling Alexei moved like a jaguar, silent and deadly.

I swung the sheets off, got to my feet, and headed to the bathroom door. I knocked softly and held my breath. Nothing. My heart thundered as I tried the handle. The door was unlocked. I pushed it open and poked my head in just in time to see Alexei pull on a pair of gray sweatpants. He already had a shirt on, his blond hair damp.

He turned around and my eyes traveled over his body. I had never understood women getting excited over men wearing sweatpants. Until now. Alexei Nikolaev was sin incarnate in sweats. Suddenly, I never cared to see him in cargo pants or a suit. While he wore those well, it didn't compare to *this*.

I swallowed hard, hoping I wasn't drooling.

"You alright?" His question startled me, snapping me back to reality.

Clearing my throat, I answered. "Umm, yes. It's just cre—" I stopped myself, unsure whether there was audio as well as camera recording us. "It was lonely in there," I finally said. He nodded in understanding. "Can I come in?" I asked him.

Without waiting for his answer, I took two steps towards him, leaving the door cracked open. I wished I could say I didn't know what I was doing, but I did.

Keeping my voice low and my back to the bathroom door, I whispered, "If we have to do *it*, can we do it here?"

I could lie to myself and say it was all for this assignment, but the truth was I wanted more of him. Maybe it was degrading, a lack of self-respect. But nobody had ever rattled me like this stoic man. No man had ever thrown me off-balance like this one. Or made me respond in so many conflicting ways.

It was confusing and intriguing. Hot and reckless. Exciting.

He raised a brow, as if my suggestion surprised him. We stared at each other, as I held my breath for his response. Fires burned in the pit of my stomach, lust slithered through my veins. It was wrong. I knew it was, yet it was pointless to fight it.

He took my chin, his grip firm, and brought my face closer to his. Our lips were inches apart and his words from the club came back. *No kissing.*

"He'll hear, but he won't see," he commented, his voice low and raspy. I nodded my understanding and something flicked across his expression. Hot, feral, and dark. It was gone so fast but adrenaline rushed through my veins.

"Yes." Jesus, what was happening to me? I had never been so turned on in my entire life.

"Brace yourself on the counter." My body obeyed without a second thought. "Bend over." I did. I watched in fascination in the mirror as his arctic gaze lingered on my ass. Then his hands came to my hips and hooked into my shorts. Slowly, too fucking slowly, he pulled them down my legs, his mouth brushing over my ass, then my inner thighs. It felt like he tattooed every spot he kissed, leaving a permanent mark on my skin.

My shorts and panties gone, thrown onto the counter; I panted with need and we hadn't even gotten started.

"Spread your legs," he ordered, his voice thick with gravel. The entire bathroom was surrounded by mirrors and I watched in fascination his reflection.

His fingers trailed a path from my ankles back up all the way to my pussy. His head leaned closer to my body, right in line with my ass. His broad shoulders hindered my view, but it only made it more exciting. My pussy clenched in the anticipation of his mouth on me. He spread my thighs wider, his breath fanning my naked skin, and goose bumps spread over my flesh. The moment his fingers brushed over my soaked folds, a loud moan vibrated against the tiles.

Shudders ran down my spine, and I arched my ass, eager for his mouth. Unrecognizable Russian words came out of him and set my insides on fire. He swept his tongue against my folds and guttural noises vibrated against my pussy.

Every fiber of my being shook with the impending release. Jesus, he just licked me and I was ready to orgasm.

"P-please," I gasped, pushing back against his mouth, shamelessly grinding against him. He made a starving noise, like he was enjoying this as much as I was. His tongue brushed against my clit, his licks rough and demanding, and an impending orgasm tingled at the base of my spine.

I wasn't inexperienced, but with this man, I might as well be, because everything with him felt so new. So deliciously dirty. And the fact that someone was getting a glimpse of this and hearing us only amplified the entire experience.

He feasted on me like he was possessed, his fingers digging into the flesh of my hips, holding me still.

"Oh God," I moaned, loudly. "I—I need more."

He tugged on my clit with his teeth, and I exploded, my screams vibrating off the tiled floors and mirrored walls in the bathroom. He didn't ease as I trembled against his mouth, licking every single drop of my juices.

I twisted my head to look at him over my shoulder, my eyes lowering to where he kneeled on the tiled floor. Our eyes connected, blue flames burning in his arctic gaze, and I shuddered.

He stood up to his full height, our body size differences striking. He towered over me, his one hand came around to my throat and gripped it.

"Ready, kroshka?"

Lust speared through me at his raspy, possessive tone. *Holy fuck*. I was ready. I was ready for round two and three. As many rounds as this man wanted.

I nodded, a delightful shiver of anticipation running down my spine.

"Hold on tight," he demanded, pushing his gray sweatpants down his muscled thighs. He dragged his hard cock along my drenched folds and my pussy clenched. I spread my legs until every inch of me was bared to him, greedy for him. "Because I'm not going easy on you this time."

My lips formed a silent O, but before I could ponder on his words further, he slammed into me. Rough and deep.

"Fuck," I choked. I could feel him so deep inside me, stretching me.

He grunted something in Russian and I glanced up, meeting his gaze in the mirror. Satisfaction curled in my stomach when I saw hunger in his expression. He might not want to touch me or kiss me, but he couldn't hide the raw need in his eyes for me, mirroring mine for him.

I arched my head, leaning into his curled hand around my throat and his grip tightened. If someone would have told me a week ago, I'd let a man squeeze my throat as he fucked me, I'd have shot them.

"Harder," I demanded, the need to see him unravel quickly becoming my addiction.

He stilled, then tore a gasp from me with a violent thrust. As if he lost all sanity, Alexei pounded into me with brutal thrusts. He thrust deep and hard. Pleasure burned through my veins and I moaned, holding on to the counter for support. Each thrust sent a delicious wave of heat searing through me.

The flames of desire burned hotter and wilder. We'd turn into a destructive wildfire if we weren't careful. Yet, I couldn't find it in me to care. His chest to my back, his hand on my throat, he pounded into me at a maddening speed. My lips burned with the need to feel his mouth on me. My lips tingled with the need to feel his hot mouth against mine. I didn't forget his words, but at this moment, the need was stronger than the reason.

"P-please," I moaned. "Kiss me."

His mouth landed on my shoulder, his tongue hot on my skin. And then he bit me where my shoulder met my neck, as viciously as he fucked me. Our harsh breathings were the only sounds in the bathroom, his hand closed around my throat. And fucking hell, I trusted him not to kill me and only give me pleasure.

A white-hot wave of sensation built inside me. Everywhere our skin brushed, mine burned hotter. His teeth pierced my skin and something maddeningly erotic shot through my veins. Each thrust of his was ripping me apart and then piecing me back together. Only to destroy me again.

"Alexei. Oh God, Alexei," I chanted. I'd never remember another man after this one. I whimpered a sob of pleasure as a violent orgasm shattered me, hitting me hard and making me see shooting stars behind my eyelids. Alexei fucked me through it with his one hand around my throat and other gripping my hip. He continued fucking me hard through my clenching orgasm, my pussy spasming with the most violent pleasure I had ever experienced.

With a rough noise, he came inside me, his hot cum filling me. Through a half-lidded, heavy gaze, I watched a tiny bit of him come undone. For me. His hand was still curled around my neck, his teeth marks visible on my skin and his breathing hard.

I had lost myself in him. In this sweet, depraved oblivion.

And I never wanted to wake up.

TWENTY-FOUR
ALEXEI

My hands laced behind my head, and I watched over Aurora as she slept. After our *show* in the bathroom, she could barely keep her eyes open. I was used to just a few hours of sleep at night. My beautiful agent wasn't.

So I lifted her into my arms and tucked her into the only bed in the room. Her eyes fluttered shut the moment her head hit the pillow and she drifted off to sleep. I climbed into the other side of the bed, and as if pulled by the same magnetic force I felt, she scooted closer to me. Her hand wrapped over my torso and her face buried into my chest. I tensed at her closeness, expecting her to snake her hand inside my shirt. When she didn't, I forced myself to relax.

I regularly slept in my boxer briefs, but I couldn't risk taking my clothes off while sharing a bed with Aurora. It would be a long night with her soft body pressed against mine. Her brows were drawn and I smoothed my hand over her brow. I didn't like her distress—not when she was awake and definitely not when she was asleep.

Clicking the side lamp off, I let darkness surround me. It matched the one lurking inside me. As I stared at the ceiling, I let my mind wander to the past.

Five years in this hellhole.

I stared at the dirty stone ceiling, a chill in the air. The room stunk of mold, blood, and sweat. The sounds of moans, flesh against flesh, a slick pounding traveled through the air and the thin glass window. Most teenagers had views of landscape out their windows, or oceans, if they were lucky. Not us here. We only had a view of orgies going on, voluntary and involuntary ones. Or fights that ended with blood and death. Every. Fucking. Time.

I'd die here.

Five fucking years. I couldn't remember the feeling of being free anymore. Maybe it was a fantasy. Or just something that kept pushing me forward so I wouldn't end it all right now. Because this was a living hell.

A bone-chilling, cold hell.

A slick rhythmical sound had my eyes shifting to the left and found Igor sitting by the only window. He watched with a sick fascination all the fucked-up shit happening in the ring while jerking off.

There were five of us left. There were thirty of us crammed into this room two weeks ago. Maybe it was three weeks, fuck if I knew. I never knew if it was day or night, what day of the week.

We killed them all. It was the only reason the five of us were still here. Because we were stronger. I contemplated so many times to let another beat me in the ring. But the instinct and the need to survive always prevailed.

There was so much blood staining my hands, nothing would save me. Even if I succeeded in leaving this shithole, I'd always be a killer. It was the only thing I knew how to do.

Igor started grunting, jerking off faster and harder. If he strangled his cock any harder, he'd lose it. It wouldn't be the worst thing. Fucking voyeur jerked off several times a day. It was probably the reason Ivan didn't bother taking him into the ring for anything but fighting. The bastard knew Igor would like being fucked out in the open. The rest of us weren't so fortunate.

I fucking hated thinking about it. It made my skin crawl. Ivan still hadn't granted us a shower since yesterday and my skin stunk like them. The women. The men.

Bile rose in my throat and I shoved it all away. Otherwise, I'd lose what little I had in my stomach.

Was it worth it to survive all those fights to endure all this shit?

Abuse. Rape. Torture.

A whimper yanked me out of my memories and I instantly tensed, searching out Aurora. She was curled into a ball, facing away from me.

I turned on the bedside lamp and was out of the bed in the same second, then rushed around the bed.

She was thrashing her head back and forth, her body curled as if she was trying to protect herself. Her lips pressed in a tight line as if she didn't trust herself not to say a secret. Her brows furrowed and her forehead glistened with sweat.

I gently shook her by her shoulder. I didn't want to scare her, but I didn't want to leave her in her nightmare. I knew firsthand how bad they sucked.

"Wake up," I whispered. "It's just a dream."

"No!" she whimpered, squeezing her eyelids shut as if she couldn't bear to see whatever was in her dreams. I couldn't help but wonder if I was in her nightmares.

"Rora, wake up." I tried the nickname I heard her brother use. It felt invasive to use it, but I didn't like seeing her distress. Her breathing labored and another whimper slipped through her lips.

"S-stop," she cried out. "P-please. Don't hurt her."

My heart tripped and my throat squeezed painfully. The vulnerability in her voice and terror on her face was the worst punch in the gut. I wanted to kill any man or woman who had hurt this woman. And how ironic that I was one of those people.

"Kroshka," I murmured in a soothing voice. "You're safe." Her eyes opened and relief washed over me. "You're safe, kroshka," I whispered, smoothing her scrunched brows.

Her dark eyes watched me, her body unnaturally still.

"You had a bad dream," I explained, keeping my voice soft. Though I worried my voice was too rough.

She didn't move, her dark hair sprawled across the pillow and pain in her dark eyes. She blinked her eyes. Then again. Her lower lip quivered and my insides physically hurt.

"What is it, kroshka?" I asked her. "Who do I have to kill?"

A lone, sparkling tear rolled down her cheek and my hand shook as I brushed it off. Maybe I was the subject of her nightmare and she was scared.

"Santos hurt her," she rasped, her voice hoarse. "He made us watch."

My shoulders tensed, her words sending a roll of shock through me.

"Raphael?" He'd be dead. If he hurt her, Isabella's brother or not, he'd be dead.

She inhaled deeply, then slowly exhaled.

Her eyes fluttered shut, the sleep pulling her back under.

"The old guy," she murmured sleepily, her eyes struggling to remain open.

"Did he hurt you?" I tried to keep my fury under bay as I waited for her answer. If he laid a single finger on her, I'd dig him up and fucking kill him all over again. I'd bring him back to life so I could burn him alive.

"Anya." Who the fuck was Anya? "He hurt Anya."

TWENTY-FIVE
AURORA

A heavy weight of a muscled arm draped over my waist. The delicious scent of a man had me snuggling closer to the heat source, as if it was my own personal security blanket. It had been a long time since I woke up with a guy in my bed. It wasn't something I cared to do even with a steady boyfriend.

The arm was strong and comforting. Protective. When I shifted, the arm tightened around my waist and pulled me closer, his chest pressing against my back. I kept my eyes closed, just relishing in his heat and amazing smell. I didn't want to wake up, forcing my brain to shut down and let me go back to sleep.

But it was for naught. Because I was intrigued and wanted to know who was in my bed. I opened my eyes and my vision seemed slightly blurry. I blinked several times, and my eyes latched on to a muscular arm around my waist.

Tattooed.

And just like that, my memory from last night poured in. The sex club. The performance Alexei and I gave to Igor. Sex. *The freaking hot sex!*

Instantly, heat bloomed low in my stomach at the memories. Sex with Alexei Nikolaev was a toe-curling, brain-melting experience. I should feel mortified, yet I didn't. How could anyone regret something so freaking hot?

Shifting my hand, I curiously eyed the complicated ink on his forearm. Just as I reached out to trace it with my fingers, I felt him tense at my back.

"Don't," he warned softly. His breath was hot in my ear and it sent shivers down my spine.

My fingers hovered barely an inch over his skin and the temptation to touch him was great. I wanted to feel him under my fingertips, roam his body with my hands.

But I didn't.

I'd never touch anyone without their permission. Though I didn't care to ponder why I allowed him to touch me. It didn't cross my mind to forbid him to touch me. It felt too damn good. Though this was just a job. A sinful, fucked-up, undercover job.

Ugh, my brothers would tear Alexei apart if they knew.

My hand fell beside me, and his own hand slid from my waist. With a heavy sigh, I closed my eyes.

We lay in silence as I struggled with this all-consuming need to touch him. Feel him against me. These emotions were tricky. Unexpected.

Maybe it was normal to feel this attraction to him after what we experienced in the club and then again last night. Though I started to suspect it had nothing to do with it.

Whatever this was, it snuck up on me over the last few weeks. And I didn't necessarily dislike it. It made my body buzz with nervous energy. The kind that I knew he could calm, as ridiculous as that sounded. He smelled so good, warm skin and a faint sexy scent that was uniquely him.

I could hear his breathing, warm and confident. And the ache between my thighs pulsed, making it harder to ignore him. I wanted him. So fucking much that I actually contemplated begging him to fuck me.

"Take your clothes off," he ordered, his words almost sounding like a challenge. My eyes shot open and met his stare, his light blue eyes sending a newly sparked current through my body. The look in his eyes made me warm from the inside out, causing a deep, throbbing ache between my thighs. "And hand me your panties."

Enigma.

He was my tempting enigma, so damn in tune with my body that I'd have sworn he knew me better than I do.

I rose up onto my knees, the mattress shifting underneath me. I held his gaze as I pulled my shirt over my head. Then my shorts followed, leaving me only in my flimsy panties.

My skin buzzed with anticipation. Alexei didn't move, his burning gaze caressing my body. When he watched me, the whole world faded out. Nothing mattered but him. Not Igor. Not the cameras. Nor the possibility that he was watching us. All that I felt and saw was Alexei.

His hands came to my hips and a shiver ghosted down my body the moment his rough palms connected with my skin.

"Da?" *Yes?* A hoarse question. His face might not portray emotions but his voice and eyes did.

"Yes," I whispered.

He hooked two fingers to my panties on each hip, then dragged them down my thighs. Gently. Slowly. As if he anticipated me stopping him. Not in a million years. Instead, I shifted, assisting him as he slid them all the way down my legs.

The room air cooled against my heated skin. I was completely bare, exposed to him. My nipples hardened and wetness pooled between my thighs as his gaze fixed on my body. I sucked in slow, deep breaths aching to feel him inside me. There was no question that he dominated my body—whether he wanted to or not. My body yielded to this attraction between us.

He leaned in, lowering his head, then licked my nipple.

A moaned gasp wedged itself in my throat and my back arched, pushing my breast into his mouth. He clamped my nipple between his teeth and gently tugged. He turned his attention to my other breast, slowly tugging, then releasing my nipple. Then he flicked his tongue over it.

"Oh." His mouth on me made my insides clench with that familiar ache. His breath hot on my bare skin, I needed his skin against mine.

"I—I want to feel you," I rasped, my fingers tangling in his blond hair. "Please, Alexei."

This need had to be quenched; it burned in the pit of my belly.

"Give me your hands," he ordered, his voice low and coarse. My body obeyed before my mind even realized it. My eyes flared to his gaze, but all I saw on his face was hot desire. The same one that burned through my veins.

He ripped my discarded panties in one swift move. He shifted my arms closer together in front of me, then used my torn panties to tie my wrists. My breasts pushed forward, brushing against his shirt. His hard muscle outlined underneath it. I wanted to feel his skin against mine, flesh against flesh.

I could see the pulse in his neck, his smoldering gaze burning right through me. He might be wielding control over his own reactions to me, but he felt this magnetic attraction too.

"I won't hurt you," he assured, his voice almost reverent.

"I know," I breathed, lifting my tied wrists and hooking them around his neck. Somewhere deep down, I knew he'd never hurt me. Despite his cold exterior and slightly psychotic personality, he'd keep me safe. Just like he had in the club. He sheltered me with his body, ensuring my pleasure.

Our eyes locked. Our faces only inches apart and I fought the temptation to brush my lips against his.

No kissing. His words echoed in my mind.

This wasn't for a show. He knew it. I knew it. There was no sense in pretending it was. Never in my entire life had I felt anything remotely like this. Languid heat pulsed through me, my body gravitating towards him.

"Please," I panted.

I craved his pleasure as much as my own. Rubbing myself against him, I wanted everything he had to give and was eager to feel his muscles against me.

He lifted my hands over his neck and then reached for something on the nightstand.

His silk tie. Expertly, he blindfolded me, blocking my sight. A smart person might be weary. All I managed to be was excited. I felt his hot breath on my cheek as he tied it in the back of my head. His mouth skimmed down my neck, searing my skin. His stubble would leave marks on my soft skin and the thought didn't bother me at all. I wanted him to mark me as his.

Being blindfolded should have left me feeling vulnerable. Yet, I felt powerful. Robbed of sight, all my other senses heightened. Harshness of his breaths. Touch of his hands, brush of his lips. His scent became a permanent fragrance in my lungs.

His hands traveled further down my body, his mouth nibbling on the curve of my neck.

He shifted and an alarm shot through me. "Don't leave me," I whispered.

"Never." It was ridiculous but it sounded like a vow. "I'm taking my clothes off."

"Finally," I murmured, my lips curving into a smile.

"You're greedy, kroshka." It was on the tip of my tongue to admit it seemed to only happen with him. But it was too soon. I didn't understand this attraction. The soft noise of him stripping, the mattress underneath my knees shifting as I kept myself balanced with my hands still tied.

My insides quivered, imagining him naked. "A-are you tattooed all over?" I breathed the question. For some reason I wanted to know every inch of him.

It took a heartbeat too long to answer a simple question.

"Da."

One day, I'd see every inch of him. I decided it would be my mission to kiss every inch of him. His flesh against mine, my mouth on his. My body buzzed with adrenaline; fire blazed through my veins.

He shifted our bodies so my back hit the mattress, his hand holding me. Then hooked my tied wrists back around his neck, our breaths intermingled. He was so close, I could almost feel the warmth of his mouth on my lips.

His body weight pressed against me and it felt like a security blanket. A wall of hard muscles. I couldn't see him but I felt him everywhere. In every breath. On every inch of my skin. And when I felt the head of his hard shaft over my clit, I moaned.

My chest rose and fell, each time brushing against his chest. I wrapped my legs around his waist, urging him forward. His cock dipped into my folds, up and down.

"Oh, God," I moaned. "That feels so good."

I couldn't see him, all I could do was feel him. He pressed further into my entrance and I clenched around him. Greedy for all of him. My fingernails dug into my palms, literally burning with the need to feel him.

Lifting my hips, he sank deeper inside me. I rolled my hips, panting with desperation to feel him fill me to the hilt.

Chest to chest. Heart to heart. Breath to breath.

In one swift move, he drove his cock the rest of the way into me, tearing a whimper from my lips. He instantly stilled.

"Don't stop," I growled. "Give me everything."

The words set him free. He thrust into me hard. Ruthless. His hands dug into my hips and he slammed into me harder, driving me to grind against his pelvis.

"Take every inch, kroshka," he growled, his accent thick.

"Yes," I gasped, my ankles clasped around his waist, holding on for the ride.

Maybe it was the blindfold, or maybe it was simply this man. I didn't know. The only thing I was certain of was that nobody had ever made me fly so high. He fucked me like a possessed man, stretching me wide.

His hot breaths fanned my neck, his hips pistoned into me. "You're so tight," he growled against my neck. "Feel so good. My own heaven."

God, his words made me fly high. His thrusts turned savage. Friction between our bodies sparked something dark and feral inside me. I feared I'd never have enough of him.

"Fuck," I moaned. "Yes. I—I'm…"

"Mine. Say it. You're mine." Each word followed up by a savage thrust.

"Yes," I screamed. "Yours. Oh my fucking God. Alexei."

I fell apart, spiraling with the most intense orgasm. My insides clenched around his cock and languid heat spread through every inch of me. Alexei pounded into me grunting, his labored breathing harsh, and I felt his cock jerk as he came inside me, filling me with his cum.

His big body slumped on top of me, my tied hands pushed into his hair and both of us panting. I wanted to see him. Kiss him. Feel every inch of him.

Our heavy breathing filled the silence, his body pressing against mine. He went to shift and I almost begged him to remain, needing him close. Instead, I kept my words to myself. As Alexei stood up, the loss was startling.

It's just sex, I tried to convince myself. Yet, it felt like so much more.

A soft shuffling noise and a sheet covered my body. More shuffling. Then Alexei removed my blindfold. Alexei stood next to the bed, fully dressed. He untied my wrists next, and he bent his head, brushing his lips against the faint marks.

The gesture was gentle. Reverent almost.

The difference between us was stark. I was still naked, as the day I was born. He was fully clothed. I had to admit, his need to be dressed struck me as odd.

"You alright?" he asked, his eyes traveling over me.

Fuck, I was more than okay. I just wished I understood this thing with him. Why was he a freak about sleeping in bed naked with me? Or letting me touch him? Kiss him? I wanted to snuggle into him and listen to his heartbeat as I felt his warm skin under my palm.

"Yes." I *was* fine. At least that was what I tried to tell myself. My body was more than fine. Sated. It was still flying high. But I'd be a liar if I said that the distance he was clearly trying to maintain didn't bother me.

God, I must have lost my head.

I was on an assignment. Alexei was part of the job. This was work. Except, this last time, I *wanted* him inside me. It didn't feel like work.

"Igor should be convinced," I mumbled, unsure why I even felt the need to have an excuse for what we just did. I was a grown woman. He didn't respond and I avoided looking into his face, scared of what I'd find there.

Whatever.

Careful not to look his way, I got out of bed, pushing my hands through my hair. Bed head never looked good on me. I had way too much hair, and it always made me look like a crazy person.

"So what's on the agenda today?" I asked him, glancing over my shoulder. Again, it struck me as odd that he slept dressed. I never met a man, or heard of one, who preferred to sleep with his clothes on.

Though I could still feel him against me as he fucked me.

"Breakfast."

My stomach promptly growled and I released an uncomfortable chuckle. "That sounds perfect. Apparently I'm starving." The man of very few words nodded. "I'll take a quick shower," I muttered, pulling my hair up into a bun.

It agitated me that the man seemed completely unaffected by the sex we just shared while I rattled like some goddamn china doll. *Maybe it was totally one-sided.* It couldn't be. Right? The images of us caught in the mirror from last night flashed through my mind, and suddenly, my insides were on fire.

Swallowing hard, I made a hasty retreat into the bathroom and shut the door behind me.

I needed a cold shower and a cool head.

By the time I came out of the bathroom, Alexei had showered, shaved, and dressed. My eyes darted behind me to find his duffle bag sitting on the counter and I frowned in confusion.

He must have read my thoughts.

"I took a shower in the spare bathroom."

"How did you get your stuff?" I choked out. This man moved silently and deadly.

He looked at me like I was crazy. Or stupid. Either was debatable right now.

"I got it out of the bag." Jesus! He entered the bathroom while I was in the shower and I never even heard him. Alarm shot through me. The man could kill me, and I'd never see him coming.

Taking a deep breath, I slowly exhaled. Panicking now wouldn't do me any good. I had to keep my cool. Not that I had a choice. We were locked in this room and who knew what the next steps would be.

"You need to eat." Alexei's voice had me focusing on him. He tilted his chin to the left corner of the room and my eyes darted in its direction to find a tray full of food. They must have brought in food while I showered. Heck, Igor, or whoever was watching us, probably heard my stomach growl. "Then we're leaving."

There was no sense in asking questions. I knew Alexei wouldn't give me any other info and we were being watched and listened to, so we couldn't blow our cover.

I took five steps to the cart and eyed the choices. One croissant and a mug of coffee later, we were en route back to the roof where a helicopter awaited. As we strode to the helicopter, Alexei slipped his arm around my waist and ushered me into the helicopter. Something pushed me to glance over my shoulder, and just as I did, I felt a sharp sting on the back of my neck.

"Alexei... I..." My voice trailed off and my vision blurred. I stumbled backwards, and as if in slow motion, I watched his hands catch me. I blinked, trying to clear the fog in my brain, but it wasn't lifting. I attempted to shake him off and step back, but all I ended up doing was stumbling backwards and my face planted onto Alexei's hard chest.

"Put her in," Igor's voice sounded distant, though he was right behind us.

"Alexei." I wasn't sure if I said his name out loud or just thought it.

Then everything went dark.

TWENTY-SIX

ALEXEI

Well, I was certainly determined to make this woman detest me. My wrongs were stacking up fast and furiously. And doing this to her right after what happened between us in bed this morning made it worse. She trusted me to blindfold her, restrain her, and fuck her. And I repaid her by drugging her.

Aurora was out cold when the door to our room unlocked earlier. Fucking Igor thought he'd caught me unaware. He never learned, and it was a miracle someone hadn't killed him by now. The slimebag was a fucking backstabber, but then it might be the reason he was still alive.

I remained still as he crept into the room, all the way until he was at the foot of our bed.

I swiftly pulled out the gun I had hidden behind my pillow and pointed it at him.

"Est' li shto-to, shto ty hoches'?" I asked him in Russian. *Is there something that you want?*

He knew if he made one wrong move, I'd blow out his fucking brains.

"I came to talk," he responded.

My gun still pointed at him, I waited. There was nothing he could say that would convince me that he'd come to talk. He probably hoped to blindside us and get his filthy hands on Aurora.

"She'll have to be put under," he finally broke the silence, his eyes hungry on Aurora. "I can't have someone like her know the location of my home."

"Nyet." He was crazy if he thought I'd let him inject her with anything.

"It's the only way. She's related to the senator."

It didn't surprise me he learned her identity. I didn't bother hiding it, and it'd make this whole thing more believable. She was the girl who helped me get out, and now I was bringing us back.

"I'll take care of it," I gritted. I didn't want to but backing out of this wasn't an option.

His next expression was smug. "I'll bring drugs—"

"No need," I cut him off, icily. "She'll be under before we get into the helicopter."

"I'll give you mine," he insisted. He was a fool if he thought I'd ever use anything he gave me. I had an emergency med kit in my duffle bag and two shots of a sedative. I'd use it for this.

Though as I pushed that needle into her neck and saw a flicker of betrayal in her eyes, it tore at my chest. She was out within seconds, and I lifted Aurora's lifeless body into the helicopter, positioning her next to me. I was doing a really good job ensuring she'd hate me when we got out of this. But it was either Igor or me, and I wouldn't trust Igor to get within five feet of her. He'd been leering at her from the moment he spotted us in the club, like she was the last drop of water he'd ever get.

The fucked-up thing was that I couldn't even blame him, because she'd become my saving grace at the tender age of five without even trying. She just had that light about her that drew you in.

The helicopter took us to the private plane, and I spent the next ten hours with Aurora's drugged body next to me. I refused to leave her alone for a fraction of a second, even to use the restroom. Igor snickered when I took her with me to the back of the cabin and locked the door. The sick bastard probably assumed I ravished her while she was unconscious because it was something he would undoubtedly do. But all I did was lay her down on the large bed and then use the bathroom. Then instead of going back to the main cabin, I remained with her, seated on the sofa, and watched the young agent sleep on the bed.

Knock. Knock. Knock.

"We are descending," Igor's voice came through the door.

I didn't bother answering. Cold sweat rolled down my back, but I ignored the dread that followed. I fucking hated this country. I hadn't been back in ten years, and before then, it was another ten. It wouldn't hurt my feelings if I never stepped foot on Russian soil again. Nothing but dark and bitter memories came with each visit. My eyes lingered on the dark-haired woman sprawled on the bed.

No matter what went down, I'd have to ensure she got out of it unharmed. I had enough blood and death on my hands without hers. And somehow, I didn't think this world could handle me if something happened to her.

I stood up from my spot and went to the bed, lifted her into my arms, and, pulling open the door to the main cabin, carried her through. I sat down with her secured next to me as I held her body upright.

Her dark, silky hair blanketed her face and I gently pushed it out of the way. She didn't belong in the cruel world of Igor and Ivan. Or in the FBI. Yes, she was strong and fiercely protective of the ones she loved. But she cared too much. It would destroy her, and my heart squeezed with contempt at myself for using her. I should have found someone else, anyone else, but the young agent was already going after the same villain I was.

"She'll be out for a while," Igor said with a stupid grin on his face. "Might be days. Kind of like when they drugged you and stuck you in the basement for those two bitches."

I had to clench my hands to refrain from reaching for him and choking the living daylights out of him. He thought I used his stupid syringe. I didn't. But the fact that he expected her to be out for days if I used his needle told me the fucker had enough tranquilizer to put out a horse, never mind a woman.

229

I tore my gaze away from her and shot him a murderous look that instantly wiped the smile off his face.

"Better watch yourself, Igor," I told him, icily. "Might end up on the wrong side of the bars. And it won't be for sex."

He knew exactly what that meant.

TWENTY-SEVEN
AURORA

D arkness dripped into my subconsciousness. Every so often, I'd hear distant noises, but I could never determine whether they were real or not.

Run, Rora.

My brother's voice full of shrill panic sent shivers down my spine.

Sharing is caring.

A whimper tore from my lips as I attempted to shift, but my body felt too heavy.

"It's okay," a familiar voice I couldn't quite place whispered. A large hand shifted me around, then lifted me up into a sitting position. "Drink."

Something cold pressed against my lips and a groan escaped me. I didn't realize I was dying from thirst until a droplet of cool water touched my lips. I opened my mouth and eagerly drank.

"Slow."

I obeyed, though I was greedy for more. The cool liquid felt good going down my throat. My mouth was dry like the Sahara Desert. Someone pulled the cup away from my mouth. Every shuffle of material sounded too loud to my ears. Curiously, my eyes fluttered open, but I closed them again when pain cut through my head.

Another groan escaped me, and I licked the droplet of water on my lip.

"Relax."

Something churned in my stomach, and I leaned over the bed just in time to throw up everything in my stomach. I couldn't remember the last time I got sick, but this sucked. Stomach acid tasted bitter and burned my throat. My body retched and a set of strong hands held me as I threw up again.

"It's okay." The voice was cold. Familiar. I couldn't place it. Yet, it didn't scare me.

To my horror, tears streamed down my face. I felt horrible. My ears rang, my throat was singed, and my head pounded. I hadn't felt like this since—

I remembered this exact feeling. The last time I felt like this was when I was put under. At the dentist. Having my wisdom teeth removed.

I wiped my mouth with the back of my hand and forced my eyes open. I ignored the pain in my head and turned my head to find a pair of pale blue eyes staring at me. We stared at each other as fury slowly rose within me and licked at my skin.

"You drugged me," I accused him, my voice hoarse like sandpaper.

The bastard didn't even bother to deny it. If I wasn't so damn weak, I'd murder him. Even in my nauseated state, his actions filled me with an anger so deep I saw red. And stars, but mainly red.

I took calming breaths, the stale acid breath that was mine, entering my nostrils, and I had to fight the urge to gag. *Breathe, Aurora. Breathe.*

Anger was so bitter that it swelled in my chest, grabbed my throat, and squeezed until I saw stars. It was my biggest weakness. My temper.

My hand shook with anger as I shoved him away and stumbled into the bathroom; Alexei right on my tail. I barely made it until my legs gave out, and I would have found myself on my knees if he hadn't been behind me to wrap his arms around me.

"I'm going to kill you," I rasped and the irony of my situation didn't escape me. I was too weak to stand after being drugged, and I was threatening to kill my abductor.

He didn't comment, and I didn't need to look behind me to feel his apathetic stare. I whimpered as my stomach rolled.

"I need ginger ale," I muttered as a shiver ran down my spine. Nobody but my brothers knew about my reaction to sedatives. It took only once to experience it and realize my body didn't react well to it.

And this fucking asshole pumped me full.

Slowly, lowering down onto my ass, I put my head between my knees and breathed evenly. This was the worst kind of feeling. It felt like it was happening to someone else, yet the nausea and pain were mine. I didn't bother to check if Alexei was with me or not. I just prayed ginger ale would magically show up in front of me so I could settle my stomach. Or sugar water... something.

The sadistic part of me wanted to call my brothers and tell them what this jerk did to me. Then I'd sit back and watch them kill him as I ate popcorn and drank soda. Gosh, I could almost picture how much fun that would be. I might save him at the last minute. Or maybe not. It was still up for debate, considering how bad I felt.

The pop of the soda sounded next to me and my eyes snapped to it. Alexei lowered to my level, handing me the soda. I cringed my nose.

"I don't drink out of the can." Okay, I sounded a bit bratty, but growing up with a germaphobe of a father rubbed off a bit. After you hear comments about rats licking those can tops in the storage warehouses for the entirety of your childhood, it was hard to not think about it while you drank directly out of cans.

Alexei straightened to his full height, graceful as a panther, and I thought he'd leave me to my own devices, but to my surprise, he retrieved a glass, washed it, then poured some ginger ale into it and came back to me with it.

Eagerly, I snatched it out of his hands and gulped it down. Just for this, I'd save his ass from my brothers.

"Don't drink too fast," he warned. He was right, of course. I forced myself to slow down, feeling the bubbles trickle down my throat.

Animosity, mixed with betrayal, hung heavy in the air as our eyes locked. *Blue*. That color would forever remind me of this man. It was his color. Blue wrapped in darkness and a flicker of something depraved deep down in his gaze.

The seconds ticked, though it felt like hours. I was stupid to offer this man even a fraction of my trust. Even now, knowing he drugged me, I had to tell myself to keep my guard up because something about this man rocked my foundations.

"It was either me or Igor injecting you." His half-assed explanation surprised me. But there was truth in his eyes. My instinct told me he'd have my back, though I didn't necessarily agree how he went about it. "I didn't trust him not to kill you. Or hurt you. I'd go ballistic, and it'd ruin our plans."

"Oh."

His voice was low but vehement, sending warmth through me. It was ludicrous. He made it sound like he *cared* about me. And the way he watched me had a shiver skating down my spine. We stared at each other, something unsettling in the depths of his arctic blues.

I studied his facial expression, or lack thereof, and all the while his eyes burned with something unsettling. I didn't understand it, but my body responded to it. I didn't understand this reaction to him. I didn't understand *him*. The moment I thought he was a psychotic, neurotic killer, he'd say or do something that would make me question whether I understood anything about this man at all.

Killer. Mobster. Protector. Fabulous lover.

I wouldn't think about the latter. It would only confuse me further.

Instinctively, I knew he wasn't the type to explain himself. I had plenty of those kinds of men in my life already—my brothers and my father. How ironic that Alexei would be so similar to them in that regard? Except that he just explained himself.

His presence was cold and intimidating, except for some idiotic reason I wasn't scared of him. My reason warned that I should be, yet I wasn't. My sixth sense told me he wouldn't have beaten a man for grabbing my ass if he wanted me dead. He wouldn't have threatened Starkov. Then there was this unexplainable attraction, or whatever this was.

Despite all my training and profiling, I had a hard time applying my learned knowledge to this man. He seemed to be an exception to everything.

"If we are to do this," I started, my voice slightly raspy, "we are to trust each other. Otherwise, neither one of us will get out of this clusterfuck alive." He watched me as if he was pondering my words. "I don't know about you, Alexei, but I'd like to get out of this alive."

Stretch of silence followed, his eyes unwavering on me.

"You would trust me?" he asked, his accent thicker than I've heard it before. His voice was soft and gentle but underlined with something raw that had goosebumps rising across my skin.

"To get us out of this alive, yes," I breathed. The scary part was that I meant those words. It confused me, yet I couldn't ignore that fragile trust. "Don't blindside me again," I warned.

My heart lodged itself between my ribs as I waited for his response. Hiding the impact he had on me, I held his gaze. Darker than usual, something depraved lurked in its depths. And much to my dismay, I wanted to feed his deprivation because somehow I sensed it was for me. The question was why?

He denied me the right to touch his body. Or to kiss him. Yet, when I stared into those blue depths, I could see the need in them.

His comfort with silence could be so unnerving, but at this moment, I suspected he debated whether I was sincere or not. I was dead serious. I wanted to get the prick that hurt little boys and was possibly connected with my brother's kidnapping.

"Partners, then," he said, his voice unemotional while my own emotions were all over the place. Alexei's hand reached out and I put mine into his. As his fingers wrapped around mine, a memory flickered in my mind.

Another place. Another time. My hand comforting a boy who was big and scary, but he had broken eyes and made me want to hug him so he'd be all better.

A sharp gasp slipped through my lips as I studied Alexei. It was the reason I gravitated towards him. He reminded me of that boy with broken eyes. A shaky shuddering breath left my lungs.

"Regretting it already?" he asked.

"No." I shook my head while he still held my hand.

The deal was sealed.

TWENTY-EIGHT
ALEXEI

"We are in Russia?" Aurora asked again, her eyes wide. I nodded. "In a castle?" she questioned.

After she showered and ate, she asked questions to her heart's content. I explained what transpired from the moment I drugged her until we arrived in Russia. There wasn't much to tell, but it made her feel better to know exactly how many hours we spent in the helicopter and how many hours we spent in the plane. Then she questioned me if I ever left her alone with Igor the Creepo.

She thought her nickname for him was original and refused to give it up.

"Are you sure we aren't in Transylvania?" she grumbled, peeking outside the window. "Are we on a fucking island?" she inquired, her delicate eyebrows furrowing.

"Yes."

Her eyes widened. "Fuck, swimming wasn't in my plans."

I frowned. "You can't swim?"

"Yes, I can swim," she answered annoyed. "But I'm not swimming in Russian waters. I'd freeze my ass off. I hate cold weather." We had that in common, then. I hate the fucking cold too. "I hate humid weather too," she added. "I want perfect tropical weather, not too hot

237

and not too cold. The Russian ocean or sea, or whatever the fuck this is, definitely doesn't qualify."

I didn't bother correcting her about the water surrounding us. It was a lake that appeared in 1957 due to the construction of a state district power station.

"Where in Russia are we?" she asked.

"Tatarstan." I'd be surprised if she knew of the city built by the order of Ivan the Terrible in 1551. The fortified city was constructed in just twenty-four days. I didn't think the world bothered learning that little useless fact, except for the Russians.

She shrugged her shoulders. "It doesn't ring a bell."

"Do you have your phone?" She glanced around the room. No land lines. There weren't any cameras either. All the action would happen in the ballroom, according to Igor.

"No."

"My brothers must be losing their minds," she murmured, concern lacing her voice. "I hate when they worry." Her eyes roamed the room again and then stopped on me. "Will your brothers worry?"

I shrugged. "Probably."

Her lips curved up in a small smile. "I bet my brothers' obsessive worry beats that of your brothers."

"Probably," I agreed. As it should. I have been on my own longer than I've known them, so they knew I'd get through. And if I didn't... Well, then it wasn't meant to be.

"Are you close with your brothers?" she asked curiously.

"Somewhat," I admitted. I'd kill for them, but I'd go on a ballistic, murdering rampage for Aurora.

She leaned against the wall, the window to her left. The sunrays against her dark hair highlighted the brown and auburn strands threaded through it. She was intelligent, classy, and brave. And so goddamn beautiful that I couldn't get my fill of her. I wanted to hear her moans, her screams, her voice. Fuck, anything. As long as I heard her.

"I'm really close to my brothers," she admitted softly. Her hypnotic, dark eyes glanced my way and a protective urge welled in my chest. Fuck, I feared I had become so obsessed with her that I wouldn't be able to let her go when all this was over. "I give them a hard time about their constant nagging. They behave like my parents since our parents." She paused for a few seconds, and I thought she wouldn't say anything else. "Well, since my mom died when I was a kid and Father wasn't around. He was too busy climbing the political ladder."

She sighed heavily and glanced back out the window, remaining quiet for a few minutes. I wondered what thoughts passed through that pretty head of hers. It was hard to guess what the next words or question coming from her would be.

"I'm suspecting swimming is in our near future," she announced and a shudder rolled through her body. The corner of my lips twitched. Her thoughts were really all over the place. "No offense, Alexei, but Russia sucks."

"Agreed."

"Does McGovan know we were leaving for the club last night?" she questioned me. "Or was that the night before? I can't keep track of time anymore."

She was out for almost a day, so it was two nights ago.

"McGovan doesn't know."

Her fingers pushed her unruly hair out of her face, and I noticed the small tremor in her hands. She was nervous. She was right to be, but it hit me wrong to see her upset. Except I didn't have much in terms of assurance. It was just the two of us. I've had it worse, but I was certain she hadn't.

"I won't let anything happen to you," I told her, though I had no right to promise something like that.

"It's just the two of us," she murmured. *Against all of them.* It was the unsaid part that got her worried. "Do you come here often?" she continued questioning. I sensed she needed words to work off her nervousness.

"First time."

"Oh." She grew silent for a moment before speaking again. "How come you only came into the picture five or so years back?" Aurora's

239

questions were all over the place. I didn't think she was doing it on purpose, but I'd admit her mind worked in mysterious ways that didn't make sense to me.

"I didn't know who my father was." It was the truth. Half-truth. I didn't know who my real mother was either. Until Vasili told me.

"Sorry," she muttered, her eyes shifting to my hand. I noticed she did the same earlier when we shook hands. "I know who my dad is, but I don't know him at all. If that makes any sense." I nodded. I guessed as much. "He has had other women too, even when he had a steady girlfriend. Or whatever you call that at his age. And I'm pretty sure he had them all along, even when my mother was alive. My brothers tried to keep me shielded from all that, except I kind of wish we'd meet the other two. I always wanted a sister and then found out that I had one. But then, do I really want to disrupt her life? She seems happy."

It didn't surprise me to learn she knew her family's secrets. Her mind was too curious and inquisitive to leave things alone and live in oblivion. She stared into an empty space, chewing on her lower lip and her thoughts somewhere far away.

"Of course, if Dad was my husband, I'd leave him." There was no doubt in my mind that she would. "And I'd take the kids," she added, her gaze coming back to me as if she wanted to ensure I agreed with her. I nodded because I did. If the man was dumb enough to cheat on her, he didn't deserve her. "My brothers remember Mom. She made them promise to take care of me." Her voice lowered, thick emotions in it. No wonder she was so close with her brothers. "My four brothers." She paused, realizing her mistake because only three were in her life. But then continued. "They always took care of me. They kept their promise for sure."

"Vasili took care of Sasha and Tatiana." I tried to share. "Their father was absent."

She chewed on her bottom lip nervously. "What about you?" I remained quiet. I didn't think my history would be the right thing to calm her down. "Their father was your father, right?" Her voice was cautious as she treaded lightly.

"Yes, but I wasn't around." She waited expectantly for me to explain. It was more than I shared with anyone in my entire life. Vasili found me and gave me the information I had been searching for my whole life.

I sat on the balcony of my villa in Portugal, the view of the sea stretching for miles. It was meant to be a view that offered tranquility. At least that was what the realtor said when I looked at it.

It didn't.

Just ask the visitor who just left, the turmoil of the sea, reflected inside me. The ripples caused by winds across the surface become unstable when reaching shallow water and begin to break.

If that wasn't a metaphor for my life, I wasn't sure what was.

On the inside, I was broken. On the outside, scarred. Though, ink covering my skin hid all the ugly. There was only one man who understood the hell constantly brewing inside me, and he needed more help than I did.

Another wave crashed against the rocky shoreline, breaking it into a million droplets.

Unlike Cassio and his gang, I didn't feel a strong connection to any of them. Though they hadn't failed me yet. Even when I didn't ask for their help, they came through. Like in Russia.

If Nico, Luca, Cassio, and Alessio hadn't come, I would have died on that rescue mission. But I lacked in forming connections.

I knew it; they knew it.

It made them wary to trust me initially. I couldn't even blame them, considering I experienced firsthand when it came down to two human beings, instincts always prevailed. We were no better than animals. Actually, we might be worse.

A shadow covered part of the balcony, signaling someone behind me. I was up on my feet in a blink, a knife between my fingers. A tall guy in a tailored suit stood there, his hands casually in his pockets.

"The door was open," he said, as if that explained why he was in my home.

I didn't recognize him. Instinct warned me he was ruthless and dangerous, but not to me. Our gazes connected, and the familiarity of his eyes washed over me. They looked like the eyes I met in the mirror every morning.

Except ghosts and demons didn't lurk in his eyes.

"Alexei?" he asked, when I said nothing.

Still untrusting, I gripped my knife, ready to deliver a stab into his gut. Though I suspected this guy, despite his suit, was just as capable in combat as I was.

"I see this will be more difficult than I thought," he muttered. "You speak English?"

I finally nodded. The families I was left with often spoke English and Russian, so I was fluent in both.

"Can we talk without the knife?" he asked, both of us still standing and facing each other.

"Nyet."

Something flickered in his pale blue eyes. "You speak Russian?"

I nodded again.

"Okay, then," he muttered. "I'll get right to the point. I'm Vasili Nikolaev." The name prompted the old hate against a woman long forgotten. The woman I hadn't seen since my tenth birthday.

When I didn't comment, Vasili continued, "We are brothers. I'm sure you gathered that by now, with our resemblance."

Brothers?

I didn't have brothers. I'd killed them all in Ivan's ring. Though how do you explain that to a mere stranger?

"Half brothers, if you want to be exact. Same father, different mother. I only found out about you a few months ago." Bitterness welled in my chest, like a bottomless pool. It tasted acrid. "I met your mother on her deathbed. She begged me to find you."

"You found me," I said, my voice hoarse.

"I hoped we could take you home," he continued, ignoring my standoffish attitude. "Sasha is my younger brother, though he's slightly older than you." It meant absolutely nothing to me. "I'd like the three of us to work together, running the Nikolaev businesses."

"Already have a job," I deadpanned.

Besides, working with two brothers who had a normal upbringing would fester this bitterness inside me. I didn't need a front-row seat to how fucked up I was, by being placed next to two versions of me who weren't. Assuming Sasha looked like his brother.

"Tatiana is our youngest sister. She's a bit wild, though she just turned twenty-two," Vasili added, as if that would change my mind. Though it was tempting. To protect a much younger sibling. But she already had two older brothers; she didn't need another one.

I said nothing, the knife still in my hand and my knuckles turning white from the force of my grip. I learned early on, there was no point to any emotions nor attachments. None of them mattered. Nobody cared whether you were jealous, sad, happy, mad. They just cared about what you could do for them.

Pashka. Ilya. Kostya. They died young. They had those emotions and they clung to them. The good ones die young, they said. It had to mean I was a bad one.

Though at this moment, it was hard to ignore this bitter envy in my chest. At Vasili my half brother. It was better not knowing.

"You also have one other sister, the same age as Tatiana." Something about Vasili's voice had me focusing on his face. Was that... regret? "Isabella Taylor. Her mother, your mother, just passed away. She never stopped searching for you." Except, she never found me. Did she? "I didn't know it, but my father searched for you too. He loved your mother and my own mother took you away."

I swallowed the need to spit. The fucking triangle. He should have kept it in his pants and saved all of us a world of suffering. There was nothing Vasili could say that would make me want to get to know them. Any of them.

"Isabella's father is Lombardo Santos." The name instantly sent a warning down my spine. He trafficked women, right along with Benito King. "He doesn't know about her, and I'll keep it that way. It's the safest for her." He paused and I watched him curiously. His jaw clenched, though I couldn't distinguish whether it was anger aimed at Isabella or her father.

When I said nothing, he let out an exhale and ran a thoughtful hand across his jaw. Almost as if he was tired of everything. Turning around, he headed for the door. He stopped, his hand on the door handle.

"Isabella is alone and knows nothing of this world," he uttered. "Nor her father. She'll need protection." He let the words sink in. "Or she'll end up for sale if her father's enemies find out about her."

Protection surged through me. No sister of mine would be put up for sale. Like damn stock. She had nobody. Vasili was protecting her, but he was only one man.

She needs me, *my heart whispered.*

"Wait."

And I made the right choice. Vasili and Sasha became brothers, not only by blood. Tatiana was just as wild as her brother described her. And Isabella was the vulnerable one who needed us the most.

But the discovery was even more bitter than I could have imagined. I had never bothered explaining to anyone what the fuck happened in our family history to get us here. Our parents' triangle damaged all of us, in one way or another.

"I had a different mother from Vasili, Sasha, and Tatiana. Isabella and I had the same mother."

An awkward tension lay between us. She wanted to ask more questions, but she didn't want to pry. I felt the tension tighten in my shoulders, but I didn't want to deny her this. So when this was all over, she could understand why I did this. At least some of it.

"Ask, kroshka."

"So you and Isabella grew up together?" Her voice was low, tentative.

"No."

"But how—" Her question lingered in the air.

"I was taken from our mother before I was out of diapers, so I never knew her."

"Jesus," she muttered, then swallowed hard. "I guess neither one of us knew our mothers but at least I had my brothers."

She was right; she had her brothers. No matter what, the Ashford brothers ensured their little sister was their priority. As it should be.

She walked over and sat herself on the coffee table, opposite me. I wondered whether it was because she didn't want to sit next to me or she wanted to see my face clearly. Aurora was one of those women who trusted people's expressions not words.

Her legs were bare, her shorts revealing most of her naked skin, and I'd be a blind man not to notice it. Every single inch of her was exquisite, and I had to clench my hand or risk reaching out to her. I didn't think she'd appreciate me interrupting her questioning. Though at least her worries of our escape seemed to pause for a moment.

"Do you know who took you?" she whispered.

"Yes."

"Who?"

"Vasili's mother."

She gasped sharply. "I hope you killed the bitch."

Turns out, my little FBI agent was bloodthirsty. A perfect combination of soft and fierce. My lip corners tugged up. In the short time I'd known her, I felt the urge to smile more than I did in all my life.

"She killed herself."

"That was too good for her."

"Agreed."

"W-were y-your—" she stammered, and I had a feeling it was because she was scared of the answer. Aurora, for all her tough demeanor, had a soft heart. I waited, letting her gather her courage to ask. "Were your adoptive parents nice?"

I thought back to the five sets of families that I could remember. There were at least two more that I couldn't.

"I was moved each year," I answered dryly. "Some were better than others. My last family—" I paused, the memory sending an uncomfortable chill down my spine. I smiled tightly. "They were good people. Vasili's mother had them murdered in front of me."

Those warm eyes widened in horror and her hand grabbed mine. It was her soft heart I loved the most.

Fuck! Did I fall for the agent while I wasn't looking? Everything about her had my blood hum in approval at having her as mine. Just the thought of something happening to her had blood rushing to my brain and my ears buzzing. It was the most terrifying sensation because this world wouldn't be the same without her.

Her soft eyes flicked to me, shimmering with tears. For me.

"I'm so sorry," she whispered softly, her small hand squeezing mine. "People can be so cruel."

God, I wanted to keep her. Forever brand her as mine.

"Yes, they can," I confirmed.

And soon, she'd realize how cruel.

TWENTY-NINE
ALEXEI

Aurora paced the room.

It drove her crazy that we were locked in here. It drove me insane too, but I hid it better. For her benefit. You'd think after all those years of imprisonment, I'd handle it better.

When dinner came through the door, I caught Aurora eyeing the open door longingly. But a guard stood there. Her eyes darted to me and remained on me, as if she needed strength to remain calm. I offered an assuring nod, hating that she felt vulnerable.

Once they were gone, we ate our dinner. Afterwards both of us showered, separately of course. The sun was yet to set. I guessed it was about seven in the evening.

I sat on the sofa, ready to pick up a magazine when her voice had me forgetting all about it.

"What are we going to do?" she asked, her voice slightly irritated with boredom. "It's too early for bed," she muttered, glancing my way, then around the room until her eyes came to the large king-size bed. She wore one of my T-shirts that reached down to her knees. "Too early for sleeping. Maybe extra-curricular activities would kill some time."

Realizing what she said, she flushed and looked back at me. Her eyes fell to my lips, she swallowed and glanced away. But not before I saw desire flash in her dark eyes.

A half-smile pulled on my lips. "I'm all for extra-curricular activities," I responded. My cock went hard as a rock, more than willing to kill all the time in the world while deep inside her.

Her soft brown eyes locked on me and I held her gaze. "Are you up for it?" I challenged her, my voice hoarse.

Her lips curved into a seductive smile. "Mr. Nikolaev, are you baiting me?" she teased, her voice breathless.

I shouldn't do it. I needed to back off. She'd already dug herself deep beneath my skin. Yet, like a depraved soul, I wanted to play. Own her. Possess her.

"I am," I admitted, those soft eyes sparkling on me. No point in lying to her. "Is it working?"

She took a step towards me. Then another. Until she was right in front of me, her toned, bare legs pressed against my own. After my shower, I pulled on sweatpants and a T-shirt. I didn't want her seeing my scars. I regretted not feeling her skin against my own.

Until this woman, a single touch sent disgust racing through me. Now, I found myself craving it. In the span of a few weeks, this woman invaded my mind and my heart. The thought of never seeing her again sent a cold sweat down my spine.

Every time I looked at her, I felt peace wash over me. And happiness; at least, I thought it was happiness. It was unlike any other feeling I had felt before. Warm, soothing, light. Whatever it was, I wanted to keep it.

I stood up, and she craned her neck, keeping her eyes locked on mine. She was so petite compared to my frame, it always sent a rush of worry through me. That I'd hurt her.

"Bed?" she breathed the question, the vein in her neck visibly throbbing. She deserved so much better than this shitty situation. So much better than me.

"You sure?" I asked, something inside me shaking with the fear of her loss. I wanted everything she had, but I knew it was impossible to demand it. Not with our complicated history. And not when I couldn't give her everything I had.

Because if I had, I'd lose her. I didn't think I could handle seeing disgust in those dark eyes.

She licked her lips, her chest rising and falling.

"Yes, I'm sure."

Aurora grabbed my hand and walked us to the bed. A shuddering breath escaped her mouth. "Might be the most exciting time-passing activity I've ever done," she teased softly.

I cupped her face, so many unspoken words burning my tongue yet refusing to come out. Instead, I rested my forehead against hers, inhaling her scent and our breaths intermixed. Her lips parted, and for the first time in my life, I wanted to brush my mouth against hers.

Yet, my mind was a fucking bitch because my body reacted against my heart. My mind was too fucked up. Too broken.

She wanted a kiss. I could taste it, almost as if it was a part of me, and it fucking burned me that I couldn't give it to her.

"Should I take my shirt off?" she rasped softly.

"Let me." I reached the hem of the shirt and pulled it over her head. Jesus Christ.

She was beautiful, standing there in nothing but her little panties. Her nipples were pink and hard. I sat her on the edge of the bed, then lowered onto my knees and took one nipple into my mouth, twirling the bud under my tongue.

Her back arched into me and she raised her hands, wrapping them around my neck. She was touching me, I realized. It was instinct on her part, yet a startling discovery on mine. It didn't send my heart into hyperactive mode. Or make old memories shatter through my mind.

I just felt *her*.

I lavished my attention on her gorgeous breasts—nipping, sucking, biting.

"Alexei," she moaned, her fingers pushing through my hair. God, my name on her lips sounded right. Like a lover's song that I'd never get enough of.

Pulling her panties down her legs, I dipped my fingers between her folds and found her soaked.

I growled my satisfaction, working my way down her stomach with my mouth kissing and licking every single inch of her. Her arousal scented the room, the sweetest addiction, and the only one I'd ever have.

My face lowered between her thighs, spreading them wider and I inhaled deeply.

The moment my mouth connected with her pussy, her fingers twisted in my hair, tugging me forward. As if I'd go anywhere else. She was my home. I licked her from her clit to her entrance, lapping up every drop. She tasted sweet, her taste bursting on my tongue.

Mine, the words buzzed in my ears as I dipped my tongue inside her pussy.

A shudder rolled down her body and my cock throbbed in my pants, demanding to be inside her.

"Oh, fuck," she cried out, her legs trembling as they spread wider. "Alexei, p-please."

Alternating from tongue-fucking her to swirling her clit into my mouth, her hips bucked under me. I raised my free hand and held it flat on her stomach, holding her still. Determined to give her everything I had. Soft moans turned louder, my name chanting on her lips.

Pressing my face into her deeper, I slid my fingers in, curling upward, then easing them back out. Then back in again.

Her legs tightened around my head and she ground herself against my face.

"Oh, God," she groaned softly. "Oh, God. Alexei, I—I'm gonna—"

I lapped at her like she was the last drop of water I'd ever get. Like she was the oxygen for my lungs. My tongue dipped in and out of her pussy, while my thumb pressed firm circles against her clit.

Her whole body started to shake and I gazed up to see the most gorgeous sight ever. Her half-lidded eyes on me, dark and lustful. Her mouth parted. Her cheeks flushed deep red.

A soft scream slipped through her mouth, her body arching off the bed and I continued lapping her, intent on drinking every single drop of her juices. I groaned against her pussy, like I was drunk from her.

Slowly her shaking turned into trembles, and I licked my way up her body until my lips pressed against her delicate jaw. Her mouth was still parted, her eyes hazed and locked on me.

For a fraction of a second, I thought she'd ask for a kiss. Something in my chest twisted, tempting me to ignore my fear. Yet, the thought of seeing pity or disgust on her face was too much to contemplate.

"Get on the bed, kroshka," I ordered. "All fours."

Without hesitation, she climbed up on the bed, her hands and knees hitting the mattress. I came behind her, spreading her thighs with my hands. She twisted her head to look at me, her eyes reflecting the desire I felt.

I gripped her throat and a moan vibrated in her throat.

All my control snapped. My one hand grabbed her silky strands and gently tugged her head back as my mouth connected with her neck, alternating between nipping and kissing. My other hand pushed my sweatpants down and found her hot center.

Without warning, I slammed into her, filling her to the hilt. This woman was my heaven. My salvation. My sanity.

I pulled out and thrust in again. Hard. Deep.

"Alexei," she panted. "Harder."

"You need deeper, kroshka," I grunted, though I still fucked her harder, causing a friction between our bodies. I wanted to give her everything she needed and wanted.

"Yes, Alexei," she cried out. "Yes, yes, yes."

"Say my name again," I growled.

I ground into her, heat spreading through every cell of me. I thrust in and out. Deep and hard.

"Alexei," she breathed, her voice hoarse, my hips powering deep inside her. "Alexei, Alexei, Alexei."

This woman was consuming me. She gave and I greedily took. My hips pistoned into her, balls slapping against her flesh, my cock filling her all the way to the hilt.

I feared I'd break her with my ruthlessness but she took me beautifully. Demanding more. I fucked her faster and deeper until I felt that familiar pressure build at the base of my spine. I picked up my pace. Thrusting in and out. Hard and fast. Every thrust stole another moan from me.

"God, Alexei," she cried out. "Please, I need more of you."

"Who else?" I growled.

"Nobody," she moaned. "Just you."

They were words spoken in the heat of passion, but I soaked them in, letting them fill the cracks in my chest.

"Look at me," I ordered, my voice guttural. Glancing over her shoulder, our eyes met and she was breathtaking. Her eyes pleasure-hazed. Her lips parted. Her little moans and my grunts filled the air. I'd memorize it all. Every single word. Every single look.

Another deep thrust and she tensed, her pussy clenching around my cock. Then she exploded with a loud cry and my name on her lips. I watched her expression as she shattered for me. Only for me.

I thrust through her orgasm and followed her right over the edge as my muscles seized and the orgasm ripped through me. My cock jerked wildly, spilling my cum inside her.

There was so much of it that I watched it trickle down her inner thigh, and for a fraction of a moment, I wondered if I could bind this woman to me by impregnating her. So she could be mine forever. So she'd never leave me.

The ridiculous idea dissipated as quickly as it came. She'd hate me enough when she found out the truth about her brother. I didn't need to add fuel to the fire.

Her breathing still labored, she collapsed onto the mattress.

Quickly pulling my pants back on, I flipped her over and cradled her into my arms. Without hesitation she snuggled into me, her eyes fluttered shut.

Her head rested on my shoulder, the palm of her hand on my heart, as if she already knew she claimed it.

I let out a breath, knowing this would lead to a catastrophe. Yet, it still didn't stop me from wanting her.

"Aurora?"

"Hmmm." Her eyelashes fluttered open and then closed again as sleep pulled her back under. Her body pressed closer to me.

"Are you on the pill?"

"Mmmhhmmm."

Our second night in this place and Igor was already hosting a party. It probably meant things were moving according to plan. And while I was eager for them to move forward, I also dreaded it.

Because I knew the time would come when Aurora would look at me with hate and disgust. I had a promise to keep, and she had a brother to avenge.

The bathroom door opened and Aurora stepped through it.

I stared at her, at a loss for words. Not that I ever said many words.

"I'm ready," Aurora announced in her smoky voice, tucking an unruly piece of hair behind her ear. Her hair was twisted up into a crown-like bun. Since our earlier talk about my past, the air between us had shifted. I explained to her what to expect when we got downstairs. She didn't flinch at it. Though her words still rang in my ears.

"You let another man touch me, and I'll slice all of your dick off. Without anesthesia." Then she added something about weirdo Russians and their orgies. She'd definitely never cower before me. Aurora's fierceness reminded me of Cassio's wife. Yes, she was soft and caring but also knew how to take care of herself.

She smoothed her hands down the dress she was provided. Igor had it brought in for her, and I fucking hated it. I didn't want anyone providing for her but me. I didn't think she particularly liked it either. It wasn't her style. She usually wore elegant, understated, beautiful dresses.

This one was too loud. She wore a shimmery dress with a slit down her leg that revealed her smooth tanned legs and high heels matching her dress. The silk straps of the dress crisscrossed around her breasts, waist, and hips, giving glimpses of her beautiful skin. A set of pearls hung around her neck that were so long, she had to wrap them around her neck several times. I was fairly certain there was another purpose to those pearls.

She shifted from one foot to another, and the material practically shimmered.

My eyes narrowed in annoyance. She'd be so fucking shiny every single pair of eyes would be on her. I didn't want the sick mother-fuckers gawking at her.

"Don't you dare call me a fucking disco ball," she huffed. Her face was free of makeup, except for mascara and light lipstick applied. She didn't need makeup to accentuate her beauty. "Fucking asshole that picked this shitshow of a dress. He should be shot for lack of taste in fashion."

My lips quirked. When she spoke like that, I could see the rich princess in her. That little girl dressed in a fancy outfit for her walk to the zoo.

I smoothed a nonexistent wrinkle from my sleeve. My suit was tailored, which told me Igor had sent a heads-up to his people that we were coming. The question was whether he sent notice to Ivan. I hoped the ass-kisser in him did.

An exasperated breath left Aurora's ruby lips and she scoffed, glancing down at herself.

It was hard for me not to look at her, regardless of what she wore. She could wear rags and I still couldn't peel my eyes away from her.

Every word she had ever spoken. Every look she gave me. And every breath she had taken had been engraved in the very marrow of my bones. It'd remain with me until my dying breath.

It was hard to believe that she was here with me. That I touched her.

Yet, the fear deep down in my chest lingered that I'd destroy her. That I'd break her. That she'd disappear just as everything else used to.

"Ready, kroshka?"

I would walk away from her when Ivan was six feet under. I knew I couldn't keep her. She deserved more. Deserved better. And I couldn't give her everything she needed. But despite odds against me, I hoped that she'd stay.

ALEXEI

She slipped her hand into mine, rolled her shoulders and sighed. "Let's go see this goddamn orgy."

I ran my thumb across her palm, her skin so soft under my rough touch. A light visible shiver shook her body and the sadistic part of me hoped she'd get addicted to me so she'd never leave me.

"Orgy, huh?" I said dryly, annoyed with myself for dreaming the impossible.

"I'm not sure what else to call it," she admitted in a low voice, rolling her eyes. I explained to her earlier that we'd be invited to an event to join Igor and his guests. Ivan Petrov could be one of those men.

We left the large room and stepped out into the large, luxurious hallway. We were staying in one of the old castles. Only in Russia will you see old historic buildings being owned by criminals and turned into some kind of freak show.

As we walked down the red-carpeted hallway, Aurora's eyes darted left and right. The house was lit by electric lights but dimmed low. The thick stones and small windows didn't allow much sunlight in.

There were dozens of rooms, though it sounded like they were mostly empty. I wondered if Igor's guests were visiting or staying here. Oriental rugs covered certain walls, murals the others.

Igor seemed to be doing well for himself. He even succeeded in securing himself with a few paintings.

"Well, the creeper has some valuable art," Aurora commented. "Not sure if I'm impressed or disgusted that someone like that owns these pieces."

"Disgusted," I told her.

A soft, mischievous smile played around her lips. "You're right. Totally disgusted," she remarked.

We walked down a set of stairs that must have seen royalty descend for centuries. I didn't belong in such a grandiose ambiance, but Aurora did. She moved with grace, as if she was the queen and all present here were her subjects.

The staff who scurried up and down, kept throwing their glances her way. She didn't fit the caliber of the usual attendees by Igor.

We passed a large formal dining room and finally approached the ballroom. I noted the grand lobby and front door on the other side and took a note of it. It didn't escape me that Aurora's eyes fleeted that way too.

We locked gazes for a fraction of a second and she nodded.

We stepped into the large ballroom, and instantly the room grew quieter.

"Showtime," I muttered under my breath.

Aurora's hand squeezed mine and she pasted on her best fake smile. I pulled her closer to me and leaned in, my lips brushing against her earlobe. "Breathe, kroshka."

She turned to glance up at me and flashed me an automatic smile. Putting on a façade was something she had experience with, considering who her father was. But she didn't like it. What you saw with this little agent was what you got; and I loved every single thing.

"My guests of honor," Igor's voice came from behind us. The fucker always did like to stab people in the back. The alarming part was that I hadn't sensed him because I was so lost in this woman.

Schooling her features, Aurora turned around slowly and smiled at him. It was a perfect smile for a politician's wife.

"Hello, Igor," she greeted him, feigning excitement. "What a beautiful home," she commended.

Igor laughed, and it sounded demonic. Aurora's expression didn't change, but her nails dug into my hand.

"I hope the helicopter and plane ride method didn't offend you," he sneered, his gaze devouring her body. I wanted to grab the nearest fork and poke his eyeballs out.

Aurora chuckled, as if amused, while I knew she wanted to kill him. If she had her sidearm, I was certain she'd put a bullet in his brain, and I'd help her bury the body.

"It happens more than you know," she responded, waving her free hand, like it was no big deal that we drugged her and smuggled her into Russia.

Igor cocked his eyebrow, surprised by her response and temporarily at a loss for words.

"Well, we are going to make our rounds," she added, smiling wide. We made it five steps when she leaned over grinning, then whispered, "I bet that fucker didn't see that coming."

Aurora enjoyed her victory a bit too much. I should have known it would be short-lived.

THIRTY
AURORA

I gor the Creeper. Forevermore.

He had officially gotten a last name. Maybe I'd even convince him to get christened so that all the humans of this world could be forewarned.

Alexei might be psychotic in a protective, weird kind of way. Igor was just a plain psycho. Back in his sex club, he hid it. Here, in his domain, he flaunted it. Just feeling his gaze on me made me sick and had my skin crawling.

It felt like a million pairs of eyes were on us as Alexei and I glided through the ballroom. I was surprised there was nothing X-rated going on. So far, it looked like a normal black-tie affair. With the exception that my gown looked like a fucking disco ball and attracted too much attention.

"Can we kill him when this is over?" I muttered under my breath, smoothing the dress with my free hand. As if that would make it less noticeable. The only thing that this dress was good for was kindling.

"Yes." Stoic. Unemotional. Perfect.

My lips curved and I glanced up at him, meeting his eyes. "Well, mister. For that, I might forgive you for drugging me."

He let out a rough breath, watching me under his long lashes, and I caught something dark and thrilling lingering in his pale gaze.

He looked good in his suit. Truthfully, he looked good in anything, but wearing a suit gave him a darker than normal vibe. A dressed-up killer who could snap your neck with one move. You'd never see it coming. And somehow, it made him even more noticeable.

We strolled around the ballroom. I ensured not to make eye contact. Alexei didn't say the same principle applied here, but it would make sense that it did. Men here gave me the creeps. Like Igor went to all the slums of the world and picked the creepiest, though good-looking men, then brought them here. I wasn't quite sure what it said for us.

A disgusting shudder ran down my back.

"Just us, kroshka," Alexei murmured in my ear, and I hoped he was right because there were some gorgeous women here and they gawked at Alexei like it was open season. The hunger in their eyes spoke volumes. I guessed he wouldn't have issues lining up women for himself, despite all his tattoos. I swore a few women even tried to approach him, until he gave them his killer stare.

I had to bite the inside of my cheek so as not to grin. I liked that he took my warning seriously. He stuck to me, ensuring no other man had a chance to start flirting with me. So sue me; if I had to go through this kinky shit of being watched while having sex, I might as well do it with the finest specimen on this planet. And possibly all the planets.

"Ladies and gentlemen." Igor's voice boomed through the speakers and I shared a fleeting glance with Alexei. "Everyone, find your way to the back room and the stage. Tonight will be a night to remember."

"Oh, Jesus," I muttered under my breath. "This sounds so promising."

"Stay close to me." Alexei's voice was firm. "No matter what."

"You couldn't pull me away from you with a set of pliers," I said dryly.

He smiled, actually smiled, the scar on his lip stretched, and I watched mesmerized as his face transformed. My breath got stuck in my lungs and something fluttered in my chest. Maybe it was lack of oxygen, I had absolutely no idea. But I couldn't tear my eyes away.

His one eyebrow rose, as if he was wondering what I was staring at. I blinked, then cleared my throat.

"I didn't know you actually smiled," I breathed. I glanced away from him and towards the crowd that was already scurrying into the other room. "You should do it more. It's kind of nice."

I felt my cheeks heat with my words. I had sex with him in a club and in the bathroom with a door open so Igor the Creeper could watch or listen, and I blushed at giving him a compliment. So nerdy.

"I'll keep that in mind," he replied.

We were the last ones to enter the back room where the *action* was supposed to happen. I took one step inside and stopped short.

"Wow." It wasn't what I expected.

The black flooring here was shined to perfection, you could almost see your reflection in it. The chandeliers were lowered and lights dimmed, it made it appear as if you were entering a separate world. Certain people were already in their own groups, touching each other, kissing, moaning. Others mingled and some just chatted. I hated to admit this to anyone, but the room screamed of sex appeal.

My heart thundered and I had to clench my thighs. My body's response to the scenery was freaking me out.

I swallowed hard, suddenly unsure. Alexei gave me an idea of what to expect, but I didn't anticipate getting turned on. Then as if on some invisible prompt, everyone's eyes turned our way and a low murmur spread through the room.

Alexei gently nudged me forward and we slowly strolled through the room. My eyes shifted through the room, over the faces of women and men but none of them looked familiar. I couldn't see Igor either.

"Igor is not here," I muttered under my breath.

A barely noticeable nod from Alexei. I should have known he'd notice it too. An unfamiliar man approached us and I stiffened, avoiding looking at his face. I was terrified to give a wrong impression.

"Mr. and Mrs. Nikolaev," he greeted us and a slightly hysterical laugh escaped me. Two sets of eyes turned my way and I silently cursed. "Sorry," I mumbled. "Nerves."

Somehow, I didn't think anyone here took me for Alexei's wife. Maybe they resorted to his last name since they didn't know mine.

"Since you are our honorable guests," the man continued, probably labeling me an idiot in his mind, "you get to sit on the throne."

He pointed to the center of the room. Alexei and I followed the direction of his hand and my jaw dropped. There was a throne, a real motherfucking throne, placed on a round, elevated landing in the center of the room.

This had to be a joke. My mouth dried out and suddenly oxygen seemed in short supply. Back at the sex club, it was semi-private in the VIP room. But this... this was wide open. In the center of the motherfucking room.

My eyes snapped to Alexei. My eyes had to be wide with a deer-in-the-headlights look in them.

"Perfect," he answered the man and guided me to the throne.

"Breathe, kroshka." His hot breath in my ear had me inhaling deeply, then slowly exhaling. I followed his lead in a haze, each step of my heels loud like a hammer against the marble floor. It was *that* quiet in this room.

I just had to focus on Alexei and I could get through this. He was my rock in this ocean. Or however the fuck the saying went. I just knew he made me feel safe. I trusted him to get us through this, catch the fucking pervert that was kidnapping boys, and then we'd get out of this freak show.

Maybe I won't arrest Mr. Nikolaev after all, I mused to myself. He kind of grew on me. I wasn't sure how or when, but I started to see his appeal. Yes, it was rough and edgy but there was light in his darkness. It was raw and rare.

Alexei sank into the chair, like he was a king and belonged in it and pulled me down onto his lap. I half expected him to wave his hand to his subjects and order them to continue their sexual charade.

Then as if he read my thoughts, he did exactly that.

"Bow-chick-a-wow-wow," I muttered from the corner of my mouth, just because I couldn't resist.

Alexei sank farther into the chair, his hands on my hips, pulling me deeper into his lap. He rearranged me so my back was pressed against his chest. I shifted lightly and my ass accidently ground against his hard cock.

I glanced at his face over my shoulder and he raised a brow, as his arm wrapped around my waist.

"Relax, kroshka."

I forced a smile on. "Easy for you to say."

It was impossible to relax with his hands on me. His thighs were firm beneath me and the man was hard. I shifted my hips just a little and felt his thick cock against my ass, which had me forgetting about everyone around us. His face was expressionless. In fact, he looked bored.

A loud moan had me turning my attention back to the room around us. There were at least fifty people in the room. And for the moment, I forgot all about Alexei as a dress slipped off a plus-sized woman, leaving her naked for all to see.

She had no panties. No bra. Though I had to admit, she was stunning. Luscious curves. Long dark hair. Her eyes roamed over a crowd of men, an invitation clear in them, and I held my breath as I waited.

A man stepped forward. Then another. And another.

I turned my head just slightly, unable to look away from the scene. Surely all three wouldn't—

I couldn't finish the thought.

"Does she pick one?" I whispered. Yes, my eyes were on the woman and three men, but my body and my mind held on to Alexei.

"Or all."

A smile spread on the woman's face, and she whispered something that only the three men in front of her could hear. The next second, the three men circled her, their hands gently sweeping over her body.

"Fucking Russian orgies," I muttered under my breath though I couldn't deny the impact this scene had on me. Desire shot through me and my thighs clenched. I relaxed further back against Alexei.

The woman must have been enjoying the lavish attention because her eyes fluttered shut and her head fell back. The three moved the woman five steps back where I noticed a St. Andrew's cross stood.

How I could miss something so large when we entered, I had no idea and could only blame my nerves.

Despite myself, I was unable to look away from the group and held my breath as the woman lifted her arms up into the air. One of the men reached out to the side of the cross and reached out into a bag. He grabbed a rope and started to bind the woman's wrists while the second man grabbed another rope, then kneeled down. He started to bind her ankles, leaving her spread eagle. The third man was trailing kisses down her neck.

I swallowed hard, then took a slow breath in. The desire between the four of them was palpable and visible, even from our spot. With each second that ticked by, the pulse between my thighs increased and my breathing became choppy.

The woman was spread open not only for the three men to see her but also the entire room. The moans leaving her lips, the ecstatic look on her face told me she was enjoying every single thing these men were doing to her. The flush spread across her skin, and for some crazy reason, I almost wished I could experience the pleasure she was.

Almost. But only with one man. The one who had his big hand firmly on my hip.

I shifted uncomfortably and felt his bulge even harder under my ass and a sharp gasp slipped through my lips. I felt Alexei's hot breath against my neck, his lips so close I could almost feel them on my skin.

His hands trailed down my stomach, his fingers making lazy circles over the exposed skin and a shiver ghosted down my spine.

"Want me to touch you, kroshka?" he breathed into my ear, then gently bit my earlobe.

This was insane. He was barely touching me and hungry fires licked my skin. My core ached with need, and I knew only he could sate it.

I shifted slightly and my legs parted. It was my answer, but I should have known it wouldn't be good enough for him.

"Tell me," he demanded, his voice rough in my ear.

"Please touch me."

He dragged his finger further down my waist, slipped it under my dress. The side dress slit gave him the perfect opening. He was closer and closer to my core, and I shivered in anticipation. My legs parted wider and his index finger brushed over my panties causing a muffled moan to slip through my lips. I leaned further into him, craving more of him. More of his heat.

My hand covered his and my hips ground greedily against his palm.

"You're soaked, kroshka." His accent thickened, and damn if it didn't turn me on even more. Was this just lust? Because I trusted him to see me through this and not allow anyone else near me. I had no idea why.

I licked my lips and my breasts felt heavier with each labored breath I took. He moved slowly, too damn slow, and when he finally cupped my pussy, another moan vibrated through me as my eyes fluttered shut. The whole room was forgotten. The only thing I could feel was Alexei.

"Please," I moaned low, grinding against his hand.

His other hand clutched my hip and he tightened his grip.

"We do this my way," he groaned in my ear.

I spread my legs wider, with a small whimper. "I need more."

He slipped his hand into my panties, and the moment I felt his fingers against my clit, my back bowed and my head fell back against his shoulder. This was different from what we had done so far. It was slower. Lazier. More sensual.

Somewhere in the deep corner of my mind, I could feel everyone's eyes on me, but I didn't care. At this moment, all I cared about was chasing this pleasure. His finger brushed against my clit, spreading the wetness over it, and I had to swallow my moan.

"I'm going to ruin you, kroshka." His voice had gotten deeper and guttural. And that damn Russian accent was killing me. Slowly, in the most exquisite way. His finger slipped inside me and my pussy clenched greedily for more. He shifted his hand so his palm rubbed against my clit as he thrust his fingers in and out.

My hips lifted again. Fire burned in the pit of my stomach. I needed more, so much more, and I knew he was the only one to lift me to unimaginable heights.

My entire body clenched, my inner walls gripped his fingers, but it wasn't enough.

"Your pussy is mine," he grunted in my ear. Possessive and harsh, as his fingers thrust deep into me.

"Yes," I whimpered, mindlessly chasing the pleasure. With my right hand, I reached behind me and pulled on his neck, my soft body pressed against his hard one. His thumb circled my clit as he added another finger and thrust deep inside me, hitting my G-spot. "Ah, fuck," I moaned loudly.

Somewhere distant, I was aware of flesh slapping against flesh. Another set of moans and grunts. But all my senses were zeroed in on this man. My lips burned with the need to feel his mouth on mine. I would have given anything to have him kiss me, with lust shooting through my body. I was intoxicated with this need. For him.

He kept thrusting in and out. Hard and deep. I was close. So damn close.

"Such a tight pussy," he groaned. My hips rode his hand, hard and needy. Working myself up. My pulse drummed frantically in my chest. I could feel Alexei's gaze on me, his lips on my earlobe, whispering filthy things. "Show everyone what they can't have."

My exhale came out on a small sob as his fingers thrust, my insides shuddered and my ears buzzed. My legs on either side of his thighs, there was no mistaking what we were doing. I was on display for everyone to see. Yet, they couldn't see my pussy, because Alexei ensured my dress and his hand covered me from their view.

My orgasm danced at the bottom of my spine. Impending. My breaths came out ragged and hitched with each roll of my hips against his hand. His other free hand came up to my breasts and he pinched my nipple through my dress.

My one hand behind me, wrapped around his neck and my other clenching his thigh, I rode his fingers as pleasure coiled tighter and tighter around me. I was so damn close. Alexei bit into my earlobe, his fingers pinched my nipple, and I came harder than ever before. It felt like falling off the highest mountain.

Incoherent words slipped through my mouth mixed with moans as I rode wave after wave of the most beautiful pleasure. And then all I could muster up the energy for was to fall back against him as he held me.

His fingers slipped out of me and he brought them to my lips. Without prompting, I parted my lips and tasted myself on his fingers. He hummed his approval, and I swore my chest beamed like a hundred-watt bulb.

"My kroshka."

"I forgot to look up what that means," I breathed, because I didn't know what else to say, and I've been curious what it meant from the first time he called me that.

"My baby girl."

"Oh." Blush heated my cheeks and something giddy swirled in my chest. *His baby girl.* I wanted to dial up Sailor and Willow and scream, and tell them what just happened. Yes, my reason had left me and probably went back to New Orleans.

As my senses slowly returned, I realized everyone's eyes were on us. It was official. I had lost my mind. Embarrassment wound through me, but before it could fester, Alexei's voice whispered in my ear. "You are beautiful when you fall apart for me."

And just like that, any insecurities evaporated. Nobody else mattered, but him. Yes, my mind was gone. Quite possibly my heart too.

"What about you?" I murmured under my breath, risking a glance over my shoulder. A dark desire flickered across his expression and heat flared in his gaze. It sent burning lust through my bloodstream.

"Lovebirds, that was quite a performance," Igor's voice sounded behind me and I startled. Alexei's expression changed to his usual one that sent ice down your veins. Except, it no longer did for me. "You stole the spotlight."

Alexei said nothing, but I slowly turned my head to see Igor's eyes hungry on me.

"Sorry." I didn't know what else to say. The lines were getting blurry. This was my case to bring a child predator to justice, yet here I was in the middle of a sex performance, and I let a man finger me. Even worse, I liked it.

"Will we see you reciprocate?" Igor's question had my spine go rigid. "I forgot to mention… clothing is not optional during pleasure." Alexei's palm landed on my lower back, the touch comforting and warm. I sincerely hoped Alexei got to kill this little weasel.

My lips curved into a smile and I'd even dare to say it wasn't terribly forced. It could be because of the orgasm I just experienced. I turned my eyes to Alexei.

"Yes." Fuck, did I say *yes*? I must have surprised Alexei too because his eyes widened just the slightest before returning to their normal blank glare. "Of course, there is room only for two on this pedestal," I added breathlessly.

Someone please knock some sense back into my head. If something like this slipped to the reporters, undercover job or not, my father's career would burn to the ground. And Byron's chance at a political career would end before it even took off the ground.

Sweet Jesus.

"Of course, of course." Igor rubbed his hands together and I wanted to smack him. "Let me help you disrobe before I leave you two love-birds to it."

"No," both Alexei and I said at the same time. Except his *no* was more of a growl. "Only my hands on her," he warned, his voice scary as shit but I was glad for it.

Igor scurried away and I slowly stood up, my knees slightly wobbly. Alexei's arm wrapped around my waist as he stood up.

"Are you sure, kroshka?" His breath was hot in my ear, his mouth on the sensitive part of my neck. To anyone else, it looked like he was showering my neck with kisses.

"Yes," I breathed. I'd just focus on him.

I sensed his body tense and I pulled slightly away to look at him. Our gazes met and something dark lurked in his glacier-blue eyes.

Dark and cold. It wasn't aimed at me, I was certain, but if it was, I'd be scared.

He lowered his head again and pressed his mouth on the sensitive part of my neck, right below my ear.

"Don't turn your head away from me"—his mouth moved over my skin—"Ivan is on the balcony, on our right. This is our last test."

My heart tripped, then sped up at a dangerous speed. I had to fight the urge to glance that way, instead I focused on Alexei's mouth on my neck and his hands on me. The soft sound of the zipper filled the air and my dress slid down to my feet. Stepping out of it, cold air sent goose bumps through my body.

Chest to chest, he stood a whole head taller than me and I nervously chewed on my bottom lip. I was so out of my element here. Willow would know exactly what to do in my place. She'd confidently lower herself down onto her knees and get to work, looking like a damn goddess while at it. Yet all I managed to do was stand and stare.

I swallowed hard, while my heart hammered against my chest. Alexei came around me and his hands reached around my throat to take my ridiculously long pearl necklace off.

Before I could even ponder why, he rasped a command. "Your wrists."

My head whipped around to look at him over my shoulder. "Why?"

"It's the only way."

His explanation made no sense to me, but obediently, I put my hands behind me and he tied them together behind my back. With my pearls. Probably the best use for pearls I had ever seen, but disappointment tasted slightly bitter. He didn't want me to touch him.

He came around and sat himself down on the throne chair, his legs spread wide.

"Come closer, kroshka." God, his accent was thicker than I'd ever heard. There was erotic darkness lurking in his gaze, pulling me in.

I stepped between his legs, the two of us staring at each other, a clear command in his eyes.

Without delay, I kicked off my heels and slid down to kneel between his thighs.

THIRTY-ONE
ALEXEI

A urora kicked off her heels, then lowered onto her knees, wearing nothing but black panties and a matching lacy bra. Her dark eyes watched me with hunger, her lips slightly parted. It took all my restraint not to bend her over the throne and fuck her senseless.

"Why can't I touch you?" she whispered, disappointment coloring her voice and her expression sad.

I brushed my fingers across her cheek, her skin soft under my knuckles. It pained me, actually fucking pained me, that I couldn't give her everything she needed. But she'd never look at me the same again if I let her touch me. If she felt the scars. I'd rather have her hate than pity.

Kneeling between my thighs, she gave me an expectant look. I had to shove all my feelings aside and focus on now. Keep her safe. Get her out of this alive.

"No touching, kroshka."

A sad sigh left her and my chest squeezed, then she smiled.

"Then give me your cock," she murmured, rolling her eyes, and it made me want to spank her. Then rub her round ass and kiss it all better. Nobody had ever made me feel this way, and I suspected nobody ever would again.

My heart gave a dull thump, and something in my chest hurt, but I squashed it deep down.

I unzipped the fly of my pants and my cock sprang free, reaching for her. Her dark eyes hazed over, then she licked her lips. I was rock hard and pre-cum glistened at the top of my cock.

She leaned forward, her pearl-bound wrists behind her, and took my cock into her pretty mouth. My cock pulsed as she sucked me, her small moans vibrating through me. Every muscle in my body tensed, and I had to fight the urge to thrust deep into her throat. I wanted to let her explore, enjoy this as much as I was enjoying it.

Fuck, if I died this way, it would be a glorious way to die.

She laved my cock with her tongue like it was a fucking lollipop, making small breathy noises of approval. Just hearing those noises could make me spill, but I wasn't ready yet. Her eyes lifted to me, and the look on her face stole my breath away.

My hand fucking trembled as I smoothed her unruly strands off her face.

My hips thrust deeper down her throat. She blinked and I stilled. I didn't want to hurt her.

Though the little noise of protest she gave me, almost made me smile. I wanted her more than I've wanted anything else in my life. To be perfect for her. Yet, it was so glaringly obvious how fucking broken I was. I couldn't even allow her the touch that she needed. Or kiss.

And she was giving me so much.

I pushed slowly to my feet and my cock slid out of her lush mouth with a soft pop sound.

"What's the matter?" Her voice was husky, soft and breathless. Her cheeks flushed with her arousal.

I tapped her bottom lip gently with my thumb. "I need it harder." A soft gasp and desire in her eyes told me she was up for it. "If it gets too much, blink twice."

"It won't be too much." She sounded convinced.

I eased my cock into her waiting mouth, slowly pushing deeper until I was buried all the way down her throat. She moaned low, and it was so fucking erotic a shudder rippled through my entire body. Aurora's eyes watered, but she refused to blink, those eyes the color of chocolate pulling me in.

I started off slowly to allow her time to adjust to my size. She sucked and licked greedily, bobbing her head up and down snapping the thin thread of self-control I had remaining. The dark desire took over and her moans sent vibrations all the way up my spine.

My pace picked up, thrusting deeper and faster into her mouth. The audience held their breath, but I was so fucking lost in her, I couldn't distinguish between anyone. My breaths turned ragged. The only sounds were flesh slapping against flesh and her small moans. I was buried so deep into her throat, I half expected her to finally blink.

Her eyes fluttered shut and the irrational jealousy that she'd think about another man with her eyes closed slithered through my veins.

"Look at me while I fuck your mouth," I grunted.

Her beautiful dark eyes opened and the look in her eyes could almost make me believe she wanted this too. That she could love me. Her submission at this moment was complete. Pleasure built in my spine with each thrust, threatening to tear me apart.

Tears slid from the corners of her eyes, and I gently cupped her face, then wiped them away with my thumbs as I continued brutally thrusting into her.

Another moan of hers vibrated through me and I spilled into her mouth. She sucked me through my orgasm that burned like a wildfire. She was magnificent.

I watched my cum trickle down the corner of her lip. She darted her tongue to lick a drop of cum from the corner of her mouth. I swore I never saw anything so erotic.

This woman owned me, and she didn't even know it.

I pulled her up onto her feet and reached behind her to untie her wrists. She smelled like chocolate and sex, and I couldn't resist inhaling her scent deeply into my lungs. So she'd stay buried there, part of my oxygen.

"Kroshka." I rubbed her wrists, searching out her face to ensure she was okay. She looked so damn beautiful.

Horror entered her eyes, but before I reacted, I heard the long-dreaded voice.

"Alexei."

S *haring is caring.*

I recognized him the moment I saw him. I wanted to run. I wanted to scream. But I stayed frozen while my heart crashed against my chest, making it impossible to breathe.

Sharing is caring, little girl.

Hate slithered through my veins and nerves crackled beneath my skin.

"Ivan," Alexei said coldly as he took off his jacket and slipped it onto my shoulders. I quickly shoved my arms into the sleeves and buttoned it up, so it'd cover my chest. Alexei's unique scent enveloped me and it was like an injection of strength. The fact that most of my body was sheltered from Ivan's view by Alexei's jacket helped.

"So nice to see you," Ivan drawled, his eyes glancing at me. I hated his eyes on me. Dark and cruel. Evil and menacing. This man enjoyed inflicting pain—physical and mental. I'd stake my life on it.

My eyes traveled over his entourage. His large bodyguards and a woman who stood next to him. No, not a woman. A shell. Her eyes were empty. She was thin and frail. It felt like looking at a ghost. Her white hair was in a perfect chignon, the diamonds around her neck glittering. As if they tried to make up for the emptiness of its owner.

Yet, there was something off about it. Like she was hiding something. Though what could it possibly be? She had to be in her seventies, though I couldn't be sure.

"Can't say the same," Alexei deadpanned icily and my attention left the woman to return to Ivan.

I found Ivan's eyes already on me, leering at me, and a disgusted shiver ran down my spine. Though I claimed the MO to kidnapping matched my brother's, I never really believed I'd come face-to-face with him again.

"Miss Ashford." He knew my name.

So much for being undercover, I thought to myself wryly.

His eyes zeroed in on me. Taunting and cruel eyes. An even crueler smile. He looked just as disgusting as I remembered him. Terror clawed its way through me as his eyes roamed over my exposed body.

"Are you enjoying yourself, Miss Ashford?" Something about this didn't feel *right*. A warning raced up my spine and every single hair on me stood up. "You've grown into a beautiful woman."

My heartbeat whooshed through my ears. This man took my brother. Destroyed my family. Took so much from us. Enjoyment was the furthest thing on my mind.

"Where is my brother?" I spat out, anger boiling inside me.

His eyes darted to Alexei, whose one hand was wrapped around my waist and Ivan's smile twisted into something ugly. A warning tingle turned into a full-blown alarm. Suddenly, I wasn't so sure our plan was that great. I should have asked my brothers for help. Alexei and I alone were too vulnerable here. Ivan had too many men and Alexei was just one man. I could shoot but hand-to-hand combat wasn't my forté.

Ivan uttered something in Russian, his gaze locked on me. Alexei's expression turned to frost and a cold shiver erupted at the base of my spine. Dread settled in my stomach and internally I cursed myself for not knowing Russian.

"Nyet." Alexei's negative response in his cold voice was the only word I understood. *No.*

Ivan's laughter followed, and it was the first time I'd ever thought a laugh actually sounded evil. I instinctively shifted closer to Alexei.

"This will be fun." Ivan switched to English. "Just like the good old times. Da, Alexei?"

My heart went ice cold. This didn't bode well. Before I could inhale my next breath, all hell broke loose. While Alexei and I were focused on Ivan, his men circled us. A hand landed on my shoulder, but before I could shake it off, Alexei's inked fingers snatched the arm and broke it in one move.

Igor showed up behind Alexei with a knife, ready to stab him. Before he could do that, I launched at him and threw a hook to his cheekbone. Then immediately after, I landed a blow to his ribs and his blade flew through the air. Alexei caught it and lunged forward at the guard closest to Ivan. The blade pressed against the guard's throat, and in one swift move, his neck was fileted open.

"Stupid to come back, Alexei," Ivan laughed, taking two steps backwards. The woman stood there, motionless, her eyes locked on the sliced neck and blood gushing out of it. It was like she was in a trance.

While Ivan took a step back with two guards, two guards remained with the old woman who seemed mesmerized by the man gurgling in his own blood on the floor. If I had time to absorb it, I'd certainly be freaked out.

All the while Alexei was making his way from one man to another. And he wasn't just cracking their bones. Dead bodies were piling up.

He was magnificent.

So sue me for taking a moment to admire his handiwork. I went for the weakest amongst the men, ensuring I didn't get in Alexei's way.

Teamwork.

Alexei's movements were calm and precise. It was eerie how a man that size could move almost gracefully across the room, killing men along the way. My brothers would be impressed by Alexei's efficiency.

All three of them were ex-Special Forces, but I was certain Alexei's skill matched theirs. Might even supersede them.

Alexei attacked the next guard, while Igor tried to run away. I refused to let him. He deserved to die just as much as Ivan. So I tripped him and then twisted his right hand behind his back, the way Royce taught me it would hurt the shoulder most. Using all my strength, I pulled on it and heard his shoulder crack.

"Fucking bitch," Igor hissed as I twisted his arm further behind him.

Ignoring him, I kept an eye on Alexei. It was stupid, I know, but I didn't want anything happening to him. He kept trying to get the guards closer to us. I was guessing, but I thought he didn't want to leave too much space between us. The man just killed seven men and he hadn't even broken a sweat.

I noticed too late Ivan and his bodyguards approaching from the opposite side.

Jumping up onto my feet, and leaving Igor with his broken shoulder on the floor where he belonged, I took a fighting stance. Mentally I took note to thank my brothers for teaching me all these tricks.

"Let's see how you fight now, you dumb bitch," Igor taunted from his spot on the floor, though his voice sounded whimpery. He should really learn when to keep his mouth shut.

Ivan's bodyguard came at me. Going with the momentum, I launched a hook right to his eye, just the way my brothers had taught me, and I watched his face plant the floor.

"Who's the bitch now?" I gloated, but it was short-lived as I felt the cold, metal barrel of the gun pressed against my skull and I instantly stilled. Ivan had gotten to me.

"Blyat," Alexei growled, immediately stopping his movements.

"Fuck," I cursed at the same time.

Alexei's body stiffened and his eyes filled with cold fury at the man next to me. He took a step toward me, and Ivan's fingers gripped my jaw so hard, I was certain I'd have bruises on my face. Assuming we got out of this alive. He shoved the gun into my mouth and my eyes widened with fear.

"One more step, Alexei, and I blow her brains out," Ivan warned, his voice eerily low.

He instantly stilled, his eyes on me. Now both Alexei and I had guns pointed at us. The guests to this shitshow were glued to their spots, some of them seated comfortably in their seats. The only thing they were missing was popcorn. This was such a stupid plan.

And what kind of people were they not to come to our rescue. Bastards. Just as I thought, Igor probably picked out the worst kind of criminal minds to come join him in his orgy party.

Though it got us close to Ivan who took three steps over to me, grinning darkly.

"I'm going to have so much fun with you," he purred into my ear, licking my earlobe. "I'll fuck all your holes, just like I had done to your brother."

I flinched at his words, and suddenly, I wasn't sure whether I should hope to find Kingston alive or dead.

My lungs squeezed tight, flashes of the young Kingston I remembered played inside my mind.

Him chasing me around our pool or up and down our grand staircase. His laughter. His dark brown eyes. The bedtime stories he'd read to me. Or how he'd eat my broccoli because it made me gag, but our cook insisted I had to eat it.

Each memory stung, ripping my chest open and slicing into fresh wounds. Lashes from a whip must hurt less than this. But I wouldn't let myself cry.

Instead, I let hate swallow me. I let anger fester inside me and boil over. It flooded through me like hot lava.

I met Ivan's ugly stare head-on and curled my lips into an ugly smile.

Waiting. Waiting. Just another inch. Copper pooled in my mouth as I bit inside my cheek. *Another inch.*

And then my head swung forward with a swish as I headbutted him.

"Fucking Italian bitch," Ivan spat out, holding his nose. "You didn't get the fight from your father. So it has to be that filthy DiLustro Kingpin blood."

The woman who came with Ivan stared at me, the void of her stare no longer empty. But there was something unhinged in her eyes, sending alarm through me. She took a step forward, and I backed away a step.

Her eyes almost scared me more than Ivan's. Anxiety swarmed every fiber of me, making it hard to breathe.

Her hand shot out and she slapped me across the face with such force that it sent my head swinging to the side. Alexei growled, fighting against the four men who constrained him.

I gritted my teeth, my cheek stinging from the burn, but I never removed my eyes from her.

"Take them to the dungeons." Her voice was low and soft. Yet, it was one of the creepiest sounds I have ever heard.

The next second Alexei and I were dragged out of the room, then down more stairs. With each step we took, we were further and further away from luxury. This side of the castle was empty, damp, and dark.

Fuck!

THIRTY-THREE
AURORA

"Well, these accommodations suck," I muttered. "Downgrade for sure."

My eyes roamed over the little room, stone walls, and one twin bed. No bathroom. It wasn't exactly a cell, but it wasn't a room either. I paced back and forth, trying to come up with some ideas. I was still in my panties and bra, wearing Alexei's suit jacket and barefoot. Not an ideal scenario. Even if we somehow got out of here, I couldn't run barefoot.

Though I'm all set for swimming, I thought wryly.

I forced myself to think about anything and everything, just not the fact that the man who had taken my brother twenty years ago was here. In this building. And he was Ivan Petrov.

Sharing is caring.

Cold fear was enough to paralyze me, but I kept moving. One step. Two steps. Breathe in. Breathe out.

I glanced at Alexei. He didn't seem worried. Though he seemed slightly pale. I assumed it was an adrenaline rush or something. I kept pacing.

I *have to keep moving*, I kept telling myself, though I knew there was no escaping this cell.

"Do you know that woman?" I asked him, just as I made another U-turn.

Alexei shook his head. "Nyet."

"I think she's fucking crazy," I muttered.

"Da." Another U-turn. I cracked my neck, heavy tension tightening my muscles.

My eyes sought him out as I made another U-turn in our little prison cell, and to my surprise, Alexei pulled out a knife. Out of his left sock.

"What are you doing?" I asked in a whisper. My steps stopped and I glanced over my shoulder at the heavy wooden door, then back at him.

"Sending our location." His explanation didn't make any sense to me, but he didn't pause. He twisted his left forearm. Then he stabbed the point of his knife into the back of his forearm.

"Whoa," I exclaimed under my breath and rushed to him. Blood trickled down his skin and I desperately searched for something to put on his wound. "Are you nuts?"

He didn't even flinch, the point of his knife digging further. I had to fight the urge to gag, seeing his flesh twishing.

"Alexei, stop it," I hissed, sitting down on the dingy little bed beside him. "You are going to hurt yourself."

Ignoring me, he continued wedging the knife into his muscle and then stilled. Before I could sigh in relief, he shoved the knife deeper and a beep sounded. I stared at his arm, almost anticipating for something to jump out of it.

Then like it was nothing, he pulled the knife out of his forearm, wiped it against his pants.

I furrowed my brows. I wasn't one to cringe from blood, but for some reason, seeing Alexei hurt and bleeding didn't sit well with me. I reached inside the suit jacket and ripped through the layered piece of inner material.

"Give me your arm." Without waiting for him, I reached for it and lifted it, then wrapped the cloth around his wound to stop the bleeding.

"So what now? Somehow, I think you left out part of our plan. You told me all about the orgies but not a word about this."

The corner of his lips tugged up. It was disturbing that he didn't even flinch when he stabbed himself in his arm. What had he gone through to be able to do that without any emotion to flicker across his expression?

I eyed my handiwork. It would have to do for now. I just hoped it wouldn't get infected.

"I'm still waiting for an explanation," I reminded him, pushing my shoulder against his.

"My brothers will get this location and come."

"How long will it take them?"

"Not too long; they are already in Russia." He must have seen surprise on my face. "We knew Ivan was here, just not the exact location."

"Oh." Alexei nor his brother ever explained why they were after Ivan. "Ivan mentioned good old times." Tick. Tock. Tick. Tock. "What did he mean?"

Silence stretched and I held my breath for an explanation. I didn't want to miss a single word he'd utter. It felt important, the connection and why they were after Ivan. But he remained quiet. Disappointment tasted bitter. Something in my chest tightened and a hollow ache spread.

I thought we agreed to be open with each other. Yet, I knew he withheld information. I knew they had history together. How couldn't they when Alexei seemed so hell-bent on finding Ivan. But good old times?

An edgy sensation beneath my skin made it hard to sit still, so I moved to release the irritable energy. Jumping to my feet, I paced back and forth. It was ridiculous that I was hurt by Alexei not trusting me enough to tell me what the fuck was going on. I had gone to a damn sex club with him. Had sex with him... multiple times. Got drugged by him. Got fingered by him in front of a room full of people. For heaven's sake, I got on my knees for him and let him fuck my throat.

And he couldn't even fucking tell me his history with Ivan. The very man who took my brother. Kingston. Oh my God, I had to find out where Kingston was. I needed to know what happened to him.

My steps paused again as a thought slammed into me.

"Alexei?"

"Da."

"If you think I'll use whatever you tell me for the FBI case, I promise I won't," I started softly, "Whatever happens in Russia, stays in Russia," I joked, my voice not quite portraying any humor.

I offered him a feeble smile, hoping he'd see sincerity in my eyes. I meant those words. I wouldn't use his confidence against him. Ever! Somehow, over the last few days, things have shifted and he has become important.

That arctic gaze watched me, longing and sadness in them. *Broken eyes*, my memory whispered. I wanted to hug him, make him better.

Tick. Tock. Tick. Tock. I waited. *Nothing.*

I resumed my pacing. Breathe in. Breathe out. One step. Two steps.

I focused on the small space and each step. Dirt ground. Stone walls. No window. It took ten steps to cross the room. One camera. I took a deep breath, turned around and continued pacing, avoiding the need to look Alexei's way.

After thirty minutes, or was it an hour, I could see the path on the dirt floor from all my pacing. At this rate, I'd put a dent in it by tomorrow. Alexei said his brothers were already in Russia. They could be here very soon. I had to find a way to get information from Ivan about my brother. I couldn't walk away from this place without discovering what happened to him.

My eyes darted to Alexei, still seated on the shabby, springy twin bed. My step faltered and I gave him a double take.

He didn't look well. I studied his face. He looked shaken up. It was the first time I'd seen a flicker of strong emotion on his face. A hint of perspiration glistened on his forehead, something unhinged in his eyes. I would have missed it if I wasn't watching him so carefully.

The man's face fascinated me. Much to my dismay. It would seem I wanted him despite my current disappointment and anger.

A faint trace of perspiration trickled down his face. And something clutched in my chest. Maybe it was my nerves, or possibly worry for him.

No, no. It was just a concern for our situation. If he was worried, maybe we are in deeper shit than I thought.

I kept telling myself we'd get out of this shit, complete the assignment, and I'd be on my way. Right after I obtained information on my brother. Deep down I knew he couldn't be alive.

If he was, he would have found a way home. To us. Dad wasn't much of one, but my brothers and I were always close. All of us cared about each other and always had each other's back.

I had to focus on that. Find information on my brother. Close the case. Move on and forget Alexei. I didn't need to make my life complicated with any suspicious connections with members of the mafia. And the Nikolaev men... well, they were fucking mafia. And clearly, Alexei didn't trust me enough to share certain things with me.

Yes, I just needed them to get us the fuck out of here so we could...

A strangled, labored breath returned my attention to Alexei. Jesus, he looked worse.

"A-Alexei, are you alright?"

Those cold, pale blue eyes had a way of sending Arctic-cold temperatures right down to my soul when he looked at me. Yet, right now, there was something vulnerable in them. The stoic, arctic expression was gone and in its place was a man. A man I was sure felt something. Fear or panic, I couldn't tell.

Tentatively, I took a step towards him. Then another.

"Hey," I rasped, unsure what to say.

He didn't move, didn't speak. It was nothing new. Yet, his eyes were screaming with something. Something horrific.

Taking another step, I slowly raised my hand to his face. Any moment, I expected him to smack it away, grab my wrist, and tell me off. Yet, nothing came. As if I was watching through an hourglass, my movements seemed exaggeratingly slowed, each breath delayed, our eyes locked.

My palm connected to his clammy cheek. *He **is** perspiring*, I realized in shock.

In all the weeks I had known him, I had not seen emotions flicker across his beautiful face. Yet now, it was as if shadows danced in his pale blue eyes, haunting him. It was the most unsettling feeling, and for the first time in a very long time, fear clutched at my chest.

A fear for him. Just like I feared for my brother twenty years ago.

I swallowed and lowered so we could be eye to eye. I didn't like to see these haunting ghosts lurk in his broken eyes.

Alexei was usually maddening with his silence. His stoic face could drive a saint insane. And I was no saint. Yet, right now... I'd rather have all of that back, rather than see him suffer.

"Focus on my breathing," I whispered. I inhaled deeply and slowly exhaled. Then I did it again. And again. Just like he did it with me in the club. Except it wasn't working.

I frantically searched my mind through any and all information I knew about this man. What could have possibly triggered this?

Alexei's breathing became erratic, causing a storm in my own chest.

Fuck it!

I straddled his lap, taking his face between my hands. I leaned closer, keeping our faces only inches apart. But I was careful not to bring us too close. I wasn't about to violate his rule of no kissing.

"Hey, hey," I muttered softly. "I know, this place sucks. One-star accommodations," I joked softly. "And this is probably like the worst time to say this. But I think you are hot. Like super insanely hot." Something flickered in his eyes. Surprise, maybe? I wasn't sure, but it was better than those ghosts, so I continued. "To tell you the truth, it is unnerving. You stare through me like I'm a piece of glass, and I get all hot and bothered."

I eyed him for any signs. He was focused on me, but his breathing was still erratic. I eyed his lips. There was nothing more I wanted to do than to lean closer to him and close our distance by brushing my lips across his.

He didn't move, but his breathing eased ever so slightly. Good progress!

"You know, you are not even my type," I continued in a soft voice.

"Every man I dated or hooked up with." I rolled my eyes. "Don't you dare tell my brothers this. They are convinced I'm still a virgin. I'm pretty sure they think I'll die a virgin." I kept rumbling in a soft voice, my eyes keen on him. I didn't want to distress him and talking seemed to help. "Anyhow, back to the main point. Every man I have dated was more of an Orlando Bloom type of guy. Not in *Lord of the Rings*. Good God, that was way too blond for me. Dark hair, dark eyes was my usual go-to. Maybe I wanted them to be boring like me with my dark hair." I lightly brushed my fingers across his incredibly blond strands. He and his brothers were the only specimens on this planet that I had ever seen with such pale-colored eyes and blond hair.

He remained still, unmoving but almost as if he was hanging on to my every word.

"I like your hair though," I murmured. "Your eyes too. And those tattoos." I brushed my thumb over the one on his right cheek. The skin felt rough there. Was all his ink hiding scars? I lightly brushed my left hand over his cheek and found the inked skin under the left eyes rough and scabbed too.

Scars, I realized with a punch to my gut. He was hiding his scars.

Anger that rushed through my veins at the thoughts of someone hurting this strong man was sudden and violent. I was unprepared for it. It was the kind of anger that made you act rash and commit murder without any evidence of guilt. I wanted to be a judge and jury.

I opened my mouth to ask him about it but stopped myself. This was neither time nor place. He was having an episode, and I'd be damned if I'd add to his pain.

This is about him, I reminded myself.

"Those tattoos are pretty badass, you know." I leaned over and pressed a kiss over his tattoo under his left eye. The skin felt even rougher under the sensitive skin of my lips. "Come to think of it, I never dated a guy with a single tattoo."

I wasn't sure why my voice choked and my heart thundered. I was just trying to distract him from his panic, yet my heart raced like my life depended on it.

My mouth skimmed down his face and stopped at the corner of his mouth. Suddenly, I wanted to kiss him like my life depended on it. But I knew I couldn't do that. He set that rule back in that sex club. *No kissing.*

He didn't even like face-to-face fucking. It would be taking advantage of his vulnerable state to kiss him the way I wanted to. I went to pull away when his hand squeezed my hip, his fingers digging into my flesh almost painfully.

"Talk." His voice was hoarse. Maybe even slightly shaky.

"So bossy," I murmured softly. "Okay, then." I locked eyes with him. "Let's see. I have four brothers, Byron, Winston, Royce, and Kingston. Born in that order. I was the last one. I love them all very much, though they drive me crazy, but I can't live without them. It was the reason I picked a college at home. Kingston, he—" My heart gave a pang, just like it always did when I talked about my brother. I was used to it by now. Years of constant pain and guilt over it, but I couldn't shake it off. I didn't want to shake it off. Not until I found out what happened to my brother. "When I was five, right after Thanksgiving, I decided I wanted a hippopotamus for Christmas. We lived in D.C. at that time." Shit, why did it still hurt? "My brothers said I couldn't have a hippopotamus for Christmas, but we could go to the zoo so I could see one."

I brushed my fingers through Alexei's hair. "Kingston's hair was so dark. He, Royce, and I look most alike. Byron and Winston are probably better looking."

"You're the best-looking one," he rasped, a sweat drop rolling down his temple.

I smiled. "It might be the first compliment I have gotten from you outside the crazy exhibitionist sex we've had," I teased, though foolishly my chest fluttered with feelings.

"Finish the story."

I blinked but then remembered I was telling him about the zoo. I bit my lip, the memories in my mind like whips slicing the old wounds wide open. "Nanny took me, and Kingston came along." I inhaled deeply, then exhaled. "Byron was always protective of all of us, but Kingston was the one who always took my side. Even when I was being a brat. He was five years older than me, so he was the closest to me in age." I swallowed hard, knowing what's coming and the words felt like rust in my mouth. "Sometimes I wonder if maybe he overheard something, because he was adamant I didn't leave his side. So I promised. Even pinky promised that I wouldn't run around. But I was so excited." My fingers trembled as I continued running my fingers through his hair. Stroking his strands soothed me. "I couldn't sit still back then. And I just couldn't wait to see the damn hippopotamus. So while Nanny and Kingston were distracted, I snuck to the exhibit."

The burn in my throat choked as I thought about the next words. The pain in my chest squeezed, making it difficult to breathe. But I continued my story.

"It was just a few minutes, five or ten at most. And it changed everything. Kingston came looking for me and a guy snatched him. I escaped; Kingston didn't. My father—" My lungs closed up, I couldn't breathe, but I pushed through it. This man needed this. Maybe I did too. "I learned later that my father made deals with criminals and often brought trouble to our door. It made me despise him. But I despised myself more because if I had listened… if I'd only listened, we'd have all gone home together."

My face felt wet and I tasted salt on my tongue, but I ignored it all. My throat burned, but I ignored that too.

A heavy sigh slipped through my lips, pushing some oxygen through.

"You know, there were so many nights since then that I lay awake at night wishing I could turn back time. I would have listened. I swore I would but wishes are for naught."

Alexei's right hand came to my cheek and his thumb brushed the corner of my eye.

Tears rolled down my cheeks.

THIRTY-FOUR
ALEXEI

T he old ghosts and anguish slammed into me like a freight train. No window. Not a single damn one. I lived for almost a decade like that and couldn't handle a single day in a cold, dark basement without windows. Unless I was in charge and torturing someone. But even then, I preferred to have a window.

Irrational. Yes. Fixable. No.

I had been away from Ivan for two decades and the same old ghosts still plagued me. And she comforted me. Of all the people in the world, it was her that comforted me. *Me*, who cost her the cherished brother.

I had to tell her. Should tell her. The loss would be imminent, but I wasn't ready for it. I'd never be ready for it.

I opened my mouth to admit my sins when a loud explosion blasted, and instinctively I wrapped my arms around her and turned us over so my body sheltered hers. The next second the door blasted open.

"Seriously?" Sasha's voice was the last thing I wanted to hear. "You two are going at it like rabbits and we are saving your asses."

Aurora stiffened underneath me, her eyes flared with fire. "Your brother is a jackass."

"Agreed."

I swiftly got to my feet and pulled her up. "Jesus, she's in her bra and panties."

"Stop looking," I growled.

"Yeah, peeper," she snapped at him. "Stop looking. We got shoved in here right after—" She cut herself off and her cheeks flushed deep red. "Just stop talking, jackass."

Sasha grinned. "Fat chance. Now get moving, naked ass," he taunted, throwing me a gun.

"Hey," she objected. "I can shoot too. Give me one." He eyed her suspiciously. "I can," she hissed. "Now give me a gun, or I'll kill you and take yours."

Sasha grinned, clearly loving her challenge. She'd never be able to overpower him or beat him. I'd know, Sasha and I sparred often. We always ended in a tie and both of us were bruised up.

"Give her a weapon," I ordered my brother.

Another blast sounded off and Sasha grunted. "Damn Vasili is intent on leveling this place to the ground along with Ivan and all his men."

Aurora reached her right hand out and tapped her foot impatiently. She may have been barefoot, but she totally pulled off the boss vibe. Just five minutes ago, she was helping me through a goddamn embarrassing panic attack and now she was glaring at my hot-tempered brother.

For two heartbeats he just watched her before caving in. I knew he would. He pulled a gun out of the back of his pants and handed it to her.

"Ever killed a person?" he asked her as she checked the magazine to ensure it was fully loaded.

"I'm about to kill you unless you stop talking," she snapped back. "Now, let's go. Unless you want Alexei and me to lock you in this room."

He chuckled. "No, thank you. I wouldn't touch that bed with gloves given what you and Alexei were doing on it."

She rolled her eyes and I had enough of my brother. "Get going, or I'll shoot you myself, Sasha."

Aurora gave him a sweet smile, while her eyes shone mischievously. She liked taunting him.

He turned around without another word and flipped the bird over his shoulder. Aurora glanced at me with amusement. Leave it to this woman to find humor in our situation. Every so often we'd run into Ivan's men. Sasha and I took turns eliminating them. I had never been so goddamn happy to leave a basement.

It didn't take us long and we found Vasili. He'd cornered Ivan in his office. Dead bodies lay around, blood splattered everywhere. Aurora's gasp was the only sound that shattered the deadly silence.

Vasili glanced our way. This was the ruthless Nikolaev man everyone feared. You fucked with his family and he burned down everything you owned. Ivan had a bald patch on the left side of his head, the skin on his scalp blotchy and red. For the first time in all the years I'd known him, I saw fear in his eyes. A true terror.

It was about time he learned how it felt.

"There you are, Alexei." Vasili's grin was terrifying, but I fucking loved it. "I saved him for you."

In two large strides, I was in Ivan's face. Before he could say another word, my fist connected with his jaw, the bone crunching under my fist the best kind of music I had ever heard. The next second I pulled out my gun and shot him in his right foot.

His loud wail was enough to wake the dead. I hoped it woke up all the boys and women he killed. And when he was dead, I hoped there was such a thing as an afterlife so he could experience torture for all eternity.

"The woman from earlier," I asked. I gave a word to Bianca Morrelli. "Who was she?"

He must have been thrown off by the question because he answered without thinking. "My wife."

"What's her name?"

"What does that—"

I shot the same foot, the exact same spot again and he screamed in pain. I wasn't called the best shot for nothing.

"Sofia Catalano." Fuck, it *was* Bianca Morrelli's great-aunt.

"Where is she?" I gritted. There was nothing more I wanted than to shoot him dead. Fear pricked in the back of my mind. Terrifying and cold. It'd cost me everything.

"She took a chopper out," Ivan whined. Aurora was right; something wasn't right with that woman and Ivan's next words confirmed it. "She'll come for you all. Morrellis, Kings, Nikolaevs. Even those filthy Kingpins. You better watch out." He grinned, his mouth bloody.

I raised the gun and pointed it to his temple, my finger on the trigger. I didn't pull it fast enough. I should have killed him the moment we set foot into this room, knowing what was at risk.

"Wait." Aurora stepped forward to stand right beside me, on my left. She slipped her hand into mine, her gun in her left hand. She was left-handed. This might end up being my funeral, as much as Ivan's. "I have a question."

I should have pulled the trigger. Yet, I couldn't do that to her. I fucking loved her, and if it brought her peace, then so be it. I didn't need any more years to live, as long as she was happy.

"Kroshka." I tilted my head in agreement.

She inhaled deeply, then slowly exhaled. Her eyes locked on Ivan, the anxiety and fear rolling off her in waves.

Ivan could smell fear from miles away. He smiled a gruesome grin, blood coloring his lips.

"Ask away, Miss Ashford."

I was certain she didn't realize how hard she was squeezing my hand. So fucking symbolic that it was the same hand she took care of earlier.

"Where is Kingston?" Her voice shook and a visible shudder passed her shoulders. "Where is my brother, you bastard?"

I didn't need to glance at my brothers to see shock enter their expressions. They didn't know about him. Everything with Kingston happened before we knew I was a Nikolaev too.

Ivan's gruesome smile told me he'd tell her Kingston was dead. Fucking sick bastard! He didn't know shit. Nothing about human decency and nothing about loyalty. Just his sick and twisted games. His eyes fleeted my way, then returned to her with a malicious gleam in them.

"He squealed like a girl," he taunted and Aurora's spine went rigid. "Cried for you and his brothers. Even his backstabbing daddy."

She swallowed a gulp, while her body and my world shook, ready to tear us apart before we had even gotten started.

"You l-lie," she stuttered in a whisper.

"Do I?" he taunted her. The bomb would explode at any second. Tick. Tock. Tick. Tock. "Ask Alexei. He came back for him and found him dead." *Boom.* Aurora stiffened. "Didn't you, boy? Alexei came back for your brother and found him whipped to death. Best part, it was Igor who did it."

Ivan's maniacal laughter filled the room, and Aurora's head whipped my way, horror in her eyes hitting me right in the heart. It hurt worse than a bullet to my chest. As if the two of us were in our own bubble, the entire world faded into the background. I could hear Ivan's taunting laugh, Vasili telling him to shut up.

"Don't you remember, girl?" Ivan continued, gleefully and enjoying her pain as if he fed on it. He was the worst kind of leech. "It was Alexei who led us to you."

She shook her head. "Broken eyes," she whispered. "No, no, no."

I didn't know what she meant by it, but the clawing in my chest intensified. It made it hard to breathe. Yet, I kept myself still, unable to peel my eyes away from her. I'd need her to carry me through whatever time I had left on this earth and for the afterlife. Maybe there I'd find peace. Though it was highly unlikely considering what I'd done.

"No, no, no," she rasped again, but recognition was there. Dots were connected.

Slowly shock and horror in her eyes turned into disgust and loathing. Pure hate. She jerked her hand out of mine, then wiped it clean against the jacket.

Then as if she realized whose jacket it was, a scream tore from her lips, and it hurt me worse than any whippings I had ever gotten. It was worse than any torture I had ever endured.

She screamed in rage and pain, and I worried she'd lose her beautiful voice, though I knew she'd never let me hear her words again. She'd never let me touch her again. Even if she'd let me live through it.

"Fuuuuck," she shrieked, tears rolling down her face. I couldn't look away, memorizing every line of her, so I could store it away for the darkness that quickly approached me. Maybe God would give me this one reprieve and let me take memories of her with me.

"You fucking bastard," she screamed, tears falling from her eyes.

She raised her weapon and put three bullets into Ivan. Her aim was deadly and spot on. Then she shifted and pointed the gun at me. Instantly, Vasili and Sasha had their guns pointed at her.

"Don't shoot," I warned them. "You hurt her, and I'll kill you."

My brothers' expressions would have been comical if my heart wasn't shredding into pieces.

"You are fucking crazy if you think I'll let her shoot you," Vasili growled. "Put the goddamn gun down, woman."

Aurora didn't even spare him a glance. "All this fucking time," she accused. "You knew!"

I remained deathly still while my insides broke.

"Say it!" she screamed and I feared her throat would hurt from the force of her yell. "Fucking say it!"

"I knew." My chest hurt so fucking bad. It felt like a bullet already lodged itself into my heart and it would remain there forever. But I made a promise. A promise I had to keep. It was my debt to pay.

"Y-you broke us," she whimpered, her face wet with tears. Her eyes shimmered like black diamonds and her chest heaved up and down. "I—I told you and you said nothing." I'd do anything for her. If killing me would make her feel better, I was ready to die. "Why? What did we do to you?"

There was no justification that would work here. No words that would ever make sense.

"You didn't do anything to me," I said, my throat squeezing painfully. I wanted to tell her she saved me. She didn't know it but she saved me.

"I'm going to kill you." Her words were calm. Final.

"Fuck you will," Sasha growled, taking a threatening step towards her.

"Stay away from her," I warned my brother in a cold tone. If I had to, I'd fight both of them to keep her safe. I returned my gaze to the woman, memorizing her features. Maybe I could find her in my next life. "Do what you need to, kroshka. It's okay. Nobody will hurt you."

She whimpered, and her eyes pooled with more tears. But instead of holding her finger firmly on the trigger, she lowered the gun, holding it by her side. She looked defeated. Tired.

"You said nothing," she choked, her chest heaving and her face wet. "All that time and you said nothing."

Her accusation. My betrayal. Our future we could have had. It all swirled in this room, like a whirlwind with no way out. She couldn't pull the trigger and set it all free.

Her not killing me was worse. Because now, I'd have to live the rest of my life knowing what she tasted like, what she felt like, knowing I would never have her.

Her body hit the ground and I took a step towards her. "Don't you dare come close," she warned, her voice barely above a whisper, just as heaving sobs wracked through her. Her arms wrapped around her stomach and she rocked herself. Back and forth.

"You killed him, Alexei," she accused, sobbing. "You killed us both that day," she cried softly. "And all this time... you said nothing."

She wiped her face with the back of her hand, her gun still in her left hand. Another sob tore from her lips. Her eyes looked up, the shattering pain in them gutting me alive.

The door swung open and her brother burst through with two men at his back. They had to be her other brothers. One looked like a younger version of Byron and the other held resemblance to Kingston and Aurora.

The Ashford brothers weren't who I expected to find here.

"What the fuck is going on here?" Byron bellowed, his eyes roaming over the dead bodies in the room, then over Vasili, Sasha, and me and ending on his sister. When he saw her face, tears streaming down her face and the state of her wardrobe, he pointed the gun at my brothers and his brothers followed suit.

"Who hurt my sister?" he growled, pissed off. "Who?"

"You touch an Ashford, you die." It had to be Royce who spoke those words. "Have you touched her, you filthy scum?"

"Let's just kill them and ask questions later," Winston added, his eyes hard.

"Yeah, you'd like to try," Sasha sneered. Of course, it was always Sasha. "You'll be dead before you—"

A bullet flew through the air and Sasha dodged it at the last second. The Ashford brothers weren't fucking around.

"You fucking moron," Sasha growled as Vasili grabbed him by his neck and pushed him behind him.

"Stop, Sasha," Vasili and I warned.

"Byron, Winston, Royce. It wasn't them!" Aurora jumped up, pleading in her voice. Her face was pale and her lower lip trembled. "P-please, listen." Her words had my brothers eye her warily, but it got her brothers' attention from us to their sister. "It wasn't them," she breathed weakly.

Her voice was weak, and it was gutting me on the inside to see her defeated like this. "It was him."

She pointed the gun to Ivan's dead body. Byron stiffened. "I know him."

This had Aurora's head whip to her brother. "How?"

"From a while back." He furrowed his brows as if he was trying to locate the memory. "That's right. It was some kind of piece of land or something he wanted. It was a long time ago. Father and he had a falling out because Father refused to sell it to him. Instead, he had it sold to Nico Morrelli."

Aurora's lips thinned. She threw the gun onto the ground and it slid to my feet. Our eyes locked and something flickered in her dark gaze.

"I see you and your brothers again, I'll have you arrested."

Sasha snickered and it made me want to smack him upside his head. But that would require some effort, and right now, I didn't want to miss out on the last glimpse of the woman who stole my heart. Just fucking robbed it straight out of my chest, without even trying.

"Let's get out of this clusterfuck," Royce grumbled. "I fucking hate Russia. And Russians, but mostly Russia."

"You're just mad Byron wouldn't let you bring along pussy on the plane," Winston retorted dryly. "Your playboy ass needs rehab."

Well, at least her brothers were no different from us.

"We're taking you home, Rora." Her brother wrapped his arm around her shoulders and steered her towards the door.

"We got you, sis. And unlike the damn Russians, we have clean clothes so you can get rid of the shit you're wearing." God, they fucking sounded like Sasha.

Her brothers were right behind their two siblings. Glancing over his shoulder, Byron narrowed his eyes on us. "Don't even think about pinning this mess on her." He looked pissed off. "And stay the fuck away from my sister. You don't want me as your enemy."

Vasili didn't even flinch, but he wanted to pounce on him. The only reason he didn't was for me. We didn't need the Ashfords on our bad side. They'd be worthy and unnecessary opponents. All three of them could cause problems we didn't need.

"Our men will clean this up," I told him coldly. "There will be nothing left to find here."

Without another word, the two disappeared out of our sight, though it took only four heartbeats for Aurora's heart-wrenching, strangled sobs to echo through and travel down the hallway.

THIRTY-FIVE
AURORA

My knees pressed against my chest, I sat on my window seat and stared out, not seeing anything. It had been four weeks since we came back from Russia. Four whole goddamn weeks, and I had no idea how I functioned. But I did, though I felt like an empty shell.

Evidence of Ivan's death was delivered to the FBI. The first days were crazy busy. An abundance of evidence of the kidnappings over the last thirty years. Locations of boys who survived and who didn't. Kingston's name wasn't on either list. Days and nights of combing through all the paperwork. Sofia Catalano's name was part of that paperwork, although nobody seemed concerned with the woman. I was.

I was emotionally and physically drained. But it was better than this silence. Nothing to do but think about every single detail, while I wore the jacket that smelled like Alexei. I must have lost my mind.

The scent that lingered on it soothed me.

So fucking stupid, but it soothed me and tortured me at the same time.

I should move on to the next big case. This one was solved. The bureau recognized me for work well done, then gave me a sabbatical.

A mandatory one. An indefinite one. Apparently, the demand came from higher-ups, and I suspected it was one of my brothers. Or all three of them.

McGovan got his promotion. Everyone screamed how the world was a better place now. Yet for me, it was messier than ever.

Just as I predicted, my three brothers went on high alert when they couldn't get in touch with me. They literally waited an hour before coming after me. I was impressed they waited that long. Using all the resources at their disposal and the security company they ran, they followed the trail that led them to me. It never occurred to them that I went undercover and of course McGovan didn't enlighten them.

Byron insisted on staying around, refusing to leave me. Four weeks with Byron would drive anyone to drink. He fussed over me like a baby.

My other brothers called every damn day. I hadn't shared with any of them what I had learned. They moved on from Kingston; I didn't. So there was no sense in opening old wounds for them. I didn't want them to relive those dark times.

My phone rang. I reached for it on the little side table and answered, never moving from my spot. The view wasn't anything spectacular, but it was better than images in my mind. Of my brother's tortured body. His screams. His cries. In my mind, he was still a little boy who needed help.

"Hello. Hello?" Royce's voice shouted through the headset that I held. Fuck, I forgot I answered it.

"Hello, Royce." God, I was tired. Yet, sleeping was even more tortuous these days. My mind wandered wherever it wanted in my dreams. To Alexei, his hands on me, his scars and pale blue eyes. To Kingston and the fear I imagined he felt.

"You there?" Royce's voice pulled me back.

"What do you want, Royce?" I asked tiredly.

"Is this a way to answer your favorite brother?" he teased.

My lips curved into a soft smile. "Nice try, but you're all my favorite brothers."

"But just between us," he whispered. "I'm your favorite. Right?"

I lowered my voice. "Just between us," I started, then paused for dramatic effect, "you're all my favorite brothers."

He chuckled and I heard Winston's deep laugh behind him. "She got your sorry ass, Royce."

"You two are the worst," I muttered.

"But you almost admitted I'm your favorite brother," Royce replied.

I shook my head. "No, I didn't. What do you want?" His heavy sigh came through the headset and regret immediately plagued me at being rude. They were just worried and all I did was give him a hard time. "I'm sorry," I added quickly. "I'm just tired."

"Are you staying in New Orleans?" He knew I was on a mandatory sabbatical. When you had a lot of siblings, keeping secrets was hard. The truth was that there was no sense in staying here. I had no friends here. And the predator that was hunting children was dead. I wasn't even sure if I wanted to continue working for the bureau.

"I don't know." Going back to D.C. made the most sense. Sailor and Willow along with little Gabriel were there. It'd keep me distracted from all this. Yet, leaving New Orleans felt like cutting the last thread that connected me to... I guess it was Alexei. Or maybe it was to Kingston. I didn't know. That hope that I'd find my brother was extinguished, but I wasn't ready to move on.

He took a deep breath, then exhaled. "Father is having a political dinner." I stiffened, knowing what was coming. He'd ask me to come. It always looked better when family was around you during those political dinners. I didn't want to go. He hadn't called me once during the last eight months. Eight fucking months. "He wants us all there."

"No."

"I knew you'd say that," he drawled. "Do it for us. For Winston, Byron, and me."

I understood what he meant. He'd nag and blame them if I didn't show. It never occurred to my father that he was the reason I never went around him. I hated his schmoozing and unscrupulousness to move up in the political world. And the latest discovery made me dislike him even more.

I killed a man he brought to our doorstep. I didn't feel remorse for taking a man's life. Ivan deserved to die, but it didn't heal this hole in my chest.

"When is it?" I asked.

"In four weeks," he mumbled. He didn't want to go either. "So another month to go and let you make room in your schedule for it. And don't use the excuse of work. We all know you are on sabbatical. Indefinitely."

Jerk. Of course he'd eliminate the excuse before I even had a chance to utter it.

"If you want some peace, you could stay at my place." I could hear a smile in his voice. "Because I am your favorite."

Just as all my siblings, he had his own penthouse in D.C. though he spent more time out of it than he did in it.

"That's okay, I'll stay in our apartment, if I come. I miss the girls and Gabriel."

"Good, good," he muttered. "Spending time with the girls will be good for you."

Then he trailed off as if he said too much. A heartbeat of silence followed, both of us unsure what to say. Truthfully, I felt empty and silence felt better than talking lately.

"I'll let you know if I come," I muttered. "Besides, Gabriel is my favorite," I teased softly, trying to cut through the tension.

"You can't backpedal," he scoffed. "I'm your favorite. Besides, Gabriel is a nephew, so he can be your favorite nephew. I'm your favorite out of the three brothers."

Three brothers.

It should be four brothers. Alexei cost me one brother. Yet, I didn't shoot him. I couldn't shoot him. And I couldn't stop thinking about him.

"Okay, I have to go," I muttered, suddenly my mood soured and I quickly clicked the end button. I hated myself for not hating Alexei. I wanted to hate his guts, make him suffer. Yet, I couldn't shake off the feeling that he suffered.

"Not my problem," I muttered, annoyed. Though it was my

problem that I wanted to make him better. The urge to hug him or talk to him, not that he was a talker, constantly lingered in my heart. Yet, every time I thought of him, I also thought of Kingston. And how he cost me my brother. I couldn't think of one without the other.

The doorbell to my apartment rang and I silently groaned. I knew Byron forgot his fucking keys again. He insisted keys were a thing of the past and I needed a thumbprint lock. No fucking way. I liked my keys, thank you very much. He had to go back home to his life. At this rate, I'd go back to work more mental than before the sabbatical.

"Come in. It's open," I called out, not bothering to go open the door.

I leaned my forehead against my knees, feeling exhausted. All these damn emotions were exhausting. Maybe I should talk to a psychiatrist, like the bureau suggested. Except, I couldn't tell anyone what really bothered me. Just like I couldn't tell anyone what happened to Anya. We promised her.

Sailor, Willow, and I helped each other power through that horror. Byron, Winston, and Royce had that five-year-old girl who cried for months for her Kingston.

But now... I was alone. I wanted to talk but didn't dare tell anyone that Alexei, the boy with broken eyes, cost me my brother.

"Hello, Agent Ashford."

Not my brother's voice. My head whipped up to find Sasha Niko-laev standing in my living room, dressed in his dark expensive suit and hiding his ruthlessness. And that shark smile on his face.

"What the fuck are you doing in my apartment?" I hissed, jumping to my feet.

"Relax, sweetheart," he drawled, not moving from his spot. He even shoved his hands into his pockets, as if that would make him look less threatening. "You and I are gonna talk."

I frowned so deeply my eyebrows hurt. Maybe Alexei wasn't the true psychopath. Maybe it was this guy because nobody sane would dare to approach me after Byron threatened them.

"You're insane." I glanced around my bare apartment, trying to locate anything that I could use as a weapon. My firearm was in the bedroom, secured, and despite Sasha's big frame, I had a feeling he moved like a panther. Just as Alexei did.

"Probably a little bit insane," he admitted and I cocked my eyebrow. Yes, crazy certainly ran in the Nikolaev family.

"What do you want?" I asked him. There was no sense in debating the man's insanity.

"I want to talk about Alexei." I stilled, my heart twitched painfully and then resumed beating. I hated that just hearing his name mentioned had my chest hurting. I remained quiet, waiting. "Do you know that my mother had him kidnapped when he was two?" I nodded, remembering his story. "Did you know that she moved him every year, so he couldn't get attached to a family?" I swallowed a lump in my throat, nodding. "Then when he was ten, the first family that cared for him, attempted to defend him, they were murdered in cold blood. By my mother and Ivan Petrov. While he watched."

The oxygen seemed to be in short supply in my apartment. "Why?" I choked out.

"She was a psychopathic bitch." His voice was cold and unemotional, but something vulnerable flickered in his pale gaze. I thought my relationship with my father was shitty, but it didn't scratch the surface on the Nikolaev parents. "Ivan tortured him, abused him. Starved him." The memory flashed in my mind. Broken eyes. He looked sad, his clothes shabby. Almost rags. I slipped my hand into his because he was so sad. I remembered him. *Him.* In the zoo with me when I was a little girl. And when I ran, he was behind me. Every time I almost stopped, he urged me to keep going.

He saved me, but not my brother. Why? I remembered he ran behind me all the way home. I stopped right by the gate of our manor.

"Come with me," I begged.

His eyes were so sad. Pale like the clearest summer sky. My cheeks were wet from tears and his big hand wiped another tear rolling down my cheek.

"You were brave, kroshka." His voice was raspy, though he tried to keep it low. "Keep being brave. Go in the house. I'll stay here until you are inside safe."

"Kingston," I whimpered. "What about Kingston? My brother."

He was so big and tall, he lowered himself down and I grabbed his shirt, fisting it tightly to ensure he didn't leave me.

"I'll get him. I'll find a way," he vowed with a thick accent, his voice rough and full of emotions. "I'll find him, kroshka. No matter what."

Alexei went back for Kingston. Even Ivan said it. Alexei kept his word, except that it was too late for my brother.

"He doesn't form attachments, Agent Ashford." Sasha's voice pulled me back to the present. "He was abused so severely, he doesn't allow *anyone* to touch him. Yet, I've seen you sitting on his lap. Touching his face. Don't destroy him too."

I didn't want to destroy him. I just wanted this pain in my chest to stop. To forget him.

"He led Ivan to my brother and me," I said quietly.

"I don't know what happened, but I'm sure he didn't have a choice." I'd give it to Sasha, he cared about his brother. Just as I cared about all of mine. "Let me take you to him so he can explain."

"He sent you?"

"No."

Of course not. Though I had no right to be upset about it. After all, I told him to stay away. I threatened him.

"There is nothing to explain," I told him. "The time for explaining has come and gone. He could have explained to the police when Ivan first took my brother." I let the words sink in before I continued. "He could have explained it to me when he met me."

"So you will throw him away?" he asked, the accusation in his voice heavy. "Just like everyone else in his past has."

My throat burned and my soul shattered. Alexei suffered enough too, his entire life. Could I even fault him for saving himself? I couldn't and I wouldn't. If only it didn't cost me my brother. Or maybe it was my own guilt that ate at me. I didn't fucking know anymore.

I pressed my lips tight, my eyes darted away from the man who reminded me of the one who had somehow snuck under my skin. A month without Alexei felt long. It was just sex, I kept telling myself.

Yet, it felt like so much more. History. Words. Each breath. His fucking single beautiful smile he gave me. My eyes burned and I felt anguish deep down in my soul.

"You better leave," I told him, my voice shaking. I needed him gone before I fell apart. "My brother will be back any moment."

He shook his head, disappointment washing over his expression.

Without another word, he strode out of my apartment.

THIRTY-SIX
ALEXEI

I slowed my steps as I walked up the stairs to the estate's gate. In Florida of all fucking places.

Raphael Santos gave me the tip. I repaid it with another piece of information. He was now hunting for a woman in Washington, D.C. I dug up the information on Anya, sister to one of Aurora's best friends. Since Russia, Aurora's dream had been nagging me. The information I found was disturbing.

It had been a month since the fiasco in Russia. I resisted the urge to stalk Aurora. I wanted to ensure she was okay and safe. I missed her chocolate smell. Her soft skin. There was so much I wanted to tell her. Yet, I knew I had to stay away. Even if she somehow forgave me, I couldn't be the man she wanted or needed.

So I focused on hunting down Igor. The weasel who somehow always found a way to escape without a scratch on him. I wouldn't allow him to become the next Ivan. And he knew Aurora, so letting him live was not an option.

My phone rang and I cursed. I forgot to turn it off. It was another thing that had happened since Russia. I have been so fucking distracted I couldn't function. Pathetic really.

I answered. "What?"

It was Vasili. "What the fuck are you doing in Florida?"

"Nothing."

A heartbeat of silence. "Please tell me this has nothing to do with that agent," he grumbled.

"Has nothing to do with the agent." It had everything to do with her.

"Morrelli called," he continued, pretending he bought my response. "He's chasing down leads on Sophia Catalano, Bianca's great-aunt. He said he tried to call you but couldn't get you."

My fingers gripped the phone, agitated. "I've been busy."

"Could you send him a description of the old woman?"

"I was too busy watching over my woman," I snapped, "to ensure Ivan didn't fucking rape her. So fuck no, I can't tell him anything about her. She was old. And fucking crazy. And you can tell Morrelli if I get my hands on her crazy fucking aunt before he does, she'll be a dead woman."

Fuck, I lost my shit.

"Why?" Vasili questioned. "What has the old woman done to you?"

"She hit my woman, that's fucking what," I snapped.

Temporary silence was my only answer. It was something I usually found comfort in, but lately, not so much. I heard *her* voice and it had me searching her out, only to find it was my fucking mind playing tricks on me. Lately the silence was suffocating me, wrapping its invisible hand around my neck and choking the living daylights out of me.

"Your woman?" Vasili's voice cut through the silence. It was calm and reasonable. It only served to egg me on further. "Alexei, moy brat." He called me his brother. Vasili never got sentimental. He was as cold as I was. "The Ashfords are powerful men. If Agent Ashford hints to them what happened, they'll come back, pouncing. It's best to stay away from them."

Vasili's unspoken words were clear. *Don't fuck with the Ashford family.*

Not in the mood to listen to reason, I ended the call and turned off my phone, then continued up the luxury marble stairs. Igor always did love nice things. First that castle in Russia, now this white marble mansion.

If I knew Igor well, and unfortunately I did, he was probably hiding somewhere here and would strike me from the back. Though, the little chickenshit was a bigger coward than I fathomed. I found him cowering underneath his desk, his complexion resembling chalk, face full of dread and eyes popping in terror.

The bastard didn't even try to fight or flee.

My lips curved with disgust. I walked toward him. Before he even had a chance to move, I grabbed him by his neck and lifted him up into the air. I caught him in a chokehold.

My mouth twisted into a cruel smirk that I knew scared the shit out of people. *Except my little agent.*

My arm swept across the glass-top desk, all the shit he had on it crashing to the floor. My fingers gripped his neck so tight, making his chicken neck turn purple. I slammed him against the desk, and he cried out as his precious face hit the glass and it shattered.

I lifted him again and flung his body onto the floor, letting the glass cut into his flesh. He scrambled, attempted to get on his knees and flee. My nostrils flared with fury.

No more running for this fucker. The icy hate flooded my veins. He dared to eye my woman. He thought he could hurt her. My black combat boots dug into his back, and I pushed my body weight into his back.

Over. My. Dead. Body. Or his; preferably his.

"Wait, wait," he begged, raising his bloody hands in surrender. He hoped for mercy; he'd get none. "I'll give you anything, Alexei."

He didn't put up a fight and the itch to release tension dug into my muscles, bloodthirst demanding to be satisfied.

I grinned, leaning slightly over. I let him believe he could buy me. "The old woman," I growled. "How do I find her?"

Igor's eyes widened. I didn't think it was possible to find him more terrified, but he was. Who in the fuck was that woman for him to be so terrified of her? Yes, she was Ivan's wife. Bianca's great-aunt. Yet, I sensed we were missing something important here.

Just like Aurora, I felt there was something unhinged and crazy about the old woman.

"Where?" I gritted. Reaching down, I flipped him over, then pinned him down with my forearm on his neck. "Don't make me ask again."

"Hiding," he whimpered. "Nobody knows where she stays."

"Why?"

"I don't fucking know." This guy was useless.

My jaw clenched, my free hand reaching up and grasping his hair, lifting it up and slamming it against the floor. I pushed his face into the glass, his crying louder.

"I told you you'd find yourself on the wrong side of the bars," I sneered.

I cocked the gun, but before I even had a chance to point it at his head, he screamed. "Greece," he shouted. "She's somewhere in Greece. That's all I know."

"For that, I might kill you faster," I said conversationally. With precision, I fired two shots into his kneecaps. His pained screams rattled the glass. I pulled the knife out of my boot and dug the tip of the blade into his neck. "But not too fast," I drawled. "After all, we have a score to settle."

I took pleasure in watching his miserable life drain out of his eyes.

THIRTY-SEVEN
AURORA

"**A**re you sure you're gonna be okay?" Byron eyed me worriedly. We were in the parking lot outside my building. It was still hot and humid outside.

He was perfectly fine with leaving until yesterday. When a box was delivered. It contained hands and a picture of Igor. Dead. I knew who did it, but I kept my mouth shut. When the police came, I acted like I had never seen him.

And here we were. My brothers all panicked.

Except, I knew Alexei did it to avenge Kingston. Was it sick? Yes. Did I object? Fuck no. Maybe I was just as crazy as Alexei.

"I should stay," Byron protested. "I don't want to leave you now." I appreciated his thoughtfulness and the fact that he cared, but there was nothing more that I wanted to do but be alone.

"You have to go," I told him. "Otherwise, we are going to kill each other."

He tugged on my ear. "Brat." I stuck my tongue out at him. It wasn't very mature, but it was either that or I smack him. "A guard will be left behind to watch you."

"Byron," I protested, annoyed.

313

"You won't even know he is here," he justified. "He's been here since we got back from—"

He stopped himself. It was ludicrous that we avoided all mentions of Russia. Byron's men hacked the surveillance and what he had seen wasn't good. He said he nor his men watched it, but I knew he made assumptions. He destroyed all the evidence of me being there.

Now, I had to lick my wounds alone and in the darkness, until I could come to terms with everything that happened.

"Okay." I forced a happy smile as I pushed him into the limo. He wouldn't budge on the guard, so I might as well go along with it. "Stop harassing your sister and go back to work."

"I don't like it," he muttered and I chuckled.

"Yeah, I don't like to work either," I joked.

I nudged him into his limo, then slammed the door before he could say another word and tapped on the roof, giving a signal to the limo driver to get going.

The back passenger window promptly slid down and my brother's perfectly symmetrical face poked through. The man looked too good for his own good.

"Don't think this conversation is over," he warned, his voice carrying through the air.

Instead of commenting, I just waved.

"Love you," I yelled after him. "Don't call me."

He flipped me the bird out of the car window, causing me to chuckle. I knew he was letting me off easily. He could have easily told the driver to turn around and let him out.

I stood there, half expecting that familiar tingle at the back of my neck. That same feeling I had from the moment I met Alexei and that warned me he was following me. But since Russia, the feeling wasn't there. I couldn't quite decide whether I was relieved or distressed about it.

I did tell him I'd arrest him if I saw him again. I meant it at that very moment, but now, not so much.

I fell for him. I knew it the moment I couldn't shoot him, but it took me a while to admit it myself. Just the idea of him dead sent heavy dread through my veins. The feelings for him snuck up on me while focused on the case.

"Miss Ashford." A strange man's voice came from behind me and annoyance flared in me.

"If you are Byron's bodyguard, you can leave," I told him without looking behind me and started walking toward the lobby door. "I don't need one."

An unexpected soft female chuckle had my steps pausing, and I turned around to meet two sets of unfamiliar eyes. My eyes shifted from the tall man with dark hair and even darker eyes, wearing a three-piece suit. Tattoos on his neck. A rose tattoo on his right hand. It was a habit at this point to catalog it all.

He held the woman's hand with his left hand and somehow I thought it was on purpose. To keep his right hand free. My eyes traveled over the woman. She was startlingly beautiful, and she was pregnant. I couldn't guess how far in her pregnancy she was, but she was definitely up there.

"Then who are you?"

"I'm Cassio King," the man answered. "This is my wife, Áine."

I recognized the name. Cassio King was the son of the late Benito King. The entire family ran a crime organization. I'd even looked into Benito King, thinking he might have been the one to take Kingston. But he didn't fit the MO, and he liked to be in the spotlight too much.

"So?" I cocked an eyebrow. I behaved like a brat, just as my brother called me. "Listen, whatever it is you want, I don't have it." My eyes fleeted to the woman. "You better get into an air-conditioned room," I told her, eyeing her belly. "This heat can be brutal, and you look like you might pop."

She offered me a brilliant smile. "I thought you'd never ask." I blinked in confusion. "Lead the way, Miss Ashford." What the fuck just happened?

"Where to?" I asked stupidly.

"To your apartment," she answered with a beaming smile.

A strangled laugh escaped me. "Umm, I don't think so. I'm not taking strangers into my apartment."

"We are Alexei's friends," Cassio chimed in. Instantly alerted, my eyes roamed around. I almost expected to see him.

"Is this about the delivery?" I whispered in a low voice.

"Delivery?" Cassio asked, confusion marring his expression. Okay, maybe he didn't know about the delivery.

"Never mind," I muttered.

"Miss Ashford, are these people bothering you?" I glanced behind me, and the moment I saw the man, I knew that was my bodyguard. He looked exactly the type Byron would hire. Probably an ex-Navy SEAL.

Cassio stepped forward, but his wife took his arm and held him back. He behaved like my own bodyguard would attack me.

"Ah, no, no," I quickly answered before things escalated. "They are… old friends," I lied, blushing. "We'll go inside. Cassio, Áine." I forced what I hoped was a passable smile. "This way."

Hopefully, I wasn't an idiot to let them into my home, but considering Alexei threatened his own brothers about hurting me, I didn't think his friends would hurt me either.

Once inside my apartment, the two sat down on my modern couch. I watched them look around as I brought them each bottled water.

"This place looks like a hotel," Áine muttered. "It doesn't look like anyone lives here."

I took my spot by the window, my eyes on the door and the entire living room in my sight. "I don't spend much time at home. Now what is this about?"

Cassio and his wife shared a glance.

"I heard that you and Alexei captured Ivan Petrov." My heart twisted into a knot. "His brother gave us a rundown." I exhaled a ragged breath and ensured my expression didn't reflect any of my thoughts.

"So?"

"I have a question for you." Cassio narrowed his eyes on me, studying me. "Do you love Alexei?"

Suppressing a flinch, I held his stare.

"That's none of your business, Mr. King," I told him, impressed that my voice reflected none of the emotions swirling in my chest.

He didn't look impressed.

"I'm going to tell you a story," he started and I rolled my eyes. This guy seriously came over to bother me with some stories. He ignored my eye roll, though his wife chuckled. "A little over ten years ago, Alexei went back to Russia. He went alone." My heart hammered in my chest, worried about anyone going to that country alone. "By coincidence, Luca and I reached out to him because we needed a location to move some women."

My spine straightened. "You better be careful what you say next," I warned. "Because I won't hesitate to arrest you."

Áine chuckled. "Cassio saved women from human trafficking," she came to his defense. "He needed somewhere safe to put them."

A fleeting glance between husband and wife, and I sensed a story there.

"Anyhow, I asked Alexei if we could bring them to Russia," Cassio continued, ignoring my threat. "That's how I found out he was there. He offered me a sanctuary for them in Portugal. It was where he was prepared to take anyone he found alive in Ivan's Russian compound." A sharp inhale of breath shattered through the air. It was mine. "We asked him to wait for us. It was suicide for him to go alone."

"Why didn't his brothers go with him?" I asked, my voice trembling.

"None of us, including him or his brothers, knew at that time he was a Nikolaev," Cassio explained.

That made sense, after all, his file shows him in the picture around the Nikolaev family only five or so years ago. "Did he wait?"

My heart beat wildly against my ribs, cutting my breaths short.

"One day," he answered. "He wanted to get anyone out before Ivan got back." I nodded at the logic. It made sense, especially if he was trying to get people out of there. "Nico Morrelli, who you know, got there first," he continued, and somehow I wasn't surprised to hear he knew I met Nico Morrelli. Though I wouldn't exactly say I knew him. "And a few others, along with Luca, my brother, and I, we got there right in time. Alexei was already in the house, attacking men and getting to the captives."

"Except my brother," I muttered.

"Including your brother." Confused, I watched him. Was he lying? "He was in bad shape, but we got him out." For a moment, I forgot to breathe. I forgot to function. I just stared at this stranger in front of me.

"K-Kingston," I stammered, my voice barely above the whisper. "My Kingston?"

"Yes, Kingston Ashford. We got him out. He was in really bad shape. We got stuck in Moscow, while waiting for a way out of that hellhole. We all took turns taking care of the survivors, but Alexei stayed with your brother."

"And he died?" I rasped. Cassio shook his head. "N-no?"

I was confused. None of this made sense. "No, your brother is alive."

I glanced at his wife who nodded, a sympathetic smile on her face.

"But how?" Alexei told me Kingston was dead. Didn't he? I went through every word that was uttered in that wretched room. Ivan said Kingston was dead. Alexei didn't confirm it nor deny it.

"He healed," he explained. "It was a close call, but Alexei never gave up on him."

I blinked. Again and again. My throat burned. My damn eyes burned. Yet, I refused to fall apart. Not now when this man ignited this hope in my chest.

"But he let me believe Kingston was dead," I rasped, my heart twitching with another betrayal. Did Alexei enjoy making me suffer?

"He gave his word," Cassio explained.

I furrowed my eyebrows and pain lingered in my temples. I pinched my nose, trying to relieve some of the tension.

"To whom?" I inquired.

"To your brother."

"But why?"

"Alexei felt he owed Kingston that much," he explained. "Your brother was in bad shape. We could heal his body, but not his mind." A shudder ran down my spine. "Alexei promised he wouldn't tell his family he was alive. Kingston didn't want you to see what he had become."

A tear rolled down my cheek, and I wiped it angrily with the back of my hand.

"Why didn't he want us to know?" I choked out. "We love him. I— I never stopped hoping—"

I couldn't finish the statement. My lower lip trembled and I covered my mouth, then rushed to the bathroom and shut the door behind me. Leaning against the door, I slid down to the cold tiled floor. I kept swallowing harshly, attempting to keep the sobs at bay. But eventually they won out. My entire body shook as heaving sobs wracked through me.

Kingston is alive.

THIRTY-EIGHT
AURORA

My insides shook as I roamed the streets of Lisbon.

Portugal.

It was the only piece of information Cassio King would share. I understood his allegiance to Alexei; but then I didn't. This was my brother we were talking about. I needed to see him. Hear him. Feel him.

I felt like that little girl again who always ran after her big brother. I loved all my brothers, but the disparity in age with the others made me always run to Kingston first. Byron, Winston, and Royce were almost in the category of my caretakers. While Kingston was my brother. The one I got into trouble with. The one who supported my idea of drawing on the wall or dumping all my paint colors into the pool so we'd see an everlasting rainbow.

The other three brothers had more common sense than we did.

I held my breath until my lungs suffocated and then slowly exhaled.

Twenty years. All kinds of scenarios ran through my mind. Was he as tall as my other brothers? Did he smell the same? Did he still like gummy bears?

It was stupid, I knew it. He was an adult now. He probably hadn't eaten gummy bears since that day.

Goosebumps broke through my skin and I fought back a shiver and the images in my mind creating the worst kind of scenarios. I had to tell Kingston how sorry I was. Beg him for forgiveness. Help him somehow.

Alexei helped him. Cassio said that he set him up financially and Kingston took it from there. He had made his own fortune since that day, but Alexei visited him often and sometimes even invested in Kingston's dealings.

Maybe Kingston would let me help him somehow too.

Then a thought struck me and my step faltered. Maybe I was the reason he didn't want to come back. I swallowed hard the lump in my throat, my stomach burning with guilt. It was heavy and bitter as it weaved its way through me.

A shuddering breath slipped through my lips and I stilled myself with determination. If he didn't want anything to do with me, then I'd… My heart got stuck in my throat at the thought he wouldn't want to see me. I sniffled, already getting teary-eyed.

Fucking bullshit.

"Grow a pair, Aurora," I mumbled under my breath. Everything was making me cry since Russia. It has been almost two months since I last saw Alexei. A week since I learned Kingston was alive. And all I did was fucking cry.

All that mattered to me was that Kingston was alive. Everything else, I'd overcome. If he didn't want to see me, I'd respect his wishes. But I'd find a way to make it up to him for as long as I lived.

I picked up my pace, soaking up the old city and rushed words spoken in Portuguese as my eyes met men's faces, searching for any resemblance to my brother. Was it dumb? Yes. Kingston would be a grown-ass man now. Thirty.

His birthday was coming up in July and he'd turn thirty-one.

There was so much that was stolen from us. Maybe he'd see how sorry I was, and if he didn't want to see me, I'd beg him to see our brothers. I'd stay away. Kingston needed our brothers as much as they needed him.

An odd sense of purpose had me rushing down the streets, making me want to find out what the future had in store for us. I heard my bodyguard's steps behind me. He was always nearby. Probably thought this trip was lunacy, but I didn't care. I sold some lame-ass story to my brothers about a much-needed vacation.

It wasn't as hard to sell it to Willow. I called her when I knew she'd be busy so she'd be distracted trying to do two things at once. And I lucked out with Sailor. She and Gabriel took a little vacation, though it was odd that they went alone. They always dragged Willow and me along.

A man crashed into me, causing me to lose my balance. Before I hit the ground, my bodyguard's hands caught me. At least I thought they were until I looked up and my breath got stuck in my lungs.

Dark hair. Olive skin. Dark eyes with an almost haunting chill in their depths. My hands gripped his shirt, his tall body a solid wall of muscle.

"You alright?" His voice was deep, a light accent in his two words. Yet, I knew him. I fucking knew him.

"Kingston," I breathed. It had to be him. I'd recognize those eyes anywhere. Except, they didn't shine as they used to. The little boy who used to laugh with me was gone. In its place was a hard man. Sharp angles. Harsh expression. His jet-black hair slightly tousled.

"Not anymore."

My chest tightened. He hated me. That softened expression I remembered was replaced by something cruel and... broken. It reminded me of Alexei's eyes when I first saw him in the zoo.

"What do you mean?" I choked out, fighting the tears that threatened to spill over. I swallowed harshly to keep the sobs that choked my throat at bay. I didn't want to embarrass him, or look weak. After he had been so strong for years under Ivan's brutality.

"I haven't gone by that name in two decades."

Silence stretched. The buzz of the city around us dulled out by this moment. Slowly, almost gently, he straightened me up and our surroundings came back into focus. I glanced around but Byron's bodyguard was nowhere to be seen.

"My men took care of him," Kingston explained. My eyes widened. "He'll wake up back in the hotel," he clarified, as if he worried I'd think he killed him. My moral compass must have turned south because the concern for my bodyguard never even flickered.

I returned my gaze to my brother, soaking in the features of the grown man and replacing the little boy I remembered and who'd forever be in my heart. He was as tall as our brothers and I had to crane my neck to study his face. Memorizing every single thing about it.

My fingers still clutched his shirt, gripping him and scared to let go. Scared that he'd turn into a figment of my imagination. There was so much I wanted to say to him. Yet, I couldn't utter a single word. Words seemed to be lacking.

"Cassio said you'd be coming," Kingston added, his tone almost gentle. "You should go back home."

I wanted to cry, scream, beg. Anything to keep him with us. But all I could do was shake my head, unspoken words choking me.

"I'm sorry," I whispered finally. A knot lodged in my throat, so I couldn't say another word. But I had so many more to say.

His one hand came up and absentmindedly I noted tattoos on his fingers. I held my breath, waiting. Though not sure for what. My conscience told me I deserved his hate, but my heart wanted my brother back.

His knuckles brushed across my cheek. "Still as soft as that last day," he said.

And that did it. Tears welled in my eyes and tracked down my face, dripped off my chin and onto his knuckles.

"I'm so sorry," I choked out. "If I could change that day, I would. I'd listen. I'd never leave your side." My voice broke, but now that the words came out, I couldn't stop. "I should have listened. Stayed with you. I should have screamed. I'm so sorry, Kingston. I wished he'd taken me and not you. It's all my fault." All the emotions swirled in my chest and I sniffed, trying to stop my nose from running with my tears. And just like when we were children, he pulled out a handkerchief and wiped it. My insides fractured at the memories before everything had gone downhill. "P-please, Kingston, I—"

I swallowed hard, the words I dreaded had to be said. It was for his good and my other brothers.

"I can stay away," I rasped, my body shuddering with emotions. "Please, don't write us off, our brothers. It was me who fucked up."

My lungs hurt. It felt like acid burned in my stomach, but I ignored it all, pleading with him. My heart clawed at my chest, and both hands now gripped his shirt.

Looking straight into my brother's eyes, I searched for the little boy who always stood by me.

"P-please..." A hiccup escaped me, but I ignored how ridiculous and weak I appeared. "Please, Kingston. I'll do anything."

My insides were twisted as I stared at him. Against all odds, I hoped for the impossible. Maybe it was the dreamer in me? Or the little girl who loved her family? It never felt complete without my brother. It was the five of us together that made a family unit.

My nerves tethered as I waited for his lashing. For him to tell me how much he despised me.

"It was our father's fault." His words stunned me and I blinked in confusion. His palms took my face between his hands. "It was the old man's fault they came for us. Not yours, my little dawn."

His little dawn. My brothers told me only my mother called me that. She named me Aurora, because I was born at the crack of dawn, and she found it to be a perfect name after enduring two days of labor.

Our father has torn our family apart. Kingston paid the price. Every single brother of mine paid some kind of price thanks to Father. Kingston used to be the brother who always found time to hug me, offer me comfort and warm smiles. And now, in front of me stood an emotionally detached grown man. So much like Alexei. Did he have to learn to detach himself from emotions to cope with everything he had to endure?

This time I broke down. A sob broke free, and I buried my face into my brother's chest, trying to muffle it. We were in the middle of a city, in broad daylight and I cried like a baby.

"I love you, Kingston," I muttered into his chest. "Please don't send me away."

THIRTY-NINE
ALEXEI

M oron.

It was the only conclusion I could come to as I watched Aurora glide through the large, fancy ballroom. I was a moron to come, thinking somehow we could talk. She'd let me touch her one more time.

But seeing this glittery world she grew up in, among the wealthiest and fanciest of the D.C. political scene, I knew we were as different as the sun and moon. I grew up in the slums among the scum of the earth, in the dark of the night. There couldn't be starker evidence of our incompatibility.

Two months without her were hell. I couldn't even fucking think about the rest of my life. The little girl from the zoo took a piece of my heart with her kindness. The woman in front of me claimed every ounce of it.

Each fucking breath. Each heartbeat. Every goddamn thought.

This had to be God's form of punishment. Some sick karma. For all the death I caused and blood staining my hands. I was given a glimpse of what I could have had, and then it was snatched away from me.

But there was nobody else for me. Just this petite woman with the softest skin, the sassiest mouth, and warmest smile. I hadn't seen her in two months. Two fucking months. I kept away from all the gang and my brothers. I hadn't gone to see Kingston either. Nor did I talk to him. I sent him some pathetic excuse. Though he let me get away with it.

I couldn't see him yet. His eyes would remind me too much of his little sister. I'd have to get over that shit. I thought coming here would help me move on. Yeah, that was dumb. Now my fucking hands shook because I craved to touch her.

Men's eyes followed her greedily, but she ignored them all. She stood with her brothers, champagne in one hand while they entertained her. The three brothers circled her like her protectors, scaring away any man who tried to get close to her.

Her smile though wasn't quite as happy, her complexion slightly paler. And the idiotic bastard in me hoped it was for me.

Like I said, a moron.

I found comfort in the fact she didn't spare a single glance to any other man. Her eyes were only on her brothers, her smiles only sincere with them, and I fought the urge to kill the bastards. It was impossible to squash the killer in me. It was who I was.

Eight weeks and three days since I'd last seen her. Tasted her. Fucked her. And it was the worst kind of withdrawal.

"Alexei, people are shitting their pants," Vasili muttered under his breath. "Stop growling and unclench your fists. We are not here for a fight."

Right! We were here because I wanted another glimpse of her. Senator Ashford invited Vasili, trying to secure the votes for New Orleans. Everyone knew Vasili ran Louisiana and whoever he backed would get the majority vote in that state. Of course, Senator Ashford didn't know what went down in Russia.

Bottom line, like a moron, I came along unable to resist the opportunity to see Aurora one more time. Of course, this wasn't Vasili's idea of moving on for me. Well, too fucking bad. If he would have refused, I'd have gone to Cassio for an invitation and then worked down the list. Fuck, I'd cash in on everyone's debt until I ran out of options.

Another woman walked by, throwing us a glance that clearly said we didn't belong. Fucking schmoozers and snobs.

"Alexei," Vasili warned on a hiss.

I forced my palms open. As if that would make me less threatening. I was fully aware of glances thrown my way. My type wasn't the kind that schmoozed in high society. I was the type to lurk in the shadows and scare these motherfuckers.

Senator Ashford joined Aurora and his sons. His hands wrapped around his daughter on one side and Byron on the other. As if in sync, every single sibling stiffened ever so slightly. The old man said something and wholeheartedly laughed, but his children didn't join him.

Then he tugged on his daughter, and unless she was ready to make a scene, she knew she had to go along with him. Though as she walked away from her brothers, she threw a pleading glance over her shoulder.

"Help me," she mouthed to her brothers, then was forced to turn around.

The senator and she joined a group of men and then introductions started. It only took five minutes and Aurora excused herself, a forced smile on her lips.

"Alexei, are you okay?" My sister's hand came to my arm, gently patting my hand. I didn't like it. The only touch I could remotely bear was Aurora's.

"Da."

Isabella's hand dropped to her side and Vasili swiftly took it into his. It was all kinds of fucked up, but I preferred not to be touched. And the only one I could even entertain touching me was the young woman who couldn't stand me because I took away something she loved. I couldn't blame her for hating me.

I watched as a man stopped Aurora as she headed back to her brothers. She tilted her head to the side, listening and smiling. My teeth ground, my blood on fire, and my breath stolen from my lungs.

She's mine, I wanted to shout to the entire room and threaten the worst kind of torture to anyone who looked her way.

My fucking hands shook with the urge to go on a killing spree. But I knew it would push her even further away. And she was already so fucking far away. Maybe the two of us were like the sun and moon, always passing each other, but never actually meant to be together.

Now I sound like a goddamn pussy, I thought wryly. That was what love did to you. Who in their right mind needed this headache?

"Go talk to her," Isabella whispered next to me. My sister didn't know what happened. Only that the two of us eliminated the threat together. If she knew I cost Aurora her brother, put him through the hell that I experienced, and he'd probably be fucked up for the remainder of his life, she'd tell me I had no chance with the FBI agent.

"I'm getting a drink." I strode away without another word. The tie around my neck was fucking choking me. The suit was too tight and too constricting. Vasili wore suits like a second skin. I wore weapons and a military wardrobe like it was part of me. Not this shit.

In ten large strides, I found myself by the bar.

"Whiskey," I told the bartender. "Straight up."

This was a bad fucking idea. I knew Vasili often got invites to political fundraisers. Two months without her fucked with my mind. I couldn't function.

"Do you work here?" An elderly woman with a cane stood next to me, eyeing me like I was scum of the earth. There was no *like* in that statement. I was among the worst scum to walk this earth. "I need—"

"No," I told her icily.

"You look like you work here," she babbled on when all I wanted was her to shut the fuck up.

The bartender saved her by putting my drink in front of me and I downed it in one gulp. I needed a whole bottle. I had never been big on drinking. The need to maintain control was ingrained in me. Yet, since meeting Aurora as a grown woman, my blood pressure constantly skyrocketed, my breathing was ragged, and my mind was a scrambled mess. And I needed alcohol.

Control flew out of the elevator the day she walked into it, back in the FBI building.

"I need someone to go get my car," the old woman demanded. Jesus, did she want to die?

"Mrs. Kennedy, how are you?" A soft voice came from behind me. The scent of chocolate. I stiffened. "This is Alexei, my boyfriend."

My head snapped her way. Was she making fun? Aurora didn't look my way, her eyes firmly on the old woman.

"Oh, my dear, I don't think your father will approve." I knew he wouldn't. Nobody in their right mind would approve of me. "He looks like a brute."

Aurora's hand slipped into mine, though she still didn't look my way. As if she couldn't stand to look at me. Though why did she call me her boyfriend.

"Maybe, Mrs. Kennedy." Aurora's slim shoulder shrugged and I wanted to bend her over, sink my teeth into her skin and mark her for the whole world to see. "But he's my brute. Now please apologize to my boyfriend."

The woman's eyes bulged and an undignified gasp left her. She didn't find me worthy of the apology. I didn't care about her opinion nor her apology. All I cared about was that my woman was touching me.

"I'd never," the old woman scoffed and scurried away, her diamonds glittering under the bright lights of the ballroom and hiding her shallowness.

Aurora pulled her hand out of my grip and took a step backwards, then met my eyes. Dark chocolate brown pulled me into a sweet oblivion. I didn't need a stiff drink when she looked at me like that.

"Why are you here, Alexei?" she asked in a soft, husky voice.

She still had that polite smile on her lips, and I fucking hated it. Because it was the same one she gave everyone else. I wanted her real smile, her real frowns. I wanted the real her.

"You're mine." Fuck, the statement slipped out before I could stop it. I should sweet-talk her, seduce her. Except, I didn't know how to do that.

Her eyebrow rose up in question, waiting for me to elaborate. But there was nothing else to say; nothing she would find acceptable.

She exhaled slowly, her eyes darting behind me. I knew Vasili and Isabella approached us.

"Agent Ashford." Vasili's voice came behind me. "Nice to see you again."

"Wish I could say the same," Aurora responded dryly. Her eyes shifted to Isabella and she nodded. "Mrs. Nikolaev."

"Please call me Isabella." My sister hated conflict and disagreements. She just wanted everyone to get along and be happy. "My husband told me y-you helped eliminate a threat to our son."

Annoyance flashed in Aurora's eyes. "Ah, so it was for your son?" she scoffed. "It would have been nice if the Nikolaev men would have told me the truth from the get-go, you know. Instead of playing me."

This had to be what being stabbed in the heart felt like. Her words filled the silence, the meaning behind them dancing in this fancy ballroom. Sadness crossed Isabella's features and Vasili growled, taking a threatening step towards Aurora. I cut him off, getting in front of Aurora.

"Ne." *No.* One word but he knew I'd fight him over her. I'd never allow anyone to hurt her. Not my brother, not my sister. Anyone!

"I'm sorry, Aurora." Isabella took Vasili's hand and pulled him back. "Vasili, stop acting like a beast," she scolded him in her soft voice.

"Sister, is everything okay?" I knew her brothers would find their way here. After all, she was their little sister.

"Are these men bothering you?" Winston growled, his eyes darting between Vasili and me. He looked like a perfect gentleman, although taller and bulkier than most other sissy pricks around here. "I thought we told you to stay away," he hissed at me, resentment in his eyes.

"I can call the guards," Royce chimed in. The three of them were already her guards, she didn't need more.

"Yes, I'm fine," she assured both of them. "Brothers, you remember the Nikolaev family, right?"

Byron's hands slid into his pockets, though I could tell he was clenching his fists in his expensive suit. Vasili told me her brother hacked all the surveillance from the castle in Russia. I'd imagine he probably detested every Nikolaev man.

"I remember them," Byron gritted, barely keeping his composure. "It's hard to forget men who almost cost my sister her life."

"Byron—"

He didn't even bother to listen to what his sister had to say. "I'm going to tell you this, Nikolaev." I wondered if he was talking to Vasili or me, because his eyes darted between the two of us. "Fuck with my sister again..." He glared at me and I got my answer. The threat was mainly aimed at me. "... I'll tear your family apart. And I don't make empty fucking threats."

Yes, the Ashfords were just as savage as the men in our world. They just hid it better.

"I'll drink to that," Winston chimed in, his smile vicious and matching the expression in his eyes. Of course, he'd never match the Nikolaev brutality. Though I suspected he'd come close.

Byron turned to his sister and his eyes instantly softened.

"I want you to meet Kristoff Baldwin," he continued, ignoring us. Not that I could blame him. It was probably impossible for him to see us and not think of the brother we cost him. Or the brother *I* cost him. I was certain by now Aurora had filled in her brothers about her findings. "I told you about him."

My teeth clenched. I'd lose my shit and that would be bad for everyone in this room. *Mine. Nobody touches what's mine.* The words buzzed in my head, and I wanted to smash her brother's face into the marble floor.

"No." A single word slashed through the air, like a whip. Her brother's eyes snapped my way, a dark challenge lurking in them. He wanted a fight and I was more than happy to give him one. "Aurora is mine and nobody touches what's mine," I growled. "I even fucking hate it when people look at what's mine. Touch her, and I'll murder you."

The threat was clear, rough, and untamed.

Except I tasted my own panic underneath it all.

FORTY
AURORA

A shot of adrenaline rushed through me at Alexei's open claim. It wasn't smart, but then I never claimed to be. Not when it came to him. An uncomfortable silence followed, Alexei's possessive darkness surrounding us all.

It was twisted. Yet something about him set me aflame. For the past two months, I felt like a zombie. I wasn't living, but simply existing. Ever since I met him, he somehow became as important as my limbs or my heart.

And of course, there was the discovery of Kingston who had told me what Alexei had done for him. The two became as close as brothers over the last decade. I recognized how much Alexei helped Kingston heal. My Kingston wasn't a sweet little boy anymore. He was hard, ruthless, but also good. And most importantly, he was alive.

He wasn't ready to come out and make himself known. He promised we'd tell our brothers. Together. I got back from Portugal yesterday, barely tearing myself away from him. Scared that I wouldn't see him for another twenty years. There was nothing more I wanted than to tell my brothers about Kingston. But Kingston and I agreed, we'd tell them together. In a week.

Kingston deserved to come back any way he saw fit or that he could handle. He wasn't able to open completely. But the torture he suffered. The abuse. The little he told me tore at my heart. Abuse. Rape. Torture. Kingston admitted that to this day he couldn't handle basements because he'd been chained and tied in them. It reminded me of Alexei and Russia. His reaction while we were locked in the basement.

It was no wonder Alexei and Kingston bonded. They both shared traumatic experiences.

My eyes sought out that arctic gaze. The familiar cold sensation rushed down my spine. I felt it the moment Alexei stepped into the room. It was a welcomed feeling. Like a shadow you missed.

The scent of his cologne lingered in the air. I could feel his heat from here. My heart drummed in my throat and against my ribs. Was it wrong that his threat turned me on? Yes, on so many levels. Somehow over the few days we spent in Russia, I fell for him, hard. Or maybe it happened in the weeks leading to our trip to Russia. I no longer knew.

All I knew was that I loved him. All his broken pieces. All his psychotic pieces. And most of all, his heart. Yes, he was rough and nothing about him fit the mold, but it was exactly that which made him perfect. He kept his word to a little girl. He saved my brother. And he saved me.

Butterflies fluttered in my stomach. I wanted to go home with him. I wanted to thank him for saving Kingston. I wanted to apologize for those cruel words I uttered to him. And most of all, I *needed* to tell him that I loved him.

My eyes roamed his body. His dark blue Armani suit made his eyes appear even lighter. Like the brightest summer day. It hurt to look at him. He filled the suit, his broad shoulders enough to make any woman's mouth water. The tattoos on every visible inch of his skin set him apart from the rest of the men in this room—in the best way possible. Since I met him, it was the only form of art I found fascinating. I didn't care about paintings, ballet, anything. Just tattoos—his tattoos.

"Aurora, let's go," Byron gritted.

My eyes darted back and forth between Alexei and my eldest brother, holding my breath. I knew if my father joined in, all hell would break loose here. He'd have a heart attack. Alexei was the type of man he'd warn me off. And Vasili Nikolaev wouldn't stand back and watch. The man was lethal, though my brothers were no less so.

Byron and Alexei stared at each other, both of their expressions dark and volatile.

"I'll stay," I said with determination, my eyes locked on the man I'd fallen in love with. Broken eyes flickered with something raw that sent a shudder through me.

I knew he didn't do kissing, or touching. Maybe not even love. But maybe slowly we could work on it. Together. I refused to believe Ivan extinguished it all in him.

"Rora, I don't—" Byron tried to change my mind, but my decision was made.

"I said I'm staying," I cut him off.

Alexei was my other half, and if he'd take me, I'd stand by him for the rest of my life. I didn't care about what the world nor my brothers thought of him. As long as he was mine and I was his.

My brothers knew there wouldn't be any changing my mind. I chose Alexei. I should have chosen him in Russia. Or when his brother came to my apartment. It would seem I owed Sasha an apology.

"You're not good enough for her," Royce and Winston spat out.

"I know." Alexei's voice was low. Emotionless. Resigned.

I loved my brothers, but I knew they wouldn't understand this love I had for Alexei. They'd called it Stockholm syndrome. All I knew was that last two months were torture without him.

Yes, he hurt me by omitting the truth and shutting me out. Though after hearing the story from Cassio King, I came to terms with my love for him.

I forgave him for keeping me in the dark because he went back to save my brother. First chance he had, he went back to save him and helped him heal. He didn't forget him and leave him to rot. And for that I loved him even more. Alexei was a victim of circumstance, just as Kingston was.

"What's going on here?" My father's voice came behind me, the hint of anger underneath his cold, snobby politeness. "Mrs. Kennedy tells me you have a boyfriend, Aurora. A brute."

His eyes traveled over the Nikolaev family, his eyebrows furrowing. I wondered if he evaluated them for potential campaign donations. But then his eyes landed on Alexei and the undignified scoff passed his greedy mouth. "Don't tell me it's this gang member."

My spine straightened and anger coiled in the pit of my stomach.

"Mrs. Kennedy really ought to mind her own business," I spat out. A man walked by with a woman on his arm and my father instantly went into senator mode.

"Ahhh, you're Byron's friend." Father beamed, ignoring the Nikolaev family and me. He extended his hand and the man glanced at it, his eyebrow cocked. He paused just long enough to make my father squirm and my lips curved into a smile. I had no idea who he was, but I liked him already.

"Kristoff, Gemma. This is my father," Byron chimed in.

Kristoff Baldwin finally accepted Father's handshake. "Senator Ashford," he greeted him coolly.

My eyes locked on Kristoff's face. His eyes were an odd mixture of greenish blue. Wrong shade. Too dark. Too stormy. Face too clean. Our eyes met, neither one of us speaking a word. He was older than Alexei. Hot. Clean cut. Strong, alpha billionaire screamed from every look he gave. Before Alexei, Kristoff Baldwin would have been exactly my type.

Except now, Alexei was my only type.

"Ah, Kristoff and Gemma. This is my little sister." Byron took my hand and squeezed it gently. "Aurora, this is a good friend. Kristoff Baldwin and his other half."

My eyes traveled to his date. She was pretty. Dark hair, dark eyes. Petite. With a soft smile. I liked her too. And if Kristoff's fleeting glance to his date was anything to go by, he was infatuated with her.

Absentmindedly, I nodded and my eyes fleeted to Alexei just in time as his glass landed with a thud, the little bar shaking with the force of it. He turned around and left without another word. Without a glance my way. And ripping my heart out of my chest, leaving me without it.

"I cannot thank you enough for your campaign contribution." Senator Ashford was in full politician mode, but I ignored it all. It was just noise to me. "We're so glad to have you here with us. My daughter wants—"

I tuned him out, my eyes glued on the door that Alexei disappeared through.

"Right, darling?" Royce's shoulder bumped into me, and when I glared at him, he gave me a pointed look, then looked at Father.

"Huh?" I muttered, still distracted.

"You'll sit with Mr. Baldwin, and his lovely companion will sit with me. I want—"

"Excuse me," I interrupted my father. He was nuts if he thought I'd stay another minute. My eyes darted back to the door. Did he leave? His brother and Isabella were still here. I glanced at the two, then back to the door. Yes, he left. "I just remembered I have somewhere to be," I muttered.

I scurried away, leaving Vasili and Isabella behind along with my brothers, Father, and Kristoff Baldwin. I waved through the crowd of men in suits and women in elaborate gowns, past the guards at the entrance of the ballroom.

"Aurora." Someone called out my name.

My steps faltered and I glanced over my shoulder. Isabella rushed after me, Vasili right on her heels. I wasn't in the mood for either one of them and I took a step to rush out of there when her voice stopped me. "Please wait," she cried out, attracting unwanted attention. I swore she did it on purpose.

I cursed my proper upbringing, whirled around slightly annoyed, and waited, tapping my foot impatiently. Vasili shot me a threatening look, his huge body stalking behind his wife. Damn it, Alexei was usually next to me, shooting his big brother killer glances right back.

"Thanks for waiting," Isabella breathed. It wasn't as if I had a choice, not unless I wanted every single pair of eyes to be staring at me.

"What do you want?" I asked, a tad bit sharper than I intended. Her husband promptly growled and my eyes snapped to him. "And for the love of God, would you stop growling at me?"

Our eyes locked, his pulse thundered in his throat, our wills battling in a silent stare down. Isabella chuckled and her right palm came to her husband's arm, squeezing gently.

"He's protective," she justified him.

"You don't say," I retorted dryly.

"I can see why Alexei fell in love with you." Hearing Isabella's words, I forgot all about Vasili.

"H-he said that?" I whispered, swallowing a lump in my throat.

Isabella chuckled. "Does Alexei strike you as a man who would say anything?"

No, he certainly didn't. His experiences have scarred him, in lots of ways.

"What hotel are you guys staying at?" I asked.

No matter where it led, I'd be with him.

FORTY-ONE
AURORA

I knocked on the door of Alexei's penthouse.

One. Two. Three. Four times.

He told me he could never give me what I needed. Yet, without him it was even worse.

If the only thing he could offer me was no face-to-face fucking and no kissing, I'd take it. Like a pathetic, weak woman, I'd take any crumbs. Because without him, I felt empty. From the moment I walked away from him, every cell in my body rebelled and demanded I go back to him.

I held steady. Barely.

I kept busy. Barely.

He was all I could think about. Each breath and heartbeat was for him. Nights in my bed were too cold. Dreams too vivid. Alexei in my dreams held me close, whispered words of love and a future together. I woke up each morning with an aching heart and the pain got worse with each breath. Until I finally found reprieve in my sleep where he waited for me.

Holding my breath, I waited while nervous energy hummed in my veins. He was so close to me this whole time. The entire floor of this building belonged to Alexei. Guess who the building owner was?

Kristoff Baldwin. Awkward, right? Especially since I ran into the man in the fucking elevator. The longest elevator ride ever.

No answer.

I raised my hand to knock again, just as the door opened and I came face-to-face with Alexei's arctic gaze that no longer chilled me to my bones. My heart sped up, then stilled as warmth washed over me.

"Thank you for saving my brother," I blurted out.

Surprise flashed in his eyes, then he nodded, neither one of us moving. The feelings in my chest grew heavier. There were so many things to say, I didn't know where to start.

I miss you, I wanted to say. Yet, it didn't seem adequate. *I need you; I crave you; I love you.* None of the words passed my lips. I didn't know what held them back, because they screamed in my head.

Alexei stepped aside, opening the door wide. Again no words. But it was as unnerving as before. It was who he was. It was who I loved.

I walked past him and into his penthouse.

The door shut behind me with a soft *click*, and I turned around to see him leaning against it. He crossed his arms, his large biceps pulled tight. He no longer had his suit jacket nor a tie and his white dress shirt sleeves were rolled up. This was him. Fuck the suits or glittering ballrooms. I wanted him as he was.

He watched me with a half-lidded stare, his pale blue gaze burning up like fuel. He waited for me to make the first move. For me to choose him.

I took a step towards him. And another. He watched my every move, like a panther stalking its prey though he wasn't the one moving. I stopped toe to toe with him, our bodies almost brushing against each other.

"I'm yours," I rasped.

His stare on my skin burned and the tension seemed to stretch on forever.

"If you want me," I spoke softly, my heart thundering in my chest, right above the life we created. It turned out my crying was very well founded. "I'll choose you forever. Every time. I'm sorry about Russia,"

I murmured, the damn emotions threatening to overwhelm me. "I should have chosen you then too."

"Kroshka," he said roughly, his voice hoarse and full of emotions. How could I have ever thought him cold? There were so many layers to this man, there was nothing stoic or cold about him.

"You're mine too," I said in a shaky voice. "I don't want anyone else. Just you."

He stayed still for so long, and fear slowly snuck into my bloodstream and spread. Maybe he changed his mind.

Then he took my hand and I watched our fingers interlock, his tattoos stark against my skin.

"Come with me," he demanded, his voice accented. I learned by now that his accent became thicker when he felt a lot. As we strode through the room, hand in hand, I noted he only had a few pieces of furniture. No personal effects.

He opened the door at the far end of the hallway, letting me walk in first. My steps faltered and I stared at the large bed in the middle of the room. Instantly, my insides quivered.

He strode in behind me and headed for the couch. I watched, curious, waiting for his instruction. Our eyes locked, two heartbeats passed. He started unbuttoning his dress shirt. My breath hitched, my eyes hungry on his every movement. He slid his dress shirt off his shoulders, and my mouth watered at the sight. Every inch of him was hard, covered in ink.

His pants followed and lust shot through my veins while my heart thundered hard against my rib cage. In all the time I have known him and all the times that he fucked me, it was the first time I actually saw him naked. His cock sprung forward, hard and ready for me. An ache throbbed between my thighs and I clenched them together, hoping to relieve it. Two months without having his length inside me was too long.

Yet, it struck me all wrong. Despite his obvious arousal, he looked so nervous. His hands visibly shook as he'd unbuckled his pants just minutes ago. His forehead was slightly glistening.

"Alexei—" I started but he stopped me.

"Tie me up," he ordered, lying down on the bed. He looked like a god, sprawled across the bed. His arms reached up and he gripped the iron bars on the headboard. "There is rope in the nightstand."

I gasped, knowing exactly how much he hated being tied up. After learning what happened to him, I didn't blame him.

"But please, take your dress off," he pleaded in a hoarse voice. "I have been dreaming about you for eight long weeks, kroshka. Let me see you."

My hand shook as I obeyed, struggling with the zipper. Finally tugging it down, the dress slid off my body, leaving me only in my bra and panties. I stepped out of the pool of fabric at my feet.

"Turn around," he ordered. "I want to see your ass." I did as he asked, turning slowly, giving him a show. His gaze burned my skin in the most delicious way.

"Come and tie me up, kroshka." His voice was thick with emotions, full of a vulnerability I wasn't used to seeing or hearing from this strong man. He had spent a lifetime perfecting the ability to hide his emotions under a cold mask. It was something he needed to do to survive and now... *I'm selfish*, I came to the conclusion. It wasn't fair that I demanded to tear it all down; that I demanded his everything because I wanted to give him my everything.

It should have been his to give all along.

"Alexei, I don't want to tie you up," I whispered, my pulse thundering in my ears.

"I want to be what you want, Aurora."

My eyes burned with unshed tears. "You are," I assured him, choking with intense emotions. "You are everything I want." My voice cracked. "I—I can't tie you up, Alexei. Please don't ask me."

He would let me tie him up, but it made me physically sick to do it to him, knowing how much it impacted him. There were so many words I wanted to say to him. How much I loved him, the good and the bad, the broken and the fucked up. I wanted to fall apart in his hands. For him.

"Come here and touch me, then," he demanded, his voice thick. "You need that and I want to give it to you, kroshka."

He stared at me intensely. Possessive. And I willingly drowned in the depths of his arctic blues.

My chest swelled with love. I would have never thought it possible to love someone so much that it hurt. Yet, here I was. I loved every single piece of him—all his perfections and imperfections. His ruthlessness. His protectiveness. Everything.

My gaze flicked to his chest, studying his tattoos. Skulls. Symbols. A heart with a knife through it and blood dripping from it. His story was written all over his body. Slowly my eyes lowered over his abs and torso, then lower over his legs. Greek gods would be jealous of him; he was all muscle, not an ounce of fat.

I took four steps to him and climbed onto the bed, straddling him. His hard length pushed against my inner thighs, making my entrance throb with the burning need. Yet he didn't move. He didn't take control, like he usually did. My hand reached out to touch him, then I remembered how much he detested people touching him. Unsure, my hand lingered in the air.

"Touch me, kroshka."

His muscles shook. My eyes gazed at his face, worried about hurting him. Not physically, but emotionally. He nodded, with an almost resigned look. As if he was saying goodbye.

Tentatively, with a featherlight touch, I brushed my fingers over his chest. The skin was rough, indented, bumpy. Scarred. It had me pausing, insecurity slithering through my veins.

"Don't be disgusted." His voice was detached. His walls slowly rose between us. My heart broke at his words. My poor Alexei.

Leaning over him, I lowered down and brushed my mouth over the scar I just touched. Then I trailed my mouth over his chest, pausing over each scar and kissing it, then licking it. His skin was hot, burning my lips in the best way possible.

He tasted like a sinner and a saint. And my man.

"I love you," I murmured against his skin. I felt him tense underneath me, and I raised my eyes to meet his gaze burning into me. "I can't stop it any more than I can stop breathing." He took a deep breath but said nothing, so I continued, "I love your scars, Alexei. The man you are. I love your heart. Your soul. Everything about you. I know." I swallowed hard and decided to be brave for both of us. "I know it's not what you are looking for. I can love you enough for both of us."

His breathing hardened, and for a fraction of a second, I worried I said too much. But it was the truth, and I didn't want to take it back. I loved him. I'd greedily take what he could give me, and the rest, we'd figure it out.

"I broke your family," he said, his accent so pronounced, it almost made it hard to understand him. "I don't deserve your love. Anyone's love."

I put my finger over his mouth, shushing him.

"You didn't break my family. You were an instrument Ivan used." I lightly traced his lips with my finger, the scar over his lip rough under my thumb. "It was my father's fault too. He dealt in shady deals and is more to blame than you ever were." I wanted to kiss him so badly, but he was already giving me so much. "You deserve everything. Every goddamn thing."

The air stilled, my heart threatened to come out of my chest.

"I can't let you go, kroshka," he rasped.

"Then don't." My skin burned under his hot gaze. I had to resist the urge to rub myself against his hard length. "I don't want you to let me go," I told him. "We might argue and disagree on a lot of things. But I'll always stay with you." I leaned over, resting my forehead against his.

"Always," I promised.

Heat flared in his gaze and dark expression across his face. "Then you're mine."

"Yours," I confirmed again, my voice soft. My heart burned with love for him. It was in my every breath, every heartbeat, every thought. His hands let go of the rails he held tight, he took my face between his hands and brought us so close, his lips were barely an inch away.

I could almost taste him. Almost feel his lips burning mine. But I remained still. I wouldn't push him. Not now that I knew life without him was so bleak. So empty. His palms gripped my jaw as he pressed his mouth to mine.

His tongue swept across my lower lip, wet and messy, and my mouth parted. I felt his scar brush against my lips.

"I love you so goddamn much," I breathed against his mouth. He pushed his tongue into my mouth, a deep growl resounding in his chest. Our tongues slid against each other, in perfect harmony.

Our first kiss. It was perfect. Lazy and sweet. Delicious and sinful. Wet and messy.

I moaned into his mouth and my fingers dug into his hair, needing him closer. Devouring him. The taste of him was an addiction I'd never quit.

"Alexei," I murmured against his lips, bringing my half-lidded, lust-filled gaze up to his. My palms were pressed against his chest, his rough skin under my fingertips. I gently licked the scar on his lip, then showered it with little kisses.

"Mmmm."

"Tell me if it's too much," I whispered. "I—I don't want to hurt you."

I wanted to protect him. Go and find every single person who had ever hurt him and kill them all over again.

"My little agent is worried about hurting me," he teased softly. But the perspiration on his eyebrow didn't escape me.

"Give me what you can," I told him, nuzzling against his neck and inhaling that scent I missed for months. "We can take this slow. I don't mind when you are in control."

In one swift move, he flipped us over, his big body covering mine and the shredding sound of my panties and bra filled the air. A little squeal escaped me. I didn't expect him to take me up on the proposal that same second.

"You offered, kroshka," he groaned, his breath hot against my lips. His brows were furrowed, his muscles straining as his skin touched my flesh.

I raised my hand, smoothing his brow and wiping the glistening off of it. I couldn't even imagine what it cost him to let me touch him, be on top of him, or kiss him.

"I did," I murmured. "You can tie me up," I rasped. "I won't mind."

He had given me a lot already. His eyes searched my face, as if he worried it would push me too far. I smiled reassuringly. "I'm sure."

He lifted up onto his knees and reached to the drawer. He dug out a black rope, but when he returned to me, an uncertainty flicked across his expression.

I offered up my hands to him. "It's okay," I whispered. "You got me."

"Kroshka—"

I stopped him. "You gave me what I needed. Now take what you need." I watched his Adam's apple bob as he swallowed hard. "I want this too," I assured softly.

Resolve settled in his expression. He slipped the rope around my wrists, wrapping it around twice, then tugged gently. I lifted my hands above my head and he tied the rope to the headboard. I was exposed, at his mercy, and I knew he'd catch me if I fell. No matter what.

I was laid back on the bed, sprawled with my hands above my head tied to the headboard. Just for him. If this was what he needed, I'd give it to him. His eyes roamed over my body and my skin burned at his hot appraisal. His big body hovered over me and pulled the rope taut as I watched his every move. A little sting of pain shot through me as the rope cut into my wrists, but I didn't flinch.

He brushed his lips against mine and my chest glowed with warm satisfaction.

"You're so fucking perfect, kroshka," he growled and I thought I'd shatter at his words. His hand trailed a featherlight touch down the curve of my elbow, over my neck and all the way down my stomach until it reached its destination. The pad of his thumb put pressure on my clit, and I felt slick wetness trickle down my inner thigh.

Two months without Alexei felt like a century. I didn't want him to go slow. I needed him inside me. Now. I lifted my hips and rubbed against him.

"Don't make me wait," I begged.

"Soon, kroshka," he whispered, laying his forehead on mine. "I want to enjoy you first." His voice was hoarse. "I missed you."

My throat tightened with emotions I heard in his voice. Our faces close together, I nuzzled my cheek against his. "I missed you too."

His muscled legs straddled me across my chest, and my gaze lowered between our bodies. It was the first time I had a full glimpse of him. Alexei was a work of art—every single inch of him. And his shaft was no different. Big. Hard. Mouthwatering.

"I want to taste you," I murmured, lifting my eyes to meet his hot gaze. "Can I?"

His face was hard to read. Like he had an internal battle going on what was okay or wasn't okay to do to me.

"Alexei," I whispered. "I can take it. Whatever you want to do to me, I can take it."

That must have been reassurance enough, because he leaned forward so his cock was just inches from my face. My tongue licked the tip of his swollen head and his loud moan filled the room. Encouraged by his response and the way he looked at me, dark and hungry, I ran my tongue across his crown and slid him deep into my mouth, keeping my eyes on him.

Without warning, he grabbed my hair with one hand and drove forward deeper into my mouth. I hummed my approval while heat bloomed in my stomach, moving lower. I squeezed my thighs together as he pushed in and out of my mouth in short strokes. He slid deep into my throat and I kept my lust-filled gaze on him. The bliss on his face was the most beautiful thing I had ever seen.

"Relax your throat, kroshka," he rasped. "Let me in," he soothed, his tone slightly desperate. I wanted to be everything he needed. I relaxed my throat, following his instruction and his rough hand caressed my cheek with such devotion. It overwhelmed me and I couldn't get enough of him. I began to lick and suck desperately, urging him deeper with the curve of my tongue, breathing in his delicious musk. He was my sweetest poison.

"You look so pretty swallowing my cock," he whispered and I moaned, watching the bliss on his face like my life depended on it. He gazed down at me, his eyes glimmering like sapphires. He held my face as he jerked his hips faster and deeper. My eyes watered, but I didn't want him to stop. I let him fuck my mouth because I wanted him to use me in any way he needed. Any way he wanted. He fell forward, his hands bracing the headboard as he thrust harder into my mouth. Each thrust of his hips matched the aching throb at my core. My body was sensitive to every sound, every move of his.

I watched in fascination as his groans became louder, his eyes glassed over and he stiffened as he finished in my mouth. He was beautiful as he lost control. I sucked him eagerly, swallowing every drop of his cum as my skin warmed under the heat of his stare. I sucked every drop of him, lapping at him, swirling my tongue over his crown while he panted.

He pulled out of my mouth with a pop, growling deep in his chest. This felt like our first time, and I never wanted it to end. He hovered over me, chest to chest, his breathing still slightly rough.

"Does my kroshka want to come?" he growled as he reached behind him and slid his fingers into my folds. A loud moan escaped me and my hips jerked into his touch.

"Please," I moaned, the ache in my core throbbing with need. I writhed underneath him, hot with need. I tugged at my bound wrists with desperation and he smiled darkly. Sinfully.

It made me part my thighs and rub my pulsing core against him. Alexei licked my lips but he didn't kiss me. It was so damn erotic. He trailed his mouth down my neck, licking and nipping. Marking me.

The bed shifted under his weight. "Spread your legs."

I did without delay. I physically ached to feel him there. His hand slid between my legs, his rough palms marking my soft skin. When he slid his two fingers inside me, I arched my head back and my eyes fluttered shut.

"Alexei," I breathed.

His lips nipped the skin where my shoulder and neck met. "You're so soaked," he rasped, slipping his fingers in and out of me, spreading my arousal around. I shivered with need, each breath I took labored.

"I missed your taste," he murmured. "You're the only dessert I can stomach, kroshka." I whimpered underneath him, grinding against his hand. "Don't ever leave me."

"Never," I vowed, as his mouth trailed kisses down my stomach. In a smooth, sudden move, he grabbed the backs of my thighs and hooked them over his shoulders, then pressed his face between my legs.

"Ah, fuck," I breathed as pleasure tore through me as he licked and sucked my folds, teasing me. He was drawing it out, his tongue never touching my clit. I writhed and grinded against his face, desperate for him to hit *that* spot.

"You're greedy, kroshka," he purred. I watched him through heavy eyelids, his eyes on me as he ate me out.

"Only for you," I breathed.

It must have been the right thing to say because his mouth latched on to my clit and sucked hard. The orgasm exploded through my body and rocked through every fiber of me hard as light shot behind my eyes.

I moaned, my fingers clutching the bars on the headboard as they dug into the palm of my hands. My hips grinding against his mouth, riding the wave of pleasure and milking it for all it would give me.

My body went limp and he pulled back, his eyes meeting mine. There was satisfaction in his blue gaze and I watched him wipe his mouth with the back of his hand. A shudder ran through me and I was ready for round two. Or was it three?

He climbed up my body, then he dragged the hot tip of his shaft over my sensitive flesh. He pushed against my entrance, and my pussy clenched greedily for him.

"I love you too, kroshka," he murmured, nipping at my jaw and neck.

My pulse sped up at his words, his mouth closed on my pulse and sucked as my heart fluttered up into the clouds. He thrust all the way to the hilt, filling me, and happy tears pricked at my eyes.

He started to thrust. I pressed my mouth against his neck, licking his flesh, whispering love words against his skin as he thrust into me over and over again.

"This pussy is mine," he growled as he pounded me into the

mattress. My shameless moans soaked the air. He was rough, the head-board slammed against the wall. "Say it, kroshka," he demanded, his voice guttural.

"Y-yours," I moaned. "Please don't fucking stop."

My breaths came out in short pants as he pushed deeper inside me, his pelvis grinding against my clit. A tingling sensation blossomed in the pit of my stomach. I was so close.

Alexei grunted with every stroke, grinding me into the mattress. Our grunts and moans filled the bedroom, our bodies slick with sweat, flesh smacking against flesh. He slammed into me hard and ruthlessly, the flames of desire burned and licked my skin. My sensitive nipples scraped against his chest as he fucked me as viciously as he killed.

And I fucking loved it.

He was the only thing that filled my mind and my body. My soul and heart. I was so lost into him, in this fog of lust.

A scream shattered through the air as he hit a spot and my back arched. He pounded into me mercilessly, as if he wanted to punish me for withholding my body from him for the past two months.

"Say you'll never leave," he demanded.

"Never," I cried out, my body shuddering with the force of another hot wave of pleasure that crashed through my veins. "Oh God. Never," I repeated. "Please. Give me more. *Oh God, oh God.*"

He fucked me harder and deeper, right through my orgasm. His strokes were long and short, fast and slow. Deep and shallow. I screamed his name as he continued to ride me mercilessly, extending my orgasm until I thought I'd die from the immense pleasure.

Both of our bodies were sweat-drenched, his cock driving brutally into me.

"Fuck," he growled, plunged into me with a last punishing thrust and finished inside me with a shudder and his face buried into the crook of my neck.

Our heavy breaths filled the silence, his mouth skimming the crook of my neck. He reached above my head, then loosened the ropes and brought my wrists to his mouth. His lips showered the red marks.

"It doesn't hurt," I assured him softly.

"You deserve better," he murmured, pressing kisses on my palms.

I tugged my hands free from his grip and wrapped them around him. My palms pressed against his back, the skin rough there. I gripped him tight against me, scared of losing him.

"There is no better than you," I told him, holding his gaze. "Not for me."

He took my one hand and interlocked our fingers. It started with my hand in his, and it will end with his hand in mine.

"Then I'm yours," he vowed.

FORTY-TWO
ALEXEI

I blinked against the sunlight streaming through the windows.

It had been years since my mind had been so quiet and my dreams absent. It was all thanks to the woman in my arms. I felt rested and in an exceedingly good mood after six hours of sleep.

My hands tightened around Aurora, scared she'd slip away. It was irrational. Just the thought of losing her sent knives rippling through my chest.

When I saw her brother introducing her to Kristoff Baldwin, something jackknifed in my chest. I could kill him, but that wouldn't eliminate all the other men like him in this world. Men who didn't have scars and ink marking their body.

So I left.

Or risked killing that bastard father of hers, her brothers, and then killing any male prospects they had in mind for Aurora.

But this was so much better. My woman came to me; she wanted *me*.

I leaned down, breathing in her scent and my cock instantly thickened against her backside. It was my first time waking up with a woman in my own bed. The whole ordeal with fucking Igor aside. It felt right having her in my home. I wanted to wake up beside her until the day I died.

I was surprised to hear she found out about Kingston. But then I got a text from Cassio in the early hours of the morning. Right after Aurora begged for some rest; otherwise, she threatened she'd doze off while I fucked her. It would seem Vasili called Cassio, and like the two old women they were, decided to play matchmakers. And Cassio had the ammunition since he was there with me that night I went back for Kingston.

I should be pissed off, but I was too goddamn happy.

Aurora stirred in my arms and her eyes fluttered open. God, she was so beautiful. So soft. And all mine.

"Good morning, kroshka."

She smiled, her sleepy eyes on me. When she looked at me, all the past, present, and future disappeared. All I saw and felt was her.

"Good morning," she murmured sleepily, pushing her body closer to mine and her face nuzzling into my chest. I stiffened, worried she'd find the scars disgusting in the daylight. But all she did was press her mouth on my chest, then lifted her head to search my face. "Want some personal space?"

God, this woman thought I wanted space from her. I never wanted her out of my sight. I wanted her flesh against mine. But old ghosts were hard to extinguish.

I tightened my hold of her. "Nyet. I'll never want space between us."

Her face lit up with a happy smile. "Just tell me when something is too much. Okay?"

A rough sound rumbled in my chest and I took her face between my hands.

"Kroshka, I fear you'll find me to be too much." I held her face and kissed her lips. Now that I tasted her lips, I couldn't get enough of her mouth. She was the only one who would get all of me. My obsession, my possession, and my love.

"Nah," she murmured softly. Her nose brushed against mine. "I have to tell you something." I sensed a slight tension in her body and I stilled. "No matter what, I love you and what I'm about to tell you puts no expectations on you. Okay?"

"Da, kroshka. Tell me," I demanded.

She took her bottom lip between her teeth, chewing it nervously.

"I'm pregnant," she blurted out. The air stilled and my heart paused. And then my blood flooded with something dark and possessive. "Are you mad?"

My gaze dropped to search her face. "Are you happy about it?" I tried to keep my voice measured, but it came out coarse. I didn't want to scare her with the intense possession that swam through my veins right now.

"I—I am," she replied softly, pushing her face into my chest and inhaling deeply. "I know what to expect after Gabriel. You don't have to worry about any of it."

A sardonic breath left me. If she thought I'd ever let her out of my sight now, she was out of her mind. "Kroshka, you are mine and I'm yours. The baby is ours." I shifted us over so I hovered over her, our eyes connected. "Now, you cannot leave me."

She chuckled. "And here I worried that I was shackling you."

My hand skimmed down her body and gently covered her belly.

"Mine forever. I'm never letting you go," I muttered as I leaned over to press a kiss where our baby grew inside her belly. "We'll have at least two babies. Da?"

I raised my eyes to find tears glistening in hers and an alarm shot through me.

"What's the matter?" I choked out, worried it wasn't what she wanted.

Her lips trembled as she smiled and she waved her hand. "It's nothing. For some reason, everything makes me cry. I'm sad, I cry. I'm happy, I cry. I'm hungry, I cry."

I blinked in confusion. I didn't remember Isabella doing all that. Or maybe I didn't notice it.

"Is that good or bad?" I asked unsure.

"It's good," she assured me. "It's normal."

Relief washed over me and my hand shook as I cupped her face with my palm, running a thumb across her lip.

"I'll watch over you and the baby," I vowed. "I won't let anyone hurt you."

She smiled, her eyes full of trust. "I know you will." Her tongue swept across her lower lip. "And yes, at least two kids. Maybe four?"

A smile pulled on my lips. "Let's make it five."

Heat burst in my chest. I never thought this would be my fate. A woman. A baby, maybe five.

"I want to know everything," I told her. "Did you see a doctor? Where is he? I have to check his background. Are you taking vitamins? Isabella had to take some."

Her laugh rang through the air.

"I only found out a few days ago. Maybe you and I can pick a doctor together. Kingston actually thought I should take a test."

The all too familiar feeling of guilt came back. It would plague me for the rest of my life. It wasn't something that can be washed off.

"I'm sorry, kroshka."

"You have nothing to apologize for, Alexei," she whispered, her mouth moving against my skin. "We were all victims of bad people. We won't let them ruin our happiness. Okay?"

"It doesn't wash off my wrongdoings." And she had no idea how much blood I had tainting my hands.

"Nor does it wash off mine," she claimed softly. "You're a good man. As long as we're together, we power through it all. We have our families. My brothers will growl at yours."

"That ought to go well," I retorted dryly.

"Well, you have the upper hand." She beamed, her eyes shining mischievously.

"How is that?"

"You saved Kingston."

EPILOGUE
ALEXEI

Three Months Later

"Uncle Alexei, we sent you a picture of Dad's opened safe." Hannah, one of Nico's twins, had her hands on her hips and glaring at me. It was kind of cute. "Where is our money? It took us three months to get it to open!"

I chuckled. These little criminals would take over the world one day.

"I got it, thank you for that. Your faces inside his safe were priceless," I praised, hunching down to my knees. "For that, I'll add an extra two hundred bucks." They both started cheering. "Can I Zelle you the money?"

"Cash only," Arianna demanded. "We don't want it traced."

I raised my eyebrows. "Does Nico not give you enough spending money?" I inquired curiously. Though they were six. What could they possibly spend money on? Bubble gum?

"Nah, it's better when we earn it," Arianna retorted. "Have the cash ready by the end of today."

Then they both took off through the yard filled with people. I rose to my full height while my gaze traveled over everyone.

I used to hate social gatherings.

Not that you'd know it from the way I stood next to my wife and mingled with our guests all day today. My eyes sought her out whenever she wasn't with me, her belly swelling bigger with each passing day.

It was official. She was mine.

After the spoken vows and rings were exchanged in front of our families, Aurora Ashford became Mrs. Alexei Nikolaev. The rays of the Portugal sunshine covered the lawn of our little villa overlooking the sea. Laughter, chatter, and local traditional music carried over the breeze.

Senator Ashford refused to give his blessing for our marriage. I didn't give a shit. I only wanted it for his daughter's happiness. Turns out, she didn't give a shit either. She just wanted her brothers and her girlfriends around.

Family. Happiness. Love. I felt like the richest man alive.

My chest grew heavy each time I looked at my wife. She looked stunning in her simple wedding dress. She refused to hide her bump, and I completely agreed. I wanted the whole world to see it. To know she was mine.

There were still days and nights when my ghosts came knocking on the door.

Nobody said it would be easy. But fuck, it was all worth it when I'd look at Aurora. Or when I'd think about that little life growing inside her belly.

My family grounded me. Aurora and our unborn child gave me happiness and a future.

I watched as my wife threw her head back and laughed at something Royce said. Her brothers, girlfriends, Cassio, and Raphael stood with them, an amused expression on their faces. Kingston was with them too. But just like me, sometimes he felt like an outsider. The shit we went through made it harder to relate.

A week after Senator Ashford's fundraising campaign, Aurora and I came to Portugal and stayed at our place by the sea. She asked her brothers over too. Kingston was ready to tell them he wasn't dead, but he still wanted to keep it from the world. It was rough seeing the reunion. And I knew it was hardest on Kingston, though he handled it well.

Better than I did.

"I'm so happy for you." Isabella's voice came from behind me, and I turned to see her with our little Nikola. "There is nobody who deserves it more."

A small noise of amusement left me. I knew many who deserved it more. But it didn't matter because I stole this happiness and I'd keep it. For Aurora. For me. And for our little Kostya. Aurora complained Konstantin was too much of a mouthful.

I brushed my fingers over Nikola's cheeks and he gave me one of his innocent grins. He spoke more and more each day.

My sister's hand reached out and squeezed mine gently. I allowed it but my wife's touch was still the only one I liked. Scratch that, the only touch I loved. Craved it. Needed it. For someone who went without a touch for a good part of my life, I couldn't survive a day without hers.

"Got that right." Vasili came from behind his wife, little Marietta in his arms. He wrapped his free arm around Isabella and she instinctively leaned back into him. I finally understood that crazy obsession my brother had with his wife, because I felt it too.

"We'll flood this earth with Nikolaev boys," he joked while Isabella rolled her eyes. "Now, we just have to get Sasha married."

"Yeah, fuck that," Sasha grumbled, approaching us. "Isn't it bad enough every goddamn one of you is having babies?"

My eyes searched for my wife again. This time, she stood aside with Cassio and Áine, cooing to their little daughter and son. Little Océane and Damon. They had twins. It would seem the Morrellis and Kings decided to flood the earth with their little offspring too.

"Unless we start producing twins," I mused, "we won't succeed flooding this earth with little Nikolaev boys nor girls. Morrelli is probably working on another set of twins."

The words barely left me when Morrelli and his wife scurried into the house, behaving like two teenagers. They were horny like two teenagers too.

"Umm, are those two disappearing again?" Aurora asked as her hand slipped into mine.

"So it seems," Sasha mumbled. "I swear, that man is getting more ass than a damn rabbit."

Aurora chuckled. "Having a dry spell, Sasha?" she teased him.

Surprisingly, she got along with Sasha the best. For some odd reason, she was able to put him in his place without threatening to beat him. It was quite useful. And entertaining to watch.

"Pfft, I have women chasing me left and right," Sasha retorted.

Aurora scoffed, while Vasili, Isabella, and I watched the exchange amused.

"I'm sure they are," Aurora agreed. "Either to beat or murder your ass."

"Woman, aren't you supposed to be tame when pregnant?" Sasha grumbled. "Isabella was more mellow."

Aurora offered him a sweet smile. "Isabella was probably too nice and didn't want to upset your fragile feelings."

Vasili's booming laugh attracted all eyes on us. The rest of the gang joined to hear what was so funny since my eldest brother didn't laugh that often. It had to run in our family. But our children would break that tradition.

We'd give them a happy life.

Aurora's hands came around my waist, lifting up on her tiptoes and pressing a fleeting kiss on my mouth.

"I love you," she whispered, her soft lips moving against mine.

"And I love you too, my kroshka. You and our baby. Until my death and even after it."

Worry still swarmed my mind. I had added extra security to all my homes and hers. Fuck, even Raphael's since she spent so much time visiting there. It drove him nuts. Whenever Aurora wasn't with me, I checked on her and our unborn baby. It gave me peace. She knew it, grumbled softly, and then kissed me, assuring me nobody would ever keep her away from me.

"I have something for you," I told her, pulling her closer to me.

"You better not have gotten me another gift," she scolded softly. "I don't know what to do with the last one."

I bought my wife a hippopotamus and had it housed in Washington, D.C.'s, National Zoo. We'd have a story to tell our children. How a little girl who wished for a hippopotamus for Christmas saved a boy.

"It's not another pet," I said, unable to resist kissing her again. Fuck, this heaviness in my chest felt good and scary as hell. The fear of losing it was a constant lingering feeling in the back of my mind. "It's your little sister's cell phone number."

Her soft gasp filled the space between us. I couldn't forget her words, how she always wanted a sister. And I knew she looked her up. I've seen her check on her more than once since we moved in together. As if she worried about her.

Aurora chewed on her bottom lip, a pensive look in her eyes.

"You don't have to reach out to her," I said, my voice guttural. I knew how it felt to find out I had siblings that I grew up without. I told Aurora the story, and now I worried it'd hold her back. "Just think about it for a bit."

Her neck bobbed, conflict strong on her face.

"She's in her last semester at Yale, and then she'll be having her finals over the next few months. Yale is no joke." I nodded in understanding. "Maybe after she graduates, I'll reach out."

"That's a good plan."

"I just don't want to pull her into—"

She trailed off but I knew what she meant. She didn't want her to be scrutinized by the public and she worried about her being endangered in the underworld.

"We'll figure it out together," I assured her. "And we'll keep her safe too."

After all, I was good at lingering in the shadows.

"Now tell me," I tried to distract her. "Is today everything you dreamed of, kroshka?" I asked my young wife. It wasn't a lavish wedding. I didn't think I could handle a wedding filled with people I didn't know. But I was willing to do it for her.

I wanted to be everything she wanted.

"It was even better." She beamed as she rose to her tiptoes and kissed me on my mouth. "So much better. You are everything—my heartbeat, my heart. You're all I want in my life. I love you."

A rough sound rumbled in my chest, just as it did every time she said those words to me. I'd never tire of hearing it.

"I love you too, kroshka." My chest grew heavy with all the emotions. I didn't deserve her, but I'd keep her all the same.

Her and our family.

Because we are doing this together.

THE END

If you'd like a preview to Belles & Mobsters, Book Five, make sure to keep reading and check out the prologue to Raphael.

Want to learn more about the Kingpins, Aurora's cousins?

Get your copy of book one in Kingpins of the Syndicate here

https://amzn.to/3Mq8oVf

Want to meet Aurora's younger half sister, who is not as devoted to law and order as Agent Ashford?

Corrupted Pleasure is available here https://amzn.to/3s6Kbuu

For a sneak peek at her story, keep reading after Raphael's prologue.

Last but not least, get to know Aurora's brothers in the Billionaire Kings series.

Book one link https://amzn.to/3s6Kbuu

RAPHAEL PROLOGUE

My driver opened the door and I stepped out of the car. The moment my feet hit the pavement, I inhaled humid Washington, D.C., air as I walked towards the D.C. Circuit Court of Appeals on Madison Place.

I climbed up the stairs of the large brick building and at the top entered through security.

I spotted her right away. The woman Alexei tipped me off about. Sailor McHale.

I'd been trailing her the past two weeks. The moment Alexei gave me the tip on Anya and Sailor McHale.

She was already there, putting her phone into the bin. I put mine in the one right behind her. I wasn't exactly a small man and usually women always glanced my way. Yet, this one never bothered to glance in my direction. Either she was completely unaware of me or she just had a habit of keeping her head down and staying out of sight.

"Miss McHale," the guard greeted her.

"Mr. Roberts, how nice to see you." Her lips curved into a smile, reserved but still a pleasant one. "Has your wife had the baby yet?"

"Any day now," he chuckled.

She grabbed her phone and continued on. She was in this building often. More than at home. Sailor McHale was the lead reporter on the

367

whole clusterfuck with the Tijuana cartel who happened to be rivals to my own. The idiots tried to expand their territory and poach on D.C. and Maryland.

Nico Morrelli put a stop to that shit right away. Though he didn't expect help from the most unlikely petite woman with long, blonde hair.

Turns out, Miss McHale had been tailing the high-ranking member of the Tijuana cartel and inadvertently witnessed the killings and drug smuggling in the Port of Washington. It was her presented evidence that put Santiago Tijuana, the fucking asshole, and others behind bars. It was only a matter of time before they made deals with the feds, ratting out their top boss. This woman became the prosecutor's main witness, and it was clear she wasn't happy about it.

But that was the second reason I was here. There had been whispers that the Tijuanas would be making a move to get rid of Miss McHale—no witness, no case. It was one of the oldest known facts in the world. I knew it would only be a matter of time before they made a move to eliminate her, but I couldn't allow that to happen.

Police and agents guarded her apartment building, her son's school, and her place of work. Then there were the undercover agents who were always tailing her.

Much to my dismay.

It made it harder to bump into her. To talk to her.

I couldn't repeat the mistake that I'd made with Bella. No assumptions this time around. There was too much at stake. Although I did have men watching her too, discreetly. If her son was indeed my half brother, I'd be responsible for them.

I grabbed my own phone and left some space before I followed. She sauntered down the large lobby. One of the agents muttered something to her and her head whipped his way. Whatever he told her, it seemed to visibly agitate her and her step faltered.

"Are you fucking kidding me?" she hissed quietly.

I acted like all my attention was on the phone, while I eavesdropped.

"No, he was bailed out."

"You fucking fools," she mumbled. "What happened to no bail?"

They lowered their voices further, but I couldn't risk getting closer and being caught. Not that hearing them mattered. I already knew what the conversation was about. Like the rest of us in the underworld, the Tijuanas had their own powerful people in their pocket. It wouldn't have taken much to slip money to the right people and get the judgment of "no bail" changed to "released on own recognizance." The only surprising thing about all of it was that it took them as long as it did. So maybe they didn't have as many powerful people to grease the wheel for them in D.C. as I thought.

"Just give me a minute," she muttered, clearly still agitated. The two agents walked away from her but kept eyes on her.

I started walking down the large, long hallway, toward the courtroom where the hearing was designated to take place.

Just as I was passing her, she swayed and I swiftly caught her elbow. An abundance of smooth, long, platinum-blonde silky hair brushed over my sleeve.

"Fucking heels," she muttered, gripping my sleeve.

Her soft body leaned into mine and the attraction was instant. At least on my part. It took me all of two seconds to notice the generous curve of her breasts. The sweet primrose scent. Porcelain skin. Smooth cheekbones. Pink lips calling to me. And a sexy, determined look on her face.

When her body brushed against mine, the attraction caught me by surprise. Yes, she was beautiful. A blind man could see it. But it wasn't about that. It was about the way her body fit against mine. A dusting of freckles on her face that I wanted to devour. Everything about her pulled at a string that I considered dead.

"Not a fan of heels?" I asked.

"Fuck no."

I chuckled softly. I never expected a member of the McHale family to have such a foul mouth. Sailor McHale came from one of the oldest families in the States, with a long history of being prominent in American politics.

Straightening up, she glanced my way and our eyes met. Her blue eyes slammed into me, and for a moment, I drowned in them. They reminded me of the waters along the shores of Miami... a beautiful clear blue along the edges that became darker the closer it drew to the pupil.

She was breathtaking.

Though I didn't think Miss McHale felt the same attraction, because her eyes widened in horror. But she quickly schooled her expression.

"Thank you," she murmured, glancing away from me.

"Is everything alright, Miss McHale?" If these damn agents took this long to get here, they were incompetent. She could have been dead already.

"Yes," she answered before I even acknowledged the two incompetent morons.

Sailor took a step away from me, and to my surprise, she went back in the opposite direction. Towards the exit of the building. I watched as she hurried down the hallway and I took a step to follow her when a massive explosion ripped through the building. Glass shattered everywhere and debris flew through the air. I watched as Sailor fell onto her knees. I had just enough time to run to her and cover her body with mine before another explosion rocked the building.

This attack was because of this woman. Because of what she had seen. I needed to get her the fuck out of here. Her and my little brother.

"What's happening?" she yelled above the sirens and alarms blaring through the courthouse, the fear clear in her voice. Her body tried to move beneath me, as she pushed away chunks of debris. "I have to get to my son." Fear taking a back seat to the urgency now in her voice.

"I can protect you and Gabriel," I gritted out, trying to keep her safe beneath me. I wasn't sure what to expect... another explosion, a round of gunfire, a fucking hell to break loose. Whatever was coming, I didn't want her to hurt... I needed to protect her.

Transferring my weight to one side, I reached in my pocket and yanked free my cell phone. It was time to move.

The Tijuana cartel had come for them.

CORRUPTED PLEASURE PREVIEW

DAVINA

08-29-19-98. Combination code.

My heart pounded with each code I punched in. Blood rushed through my veins and anticipation buzzed in my system. Everything depended on this going right.

With a trembling finger, I entered the last number and a soft click sounded.

My soft gasp broke the silence in the room as I stared dumbfounded at the cracked safe door. Too afraid to peer inside. What if we robbed the head of the Irish mafia for nothing? It didn't matter that he was Juliette's father… he was a mobster first and foremost.

Swallowing hard, I pulled the door open and a sharp inhale slipped through my lips. There were stacks of money. Stacks and stacks of money. More than I've seen in my entire life.

Glancing around, I spotted the black backpack that Juliette had said Quinn always left here. I picked it up, unzipped it with shaking hands, and started shoving the money into it. I had no clue how much was in each stack, so I estimated.

Then as a thought struck me, I paused.

"I should take all of it," I muttered under my breath. "Just in case."

If Wynter's friend didn't come through, I wouldn't put it past Garrett to continue blackmailing us. Again and again.

Determination settled within me. There was no sense in doing it half-assed. So I'd take it all. My hands shook badly. Every so often, I'd miss the bag completely and the wrapped-up stack of bills would end up on the floor.

"Focus, Davina," I scolded myself softly.

Another stack of bills into the bag. Jesus Christ! There was more money in here than most people see in their entire life. Once the safe was emptied out, I lowered onto my knees to pick up the ones that didn't make it into the bag.

Tugging on the zipper, I attempted to close the bag, but it got jammed.

"Fuck, fuck, fuck," I cursed softly, struggling with the fucking zipper. It finally gave and I exhaled a breath of relief.

"Filthy words from such a pretty mouth." A deep voice filled the room.

My head shot up, the zipper forgotten while a little scream shot out of me. Trying to jerk upright, I lost my footing and fell back on my ass, all the while staring into a stormy ocean gaze.

What bad fucking luck! To be caught red-handed. This hasn't been my week at all. I hoped my girlfriends had better luck than I did.

My breathing hitched as I waited for Liam Brennan to call the police. Or kill me. Something. Anything.

Jesus, two crimes in a single week. Could this get any worse? I wondered what the sentence would be for arson and larceny.

Shit!

I couldn't get arrested. I was about to graduate from Yale.

"Let me guess," Mr. Brennan drawled, his tone lazy with the hint of something dangerous and ruthless in it. I imagined the head of the Irish mafia might contemplate tying my feet to a cement block and throwing me into the Hudson River.

"The other three are meant to be a distraction while you are here robbing me," he continued, almost sounding amused.

I looked away, scared he'd see the truth in my eyes. Besides, he was way too good to look at. Something about him ignited my skin and warmed my insides. He was just as good looking as I remembered him. I wondered how good the sex would be with him. He was so tall, all muscles and raw strength. God, I bet it would be a treat to explore his body.

Great, now I was turned on and scared.

"Fucking wrong," I protested, sounding stronger than I felt.

My eyes glanced at the door he blocked. I wished he'd move from it. Maybe I could sprint past him and out of this crazy club.

"Enlighten me, then. Why is my safe open, and why are your hands on my money?" he asked.

Wasn't that the question of the century? Of course, telling him the truth was out of the question. So I shrugged nonchalantly, slightly annoyed.

"Safekeeping," I blurted out because it was the only stupid answer I could come up with.

Hopefully, the man wouldn't kill me, his own daughter, niece, and Ivy.

"I love your sassy mouth." He smirked. "Keep it up, and I'm going to find out just how good it works."

I gulped, his words sending heat through my veins. Jesus, why did I find that so hot. Clenching my thighs, I tried to ignore the throbbing in my sweet spot.

Wrong time. Wrong place. Wrong man.

Who looked so damn tempting. "You're my best friend's father!" I rasped, though I wasn't sure if I was trying to convince myself or him that his insinuation was improper.

"What makes you think something so small will keep me away from you?"

I shook my head, while a shudder traveled down my spine. I opened my mouth to tell him he was a gross old man, but I was physically unable to utter those words. Because Mr. Liam Brennan was the hottest man I had ever seen.

"Stand up," he ordered. I blinked in confusion. "Now!"

I narrowed my eyes at his rudeness, but I got to my feet. Though I ensured I grabbed the backpack and finished zipping it. I still hoped I'd keep the money. Somehow.

The girls and I needed to stay out of jail.

"Now what?" I challenged, with bravery I didn't have.

His eyes traveled down my body, and suddenly, it felt like my minidress was too revealing. My skin flared from the weight of his stare, leaving a trail of fire in its wake. Then his eyes came back to my face and something about the way he looked at me stole a breath of air from my lungs.

The door shut behind him with a soft click and adrenaline rushed through my veins. With anticipation and excitement.

This was wrong. Oh so wrong. But I wanted to see where it went.

He moved towards his desk and casually leaned against it; his eyes locked on me.

The door swung open.

"They got away," Quinn told Mr. Brennan. "Wynter took her damn clothes off."

It would seem everything out there was going according to plan. I had to succeed too. For the four of us.

Mr. Brennan's eyes came back to me, his expression cold.

"Miss Hayes, tell us what it is that you and your friends are up to." This was a man used to getting whatever he wanted.

"No," I snapped.

"Want me to turn in the evidence to the police?" The dreaded question. Why even bother asking it? Nobody sane would say yes.

"Like what? The backpack?" I sneered. Technically, I hadn't stolen anything yet.

"For starters, yes. That backpack belongs to Quinn and the money you stashed in it belongs to me."

My eyebrow rose, seemingly unconcerned with his words.

"There are a million backpacks like this and possession is nine-tenths of the law." I prayed my bluff was right. I studied business, not fucking law. "So don't touch my stuff."

I tilted my chin up, daring him to dispute it.

He pointed to the corner of the room where a camera was. Well, fuck me. Juliette must have forgotten about the security. Fuck, and I didn't even think to ask. Anyone with that amount of cash would have security cameras.

The. Worst. Criminals.

"See that, sweetheart." His voice was deep and almost seductive. "That's our evidence."

"Shit," I grumbled. "Fucked. Just fucked."

"Pretty much," he agreed.

It was time to run. It was the only thing left to do. Goddamn it. And there were two of them now. I glanced between the two of them, wondering what the best way to slip between two men was when Mr. Brennan asked a question.

"The Italians here?"

His man nodded.

"Deal with them and keep them away from here," Mr. Brennan ordered.

Before he left, the man's eyes came back to me.

"I see the girls are following in our footsteps. One hour," he announced and then left us, shutting the door behind him.

"Let the fucking fun begin," I muttered low to myself.

Apprehension twisted in my stomach as I waited for Juliette's father to do something. Anything. A cold shiver erupted at the base of my spine, along with all kinds of scenarios playing through my mind. Sweat-slicked bodies. His deep voice would whisper words in my ear. His strong body would pump into me fast and hard, each thrust breaking me apart.

Keep your head, Davina.

God, I wished he'd make up his mind already. Either kill me or call the police. Or fuck me, so we could end this tension and silence. It was killing me, making me anxious.

"What do you want, Mr. Brennan?"

"What do you think?"

It sounded suggestive, making me feel hot and edgy. "Probably your money back," I said dryly. Though I wished it was something else. "But it's our money."

A soft scoff. "You haven't earned it." So there was a way I could earn it. Best news tonight. "Yet. But we can fix that," he added.

"How?" I asked. The look he gave me seared into my flesh, dark and hot. And possessive. "Something freaky probably."

I really tried to sound dignified. I really did. But my words came out breathy, something hot burning in the pit of my stomach. Butterflies fluttered through my veins, a heavy anticipation in my every breath.

"Well, I'm not into freaky shit," I breathed, my cheeks burning and my blood sizzling. "Nor old men."

Mr. Brennan wasn't old looking. And he was the hottest man I had ever seen. Hands fucking down. Yet, I couldn't tell him how hot and attractive I found him. I embarrassed myself enough the last time I saw him.

"I'd bet all the money in that bag, and in my bank account, that you are into freaky shit," he baited me.

I scoffed. I was tempted to bet him, but then I feared every word of his was a trap.

"Now what?" I asked instead.

"Are they waiting for you?" My eyes widened slightly. I shook my head, not trusting my voice to betray my lie. He must have read the truth in my eyes though. "You will send them a text and tell them to go back to the university without you."

My lungs couldn't get enough oxygen. This man had to be stealing it all. One part of me thought he felt this sizzling attraction, and the other part of me thought he wanted to kill me.

"Now," he clipped and I jumped. I rushed to obey his order. There was only so much disobedience I could give to a fucking mobster. "I want to see the message before you send it."

"Control freak," I mumbled, glaring at him.

I took a few steps towards him and showed him my phone screen. "Here. Happy?"

He nodded and I pressed the send button.

Now that I'd taken those few steps closer to him, my heart thundered even harder. The scent of his sandalwood cologne reached me and I inhaled deeply. It was like extinguishing a fire with gasoline because my body burned for his touch.

"First you drink my most expensive bottle of cognac," he drawled. I had no idea how he knew that. We just did that yesterday. "Then you steal from me."

"Sorry." Yeah, sorry would not suffice in this instance.

"Take your panties off," he ordered and the ache between my thighs throbbed with greed. While my body wanted to obey, my mind warned.

"W-what are you going to do?" I hated that I stuttered. Yes, he was older than me. But I certainly wasn't a blushing virgin.

He let out a breath of amusement.

"Take. Your. Panties. Off."

Asshole. "Fine, old man."

Putting the backpack with cash next to my feet, I reached under my tight minidress and slid my panties down my legs.

"Now what?" My cheeks burned, though I suspected it had nothing to do with embarrassment.

He extended his big hand, palm facing up. Did he—

Yes, he did. He wanted my panties. I threw them into his face but he caught them.

"Now turn around and bend over my desk."

Holy fucking shit! Would he fuck me now? My body sang yes, yes, yes. My mind warned it was a bad idea. I just got out of a relationship that caused all kinds of problems.

"Are you waiting for written instructions?" he barked.

Jackass! "Fucking mobster."

I did as he ordered and bent over his desk. He took a step and came up right behind me. His finger traced down along my spine and I had to fight a delightful shiver. He barely touched me and I felt his touch unlike anything ever before.

His big hands came down to my thighs and my body reacted, pushing into his touch. God, I was losing my mind. He pushed my dress up, leaving my ass bare for his viewing.

"So beautiful." His voice was like a lover's caress. "I'm going to punish you for stealing from me."

Oh my God. I was so turned on, I wanted to beg him to punish me, fuck me, make me come. But that would be a reward. He must have something else in mind.

"I hope you're not fragile," he said, his voice dark and sinful.

"Bring it on, old man," I breathed.

God, did he ever!

ACKNOWLEDGMENTS

Holy moly!

Can you believe I've written fifteen novels? Fifteen! And all in the span of two years. I can't. Though I love it. I told a friend it feels like playing pretend while jotting down English words on a piece of paper.

Thank you to my wonderful readers for reading my books and going through this journey with me.

Thank you to my family and friends for not giving up on me. Even when I fake a headache. What? I never do that. LOL

Thank you to my editor at MW Editing for catching my weird non-English phrases.

Thank you to my cover designer, Victoria at Eve Graphic Design, for giving my books a face.

Thank you to Susan Hutchinson and Beth Hale for catching my snafus.

Thank you to my wonderful beta readers for not giving up on me—Christine Stephens, Jill Haworth, Mia Orozco, and Denise Reynolds.

Thank you to my high school teacher who let my imagination thrive and let me distract her by reading my thirty-page story. I saved my classmates that day.

And last but certainly not least, to my daughters. You are now, and forever will be, my reason for everything.

XOXO

Eva Winners

Made in United States
Orlando, FL
03 October 2024

52341676R00231